THE BODY ELECTRIC

a novel

NEW YORK TIMES BESTSELLING AUTHOR

BETH REVIS

OF THE ACROSS THE UNIVERSE SERIES

SCRIPTURIENT
BOOKS

SCRIPTURIENT
BOOKS

First paperback edition: 2014
"The Turing Test" © 2013 by Beth Revis. Originally published in *Lightspeed
Magazine*. Reprinted by permission.

ISBN-13: 978-0-9906626-0-0 (signed, limited edition)
ISBN-13: 978-0-9906626-1-7 (special edition)
ISBN-13: 978-0-9906626-2-4 (paperback)
ISBN-13: 978-0-9906626-4-8 (ebook)

- THE -

BODY

ELECTRIC

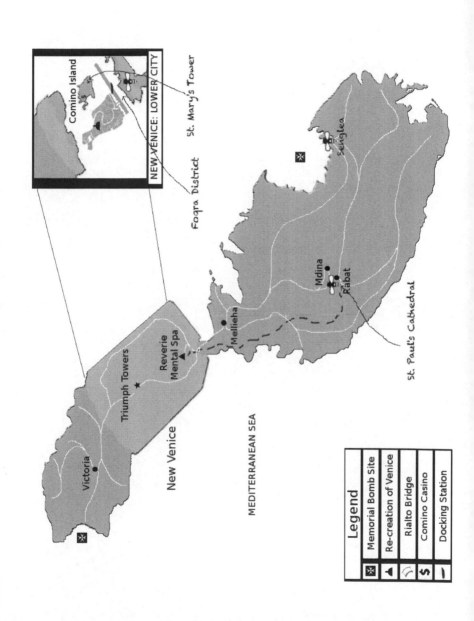

NEW VENICE: LOWER CITY

Comino Island

St. Mary's Tower

Foqra District

New Venice

Triumph Towers

Reverie Mental Spa

Victoria

Mellieha

Mdina

Rabat

Senglea

St. Paul's Cathedral

MEDITERRANEAN SEA

Legend	
✳	Memorial Bomb Site
◢	Re-creation of Venice
⌒	Rialto Bridge
$	Comino Casino
⚊	Docking Station

For the ones I can never forget.
Dei gratia.

The question, O me! so sad, recurring—What good amid these, O me, O life?

—*Excerpt from Walt Whitman's "O Me! O Life!"*

ONE

"DON'T EVER FORGET HOW MUCH I love you," Dad says.

I dig my toes into the warm Mediterranean sand. The water is a perfect blue, speckled with the white foam of cresting waves. When I tilt my head back, I can feel the warmth of the sun, a gentle sea breeze lifting strands of my short, brown hair and blowing them into my face.

But none of this is real.

"It is real!" I shout.

Dad turns around, a look of surprise on his face. "What was that, Ella?" he asks.

"Nothing," I mumble.

"Are you ready to come in, you two?" My mother stands at the top of the beach, near the road, her cupped hands amplifying her voice.

"Not just yet," Dad says, winking at me. He takes off at a run, kicking sand on me as I jump up, chasing after him. I can hear my mother laughing behind us. The sandy beach gives way to pebbles and bigger rock formations, and soon neither of us is running as we pick our paths through wave-worn rocks. Mom and the road and the beach are far behind us. It's just me and Dad and the sea.

It's fake.

"No!" I say, just as my bare feet slip on the wet rock. I crash down, pain shooting up my scraped shin. Dad turns back and helps me up.

"Are you okay, Ella?" he asks.

No. NO.

"Yeah," I say.

"We shouldn't run," Dad says. "We should take the time to appreciate this area. You know where we are, right?"

I hadn't recognized it before, but now that Dad says it, I do know where I am. From the cliff above us extends a giant arm of rock, arcing over the sea and then reaching back down into the water. The rock formation has created a perfect arch—large enough to fit a house under— through which the sea flows. Waves crash against the sides of the rock, sending up salty sea foam.

"It's the Azure Window," I breathe, staring at this natural wonder.

It's not. Not really.

THE BODY ELECTRIC

"Eyes are the window to the soul, Ella, don't forget that," Dad says. He's not looking at me; he's watching a girl swimming out in the ocean, so far away from us that I cannot recognize who she is.

"I... I thought the Azure Window was destroyed," I say slowly. "In the Secessionary War. The bombs broke the arch, the rock crumbled into the sea."

As I say the words, the natural bridge of rock cracks with an earsplitting snap. First pebbles, then boulders fall from the arch. The water churns with the destruction. Giant clouds of dirt and debris mar my vision of the crumbling rock formation. When the dust finally clears, there is nothing there but a pile of rocks and swirling, dirty water.

I turn to my father.

He's dead.

He's dead.

As I watch, the skin of his face cracks, like the rock did, exposing red blood. His flesh falls away from his skull like pebbles crashing to the sea. A waterfall of cascading blood and gore falls from his head, down his neck. His shoulder chips away, and, with a giant crash, the flesh from his chest falls from his body, an avalanche splattering into the sea at our feet, now stained red. I can see, for just a moment, his beating heart in his ribcage, and then that, too, withers and dies, the useless, blackened lump tapping

- 3 -

against his ribs before plopping out of his body. He's nothing but bones, and then the gentle warm Mediterranean wind blows against him, and his bones break, clattering down into the pile of muck and flesh swirling in the salty sea.

"This isn't real," I say.

Because it isn't.

TWO

I WAKE UP WITH A VIOLENT JERK, running a shaky hand over my sleep-crusted eyes.

Ever since last year, the nightmares have been getting worse. More vivid. The line between what's real and what's not is so blurry.

Ever since I started working at the Reverie Mental Spa.

I sigh, throwing my blankets back and getting out of bed. By the time I make it to the kitchen, my mother's already slicing tomatoes for breakfast.

"Sleep well?" she asks cheerily.

"Yeah, no," I say, slumping into the chair. But when she turns back to look at me, a curious smile on her lips, I just grin at her as if I'd woken up from the best dream ever.

Mom hands me the plate of tomatoes. "Forgot the basil," she mutters, turning away before the plate's fully in my hands.

They're real tomatoes, grown on our roof, not the perfect spheres from the market. Of course, they taste pretty much exactly like the genetically modified food the government stamps approval of sale on, but I like the weirdly discordant shapes of the tomatoes we grow ourselves. They're lumpier, as if they have only a vague idea of the round shape they're supposed to be. The rich, red insides glisten with the sprinkle of salt Mom threw over them before she handed them to me.

Then I notice the blood.

"Mom," I say evenly, trying not to make it sound like a big deal.

"Mmm?" she asks, not turning.

It's rather a lot of blood, mixed in with the slices. It's darker than the tomatoes' juice, smeared across the plate.

"Mom," I say again.

Mom turns, still holding the knife. I see the cut pulsing blood down her hand, cutting a dark path through the chopped green basil clinging to her skin. She's shorn off the tip of her second finger.

"Mom!" I say, dropping the plate on the counter and rushing to her. She looks down at her hand and curses, tossing the knife into the sink.

"Damn, damn, damn," she says. "It's ruined, isn't it?" She looks past me at the plate of tomatoes. "All ruined. Damn!"

"I don't care about the tomatoes," I say, wrapping a tea towel around her finger as Mom reaches past me, grabbing the plate and sliding the tomato slices into the rubbish bin. "Be still," I order, but she doesn't listen. She tries to shake me off.

"Forget about the damn tomatoes!" I shout, snatching her hand again and pressing the towel into the cut. Mom stares down at it dispassionately, watching the red blood soak through the white cloth.

I slowly raise my eyes from Mom's hand to her face. There's no emotion on her face. No pain.

"You didn't feel it, did you?" I whisper.

"Of course I did," Mom says.

I squeeze the cut finger, just a little, just enough pressure that she should feel a spike of pain. But Mom doesn't notice.

I drop her hand, and Mom peels away the tea towel. It's ruined—but Mom's finger isn't. As we watch, the raw, bleeding flesh slowly knits back up, and the skin starts to regrow.

Mom snorts. "At least the bots are good for something."

"You're getting worse," I say. It's not a question.

"Ella—" Mom starts to reach for me, but I wrap my arms around myself. The back of my tongue aches as burning tears fill my eyes. "Ella, it's not that bad."

"It *is*!" I shout, staring at her. Mom's eyes plead with me to forget what I saw, to pretend that everything is okay. But it's not. It's not.

It's the beginning of the end.

This is the way things are:

Almost two years ago, Mom was diagnosed with Hebb's Disease. It's rare, and it's fatal. Some people think it comes from the universal cancer vaccination since it was developed a short time before the first case of the disease, but no one's sure. All we know is that, for some reason, the space between neurons starts to grow wider. Your brain is *yelling* at you to move, but your nervous system can't hear it.

Most people don't last more than half a year with Hebb's, but Mom's survived two whole years thanks to the research on nanobots Dad did. He was close to finding a cure, I know he was. He used nanobots to help alleviate the symptoms, using the tiny, microscopic robots to communicate the messages between Mom's brain and nervous system. The bots have the additional advantage to heal other areas where Mom's been hurt, like the cut on her finger. Medical nanobots are no new thing—everyone has vaccination bots when they're born—but the way Dad used them on Mom's illness... it seemed like a miracle.

But then Dad died.

And now Mom's...

Not being able to feel anything is the first warning sign. If a knife nearly sliced off her finger, and she didn't even freaking *notice*, that means Dad's temporary fix for Mom is failing. The bots aren't working. The disease is taking over. The disease that eventually kills every single one of its victims is winning.

"Mom," I say, my voice eerily calm. "How long have you had trouble feeling things?"

"It's not been long, Ella, please, don't worry about—"

"How long." It doesn't even sound like a question any more, just a demand.

Mom sighs. "A few months. It's... been getting steadily worse."

My hands are shaking so violently that I curl them into fists and hold them behind my back so Mom doesn't see. I can't be weak, not in front of her, not when she needs my strength.

When Mom was first diagnosed, I practiced saying "My mother is dead," until I could say it without crying.

And then Mom didn't die. Dad found a way to stave off the disease, and she lived.

But he didn't.

Dad's death was sudden, and violent, and it gutted me like knife guts a fish. An explosion in the lab where he worked, about a year ago, killing him and several other scientists. No one expected it—no one except the terrorists who planned it. I was so *angry*. He left me with a sick mother and no hope. And when I woke up the next morning, and every morning after, there would be a moment, a brief moment, where I'd forgotten Dad was dead. And every morning, I relived every ounce of pain when I remembered again that he wasn't here with us. With me.

"Ella." My mother speaks loudly, drawing me back to the here and now. "I don't want you to worry about it, really. Jadis is taking me to a new doctor, one of the ones in the lab that gave us the grant money, and well—don't give up hope on me, okay?"

I jerk my head up, staring at her fiercely. "Never," I say, and I mean it more than anything else I've ever sworn.

I'm not ready to be an orphan.

THREE

I WATCH MOM LIKE A HAWK, EVERY nerve in my body strung out. How could I not have noticed her condition worsening before? She moves slower than normal. When I stare at her face, I notice that the skin just under her jaw is a little looser, as if she's shriveling from the inside.

When the buzzer at the door sounds, I nearly fall out of my chair. I tap my fingers across the cuff at my wrist quickly. My cuffLINK is connected to our apartment, and my commands for the door are received immediately. It slides open noiselessly and Ms. White steps inside.

"How is everyone?" she asks cheerfully. Then, seeing my grim look, she asks again in a lower voice, "Is everything okay?"

"Everything's *fine*," Mom says, crossing the room. She picks up her brown purse from the bench by the door, but weighs it in her hand, as if the small bag was too heavy. She drops it back down; all her information is contained in her cuff, and she doesn't really need anything in her purse, but I can't help but think this is another sign that she's growing weaker.

Ms. White's eyes shoot to me for a more truthful answer about Mom's condition. Ms. White is Mom's best friend and my godmother, as well as manager of the Reverie Mental Spa—the business Mom developed before she got sick and where I intern. When I was younger, I tried calling her Aunt Jadis, even though we're not related, but it was weird, like calling a teacher by her first name. She's just always been Ms. White to me, even now, when she's one of the few still standing beside me after Mom got so sick.

As I fill Ms. White in on this morning's tomato episode, her mouth narrows to a thin line and her skin pales even more. Ms. White is originally from Germany, and her pale skin and platinum blond hair has always stood in contrast to Mom's and my Mediterranean darkness. As Ms. White listens to me, I can't help but compare her to Mom. In many ways, Ms. White looks like everything a responsible adult should be: she dresses in immaculate, designer linen suits, her hair is always razor-edge straight, and she just has the appearance of someone who gets things *done*. She looks exactly like what she is: a business manager. Beside her, Mom looks like an adult dressing up as a disheveled teenager, but it's Mom who's a literal genius and scientist.

"I'll take her to Dr. Simpa, and let him know," Ms. White tells me as we all head to the lift across from the apartment.

"I can do it," I say immediately.

Ms. White smiles at me kindly. "Let me. It's no trouble. And you look like you could use a break."

The lift doors open to the lobby of the building. Mom bought this building specifically for the development of the Reverie Mental Spa—we only moved into the apartment upstairs after Dad died.

"Don't you need me to work today?" I ask Ms. White as we move across the lobby floor.

Ms. White pauses. "I cancelled our appointments," she says.

I stare at her, surprised. She didn't know Mom was ill; how could she have known to clear the schedule?

"Something's come up," Ms. White says, lowering her voice. She drops back, letting Mom walk to the door on her own as she draws me to the side. "I'll tell you more about it later, but we have a very special... er... client coming in tonight. You don't have plans?"

I snort. I never have plans. All I do is work.

"We'll meet back here, then. But for now—you should go out. Try not to worry."

Ha. The only thing I do more than work is worry.

Ms. White leads Mom to the door, where she has a private transport waiting to whisk them to her doctor. I stand in the empty lobby, considering my options. With no clients, the spa is empty, and there's really no point in my staying here.

The lobby is all glass and chrome, and immaculately appointed. The front wall is made entirely of glass, and is illuminated with our logo: a giant neon sheep. The sheep bounces over the letters of **REVERIE,** making them melt into our slogan: **RELIVE your fondest memories with Reverie Mental Spa.**

People from all over the world come here for Mom's invention—a process that allows people to lucidly dream in a state of utter relaxation. It's expensive, but worth it: Having a reverie is like reliving the best day of your life in perfect clarity.

I briefly consider ignoring Ms. White's advice about going out. I could go to the basement level of the building, where Mom's reverie chairs are set up. I could give myself a reverie and get lost in the past, forget about this morning, and Mom's blood, and Mom's disease, and everything else.

I could relive a day when Dad was still alive, and Mom wasn't sick.

But then I remember the image of Dad's flesh melting from his skin in my nightmare.

Maybe I should go out.

FOUR

WHEN I STEP OUTSIDE, THE GLASS doors of the Reverie Mental Spa closing behind me, I allow myself a moment to get lost in the chaos of the city. Our building is on one of the busiest streets in the city. The autotaxis and magnatram zip by the road in front of the spa, with dozens of e-scooters weaving in and around the traffic. A crowd of people gather in front of the Reverie Mental spa—tourists, snapping pics with their cuffs of the elaborate iron gates that lead into Central Gardens, just across the street from us.

New Venice was one of the first good things to come of the Secessionary War. After more than a decade of violence, the war ended a year before I was born with the formation of the Unified Countries, a republic designed to govern global issues. It took a while for the new government to decide on a city to be its seat of operations, and ultimately, it decided that a new government deserved a brand new city.

Originally, the island nation of Malta consisted of two landmasses, but New Venice was built as a giant, ten-kilometer square bridge connecting the two large islands. Right now, if I were to blast through the walkway, I'd land in the Mediterranean Sea.

"Excuse me," I say, squeezing past a tour group. It's easy to spot the tourists, even if they didn't have a red band across the tops of their cuffLINKs. The tourists are the ones who stop in the middle of the street to stare at simple things like street androids. They're the ones who lift their feet and stare at them as they walk on the rubberized cement of the kinetic energy generator sidewalks. They're the ones who are *always* dressed in shorts and tank tops, no matter what the weather, because they cannot imagine this Mediterranean island being anything but warm and sunny.

They also tend to look at the city through tourist programs. Most of their pupils flash silver, a sure sign they've connected their eye nanobots to some sort of program—history walks through the city, or news, or chats with their friends back home, or just recording everything they see.

I slip around the tourists gathered at the gates of Central Gardens. A street android stands at attention just on the other side, and I go to him before the tourists spot him.

"A pastizza please," I say, pointing to a pastry filled with cheese. When I touch my cuff to the scanner attached to the street android's cart, my credits go down and my caloric counter goes up. I consider buying two pastizzi, but if I go over my daily calorie count, I'll have to add at least an hour of exercise to my day.

I idly wonder how much trouble I'd get in for cutting off my cuff. One more pastizza wouldn't hurt anything. But, of course, if the cuff comes off, all the links to my health status go offline and an alert is sent out.

I stuff my single pastizza into my mouth, relishing the warm, gooey cheese. The flaky crust crumbles down my shirt as I tap my cuff against the scanner by the gate. Four armed guards stand at attention, and another one checks my info before allowing me into the gardens. The Secessionary War ended before I was born, but there are still threats against our blossoming global union.

While I eat, I check my messages on my cuff. An advertisement for a clothing store I went to once, a summary of articles that mentioned Dad or Mom's names published online this week.

"Look, Harold!" a woman exclaims, stopping in the middle of the path so suddenly that I bump into her. "Sorry, sorry," she says, grinning at me as I step around her. "I just got so excited!"

I glance up to see what she's looking at—Triumph Towers. The path through Central Gardens is designed to wind around, showing off the city's skyline at strategic points.

I step off the kinetic walkway, cutting through the manicured lawn. New Venice is the capital of the world—not just in politics and economy, but everything else, too:

fashion, art, technology. While I've never left the shores of Malta, I feel as if I'm more global than a world traveler. Everything comes to us.

My wrist buzzes and the tech foil vibrates against my skin. I look at the words that flash across the top of my cuff, then glide my fingers over the surface, answering the call.

My cuffLINK—the licensing, identification, and networking key I wear around my wrist—is linked to the nanobots inside me. Twenty years ago, the only bots people used were for vaccines, but now everyone has nanobots. Enhancement bots ensure that everyone has good vision and hearing throughout their lives. Media bots connect to our wrist cuff, giving us the ability to display information directly into our retinas, or to listen to music or have conversations through the interface without using an earpiece.

Now, as I answer the call, my vision fills with a holographic image of my best friend, Akilah Xuereb. Her voice rings in my ear—"Hella', Ella!"—all of this directly fed from my cuff to the nanobots in my eyes and ears.

"Hi, Aks!" I grin. I keep walking through the park; the image of Akilah floats in front of me, as if she's walking with me.

"What are you up to?" she asks. She sweeps her hair—done up in long Havana twists—off her shoulders, shaking it behind her.

"Just on a walk."

Akilah doesn't speak for a moment. Her eyes narrow. "What's wrong?" she asks.

"Nothing."

Akilah purses her lips.

"*Nothing*," I insist.

"What happened?"

I sigh. I can never get anything past Akilah. We've been friends since primary school, when she let me twist her fluffy hair into dozens of braids during recess.

"Mom's worse," I confess as I veer deeper into the gardens, heading toward the trees.

Akilah curses, and I note that she's picked up some more colorful words since starting her service year in the military. Before becoming a full citizen, everyone must complete a year of service at the end of secondary school. A white band illuminates the top of my cuff to indicate that I'm serving as an intern; Akilah has a yellow band on her cuff since she was assigned to a year of military service.

"But does this mean your father's treatment isn't working any more?" Akilah asks.

I shake my head. "And we've had to scale back on it, anyway. She's overloaded with bots."

Dad's medical nanobots in Mom's system work to replace the synapses that the disease destroyed, but there's a limit to the number of nanobots someone can have. No one realized nanobots were dangerous until the Secessionary War. That's when the government started giving the human soldiers new enhancement bots. Bots in the eyes to make a soldier be able to see in the dark. Bots in the muscles to give superhuman strength. Bots in the mind to make a soldier go for days and days without sleep.

Too many bots. And one by one, the soldiers started to develop bot-brain—their brains literally turned to mush. It was a quick but gruesome death as the very bots they'd taken to live destroyed them from the inside out.

Which is exactly what will happen to Mom if she takes more bots.

"What are you going to do?" Akilah asks.

I pause, looking at my friend. It's almost like she's here with me, but of course she's not. I glance up at the moon, nothing more than a pale white shadow on the rich, blue sky.

Akilah's somewhere there, at the lunar military base. And while I can see her, thanks to the nanobots projecting her image directly into my eye, I can't feel her. I can't touch her.

"There's nothing I can do," I say finally, defeated. "Listen, I've got to go."

Akilah shoots me a sympathetic frown, then her face freezes. "Wait... you said you were going for a walk. You're not... Ella, where are you?"

"Nowhere," I say too quickly.

"Ella! You *can't* obsess! You really shouldn't—"

"Gotta go, bye!" I say quickly as I swipe my fingers across my cuff and disconnect the call. Akilah's right—I shouldn't obsess over my father's death. But after that nightmare and Mom's health, I just... I need to see it again. Dad's grave.

FIVE

A LONG, LONG TIME AGO, PEOPLE USED to bury the dead. But New Venice is a modern city, and there's no room for carved stones and wasted earth. Instead, people are cremated, and their remains are used to fertilize the roots of trees and other plants in Central Gardens. On the far side of the park, near the perimeter walk, the trees are larger, some of them planted from the remains of people who died before the city was finished being built. Not everyone who dies has a tree planted— only the people very important to the city.

Like my father.

The groveyard is my favorite place in the entire city. It's the only place in New Venice where real trees grow. I know that if we dig down far enough, the base of my city is steel rafters and concrete, not solid earth. But it *feels* real, here, where the trees are growing up from the gently rolling slopes of the cemetery that's really a forest.

My steps slow as I reach the groveyard. The trees waft gently in the breeze, but my attention zeroes in on one in particular—a small holly with a plaque encircling its base.

Philip D. Shepherd
2299-2341
Truth lies in the heart of fortune.

I stand there, blinking away tears as I stare at the hard, prickly leaves. The world grows cold and still. There's a sort of bitter finality to seeing his death date right there in front of me.

And there's something worse inside of me, a weight tugging my heart out of my chest at the way I notice, for the first time, the way there's space under Dad's epigraph. Space for Mom's name to be inscribed. She'll be planted here, too, her ashes mingling with Dad's, growing from an ivy that will wrap around the holly tree. I was the one who set up Dad's funeral arrangements; I saw the ones she'd already prepared after she was diagnosed.

I grit my teeth together.

I can't lose Mom. Not her, too.

"Um?"

I turn around, surprised that anyone else is here. The groveyard isn't exactly popular, not when you could pretty much do anything else in the city. The guy who spoke is about my age, a little taller than me (which isn't saying much), and he barely fits in the worn black jacket covering his cut biceps despite the warm day. I wouldn't say he's handsome, or even particularly good-looking, but there's something about him that makes my heart clang like a bell. He has dark, cropped hair, but the most striking thing about him his is pale blue eyes.

Or maybe I just notice his eyes because he's gaping at me.

"Yeah?" I ask, impatient when he doesn't say anything else.

The guy reaches for my arm, pulling me closer to him. I wrest free—I don't like strangers touching me—and he reaches for me again, his wrist encircling my arm and yanking me painfully several steps forward. I act on instinct, twisting my wrist out of his grasp and slamming the end of my palm against his face, connecting with an audible crunch against his nose and splitting his lip open. "Don't touch me!" I shout at him. My muscles are tense, ready to spring into action. I'm suddenly aware of how very alone we are.

"Look—" the guy starts, but I jerk around my elbow blocking him from coming closer.

It's like the guy's face snaps into a mask, one made of hard edges. All the color drains from his face—except for the bright pink of the blossoming bruise on his cheek and nose. His heavy eyebrows pull down into a scowl, and he glares at me so much that I take an instinctive step backward. My movement makes some sort of emotion flicker across his face—regret?—but it's quickly masked again.

"Look, I'm only here to warn you." There's something of desperation and danger in his expression; he looks like a caged animal, despite the fact that we're in an open area.

My eyes grow wide, and I look around me, half expecting to see attackers jump out from behind the trees.

He rubs his hand over his short hair. "It's not—it's—"

"What?" I ask. I wrap my right hand over my left wrist, over my cuff, where there's a panic button that will bring police to my aid if this guy turns dangerous.

The guy's eyes narrow when he sees. He curses. "I just wanted to warn you about Akilah," he said. "There, I said it, I'm gone now."

"What?" I ask again as he turns away. "What about Akilah?"

He hesitates.

"How do you even know Akilah?"

He stops entirely.

"Don't be like that," he says without turning. His shoulders slump, defeated, and I almost don't catch what he says next. "I know it sounds crazy, but... listen, you can't trust her."

"Of course I can; she's my best friend!" My only friend.

He still doesn't turn around. "Not any more," he says.

I start to object, but he turns, throwing up his hands. "I only came here to say that. Out of... respect for you father. That's all. I'm going."

He starts to walk off—and I let him, there's no point talking to crazy—but he pauses at Dad's grave. He stands there respectfully, his eyes lingering on the little stone marker that encircles Dad's tree. His face is hidden as he leans down, his mouth muttering words I cannot hear.

I glance away, tucking a piece of hair behind my ear. He's talking to Dad the same way I do. His face is full of sadness, his tone, regret. He looks kind.

He looks as if he misses Dad as much as I do.

SIX

I WALK SLOWLY BACK TO MY apartment and the Reverie Mental Spa. I have no idea who that guy was, but there's something about him that feels like déjà vu. I shake my head, trying to clear it. I'm tempted to call Akilah, but she only has certain blocks of time she can use her cuff; the military is strict about communication on the base. I have no idea how that guy knew Akilah, but he was clearly—

I stop in my tracks, almost slapping myself on my head. *Of course.* He was wearing a jacket, even though it's so hot outside today. He was trying to cover up his cuff. He was my age, he knew Akilah, and he didn't want anyone to see his cuff.

He's a defector.

Anyone assigned to the military has a yellow band on their cuff. After their year of service, the band turns gold. But if they scamper, then their cuff turns black so everyone can see.

That guy was probably assigned military for his year of service, just like Akilah. And instead of serving it, he defected. He must have been enlisted long enough to meet Akilah—he knew her well enough to learn who I was, at least—but then dropped out. What a loser. Without completing his year of service, he's lost all chance of going to university, he can't vote, he might as well pack it up and go to a Secessionary State. I don't know why he bothered to try to say something to me about Akilah, but someone willing to defect has more issues than I care to try unravel.

By the time I get back home, Mom and Ms. White are already there. Mom assures me everything's fine, but my eyes shoot to Ms. White's grim look.

"Oh, don't be so doom and gloom!" Mom says. "Look what Dr. Simpa gave me!"

Mom points to Ms. White's office. I shoot her a confused look, and then someone steps out of the office.

Not someone.

Something.

"No," I groan.

"A new nursing android!" Mom beams. Her old one had broken down a few months ago, and I'd done my best to delay her getting a new one. During the Secessionary War, androids played a huge part in suppressing the uprising and helping end the violence. Now, decommissioned androids are cheap, and everyone has at least one. We have cleaning androids and a few working in the spa, but a nursing android will be around Mom all the time, impossible for me to avoid.

This one moves to stand beside Mom. It's wearing normal clothes, the only sign that it's an android from the label pinned to its chest: Robotic Operations Service Interface E-assistant.

"I'm going to call her Rosie," Mom says proudly.

"It doesn't need a name," I say, even though it's useless to argue. Mom always names the androids like they're human.

Maybe that's why I *don't* like them. They wear human clothing over human skin—not literally, it's really just a finely textured rubber and silicone mix—and they have perfectly groomed features. From behind, all androids look human. They sound human, too, if you ignore the fact that they never say anything worthwhile, only spitting out programmed phrases and responses. It's really only when you see an android's face that you know something's... off. Every effort has been made to design android faces to look as human as possible. But the more they try to make the robots look human, the more I'm unnerved by the little things that remind me they're *not*. Eyes that are lenses. Facial features that respond to a program, not self-will. Too-even smiles hiding porcelain teeth.

The more human they try to make androids look, the more they just remind me of death.

I've only seen death once. But at the funeral, when I peered down at my father, I remember thinking that although the body looked like Dad, it wasn't, not really. The thing in the casket wore his face, but not his life.

That's what androids remind me of. Something with a face, but nothing behind it.

"I was about to have Rosie give your mother a reverie," Ms. White says. "I've already programmed her to use the machinery."

I expect Mom to protest—reveries are expensive to create, and we're such a new business that she always insists we can't afford it—but instead Mom sighs. "That would be nice," she says.

My heart sinks. The news from the doctor must have been really bad.

Ms. White stands, but I jump to Mom's side. "I'll do it!" I say quickly. I don't want to be replaced by a robot.

Ms. White walks with us to the lift, and, after Mom gets on, touches my elbow to hold me back.

"Was it—?" I ask

Ms. White nods. "The nanobots are in complete remission," she says. "They're failing, one by one. And Dr. Simpa confirmed—your mother can't have any more. She's at max—over max, actually."

When she sees my face, she pushes me onto the lift. "Don't worry about it," she says. "We'll figure something out."

Mom chats as we descend, and I realize why she's had such a forced cheerfulness lately.

She knows something's wrong.

She's trying to keep it from me, to make me think it's not as bad as it is. I shut my eyes briefly, weighing my options. When I open them, I smear a grin across my face. If she wants me to pretend everything is fine, I can pretend. For her, I can pretend.

SEVEN

MOM BREATHES A DEEP SIGH WHEN WE reach the reverie chamber and she settles into the plush cushions of the chair. She runs her fingers over the armrest, tracing patterns in the fibers. I lower the hood over her head—a large, half-globe helmet that will emit sonic flashes that she won't feel or hear, but that will spark the memories in her mind. Mom shudders as I press the cool electrodes onto her forehead.

Before I do anything else, I connect Mom's cuff to the reverie chair, checking her health stats. I have to swallow back a gasp of surprise—I've never seen her with such bad stats. Dangerously low blood pressure and heart rate, low oxygen, vitamin deficiency, constant dialysis pumps... how has she hidden how bad off she is from me for so long?

"Ella?" Mom asks when she notices that I've frozen, my eyes glued to her stats.

I force a watery grin on my face. "Ready?" I ask.

Mom nods and I turn my focus to the neurostimulator and adjust the dials, setting a low direct current of electricity to her brain. In moments, Mom's slipped into sleep.

I take this moment to look at Mom, and try to ingrain her image into my memory. *This* image. The lines on her face smooth, and a small smile twitches the corners of her mouth. She looks peaceful now. Like she's not even sick at all.

My fingers glide over the controls in the room. Every single thing—from the automatically dimming lights to the reverie chair itself—was designed by Mom. People had theorized that reveries were possible, but it was Mom who made the system. It's Mom who's changing the world with it.

Reveries are a state of controlled lucid memory recall. When you're in the reverie chair, you experience a memory—your best memory, the time when you were happiest—just as if it were all happening again. On a purely theoretical level, reveries are easy—a dose of a specially designed drug plus transcranial direct current stimulation equals a state of lucid dreaming based on a pre-existing memory.

Reveries enable you to retreat into your own mind. Ms. White works with the government so she can funnel grant money into Mom's research, and she's experimented with having scientists and researchers use reveries to focus entirely on a formula or problem they have to solve. It almost always works: Reveries open your mind up so that everything inside of you becomes entirely focused on one thought.

But Mom didn't invent reveries for science. She invented them for herself, for a reason.

In reveries, she gets to see Dad again. Before she got sick.

I slip out of the reverie chamber, keeping an eye on Mom's health stats. I know from experience that Mom will be dreaming about Dad, reliving a day with him. It will feel real to her, as real as real life, and when she wakes up, maybe she'll be able to hold onto that peace and happiness, at least for a bit.

As I watch Mom's health scans, I can see everything improving—her tension, her blood pressure, her heart rate—it's all getting better with every second she's in the reverie. There's no science to that: happy people are healthier. It's not a permanent cure, but the effects usually last her a couple of days at least.

Red flashes across the control panel. I lean in, inspecting it. Her brain scan goes off the charts—her reverie is failing—and by the time I look back at Mom's health stats, every single one of them is back up.

I race back into the reverie chamber just as Mom's eyes flutter open. I can't tell if, as the reverie fades, Mom feels fear or panic first, but either way, her eyes grow wide and then suddenly narrow. Her arms and legs twitch, as if she's trying to summon the strength stand up.

"What happened?" she asks, looking at me. Her eyes are glazed—the reverie drug is still in her system.

It's just not working.

"I couldn't get you to a reverie," I say. "I'm sorry, Mom, I thought I did everything right..." I lean down, inspecting the chair, the sonic hood, the electrodes.

Mom puts a hand on my arm. "Ella," she says.

I ignore her, trying to figure out what went wrong.

"Ella." Mom's voice is firmer this time. I pause. "You know why it didn't work."

I shake my head. "That's not it."

Mom sighs, shifting in the reverie chair. "I theorized about this before. Hebb's Disease attacks the synapses in my brain. My body's not strong enough to have a reverie."

The amount of pain in her eyes when she says this kills me. Reveries were the last thing that gave her any modicum of peace. She couldn't forget about being sick, not ever, except in a reverie.

This damn disease has taken away so much. Not just her health, but her chances of happiness. She used to love to go out; now she never does. She used to run. She used to sing. But Hebb's has slowly, irrevocably taken it all away.

And now it's taken away reveries, the only chance she had to escape.

"It'll work; let me try one more time."

"Ella," Mom says gently. "It's hopeless."

"Just stay there. Don't unplug." I pause. "Actually, here." I give her a second dose of the reverie drug—it won't hurt her, just make her sleep.

She's asleep again by the time I slip back into the control room, pacing, pacing. There has to be something I can do. Mom's sick—really sick this time, maybe so sick that—

I force myself not to complete that thought.

But she's in pain. She's been hiding it, but her health stats don't lie. She hurts, she constantly hurts, but this—this—a reverie—would alleviate that pain. Just for a little. But that would be enough.

My mind races in a myriad of thoughts. *Mom can't have more nanobots. Mom can't have a reverie. There's nothing I can do.*

I pace back and forth in front of the control panel, thinking, thinking. There has to be something that I can *do.* I can't just *not* do something. I have to—

I stop.

Mom can't have more nanobots.

But I can. I'm nowhere near my limit.

On the other side of the control panel is another door, a secondary reverie chamber that's connected with Mom's. Mom theorized that someone could go inside someone else's reverie by linking two chairs together. She experimented, but it never worked—until she developed nanobots that were designed to help the observer break into the other person's mind. She ultimately decided that it was too great a risk to give someone the additional nanobots, and she closed off the room.

But if it worked...

I could go into Mom's reverie. I could enhance it, make it stronger, help her to stay in her memories, help her to remember what life was like before she got sick.

I check Mom's stats one last time—the extra dose of the reverie drug has helped, and her mind is building the platform for her memories, but I can tell it's shaky at best. She's going to wake up again any second.

It's now or never.

EIGHT

MY HANDS SHAKE AS I APPROACH THE secondary reverie chair. It's nowhere near as nice as the one Mom uses with clients—why bother cloaking it in cushions and velvet when no one can use it?

A small recess in the wall holds what I was looking for: the additional nanobots needed for someone to use the chair. I pick up the vial. The inside looks empty, all except for a tiny sprinkle of silver glitter on the bottom. When I shake the vial, the silver moves like liquid.

There are *millions* of microscopic nanobots in that vial.

I take a deep breath.

I know this is dangerous. I have no idea what my nanobot count is, but I know that I shouldn't be letting any more infect my body.

But Mom developed these. And if, by taking them, I can help her...

I stride across the room to the chair, and slide the nanobot vial next to the poison-green reverie drug in the injector. One dose will give me both the drug and the bots, administered as a puff of gas in my eyes when the sonic hood turns on.

My body wants to turn and run.

Instead, I sit in the chair. It's long and reclined, designed to make me lay down more than sit. I slide my left arm against the raised bar, connecting my cuff to the system. I jam the electrodes onto my skin and lower the sonic hood over me.

Commence joined reverie? The system asks me in warning yellow letters.

I shut my eyes, flinching even though nothing has happened yet. I think about the microscopic bots crawling over my eyes, behind them, into my brain, burrowing into grey wrinkles.

"It'll work," I say to myself, trying to convince myself that wishful thinking was truth.

I push the button.

The reverie chair hums with life. I have a moment to see the sparkle of the nanobots mixed with the green puff of reverie drug, and then I blink, and then—

—My body *explodes* with pain.

My knees jerk up toward my chest as my muscles spasm and tighten. It's like a cramp for my whole body. Pain slices through me, shredding my muscles. I gag on bile, then gasp for air, and I'm deeply aware of the heavy thump of my heart, ricocheting in my chest.

And then—nothing.

Nothing at all. I cannot hear the sound of my beating heart. I cannot feel the warmth of life within me.

I'm dead.

NINE

I HEAR MUSIC. I ALMOST RECOGNIZE the tune, something soft, played on a guitar, but then the world bursts into being. Light explodes from a pinpoint in the distance, and with the light, everything else—scents, warmth, the feel of air on my skin.

In the distance, I can see a house.

I know that house.

It's where we lived when I was a kid, before everything bad happened, a narrow two-level building in Rabat, a dusty, limestone-drenched suburb of New Venice.

I step toward the house, and in that one step I cross kilometers. The house moves from the background to right in front of me, so close that I can touch it.

Singing.

I creep around the edge of the house. It's perfect in every detail, from the stone walls to the clay tiled roof with aggressively green, stubborn ivy crawling up the wall toward the kitchen window. A potted chinotto tree standing by the doorway wafts in the warm breeze.

The window in front of the kitchen sink is open. I stand on my tiptoes, peering inside. My mother—younger than normal—dances around the kitchen, laughing, covered in flour. And Dad's behind her, pulling out a huge bouquet of yellow roses for her. I can hear childlike laughter—*my* laughter, I realize, when I was a little kid—weaving in and out of the sounds of my parents' chatter and over the whirr of the electric mixer, but my mother's reverie isn't focused on me as a little girl.

It's focused on Dad.

If my mother looked through the window over the sink, she could see me as I am now—eighteen years old with dark brown hair hanging just past my chin, my gold-flecked brown eyes staring straight at her. But I don't think Mom will do that. Her body is aware that this is a reverie and not real, but her subconscious is letting her relive the memory. I could probably stand nose-to-nose with her and she wouldn't see me. Her brain wants to live in the reverie and will do anything to protect itself from leaving it.

From becoming aware that this isn't real.

Looking at Mom and Dad now, I wish this was real. I would trade anything to be able to let my mother live this life.

But it's past. This is long ago, well before her disease ate her from the inside out. Before I grew up. Before Mom developed the technology that even makes reverie possible. Before Dad died, giving her the reason to invent the process of reveries so she could live with him in her mind.

Mom's memory falters. The house flickers.

I duck under the window, just in case this was enough disturbance to push Mom out of the reverie. Crouching against the house, I cup my hands and blow air into them, thinking *cinnamon*.

A warm, overwhelming scent of the spice wraps around me. I throw my hands up, envisioning the smell permeating every corner of Mom's dream.

"The cookies!" I hear Mom say, her voice a trill of laughter. She's fully back in the reverie now, the flicker gone.

But just in case, I do everything else I can think of to make Mom's memory even more real. I hum the opening strands of Dad's favorite song, "Moon River," the song I heard at the start of the reverie. The sound continues long after I quit humming—Mom's memory has picked it up, adding depth to her reverie. I add my memories of the old house to hers, and the kitchen grows in sharper details, like a blurry image coming into focus.

I think everything's going well. Maybe I can leave the reverie, let Mom's mind fill in everything else.

But then I hear her voice. It is so strained that I stand up and lean closer, despite the already-weakened state of the reverie.

"Philip," Mom says, her voice heavy with unshed tears. "Philip, I don't think this is real. I wish it was... but

I'm in a reverie, aren't I? You're not real. You're just a memory."

I act on instinct as I swing my arm, and the wall separating me from the kitchen and my mother disappears. The laws of physics do not apply in reverie. My mother starts to turn, but I lunge forward and grab the sides of her head, keeping her facing Dad.

I can feel, deep within me, power. Control. I can control my mother's reverie, like a puppet master pulling strings. I concentrate with all my strength on the idea of this memory.

But then I hear my mother whimper, and I know that now she's remembering the pain of her disease, and all around me the kitchen flickers, and even the memory of my father flickers.

No. I reach deep within me, to a core of power I didn't know was there, and tap into every happy thought and memory I have of my parents like this and I imagine them all pouring out of me, engulfing my mother.

warmth love heart-full joy love chaos kissing the taste of his lips the feel of his body love the child the soft sleeping noises tiny fingers tiny toes clear brown eyes open wide love love love

I rip my hands away. My mother's reverie body sags and relaxes. I reached inside her and pulled out the deepest memories in her body, the memories that words can't describe, the memories that are as much a piece of her as her arms and legs. Those are the ones she's filled with now.

Mom's face looks up to Dad's, and I know now she truly is in the reverie, and this feeling of peace and joy will stay with her long after she wakes up.

It worked.

I turn to leave. It's safe for me to go now; Mom's reverie is definitely connected.

But I glance back. I can't help it.

I miss Dad, too. I miss the way he looks. My own dreams are nowhere near as vivid as Mom's. And even though he's younger here than I remember him, and he has a scruffy bit of facial hair that makes him look reckless, and he's missing his glasses, and there's more hair on top of his head, it's still Dad.

And then he looks at me.

"Ella," he says, his voice cutting through the soft sounds of memory in sharp, precise tones. "Ella. You have to wake up."

TEN

I JERK SO HARD THAT I CRACK MY SKULL against the sonic hood. I throw it back, ripping the electrodes off my skin, nearly breaking the chain of my necklace in the process. My skin vibrates. I stare at it, awed and scared, as my flesh ripples like an earthquake. The vibrations seep past my skin, into my bones, and I feel as if I'm hearing *something*, the buzzing of my soul within the confines of my flesh.

And then I blink, and everything is silent and still.

I cover my eyes with a shaking hand, trying to regroup. A hallucination. My body is reacting to the extra nanobots I injected myself with. That last image was... disturbing. And it shouldn't have been possible. Reveries aren't real. I wasn't really there in Mom's head. Memories are nothing more than electrical impulses shooting across the brain's synapses. There is no way Dad—it wasn't Dad, it was just a dream of him—there's no *way* that could have seen me. Could have *spoken* to me.

I gasp, and check Mom's stats, worried that the last image of Dad being so weird and creepy affected her. But she's blissfully asleep, still in her dreamworld, her health stats calm and far better than they were before we started. The door slides open and Ms. White bursts in, her eyes wide and panicked. "Ella!" she screeches. "What did you do?" She rushes to my side, noting the cold sweat prickling my skin.

"I did it," I say, fully realizing what just happened.

"Are you okay?" Ms. White ignores me, checking the health stats on my cuff. "Where's your mother?"

I jerk my wrist free and grab her hand, forcing Ms. White to look at me. "I did it," I repeat, a smile breaking out on my face. "I did it!"

"Did... what?" Her voice is hesitant and wary.

A quiet beeping starts from the control panel, followed by a flash of red. "Mom's almost out," I say, jumping from the chair and pushing past Ms. White. Her head turns between me and the secondary reverie chair, and I almost wish I'd been looking at her face when she noticed the empty nanobot vial.

"Ella!" She gasps, chasing after me.

I race into Mom's reverie chamber just as her eyelids flutter open. "Good reverie?" I ask, beaming at her. My smile falters. What if she remembers when it almost broke? What if she remembers Dad being so strange?

But then I see her expression, and my heart melts in relief. "The best," she says.

I help her get up out of the reverie chair. "What did you remember?" I ask, even though I know the answer.

Mom squeezes my hand. "My last good day."

She moves forward to talk to Ms. White, but I'm paralyzed. Her last good day. Every day since then has paled in comparison to that one day, years and years ago.

Mom's new nursing android, Rosie, stands at attention by the door and Mom leans against her as she heads to the lift.

"Coming?" Mom asks, the happy glow of her reverie around her so palpable that I can almost see it.

"No—I need to talk to Ella about her internship," Ms. White says before I can reply. She shoots me a look, and I wave Mom on. After we hear the lift doors close behind Mom and the android, Ms. White turns on me, her face a mix of pride and anger.

"Ella!" she says, her voice already rising. "That was really, *really* dangerous!"

I shudder, my body remembering that moment when it seized, and then it became nothing. I'd thought I'd died.

"I was fine," I say to her dismissively. "And more importantly, it *worked.*"

Ms. White sucks in a breath. "What was it like?" she asks eagerly, the familiar sparkle of scientific discovery in her eye.

"It was amazing!" I shout, spinning around her. "I was *in* her reverie! I could *control* it!"

Ms. White's eyes widen.

THE BODY ELECTRIC

"It was just like I was there," I continue. I start to tell her everything, but she raises her hand to stop me, a grim look replacing her excitement.

"How many bots did you take?" she asks.

"Just one vial."

"One... *vial*?"

"Is that too much?"

"I... uh... you're okay?"

"Yeah, I feel fine." At least, I do now. If I took too many, maybe that's why my body reacted so violently.

"Ella, that was very irresponsible. And dangerous. You could have overdosed."

"Yeah, but I didn't."

"But you could have."

"But I *didn't*." I glare at Ms. White. What I do is not her business, especially when what I do, I do for Mom.

Ms. White sinks into the reverie chair Mom just left. Her shoulders slouch forward, the ends of her hair obscuring her face. "You're going to have to let go one day," she says.

"Excuse me?" The words sound harsh in my own mouth.

"This internship year was supposed to prepare you for college, not prepare you for becoming a nurse to your mother. The year's almost up, and look at what you're doing. You're killing yourself, just to let your mother dream for a half hour."

"It's worth it," I mutter.

Ms. White grabs my chin and forces me to look up at her. "It's not," she says.

I jerk free. "What do you want me to do?" I ask, practically shouting. "Just let my mother die?"

Ms. White's gaze doesn't waver from mine. "Yes," she says simply.

I reel back violently, as if she'd struck me across the face.

"Don't look at me like that," Ms. White says. "I just need you to understand that you're going to have to let your mother go one day. Maybe one day soon. And it's not worth risking the rest of your life to scrabble together a few more minutes for her."

"I don't want to talk about this," I say, my jaw tensing.

"El—"

"I do *not* want to talk about this."

We glare at each other. It's so rare for us to disagree. Since Dad's death and Akilah's service year on the lunar base, it's just been me and Ms. White against the world.

Ms. White sighs and pushes up against her knees. "I didn't come down here to fight," she says. "I came here because there's someone to meet you."

For one crazy moment, my mind flashes to the boy I met in the groveyard. Did he follow me home? His pale blue eyes are burned into my memory, scorching my mind.

"Are you ready?" Ms. White asks, leading the way to the door.

ELEVEN

I SOON LEARN THAT WHOEVER IT IS I'M meeting, I'm not meeting him here. Ms. White assures me that Mom's fine to stay with the nursing android alone, and she gets into an auto-taxi with me. I try to quiz her as we zip around Central Gardens, but Ms. White just smiles obliquely.

The drive isn't long. The auto-taxi stops at the barricades around Triumph Towers, the capital building at the other end of Central Gardens.

I shoot Ms. White a look, but she still doesn't answer me. My stomach starts to twist with nerves.

When New Venice was originally built, Triumph Towers were meant to symbolize the combined government—the Unified Countries—born from the ashes of war, like a phoenix. They look even more like flames now that the newly developed solar glass has been affixed to the top of each of the five towers. The solar glass glitters like crystallized amber, radiating a soft glow visible even in the bright daylight. At night, the towers cast most of the city in a warm twilight so that it's never really dark here. The giant blue-and-white flag symbolizing the UC flaps noisily just behind a beautiful marble water fountain in the plaza stretching out between the towers and Central Gardens.

Ms. White straightens her pale linen jacket and leads me across the plaza, crowded with tourists, street androids trying to sell us tantalizing snacks, and hawkers pitching tourism program downloads. A plethora of languages drifts through the air, words I don't recognize weaving together with ones I do. The nanobots in my ears struggle to translate the differing languages, but it's a mismatched mess, bits and pieces of everything everyone's saying, mostly excitement to go to the top of the world's tallest tower, from which you can see both Europe and Africa.

Ms. White leads me past the fountain and the crowds, toward a less ostentatious entrance. She flashes her cuff at one of the security guards, and we're quickly whisked away into the central tower and to a high-speed lift that carries us up and up. My heart races as we rise, and I'm deeply aware of how disheveled I look. Beside me, Ms. White looks perfect, every one of her pale blond hairs smooth, her pencil skirt straight.

"Don't worry," Ms. White says, grinning when she notices my nerves.

The lift doors slide open to one of the top floors of the tower. I trail behind Ms. White absorbing every detail.

Most of the outer walls are floor-to-ceiling tinted glass, giving me a glimpse of the world outside. The bridge New Venice is built on is nearly ten kilometers long and wide, filled with skyscrapers and city streets and buildings, but still, it's just a bridge. From the rooftop garden above my apartment, I have a great view of Central Gardens and Triumph Towers, but it's rare for me to catch a glimpse of the sea—there are too many buildings. But here, atop the tallest tower in the city, I can see the clean lines of the perimeter of the city, and the glittering caps of waves rolling from the Mediterranean. I trace the outline of the city with my eyes. I can see exactly where the bridge connects with the island of Malta, where the smooth lines of the manufactured meets the broken, rocky edges of the natural land.

"Ella?" Ms. White calls, and I rush forward to keep up. A large, ornate set of double doors is closed in front of her. As I step beside her, the doors creak open.

A woman stands on the other side, and my breath catches in my throat.

"No freaking way," I say, then I clap a hand over my mouth.

The woman smiles.

"It's a pleasure to meet you," she says.

I stutter out some sort of reply, still gaping at her. This is the most famous woman in the world. Prime Administrator Hwa Young is on her second ten-year term, and while she has a reputation of being ruthless, she has a kind smile on her petal-pink lips now, and I find myself unable to tear my eyes away from her. She's been the PA my entire life, but my awe has more to do with her power than her fame. Before she was PA, she was Secretary of War, and she, more than any other single person, ended the Secessionary War.

She is, quite simply, the hero of the new world.

She looks pretty, but not beautiful, and while she's plainly dressed, it's clear that her wardrobe is expensive. The suit jacket she wears is smooth and supple, the skirt moves like water falling over her slim hips. Although I know she's around sixty years old, she looks half her age, with her sleek black hair draped neatly over her shoulders.

"Please, come in," P.A. Young says graciously, stepping back so we can file into her office. With a flick of her fingers, the security personnel who'd been escorting us dissolves—some back into the hallway, some to an adjoining room, some beside the doors as they close with a dull thud. Ms. White touches my shoulder, gently steering me toward the cushioned seats across from a small circular table. PA Young sits first, then Ms. White pushes me into a seat before claiming her own chair.

PA Young starts to pour tea for us, adding a slice of lemon and a drizzle of honey to hers. I take a cup, but I'm too nervous to drink, so I leave it on the small table by my knee. My eyes keep darting to Ms. White. When she said we had an appointment to meet someone, I had no idea she meant *her*.

"I suspect you're curious as to why I asked Jadis to bring you to me," PA Young says.

I nod silently. My face feels like it's on fire. PA Young has this way of looking at me, as if I am one hundred percent the object of her focus, and it's disconcerting.

PA Young leans forward, concern etched on her face. "I needed to warn you."

The words are so reminiscent of what the boy at the groveyard said earlier today that I'm too shocked to say anything.

"Your mother's technology... it's groundbreaking."

A smile creeps up on my face. I'm proud of Mom and her work.

"But," PA Young continues, "it's also very dangerous."

"Dangerous?" I ask. What's dangerous about people reliving their memories?

"I've read your mother's published research. It seems possible that people could misuse it. While it's not been done before, it's theoretically possible that someone could enter someone else's reverie—"

"It's no longer a theory," Ms. White interrupts.

The silence in the room is like a physical thing, a snake winding its way around us. PA Young's head turns slowly to Ms. White.

"Ella did it. This afternoon."

PA Young whips back around to me. "Is this true?" she asks, a hard edge to her voice.

I twist my hands in my lap. "I—yes." Her gaze is so intense that I feel as if it will bore into me.

"Well." PA Young stands up. She sounds impressed. "Well, this changes everything."

TWELVE

THE PRIME ADMINISTRATOR STANDS, leaving the tea behind as she crosses her office to the glass wall showing an unmarred view of the Mediterranean Sea. When PA Young touches it, though, the interface system comes to life. A dozen or more images light up as the window turns opaque, blotting out the sky and sea on the other side. Documents with text too small for me to read from where I am, images of a military base, people I don't know.

In the center, though, is an image of my mother.

PA Young touches my mother's holographic face and moves the image to the upper corner. Beneath it, she moves an image of the Reverie Mental Spa and a reverie chair—the same chair Mom was in earlier today.

"Your mother has used her technology for recreation up to this point," PA Young says. "A plaything for rich clientele who want to amuse themselves."

Her words are harsh; I wouldn't describe Mom's work quite so dismissively. Sure, most of our customers just want to relive their glory days, but that doesn't make it worthless.

PA Young touches another image and enlarges it, putting it beside Mom's picture. It's an older man, with olive skin and dark hair greying at the temples. His eyes crinkle at the corners, and he looks as if he's about to laugh despite the fact that the picture is rather formal.

"This is Santiago Belles, the Representative Administrator from Spain," PA Young says. "I believe he's been approached by terrorists who wish to undermine the Unified Countries, and that he's considering treason."

I stare hard at the face, trying to see the evil behind his smiling eyes. He doesn't look like a traitor, but then again, no one ever does, not when you really look.

PA Young brings forward the holograms of Representative Belles and my mother's reverie chair. She turns around, looking at me expectantly.

I glance at Ms. White, unsure of what I'm supposed to do.

"Ella," Ms. White says carefully, "you went *into* your mother's reverie. Into her *mind*."

"And you can go into Belles's," PA Young continues. "You can find out who approached him, how deep the terrorist network goes. You have the potential to stop violence before it happens. We could try to trick the information out of him, or torture him, or anything else, but he could never be able to keep a secret from *you*, not when you were in his *head*."

My eyes widen at the thought, and I swallow a lump rising in my throat. Ms. White moves behind me. "We need to do more testing, first," Ms. White says firmly. "We have to make sure that Belles won't know that Ella's in his reverie, and we have to find a way to keep her safe."

PA Young stares at Ms. White for a long moment, and for the first time I understand why people are afraid of her. Without speaking, she turns back to the glass wall and brings up another image—a video clip. She enlarges it so that it fills up the entire space, then turns around to watch me with cold eyes as it plays.

I choke back my surprise.

My father. He's right there, in the lab on the screen. The audio's low, but I can just make out what's being said. Dad's talking with a few of the other scientists about a lab assistant that was recently let go while they're working on some sort of chemical compound. There's an early prototype of a reverie chair in the background—Dad had been experimenting with the chairs' functions to tap into android artificial intelligence.

Another man walks in. He looks nondescript—average height and build, wearing a lab coat—but everyone in the lab freezes. I see fear in my dad's eyes.

The man who just walked in turns slowly in a circle, looking at each of the scientists in turn. Then his gaze meets the video cameras; he must have known exactly where it was. It's not until his eyes meet mine that I realize—this isn't a man.

It's an android.

"This is a warning," the android says.

And then it explodes.

The screen goes white.

Bile rises in my throat, and I look around urgently, certain that I'm going to vomit.

I just saw my father's death.

Ms. White strokes my back, swiping my sweaty hair out of my face. "Really, Hwa, you didn't have to show her that," she says, glaring at the PA.

PA Young crouches in front of me, peering up at my face. "I'm sorry," she says. "I thought you knew."

"Of course I knew he was killed," I snap. And I knew how. The casket for my father had been shorter than it needed to be; they were only able to salvage some of his body after the explosion. And while I had known it was terrorists who set off the bomb, I never knew anything more than a nebulous idea that it had been some faceless group.

I look up at the holographic image of Representative Belles.

"I need you to understand," PA Young says. Her voice is gentle, but firm. "I need you to know just how dangerous a game we're playing. Because..."

"No," Ms. White's voice cuts across the room.

PA Young looks up at her. "We have to."

"What?" I ask.

"No," Ms. White repeats. "It's too dangerous. She's just a little girl."

"I already understand the danger," I say in a hollow voice, not taking my eyes off PA Young. "I saw my father's body, after. I understand."

Some sort of communication flashes between Ms. White and PA Young. But Ms. White steps back, ducking her head.

"I was Secretary of War for the UC before I was elected as Prime Administer, you know."

I do know. She was elected in a landslide; her work in ending the Secessionary War made her a cinch. She's the first PA who saw battle, the first to be a war hero.

"I studied war; I lived it. The Secessionary War was unlike any other. The first to use androids in battle, the first with nanorobotic bombs. And of course, the death toll was higher than any other war in history. The thing you have to remember," PA Young continues with a far-distant look in her eyes, "is that in the end, all war does is kill people. We can pretend it's something else, but it's not." Her clear eyes meet mine. "You know what my favorite war is?"

I shake my head. I didn't know people *had* favorite wars.

"World War II." PA Young's voice is musing. "In the early 1900s, there was the first World War—of course, they didn't call it 'World War I.' They called it 'The Great War,' or 'The War to End all Wars.' And then armies rose again, and we had another World War. That's why I like World War II. It was the war that came *after* the war to end all wars. It reminds me: the war is never over. We can't stop fighting it."

I stare at PA Young, unsure of what to say. The war *is* over—not just the ones she's talking about, but the Secessionary War, too. It's been over for longer than I've been alive.

When PA Young meets my eyes, I can tell that she sees my doubt. "The war never ends," she repeats, her voice more firm now, none of the reminiscence lingering. "And there is always a price to pay. Always. For some, the price was immediate."

She turns to Ms. White, who's been hanging back behind us. PA Young holds out her hand, demanding... something, but I'm not sure what. Without a word, Ms. White strips off the crisp linen suit jacket she'd been wearing and starts to unbutton her white blouse. My eyes go wide with shock, and she slips one shoulder of her shirt down.

And then I see it—the thin silver line that divides Ms. White's real body from the cyborg arm. Ms. White presses a hidden button in her arm, and twists it off, slipping it out of her sleeve and handing it over to PA Young without a word.

I stare at the arm in horror. Ms. White hardly ever takes it off, but there it is, in the PA's hand, the stump made of silver and chrome and glistening with bio-lube. The fingers still twitch—an automatic movement as it resets.

"This was the price Jadis paid," PA Young says, holding Ms. White's arm out to me. "She paid it the second she moved your mother aside to protect her during the Valetta Attack."

I swallow. "I know," I say in a small voice. Ms. White saved my mother's life that day.

"And you," PA Young says, her voice rising. "You paid the price of the war before you were even born."

My eyes flick from Ms. White's arm to PA Young's eyes. They're filled with sympathy, but I don't understand. Not until she says, "I'm right in remembering your family was from Valetta?"

My eyes drop to the floor. PA Young hands Ms. White back her cyborg arm, but I'm trapped in the dark thoughts she's led me to. A hundred thousand deaths, but I am not haunted by their ghosts. I'm haunted by my grandparents'—both my mother's parents and my father's were in the city at the time of the blast. And my uncle who I never met, my father's brother, who was engaged to be married. I might have had an aunt. Cousins.

The only family I have left now is my mother. That's it.

PA Young touches my shoulder. "The price of war is always heavy, and it must always be paid. And for some, that price isn't paid for years and years after the peace treaties are signed. Such as your father. He had to pay for the Secessionary War, too."

"He was killed by terrorists."

"Terrorists who hadn't given up on the Seccessionist's cause. Terrorists who are still fighting the war that ended nearly twenty years ago." PA Young stares intently at me. "The rebels are a very real threat. Our government is not an empire, though it is vast. And I am no dictator, gripping the nations together in an iron fist. Perhaps it would be simpler if I were. But no. We are a republic. The largest republic in history, but still—a republic. However, if we are to be truly one, a unified government..."

It's hard for me to imagine that the UC is still new— it's existed all my life. But as far as governments go, it is just a baby, only a little older than me. And while I've always felt it was stable, if someone as high up in the government as Representative Belles is contemplating treachery... well, I can see why PA Young's scared.

"The ability to stop a war before it happens—that's what your mother has truly invented. Not a plaything for the rich. A chance to make the Secessionary War the one that ended all wars."

"But the danger," Ms. White says, flexing the fingers in her cyborg arm as she reattaches it.

"The danger was always there. The terrorists know that your mother's technology exists; it will not take them long to figure out a way to use it for themselves, or to attempt to destroy it so it can't be used against them. We must strike now, and quickly."

THE BODY ELECTRIC

PA Young stretches toward me, her icy fingertips brushing my cheek. "Ella," she says softly. "They know you have access to your parents' technology. These are the people who killed your father. And now they're coming for your mother. And... you."

THIRTEEN

"I DON'T LIKE IT," MS. WHITE SAYS once we're back at the Reverie Mental Spa. She barely spoke at all after PA Young dismissed us and she kept her cool the entire cab ride back, but now that we're in our own building, she's pacing back and forth, twisting her hands in worry.

"He won't see me," I point out. "The secondary reverie chair, the one I used, is in another room. We'll just give Representative Belles a reverie, and I'll slip into it like I did with Mom's and…"

"Too much can go wrong!" Ms. White says. "It's far, far too dangerous." She spins around to face me. "Can you honestly tell me you're not afraid?"

"Of course I'm afraid," I say immediately, without thinking. The words take even me by surprise, and I bite my lip, considering.

When I shut my eyes, I see the way my father died.

"Do you really think that the terrorists will come here?" I whisper.

Ms. White wraps me in a hug. "I don't know," she says. "Your mother has kept her technology a secret, even from me. But if they can't steal it and replicate it… they may try to destroy it."

I see the way the bomb exploded, the way everything went white.

I am scared. I'm *terrified*.

"We could go somewhere," I say. "Destroy Mom's tech, sell the building, move somewhere else."

Ms. White holds me tighter. "Maybe…" she says, her voice trailing off, but we both know it would be a long shot. It's hard to disappear. We'd have to disable our cuffs, and that would make us look suspicious anywhere we go. Besides, if the terrorists could reach someone as high up in the government as Representative Belles, then how hard would it be to take us out? As long as Mom's alive, she's a threat—even if she destroyed the reverie chairs, she still has the knowledge to make more.

And we're both forgetting the most important piece of information. "Mom's too sick to go on the run," I say. I pull away from Ms. White. "And we can't tell her about this."

"But—"

"She's getting worse. You said so yourself. We can't let her know about the danger."

Ms. White nods slowly. "Are you going to do the reverie with Representative Belles?" she asks. "We could refuse. No one knows you can do this except the two of us and PA Young. If we hide your ability, the terrorists might not…"

"PA Young said they were already a threat to us," I counter. "We can't run, and we can't hide. We have to beat them at their own game."

The next morning, I watch Representative Belles arrive at the Reverie Mental Spa from the security feed while I hide in the secondary reverie chamber. His face is full, but overall he's slender and tall. He looks nervous. This is his first reverie. He has no idea how nervous he should be.

The Prime Administrator arranged it so that Representative Belles "won" a raffle for a series of free visits to the mental spa. Hopefully, even if the terrorists know that Mom's technology can be corrupted to be used for spying, Representative Belles doesn't. He doesn't appear to be suspicious, at least, and Ms. White is a master at putting clients at ease.

When they enter the reverie chamber, I start to get ready. While Ms. White is giving the representative a dose of the reverie drug, pressing electrodes into his skin, and hooking the interface system up with his cuffLINK device, I'm doing the same in this hidden room, connected by wires to the representative's reverie chair.

The door to my room opens, and Ms. White steps in. She scans the chair, checking behind me to make sure I'm fully plugged in and ready for the reverie.

"Promise you're okay?" she asks, worry clear in her eyes.

-68-

I don't bother answering; I just lower the sonic hood over my head. Ms. White pushes a button, and a puff of the bright green reverie drug bursts straight into my open eyes.

My eyelids droop and my head feels heavy, sleep starting to pull me in. There's no pain this time—*thankfully*—but the black behind my eyelids turns to bright white, and I feel a moment of nothingness before the world—Representative Belles's world inside his mind— starts to develop.

I am in the middle of a war.

For a moment, I'm struck by the horror of it all. The Secessionary War was more than twenty years ago, and of course I've seen the digi files on it, but I never... I was never in the middle of it. I never lived it.

I didn't know that wars were so dusty. The air is thick with it, swirling streams of acrid smoke and debris. I cough, choking. This isn't real, I remind myself. It isn't real. I shut my eyes, clenching them so tight that the blackness behind my eyelids bursts into my brain. When I open them, for a second I see the dream Representative Belles is trying to have—an old man and an orange grove—but then a bomb bursts, and all I can see is the war.

Representative Belles is obsessed with the idea of war right now. He can't quit thinking about it. This is the fear inside him, drowning out every single other thought. It's not different, really, from the way Mom can't have a reverie when the pain of her disease is too much to bear.

Terror creeps along my throat, like a spider trying to crawl out of my mouth. I could suppress Mom's pain, help her forget it, because I wanted to forget it, too. But this? Representative Belles's fear is my fear, too. I cannot break him from a fear that I share with him.

We're both sinking into the nightmare.

Panic rips through me. What if I get stuck, trapped inside the representative's mind? What if this is my fate, doomed to live in another man's hell?

A missile soars overhead, whistling through the sky before it crashes into Triumph Towers, the largest buildings in the city, home of all the representatives, including Prime Administrator Young and where Representative Belles works. The towers were built to look like flames, topped with solar glass that glitters day and night, rising from the ashes of the Secessionary War. But now, in Representative Belles's dream, the towers burn for real. They shatter like crystal, sparkling amidst the rubble.

A bomb lands near my feet, sending broken stone up in a shower of rocky debris. I stare down at the unexploded bomb—it's made of glass and glitters like liquid gold swirls inside. Solar glass. A recent import from the extrasolar colonies, solar glass provides a lot of the fuel needed to run New Venice, but ever since the disastrous attempts to use solar bombs during the Secessionary War, they've been utterly banned as weapons across all nations. Still—this is Representative Belles's fear, so it's real here.

I hear screaming. A long, long cry of utter sorrow. This is a dream; it is focused on the Representative's greatest fears. And his fear is personified here at my feet.

Two children, a boy a few years younger than me and a little girl. Blood trickling down their faces. Their eyes staring up, empty.

Dead.

The entire dreamscape rumbles with Representative Belles's grief. The world darkens. This is enough to rip him from his reverie, just like the pain pulls Mom out of hers.

But while I share the representative's fear of war, I do not know these children dead at my feet. And not knowing them reminds me that this isn't real.

I close my eyes again, concentrating. I sweep my arms out, and the air smells sweeter, like citrus. I bring up a warm breeze. I take away all sound, then concentrate on the soft whispers coming in through the sensory chamber Representative Belles's is in. Leaves clattering. Branches creaking.

When I open my eyes, Santiago Belles stands before an old man.

"*Abuélo,*" he says, wonderingly. *He casts his eyes back, and even though he looks right at me, he doesn't really see. His brain wants to be in this dream, the one with his grandfather. His face melts, and he looks younger as he turns back to the man beside the orange tree. Behind them, an entire grove rises.*

"*I fought in the Secessionary War,*" *the dream-grandfather says.*

Crap. I don't need his own dream kicking him back into a nightmare. I start to intervene, but then the grandfather continues.

"*Fought for the losing side. Least, that's what they told me. But I didn't really fight for either side.*" *The old man looks Representative Belles square in the eyes.* "*I fought for my family.*" *He taps the representative in the chest, just over his heart.* "*Nothing more important than family. You gonna fight for something, you fight for something that you're willing to die for. I wasn't willing to die for my government, Secessionary or UC. But I was willing to die for the people I love.*"

I choke down a snort of derision. Idealistic mantras like that are what made the Secessionary War so bad. All you have to do is look at the hole where Valletta once stood or the broken arch of the Azure Window to know that. The old buildings in the country still carry the scars of battle, two decades later. Preventing another war like that is exactly the reason why I'm in Representative Belles's mind in the first place.

It's harder to enhance the dreams of someone I don't know, especially when fighting against the worry of war, but I work with what I have. Focusing my mind on the sensory details already present, I make the smells stronger, the music louder. I add warmth from the Spanish sun, birds chirping and locusts humming. I focus on the grandfather, giving him specific details, wrinkles from every old face I've seen, clothes that smell of detergent and dirt and sweat.

As the dreamscape around me grows clearer, I slip further away from it. The mind is a magical thing, I'm discovering. A dreamscape is made of thought and is wider than the sky, able to grow large enough to fit not just our own world, but every possibility and impossibility beyond it. Once I quit thinking of it as being forced into the laws of physics, it's easy to manipulate the dreamscape into anything I want. I don't know how I know all this, no more than I understand how I know things when I dream. I just do.

I throw up my hand, and a wall rises between the orange grove and me. Behind the wall, I start creating the world I need in Representative Belles's mind.

A filing cabinet first, then a desk. This is work; Representative Belles's mind is my office.

Filing cabinets are hardly ever used any more—most records are on the interface. But the only really secure information isn't stored on the interface system—its hard copies kept under lock and key, just like Mom's research in the secured databank in England.

Representative Belles's mind opens up to me as I slide open the top drawer of the filing cabinet. The tabs are easy and expected: childhood, school, family—two children and a loving wife, Spain, Malta, Triumph Towers. Getting closer—Triumph Towers is where the government works. Campaign, compromise, duties, cabinet meetings.

Secrets.

I snatch the folder up and toss it on the desk. My mind's eye wavers as I look at the contents. Focus. I have to focus. But the insides are a jumble. Representative Belles himself isn't sure of everything he's learned—the seeds of his rebellion are just beginning to form.

I pick up the largest paper in the folder, and a moving image loops over and over—Prime Administrator Hwa Young stands at the head of a long wooden table, shouting at a representative administrator I don't know. She's utterly eviscerating the man seated before her, globules of spit flying in his face as she tears him apart. Slowly, her voice rises from the page, deep for a woman, cold, furious.

The dreamscape rumbles.

I slam the page face-down on the desk, shut my eyes, and think of sunlight and oranges and the buzzing of bees and the way old men's voices crack when they speak of the past. The more I focus on something, the more Representative Belles's mind will focus on it, and it's important that I keep him in his reverie long enough for me to discover the terrorists.

I flip to another page in his file. It's a spreadsheet of data—money. I scan it, trying to make sense of the numbers, but I can't. Sometimes the mind works that way—it remembers things in a way only that mind can interpret. This chart would make sense to Representative Belles, but not to anyone else.

This isn't working. Representative Belles might be seditious, but I've found no proof that he's a key player in the terrorist plot. The number data could be tracking where funds shift to a rebel group... or they could mean nothing. He might not even be in any rebel groups yet; he might just be considering it.

Maybe he's been approached, though...

If he knows any of the known terrorists, that might be the link we need to find them. I pluck out another file from the cabinet, this one marked simply, People. I open it on the floor, and, rather than paper falling out, a city street explodes into being around me. I'm in a crowd of people, maybe a hundred or more. These are the people in the representative's immediate memory, the ones he's been thinking about most recently. They're grouped in different places, his family in one corner of his mind, a wife and two children; his friends crowded around a bar, drinking beer; his fellow representatives in suits and business clothes, around a long, polished wooden table. And more: a group of schoolchildren—part of his charity work, I think; employees standing around a ribbon-cutting ceremony in Madrid; crowds of everyday people. Street androids selling pastizzi and honey rings. The girl who makes his coffee. The representative from Brazil who flirts with him when he works late.

A boy with dark hair and pale eyes.

My heart stutters.

"I know you," I whisper.

It's the boy from the gardens, the one who approached me with a warning and stopped to pay respect to my father's grave.

Looking at him makes my heart race, my breathing come shallow. I feel...

Fear? No, that's not it.

I sweep my arm out, and everyone else disappears. Just me, and this boy.

His face is made of sharp angles and shadows. He has the clearest eyes I've ever seen. His shoulders are broad and lined with hard muscles hidden under a long-sleeved black t-shirt. There's a flash of gold—some sort of pin—near his collar. His skin is tanned and his hair is dark, but he's white—he doesn't have the deep brown coloring of a native Maltese like me. Judging from his accent when he spoke before, he's probably English. I ruffle my cropped dark hair nervously. Despite the fact that this is all just echoes in Representative Belles's mind, it feels as if his eyes are resting on me and me alone.

I dig deeper into Representative Belles's mind, trying to figure out how he knows this beautiful boy. A name, an address, anything. A ghostly image of their last interaction plays on a loop: the boy looking around furtively, whispering something too fast for me to catch, and holding something out for Representative Belles's to take. A folded up piece of paper, or maybe a digi strip; I can't tell. And while Representative Belles's memories show that he took the paper, he hasn't looked inside it yet. He himself doesn't know what it contains.

It could be nothing.

But it doesn't look like nothing. This boy—this moment—is weighing on the representative's mind. He can't forget him, and, judging by the fuzzy outline around him, he's tried.

I peer closer at the boy. It's not really him here, just a memory of him. But he looks anxious—almost mournful. I watch the way his eyes dart, left-right. I can see a pulse thrumming in his neck.

A buzzing sound fills the air, and I notice a fat yellow-and-black bumblebee has made its way from the orange groves of Representative Belles's reverie over the wall into the area where I'm working. The wall seems thinner—through it, I can see the dreaming representative still walking with his grandfather, but I know I don't have much time left.

I turn back to the repeating image of the boy and lift my hand. A small filing cabinet rises up beside him. I lean over to open the drawer—but it won't budge.

Locked.

My eyebrows raise. This really is a secret the representative doesn't want me to know. It's buried deep within his mind, and though I might be able to extract the information I need, the reverie's already so close to ending that any effort on my part will break the connection, wake the representative, and leave me empty-handed. I release the drawer's handle and peer down at the label instead, hoping for something.

Written across the label in handwritten green, capital letters is a name.

JACK TYLER.

I look up at the fading image of the boy who gave the representative a secret message. "Jack Tyler," I whisper.

The image, which had been playing in a constant loop, stops. It freezes, the memory of Jack Tyler holding out the piece of paper, leaning forward.

And then, impossibly, the boy turns his face to me. His head turns eerily, as if he is possessed.

His pale eyes meet mine—

—And I wake up.

FOURTEEN

MY HEART THUDS IN MY CHEST. I CAN'T get the way he looked at me out of my mind—not just in Representative Belles's reverie, but in real life, too, when I saw him—Jack Tyler—at my father's grave.

I tap into the spa's security feed, watching as Representative Belles wakes up. My cuff connects automatically to the mental spa's interface system, the image crystal-clear on the thinner-than-paper responsive tech-foil skintight around my wrist.

Ms. White is all smiles and graciousness as she helps him up and leads him to the lifts that go to the rest of the Reverie Mental Spa. I count to ten, waiting for him to be well and truly gone, but also waiting for my heart to calm down. I catch a little of the representative's conversation with Ms. White before they disappear into the lift—he's completely satisfied with the reverie of his grandfather and completely ignorant of what I was doing in his mind, that I even was in in his head at all.

As soon as the representative is gone, Ms. White returns to me. She watches me in silence while I peel off the electrodes and straighten up the chair.

I take a deep breath. "He's scared," I say finally.

"Scared?" Her gaze is intent, worried.

I nod. "I think he's afraid of another war."

"A war he's contributing to." When I don't answer this, Ms. White continues, "Anything else?"

I look down, rubbing the sudden chill from my bare arms.

"Ella?" Ms. White asks gently.

"Just a name," I say. "Jack Tyler."

Ms. White stiffens, as if she found herself unexpectedly at the edge of a precipice.

"Do you know him?" I ask.

She shakes her head. "It's just—it's strange to hear a specific name, you know? That might be the person who led the terrorist attack that killed your father, and to have a name to associate with that attack, just like that... it makes it all more real. Does that make sense?"

"Yeah," I say. My stomach twists. That hadn't occurred to me—that Jack may have had a hand in Dad's death. Jack Tyler is about my age, but it's possible he helped with the terrorism attack.

A shaky breath escapes my lips. I remember the sound of his voice in my ears, the way he looked a Dad's grave, the way he looked at me.

"Ella?" Ms. White asks, her voice filled with concern. Out of the corner of my eye, I see her reach toward me, but her hand drops away before she touches me.

"I'm okay," I say softly. "I'm sorry—I just..." When I close my eyes, I see Jack Tyler's eyes. I feel the bombs Representative Belles felt.

"Sometimes," she says, "I forget how young you are. Ella, I know this is hard. This is not the life a teenaged girl like you should lead. You should be applying for universities, still be carefree, go out on dates and to parties. I'm the one who's sorry. I wish you could have those things."

"This is more important," I say, and I mean it.

Ms. White goes to Triumph Towers to report directly to PA Young, but I just go to bed. My head is throbbing, a low buzzing sound vibrating in my ears, and I just want to slip into nothingness.

By the time I wake up, it's well past lunch. I walk down the hall, surprised my mother hasn't woken me up yet. "Hey, Mom," I say softly, pushing open her heavy door. The apartment—like all buildings in New Venice—was built with a panic room. The architects of the city were the same ones who rebuilt Malta after the Secessionary War, and every home has at least one safe stronghold. We converted the panic room in our apartment into Mom's bedroom—it has a built in generator and a dedicated power and water source that we can use for the machines that monitor her health.

Mom looks up at me from her bed. She's still in her dressing gown, her hair in thin, soft wisps around her face. When she blinks, I notice that her pupils are silver—she's watching a program using her eye nanobots.

"I can't find the book I want," she says, offering me a goofy, self-depreciating smile. "You know, the one that movie was based on."

"*Titanic of the Stars?*" I ask. She's read the book at least a half-dozen times before.

She nods and holds out her wrist to me. I type across her cuffLINK, bringing up the book she wants, a historical drama about the mystery surrounding the disappearance of the world's first interstellar ship. "You know how it ends," I say, half-laughing as I download the book into her eye bots for her.

"Well, obviously," she says. "It's based on *Godspeed*. Of course I know how it ends. But I've heard this version is good."

I blink. "Oh?" I ask, trying to keep my voice light. "You've not read this one before?"

Mom laughs. "It *just* came out, Ella, how could I have?"

My stomach drops. A symptom of advanced stages of Hebb's Disease: Memory loss.

I step outside and call for Rosie the nursing android. It records this new symptom of Mom's disease without betraying any emotion.

I open the door wider, letting it into Mom's room.

"Take care of her," I say.

"Of course," Rosie replies in her even, clipped tones. "It's what I am programmed to do."

"Ella?" Mom calls, her voice cracking in a cough, the sound like splintering wood. I rush to her side, watching helplessly as she heaves.

She mutters something as I arrange a blanket around her legs after she stops wheezing.

"What?" I ask, forcing a cheery smile on my face.

"Not much longer now," Mom says, her voice barely a whisper. "Then you'll be free of me."

It takes a moment for the full impact of her words to hit me, for me to realize what she means by "free." I swoop down over her and wrap her in so tight a hug that she squeaks in protest.

"I don't *want* to be free of you." My voice is strained and raspy; I don't want her to see me cry. "Not ever."

Mom smiles up at me as I pull back, examining her face.

I can already see the goodbye in her eyes.

FIFTEEN

I WANDER INTO THE KITCHEN, MAKING myself a sandwich as I scroll through messages on my cuff. I widen the interface, staring at the holographic icons spinning before my eyes, thanks to my eye bots. I tap the communication box. The program bursts open, sparks of light shooting between my fingers and reforming into a video chat box hovering at eye-level.

"Contact: Akilah Xuereb," I say.

A moment later, my best friend fills my vision.

"Hella' Ella!" she says brightly. "Feeling better?"

"Not really," I say. I touch the charm on my necklace—a fortune cookie locket. Inside is a digi file—Akilah and I at the Summer Festa when we were eight. The UC shipped in fireflies, and we stayed up half the night in Central Gardens, trying to catch them all. Dad gave Akilah and I both a locket—mine's silver, hers in gold—with the digi strip inside it when her father left her family and she moved to the Foqra District.

Akilah leans forward. "What happened?" she asks.

For the first time in my life, I don't reveal the secrets

of my heart to her. I used to tell Aks everything, but... this is the stuff of national security, of anti-terrorism. I *can't* tell her about this.

"Is it your mother?" she asks.

It would be so easy for me to lie now, to tell her that everything bothering me comes back to Mom's illness. And, of course, I'm worried that she's worse, and the way she seems to have given up. But it's not her ghost that haunts me.

"I'm just... I'm doing some new work at the mental spa," I say.

"Gah, I wish I was there," Akilah says. She applied to be an intern for her service year, just like me, but she was selected for military instead.

"Me too," I say, my voice dropping. "But this... *this* job. It's just—it's really intense."

"What are they having you do?"

I open my mouth, but I don't know what to say. I can't tell her that I just spied on someone's *mind*—she'd never believe me, and even if she did, I don't think I *should* say anything.

Akilah's brow wrinkles in worry.

"I know you're in the military now," I say, "and basically the whole point of being a solider is taking orders. But... have you ever had to do something that..."

After a long pause, Akilah asks, "That what?"

"That scared you?" I say, the words rushing out. "I mean, you're armed, and you're trained, and it's not like the War is still happening, but it might, and you don't know what will happen, and you have to trust that the people higher up than you know what they're doing, but it's still dangerous, it's still... scary."

I almost roll my eyes at myself. I sound like such a moron. *Scary?* That's the best word I could come up with?

"Just what is Ms. White having you do at the mental spa?" Akilah looks as frightened as I feel.

"It's not—" I bite back the words. It's not Ms. White. But how can I tell my best friend that I'm taking orders from the Prime Administrator of the entire freaking world?

Akilah curses. "I *hate* being stuck here, so far away from you!"

"I'm okay, Aks, really. Sorry to have bothered—"

"Don't you *dare*, Ella Shepherd!" Akilah shoots back. "Don't you dare try to apologize for this! Of course I want you to tell me if something's wrong!"

I can hear the buzzing sound in my head again, and my skin jumps from the aftershocks of bombs that only went off in my mind.

"I—I've got to go," I say. Akilah tries to protest, but I close the screen. I can't tell her what's troubling me, and that makes it even worse than if I'd not talked to her at all.

She tries to call me right back, but I block the message. I don't have any answers—not for her, not for me.

Ms. White was right. Seeing Jack Tyler's name in Representative Belles's reverie made everything much more real for me. Dad's death, the threat of war... it's so overwhelming.

But it's worse just sitting here, waiting for PA Young to tell me what to do next. I have only one real lead to follow, and it's not much of one, but I'll do what I can. I dismiss the chat box on my cuff and bring up the search icon.

"Jack Tyler," I order.

Unfortunately, Jack Tyler is a very common name, from a prominent American politician to a British actor from the twenty-second century. I narrow the search perimeters, but still get too many hits, so I switch to an image search, plugging in his features as well as name.

Soon, I find him.

It's a picture taken in a scientific laboratory— glittering test tubes and vials shine in front of a white tiled wall. Jack stands in the middle of a group of six men, all smiling in front of the body of something that appears to be a dead girl, except her chest is open, exposing a bundle of wires and circuits, not blood and bone. An android.

But that's not what makes me hold my hand out to the interface screen as if I could reach through it and touch the people in the image.

The man with his arm slung around Jack's shoulder, the one with a crooked smile and a laugh in his eyes—

Is my father.

SIXTEEN

LEAD SCIENTIST DR. PHILIP SHEPHERD
with his team working on a prototype for meta-functioning
android technology.

While Dad used nanobots to come up with something of a cure for Mom's Hebb's Disease, his real scientific focus was on android technology. This picture must have been taken very soon before he died. I glance back up at it, taking note of everyone.

Everyone in the picture—with the exception of Jack—was killed in the same terrorist-planted lab explosion that killed Dad.

My body grows tense. "Now what are the chances that only Jack survived?" I growl under my breath. My eyes narrow as I focus on his smiling face.

I pull the photo out of the article and blow it up to life-size. I try to look at Jack, but my eyes go to Dad. He's smiling here. He looks happy. Proud. And his hand is on Jack's shoulder, as if he's his son.

I slice my arm through the holographic projection and sweep it aside, cutting Dad out of the photo. I do the same to the right-hand side of the photo, isolating Jack. In the hologram, he's just a little taller than me, like in real life. His hair is different here, shorter. I lean up on my tiptoes, nose-to-nose with a holographic image of this boy who, somehow, is tangled up in the parts of my life I've kept hidden. His eyes stare forward, glittering with the holo-light.

"Who are you?" I ask, but of course he doesn't answer.

I swipe away the photo and scan the article attached to it. Jack's listed as an intern, with a note that his parents are aides in the Representative Assembly.

I turn back to the interface system, trying to find more on Jack. I find an article dated only about a year ago—no, not an article. An obituary. Two government officials working in the Prime Administrator's office killed in a car crash near the beaches in Gozo, and a note saying they were survived by their only son, Jack Tyler. They died nearly a month after Dad.

So he's an orphan.

Like me.

I jerk back, repulsed by my own thoughts. I am *not* an orphan. I still have my mother. How could I even think that?

I swipe my arms across the holo-display, pushing away the rest of the obituary. So what if he has a tragic past? I think about the picture of him with my father. Maybe Jack Tyler contributed to my own tragic past.

I search using other perimeters, but I can find no new information. He's done a very good job at keeping himself off the interface—or of erasing things that used to be there.

I sigh, disappointed in the fruitless research. I sweep aside the search box, but another holo-icon replaces it almost immediately. I stare, reading the words across the bottom with growing shock:

Open in case of search for Jack Tyler.

I check the file information—whatever this is, it's hard-wired directly into my cuff. Only I could have put this file here, or someone who was actually feeding wires directly into my system. This is no easy hack—someone would have had to have either stolen my cuff (which is impossible, as I've never taken it off), or linked directly to it, which is also impossible as no one has shared a direct link to my cuff in years.

The holo-icon twirls inside my vision.

I know I didn't put this file here. But I also know it's impossible for anyone else to have either.

I touch the holo-icon, and it opens as soon as I select it.

Processing, the screen flashes at me. I feel a buzzing at my wrist and look down to my cuff, which is synced to the interface system. *Program complete*, it says.

Program? *Program?!* I don't want to open a program—I just wanted to see what was in the file! My eyes grow foggy—the program has already linked to my nanobots, the ones that display directly into my eyes. I blink madly, even though I know it'll do no good, but I freeze when I see the words being projected into my vision.

To find Jack Tyler.

I squeeze my eyes shut, my mind racing. This must be some sort of bot virus. Jack Tyler must have found me, hacked the code into the system.

I move automatically to my cuff. I can call Ms. White, the police—anyone. I can show this program to them, have them trace the hack, figure out where Jack Tyler is and how he's involved with all of this.

And then I open my eyes. In the reflection of the mirror hanging on the wall across from the table, I see myself, my irises silver from the nanobots.

And standing behind me is my father.

"Dad?" I whisper, my voice cracking on the word.

SEVENTEEN

MY FATHER IS STANDING RIGHT IN front of me.

"Dad?" I ask again. My eyes are watering now for an entirely different reason, my heart thudding in my chest so violently that I feel as if I'm about to throw up. I try to say his name again, but I don't have any more words within me. Instead, I rush forward, my arms out—

—And I go right through him, as if he was nothing more than a ghost.

Nothing more than a projection.

Because that's what he is. This is what the program downloaded directly to my eye nanobots is. It's a trick. It makes me see my father. *Dad's dead.* I force myself to think those words until I believe them again.

I raise the opacity of the program using my cuff, and, sure enough, my dad becomes more and more transparent. More and more ghost-like. Thinking that makes a shiver run up my spine, and I shoot the opacity back down to zero so that he appears solid and real again.

Dad—the projection of Dad that only I can see— raises his arm silently, pointing to the door that leads out of the apartment. I follow him, my eyes half-blinded with unshed tears. Out of the apartment, down the lift, across the lobby, out the front door of the Reverie Mental Spa. And all the while, Dad is just out of my reach, pointing, pointing, pointing. His eyes stare into mine.

I *know* he's not real. I *know* he's merely a projection in my tech contacts, that he's a part of a hacker's program that broke through my security and downloaded into my system against my will, that I should report the program to Ms. White and the interface police, that I should delete the program without a second thought.

But I can't take my eyes off Dad.

Wherever this computer-generated image of my father is leading me cannot be good. Someone left that file for me to find—me specifically, judging from the retina scan I had to give in order to get to it. And I can't trust anyone who would use such an underhanded tactic as to send me my father to lead me down an unknown path.

But I can't *not* follow my father. I have to see where he's leading me.

Jack Tyler—or whoever it was who hacked the Reverie interface—did an excellent job at figuring out how I ticked. He knew exactly that the only thing I'd ever follow into the unknown was something with my father's face.

Dad leads me all the way to the lifts at the center of the park. New Venice is a bridge city, a man-made metropolis that spans across the Mediterranean Sea between the two islands that make up the nation of Malta.

The upper city is where the businesses are; the work of the city happens here. But the lower city is where people go to play.

The loud *do-dee-doe* sounds of the lifts ring out across the central area as the masses of people of converge in the center of the gardens. A fat man pushes past me when I pause, scanning the crowd for Dad. My father's image stands near one of the lifts, a ghost only I can see, his image wavering as tourists pass through him in the mad scramble to the lifts to the lower city.

I approach the tills in the center of the plaza. Half-androids—the upper half human-shaped, bolted to the lower-half ticket-dispenser—accept credits as people tap their cuffLINKs against the scanners. I do the same, a red twenty credits deducting from my account on the screen when I do.

The lifts are all glass, so that tourists can have the full view of the lower city. I get crammed against the back wall as an entire Australian lacrosse team—all wearing offensively bright orange shirts splattered with their team logo—jumps into the lift after me. They're loud, but under normal circumstances, I would quite like being packed into a lift with so many good looking young men. But Dad's disappeared now, and I'm anxiously looking for him through the lift's glass walls.

The city is beautiful from up here. The ceiling—really just the underside of the bridge—is a perfect, cloudless blue, bright and shining. It's made using solar glass—a new discovery by the colony on one of the UC's space missions funded by the FRX—and it ensures that, no matter what the weather in the upper city of New Venice, the lower city is constantly and forever in brilliant sunlight, day and night.

But that's not why people come here. The original Venice—which was located in Italy, not Malta—sank long before the Secessionary War, but it had grown an almost legend-like status in history, like a real-life Atlantis, tragically lost in history. So when New Venice was being made, the upper city was turned into the highest-tech planned city in the world. A city worthy of Triumph Towers and the capital of the UC. But the lower city was an homage to the past—and to the money tourists brought in. The architects had used historical documents and photographs from the 21st century to recreate the look of Venice and built it directly into the waters of the Mediterranean. The marble and tile and hand-blown glass lamps would look out of place among the glass-fronted advertisement filled towers of the upper city, and it wouldn't even match the dusty, light-brown limestone of the rest of Malta, but it looks perfect here, rising up from the water. Rather than streets, waterways weave in and out of the city. And, just as the real Venice had once used gondolas, New Venice uses traditional Maltese boats— brilliantly painted luzzi in shades of red and yellow and green, each operated by a luzzolier.

The boys in the lift with me start talking animatedly about what part of the lower city they want to explore first, but I turn my attention to the docking platform. Luzzu boats crowd the side that's open to the water, and a floor-to-ceiling wall of lights flash advertisements on the other side. I scan the milling tourists at the base, looking for Dad.

I start to panic. I can't find him. The lift reaches the docking station and bumps to a stop. The lacrosse team shouts out something Australian and cheer-like that I can't understand and pours out. I follow, slowly, eyes still searching the crowd for Dad.

And then I see him, standing on the other end of the docking station. Luzzoliers crowd their boats near the lifts, hoping to snag tourists right away. You could, technically, walk the city, but no one ever does—the luzzu boats are too well known, too much a "must-do" part of the New Venice experience. The lacrosse players take up five boats, all rocking and nearly tipping over as they jump in a bit too excitedly.

But Dad's not near these boats. He's on the far edge of the docking station, well away from the tourists, at the Grand Rialto bridge that connects the docking station to the Renaissance recreations.

I rush past the people piling into the luzzu boats. At the front of each boat is a carved eye—a part of the traditional Maltese design, but even though they're made of nothing but paint and wood, it feels as if they're staring at me as I race down the platform.

"Pretty girl!" a luzzolier in an older boat painted yellow and black calls. "Ride my boat. Cheap! No need to walk!"

I raise my left hand at him, showing him the green stripe on my cuff that proves I'm a native to New Venice and not going to be swayed by the same pick-up lines that work on tourists. Sure enough, he shrugs and edges his boat closer to the crowd near the lifts.

When I reach the Grand Rialto bridge, I see Dad standing at the highest point of it, facing the plaza. Street androids walk up and down, selling pastizzi and hot dogs, falafel wraps and gyros. Pigeons—which had apparently overrun the original city in Italy—are a mix of the real thing and mechanical ones, each fitted with camera lens instead of eyes.

I keep racing, Dad always just beyond me. He flashes on and off so quickly now that I can barely keep up—down this street, then the next, over the bridge, past the people queueing up at a luzzu station, over another bridge, around a building, across a plaza, through an alley. The streets grow narrower, and there are less tourists and more natives like me—people who work in the city. I see their real faces now, not the smiling ones they show the tourists. They nod as I run by, watching me curiously. Probably assuming I'm late for work.

And then Dad stops. He's in front of a doorway, one that looks rather inconspicuous. It's painted a dingy burgundy, the color cracked and peeling away. The number eight is scratched into the door, followed by a capital Q and another eight. The stoop is littered with empty candy wrappers, a crumpled wad of paper, and, oddly, a small jar full of what looks like honey. A blackened silver-colored knocker shaped like a fist holding a giant ring is bolted to the exact center of the door. Dad doesn't move. His eyes stare straight ahead—not seeing me, as I know he can't.

I stop, my chest heaving from the run, my hair sticky with sweat. I try to move myself into Dad's line of vision. I want to pretend, even if for just a moment, that he's here and looking at me. But he's not. Of course he's not. I reach through his head and lift the metal ring, letting the knocker fall against the weather-worn door. It opens almost immediately, as if the person on the other side was waiting for me.

Jack Tyler.

EIGHTEEN

JACK'S EYES ARE WIDE AND SHOCKED. I notice that his nose, while unbroken, is still swollen from where I hit him earlier.

"How in the hell did you find me?" Jack demands.

My head snaps back in surprise. I thought he was the one to hack into my cuff and send me the tracking code to get here. I glance nervously behind me, half-expecting someone to pop out of the waterway nearby, as if this were all a setup.

"Shit, did you bring the police?" Jack growls. He starts to slam the door shut, but I cram my foot in the way.

"No," I shoot back. "Although you're making me think I *should* call them."

"Don't," Jack orders. His jaw clenches. He looks furious.

Like he can tell me what to do. If I have to, I'll bring down the Prime Administrator on his head. But first: "I came for answers."

"Well, I'm not talking to you. All you do is hit me." He tries to shut the door again, but my foot remains in the way. I push my shoulder against the door, and Jack curses as it opens more. I'm surprised to see that I *can* push my way through—he's far bigger than I—but I have good leverage from my spot on the stoop. I shoulder the door open even further, and Jack gives up, letting it swing open.

"Don't punch me again," he says in a defeated tone, backing into the shadows of the house.

I step inside, hesitant, my hand covering my cuff. If I have to, I can push the panic button.

"Shut the door," Jack growls.

"No," I shoot back. I want answers, but I don't want to be locked in a room with this possible psychopath.

Jack reaches around me and pushes the door. It slams shut. My fist is already curled, and he has to duck out of the way to avoid being hit. "I said don't punch me!" he shouts.

I ignore him and test the doorknob. It's not locked. I can still escape.

"Why did you even come here if you were just going to leave?" Jack's not yelling any more, but he still sounds furious. "And *how* did you find me?"

I don't answer, my eyes still on the door. Then I say, "Someone sent me a map program to my eye bots. It led me here. Did you do that?"

Jack shakes his head angrily. "I told you I didn't. Why would I even want you here?"

"The map program used my father's image." The hologram of Dad stands silently beside Jack.

Jack is silent for a long moment. "I wouldn't do that to you, Ella," he says, his voice softer. "I know how much he meant to you."

I jerk away from him. "Don't pretend that you know me," I snarl.

For the first time, Jack's face betrays an emotion other than anger and frustration: he seems surprised. Maybe even hurt. His eyes widen, and he opens his mouth, but no sound comes out.

"Regardless," he says coldly, "it wasn't me. But I need to know how you found me so I can make sure no one else can find me."

I open my mouth to argue, my mind racing. This isn't fitting together the way I thought it would, and I feel unbalanced and thrown off course. I expected to find answers, but all I have is more questions. I need to find out who *did* hack the interface system and got me the map code. It had to be someone close, someone *very* close to me—it came from my cuff, after all, to say nothing of the appearance of Dad's face. And I don't think it was Jack—his shock was real.

Jack whirls around, staring at me intently. "For there to be a tracking program, there has to be something to track. You can't just track a *person*."

"Unless they have tracker nanobots in them," I point out.

Jack's eyes widen, and he looks momentarily panic-stricken, as if he'd like to rip off his skin. But then he shakes his head, "No, that's not it," he says, almost as if assuring himself. "Xavier's meds…"

"Hmm?" I ask, watching him closely.

"I don't have tracker bots. There's something else." Jack narrows his eyes at me. "Son of a bitch," he says, wonderingly. "I know what it is." Jack rips his jacket off, his hands scrunching the black material, looking for something. There's a flash at his collar from the golden bee pin he wears, but that's not what Jack's trying to find. From a hidden, inner pocket, he pulls out an old-fashioned pocket watch.

I gasp. "That—!" I glance up at the holographic projection of Dad standing mutely beside Jack. But before I can finish the sentence—*That watch belonged to Dad!*—Jack throws it on the ground and stomps on it with all his weight. The watch crunches, and the hologram of Dad disappears.

"Why would you do that?!" I scream, dropping to my knees and picking up the bent and broken watch face. "That was my *father's!*" This was an antique, passed down for generations from father to son in my family. Dad gave to it to me a year or so before he died, after Mom seemed cured and he was promoted to work directly in Triumph Towers, researching bots and androids for the government. The engraving on the inside of the watch is still there, exactly as I knew it. *P.K.D.S.* The initials of my great-something grandfather.

Jack swoops down and picks up a cracked silver-colored bead from the shattered remains of the watch. "Well, Dr. Philip didn't put a tracker in it, that's for damn sure!" He holds the tiny object out to me, glowering.

"How did you even get this watch?" I ask quietly, staring down at the broken pieces.

Jack stands abruptly, knocking the watch face out of my hand and dropping the metallic bead into my palm. "A tracker. You put a *tracker* on me."

"I didn't do this," I say in an even monotone. I'm barely able to control my rage. I have so few things that are my father's, just his, and seeing the broken watch is like seeing a memory of him smashed against the dirty stone floor. "How did you get my father's watch?"

"Because *you* gave it to me!" Jack roars. I flinch, and he takes a step back, breathing deeply. His eyes search mine, full of scorching rage. "Are they coming?" he asks.

"Wh-who?" I stutter.

"The M.P.s. The cops. Did you lead them here with your stupid little tracker program?" He steps around me, flinging open the door and looking out into the bright sunlight.

"I didn't call anyone," I say. My voice is stronger with each word. "No one followed me. And I didn't do that. I didn't put a tracker in the watch. And I didn't give it to you."

"What are you even doing here then?" Jack says. His voice is low now, and it sounds almost disappointed. Defeated. "I know you hate me, Ella, but why are torturing me?"

"Torturing? Hate you?" I gape at him. "I don't even *know* you!"

Jack's face falls into an emotionless mask. "I'm beginning to think that might be true."

"Of *course* it's true!" I shout. "I never even saw you before yesterday! So I couldn't have put a tracker on you—and I'm still waiting to hear how you stole my father's watch!"

The color drains from Jack's face. He just stares at me, speechless.

"What?" I demand.

"You remember Akilah, though, right?"

My hand goes instinctively to my necklace, the fortune cookie locket with a digi file of Akilah and me inside. She has a matching one.

Jack runs his fingers through his hair. "I've heard that the government uses subliminal messaging to control people," he mutters. He casts an appraising eye on me. "But this is so specific..."

"How do you know Akilah?" I demand again. I don't care what kind of mind games he's playing at; I want answers.

Jack doesn't speak for a moment. He looks as if he's carefully choosing his words. "Akilah and I were in the same unit."

"She's never mentioned you."

"She probably didn't think you wanted to hear about me."

I rake my eyes over him. "Obviously not."

"No—I mean—" Jack growls in frustration.

"Let's just clear this up right now," I snap. I raise my wrist, my fingers skimming across the surface of my cuff.

"What are you doing?" Jack demands.

"Calling Akilah. If she knows you, she can tell me."

"No—don't!" he tries to knock my hand away.

I narrow my eyes. My fingers stay on my cuff—not on Akilah's contact info, but on the police's.

Jack's lips curl up, but it's not a smile. It's a grimace. There's a look in his eyes that is far sadder than I've ever seen before. My stomach drops, and dread rises up within me. A warning flashes through my head, and I'm suddenly reminded of the day my dad came into my bedroom to tell me that Mom had Hebb's Disease.

"Akilah's dead," Jack says, and it's not just the words that kill me, but the tone, full of sympathy and sorrow.

NINETEEN

THE AIR LEAVES MY BODY IN ONE
whoosh, and I stagger back away from Jack as if he'd hit
me. But then I shake my head, clearing the confusing
thoughts.

"I *just* talked to her, less than an hour ago," I say.

"You really didn't," Jack says in a terrible low
monotone.

I scrutinize his face, but even though he's wearing an
emotionless mask now, there is truth in his eyes, grief. His
shoulders are slouched in defeat. He's got the build of a
soldier boy—athletically large, quick reflexes, a certain set
of his jaw that indicates he's seen more than he should.

But no matter how much he appears to believe what
he's saying, he's obviously lying. Or crazy. Or both.

I glance down at his arm, and notice the way he tugs
the sleeve of his jacket over his wrist. I remember that he's
missing his cuff.

"You're off the grid," I say. "You're on the run. You...
you deserted the military didn't you?" This fully supports
my theory that he's tied in with the terrorist rebels
Representative Belles is getting mixed up with, and I grope

behind me for the doorknob, feeling the cool metal solid beneath my fingers, ready to run if I need to.

A muscle moves behind Jack's jaw. "Around a half a year after I joined," he says. "After Akilah..."

I wave my hand, dismissing this. Akilah's not dead.

"Don't look at me like that," Jack growls.

"Like what?"

"Like I'm a deserter."

"Akilah's not dead," I state, and saying the words makes me feel stronger. "You are a deserter, and—" I stop talking. I don't know what I was going to say next. *And I'm leaving?* No—I can't. I don't know how I got the tracker program on my cuff, but regardless, the tracker's destroyed now. If I leave, I'll never be able to find Jack again. This may be my only chance to capture him for PA Young.

My hand closes on my wrist, my finger millimeters away from the panic button that will bring the police.

"Wait," Jack says. It's the way his voice cracks over the word, desperate, that makes me look up at him. "God, I hate this," he mutters, running his fingers through his shorn hair. His clear, pale eyes—not quite blue or gray, but something in between—look up and meet mine.

"Just—here." Jack holds out the thing he retrieved from the other room earlier, waiting for me to take it. My hand shakes as I reach for it. A small, folded up piece of paper that's slick and heavier than normal paper. A digi strip. "Just watch this, then I think you'll understand."

"What is this?" I ask, opening the strip up. The screen is dark, waiting my command.

"Answers."

Exactly the thing I came here to find.

"I'll wait, here." He points to the other room. "Just— watch it. And then if you still don't believe me, I'll..." He lets the promise hang in the air between us, unspoken.

I unfold the digi strip slowly as he turns to the other room to give me privacy.

"And—" Jack says, pausing at the door.

I turn, but he doesn't speak for a long time. He just looks into my eyes, as if trying to see through me.

"And?" I prompt, impatient.

"And," Jack says, his voice low now, "I'm sorry."

I flatten the unfolded digi strip in my hand, swiping my fingers across the surface to turn it on. A date written in black letters illuminates the screen. December 26, 2341. Last year, just after Winter Festa. There's a small timestamp on the bottom, certification that this digi file was recorded on this date.

"Jack, what are you doing?"

My heart freezes at the sound of Akilah's voice. She sounds happy, playful. She sounds exactly the way I remember her.

"Recording." Jack's gruff voice.

The image bleeds onto the paper: Akilah, wearing her military uniform. She looks so professional—wild hair tamed into a beautiful twist, the crisp lines of her pants visible even on the digi file, her brown eyes big and smiling. A single star glitters on the right side of her chest—she'd only been in the military for a short time, and already had risen up one rank.

"Yeah, but why are you recording?" Akilah looks impatient, but she smiles playfully at him.

The image sweeps away from Akilah, toward a building. They're clearly both at the Lunar Base in Serenitatis—there are military grade rovers scattered on the roads, the shimmering dome in the background. But Jack's focusing the camera on one building in particular. It looks almost like a hospital or dormitory, but as Jack zooms in, I can see that the windows aren't glass but painted bricks and the doors are locked with heavy iron bars across them.

"Don't you ever wonder what's over there?" Jack says in a low voice.

"None of my business." Akilah sounds serious now, too. Maybe even a little scared.

The camera moves, as if Jack's turning to talk to Aks. "The people ordered to go into the Laboratory Facilities... they're not coming out the same way they were."

Akilah rolls her eyes. "Not everything is a conspiracy theory, Jack."

"What's going on over there?" A deep female voice shouts out, followed by a series of thuds as she approaches.

"Nothing, sir," Akilah says immediately, jumping to a salute.

Jack doesn't speak. His camera is facing the ground, hidden by his hand. "Sir, nothing sir, we were just wondering, sir."

"Wondering about what?"

"The Lab Facilities."

The woman pauses. "Soldier, it would be an honor— an *honor*—to be selected for duty at the Laboratory Facilities. It is a privilege, and only the top officers are allowed entry."

"Sir, yes sir," Jack mumbles.

There's more words I can't distinguish, but soon the commanding officer strides away. Jack seems to have forgotten about the camera, but the audio is still recording.

"Akilah, look—the people who go in that building come out different," he says in a rushed voice. "And they're targeting people from the Foqra District."

Akilah sucks in a harsh breath. The Foqra District— the poor section of New Venice—is where she lived before she was assigned to military duty for her year of service.

"The people who go in... they come out not caring about anyone or anything. What's the most important thing in the world to you?"

The camera tilts—Jack's remembered he's holding it again. It fills with Akilah's face as she touches the fortune cookie locket around her neck. I do the same, fingering the familiar smooth silver. This is the sign of our friendship, the thing that ties us together even when we're so far apart.

Akilah's father disappeared on them when we started secondary school. Her mom was financially ruined, and she and Akilah had to move to the Foqra District. When Akilah got her military assignment, her mother decided to move to Tunisia to look for work, and I know that Akilah doesn't hear from her often.

Neither Aks nor I have a sibling, and fate and tragedy has isolated us. But the one thing we always had was each other.

Akilah doesn't answer Jack's question, but she doesn't need to.

The screen fades to black, and a new date pops up: January 8, 2342. This year, a few weeks after Jack's first vid.

The image on the screen makes me feel motion sick—it's bouncing around as if the person holding the camera is running. The entire screen turns white for a moment, then a loud *boom* echoes from the digi file. A bomb. My eyes search the screen, trying to pick out Akilah in the mass of people screaming and shouting, running away from—or, in the case of the military, toward—the bomb.

The person holding the camera curses—I think it's Jack again, but I'm not sure—and a small cloud of gray dust obscures the screen.

The voice behind the camera starts again—just one word over and over: "*Nonononononono.*" And then the camera drops. I see Jack fall to his knees, gray dust smearing his clothing. And something wet. Something red.

Blood.

Not his.

An arm. The forearm shorn to the bone, white standing out starkly against dark flesh.

Jack crouches over the body of a girl, slender and tall, with wild hair done up in twists. His shoulders start to shake. I see him stiffen then, and lean back.

And I see her face.

Akilah's dead, staring eyes.

Water splashes onto the digi file screen. I smear my tears away.

Jack pushes on Akilah's chest, up-down, up-down, but it's too late. Her stomach is ripped apart, her guts spilling onto the dusty ground, turning the grayish earth dark. One leg is twisted up under her body, the other is completely gone.

I sob, choking for air. My eyes burn so much that I cannot see the rest of the film strip.

Jack wasn't lying. This isn't a lie. There is nothing truer than her death and the way my soul is silently crying out in sorrow.

TWENTY

I SLAM MY PALM ON THE SCREEN, pausing it. My legs give out and I sprawl on the cold, dusty floor, my chest heaving.

I don't want to believe this is true.

I examine the digi strip, but it's secure and sealed—it can't have been tampered with. And Akilah would never fake her death, not like this.

The evidence is right here in front of me, but it's impossible. There have been no reports of her death.

But the image of her body, torn apart by bombs, is burned into my retinas.

And... I *just* spoke to her. Not that long ago. She's fine. She's fine, she's fine, she can't be dead.

With a shaking hand, I start the last vid stored on the digi strip. The date—with the official time stamp authenticating it—glows darkly. One week after Akilah's death.

The image is of a military bunker of some sort. Cots line the building, and it appears as if the camera is propped up on a pillow, pointing to the center of the room. Jack and a few other men are talking to someone, but I cannot see the person's face. Then the crowd shifts.

I gasp aloud, my heart stuttering.

Akilah walks before a group of military men. She stands straight and tall—on both her legs. She has no scars. No sign that she was injured, let alone killed.

The group of people are just far enough away that I can't hear what anyone's saying, just that it appears as if Akilah's giving orders. I glance at her uniform. She now has six stars shining on her chest. A few weeks ago, she was barely an officer; now she's nearly a general.

Jack breaks off from the group talking to Akilah and rushes to the camera and the cot it rests on. He does something I can't see, but when he turns around, I notice a gold necklace in his hand. The fortune cookie necklace. I touch my own, warm from my body heat, and my fingers curl around the metal, squeezing it. Jack rushes back to Akilah and hands it to her.

The gold chain dangles through her fingers. She looks up at Jack, confused. Says something. I strain my ears, but there's no sound this time other than muffled, indiscernible voices. Jack says something else, as if he's trying to explain, but Akilah just shrugs as she leaves the group. The other men snap to attention, saluting Akilah, but Jack just stares at her as she passes a rubbish bin and drops the necklace in it.

The screen fades to black. It slips from my numb fingers.

"What does this mean?" I wonder aloud. That Akilah is dead... but she's not? She's fine—but different? She hasn't seemed different. But she hasn't said anything about dying, either.

There's one sure way to find out. I stand up, tapping my fingers on my cuff. My eye and ear bots connect to the cuff, and soon a hologram of Akilah fills my vision.

"What's wrong?" she asks immediately.

I wipe my face with my hands, feeling the grime smear against the tear tracks. "Akilah—you're okay, right?"

She laughs—nervously, still worried about my obvious distress. "Yeah, of course I am. What happened? Is it your mother?"

I shake my head, swallowing down the fear and sorrow that had risen inside me. I give her a watery smile. "I was just... someone lied to me," I say. "I'm sorry to bug you."

Akilah grins at me. "No worries," she says. She leans forward, reaching for something I can't see.

"Akilah?" I ask, my voice hollow.

She freezes and leans slowly back, focusing her attention on me. "Yes?"

"Where's your necklace?"

She stares at me, confused.

I reach up, tugging the silver chain of my fortune cookie locket out, swinging the charm toward her. "Where's yours?" I demand.

Akilah touches her neck, but there's nothing there but the collar of her shirt. "I... um..." Her mind's racing, as if she has no idea what I'm talking about. I narrow my eyes at her. That necklace was the symbol of our friendship. She got special permission from her commanding officer to wear it under her uniform because she didn't want to take it off, ever. And she didn't even notice it was gone?

"I didn't want to worry you," Akilah says in a rush, as if she's reading lines from a play. "It broke, but it should be fixed soon, and—"

"I have to go." I sever the connection without another goodbye.

My mind's reeling. My best friend would *never* just forget about our necklaces. Inside the fortune cookie locket is a small digi strip, one we made together. We both *swore* to never take it off.

It makes no sense that she doesn't have it. But it also make no sense that she died, and came back as the kind of person who'd throw away the locket as if it means nothing.

"Jack?" I call, striding across the room. "This was *not* 'answers.' You need to start speaking, *now*."

I throw open the door to the room he said he'd wait for me in.

It's empty.

"Son of a—" I mutter.

The window's open, a warm breeze blowing. I race to it. It's low and easy for me to hoist myself over the ledge and drop down on the street on the other side. I gaze around, trying to find Jack, but he's long gone.

TWENTY-ONE

GREAT. I HAD ONE LEAD—ONE PERSON directly connected to the terrorist attacks PA Young warned me were imminent. One. And instead of calling the police the second I saw him, I let myself be distracted by his lies and fall into a confusing world where nothing makes sense.

I need answers.

Jack's idea of answers just led me to more questions. I can't ask Mom; I can't risk triggering an attack or making her upset. Ms. White knows as much as I do.

I need answers from the person pulling the strings.

A giant fountain rises up in the center of the plaza in front of Triumph Towers. Everything here—except the glittering steel-and-glass towers—is made of gray granite and marble imported from Italy—a stark contrast to the dusty brown limestone that nearly every other building in Malta is made of. And the water here, rather than the blue of the Mediterranean, is golden like honey. I'm not sure if the water's been dyed, or if it's just a clever trick of the light, reflecting the bronze base of the fountain up through the water.

I tilt my head back, scanning the roof of the tallest tower, wondering briefly if PA Young is up there, looking down at all of us.

If anyone can tell me what's going on, it's her. I'm just not sure how much I trust her. Jack's digi strip was convincing—maybe there is something going on in that so-called Laboratory Facilities. And that's government run—which means PA Young isn't telling me everything.

But... how do you stride into the most secure building in the world and demand answers from the woman who runs the largest global government in history?

Auto-taxis from Mdina and Rabat crowd the corners of the streets, but no vehicles are allowed directly in front of the plaza—safety first. Nearly everyone in the plaza has their eyes glued to their wrists—some are on calls with others or going over their schedules or reviewing notes for the workday. The tourists are holding their wrists up, lining up photos on their cuffLINKs. The only people not staring at their cuffs or with silver eyes showing their nanobots are the security force. Dressed in all-black, the officers stand at attention, their eyes skimming the milling crowd for any trouble.

I twirl my own necklace through my fingers as I stand before Triumph Towers. Before, I had always looked at these buildings with a sort of patriotic pride—they're gorgeous, skyscrapers that are both magnificently tall and also beautifully built. But now they seem ominous. Glittering in the sunlight, but still—ominous.

A piercing, high-pitched laugh echoes through the plaza, and I'm not the only one who spins around in the direction of the little girl in the neon-bright pink dress who's half-hiding behind the statue at the base of one of the towers. An older man carrying two cups of a gelato lunges at the girl and she skitters away to her mother, laughing, before racing up to the man and snatching the chocolate gelato cup. I squint, but it's not until the man turns and sits on the base of the statue beside his daughter that I realize who it is.

Representative Belles.

He looks so different here from when I saw him earlier, after the reverie. He seems lighter, somehow, as if he has no worries. The little girl in the bright dress doesn't stop bouncing around and spinning as she eats her gelato, and the representative and his wife smile fondly at her. She tries to do a pirouette while balancing a huge dollop of gelato on the little shovel-like flat spoons the android vendors dole out, and chocolate plops down the front of her pink dress. She looks on the verge of tears until Representative Belles swoops down, whispering something in her ear and sending her into a gale of giggles.

The corners of my lips twitch up. The representative seems nice.

I hope he's not a traitor.

THE BODY ELECTRIC

I hear a small buzzing sound just before I feel a jab of pain in my hand. I smack my wrist automatically, and my palm comes away smeared with the guts of a fat bumblebee, the stinger embedded into my skin, already puffy and swelling.

"That looks like it hurts," a voice says.

My stomach drops, and I swallow nervously as I lift my eyes.

And see Dad. Real Dad. *My* Dad.

I don't know how I could have been tricked by the hologram tracker program earlier, even if for just a moment. It was nothing compared to Dad standing in front of me right now. He's *real*. His hair moves in the gentle sea breeze, his chest rises and falls with each breath, a heartbeat thrums at the vein on his throat.

I leap up, throwing my arms around him. This is Dad. He's warm and real and *here*.

"How... how?" I stammer, clutching the sides of his arms. "You... you're *dead*." I whisper the last word, dreading the sound of it on my lips.

"Ella," he says, his voice trailing off. My name spoken in his voice is heaven; my heart leaps and I want nothing more than to live in this moment, me, holding onto Dad, real and in front of me and clearly, obviously, not dead.

"What happened?" I say. "Was it fake? Your death? Are you in hiding? Is that why you couldn't come to me and Mom, why you disappeared? We thought you were dead, Dad, we thought—" My voice cracks, and words fade.

"Ella," Dad says again, and something twists in my stomach, something sickening. A whisper of doubt rises in my mind, but I push it down, my fingers seizing against Dad's linen jacket, holding him tight, keeping him here.

"What's going on?" Tears are streaming down my face now. "You were dead, and now you're not, and Akilah's dead, and then she wasn't." A horrible fear enters my mind. "You're not like her, are you? Do you remember me?" I giggle, a hysterical, bubbling sound. "Of course you remember me, you said my name. You're real. You're Dad." I say the words for me as much as him.

I search his eyes. "You're alive." Saying the words makes me—finally—accept them as true. Nothing else matters. With Dad back, he can cure Mom. He can help me solve this terrorism problem. He can fix everything.

"Ella..."

"Please!" I cry, "Say something other than my name!"

"Ella." Dad's voice cuts through every other sound in the plaza. "Ella. You have to wake up."

TWENTY-TWO

MY EYES OPEN BLEARILY. I'M ON A THIN mattress in a small but richly decorated room that smells of musk and wood oil. I'm wearing all my clothes, even my shoes, but a knitted throw covers the lower half of my body.

For a while I just lay there, staring at the taupe wall with heavy wooden accents. My father was there in front of me.

But he wasn't really.

I… I hallucinated. That's the only answer. I know he's dead—I know he's dead, but seeing Representative Belles with his family while I was thinking about Dad…

…But it was so *real*.

I could *feel* him. Touch him. I heard him. He was *there*.

But he wasn't.

It all happened in my mind.

I'm going crazy. My stomach twists and I curl up in the fetal position. I did this to myself. Those extra nanobots I injected into my body so I could help Mom with her reverie, the ones that gave me the ability to go into other people's reveries...

A person can only have so many nanobots in their system. Too many, and the body fails. The mind fails. Bot-brain... and death.

I shut my eyes, and force myself to think the words slowly. *I. Am. Going. Crazy.*

Only crazy people hallucinate like that.

Only crazy people believe their hallucination is real.

Oh, shit. I choke back a sob in this silent, unknown room. And then I wonder: *what did I do?* In my mind, I grabbed my father, I spoke to him. Did I just speak to the air? Did I grab a stranger? Is this a waiting room to a mental institution?

And what if... what if I lose my mind more? What if I disintegrate into nothing? Or worse—what if I hallucinate with Mom around? What if I hurt her?

I feel sick—physically sick, like I'm going to throw up. I feel as if my brain is turning to jelly, and there is nothing I can do but feel it leak into my blood, twist around my veins, and seep out of my skin. I swallow down the bile rising in my throat and squeeze my eyes shut. I can envision the microscopic nanobots in my body wiggling over my brain and crawling into the wrinkles. I grip the sides of my head, pulling my hair. A part of me wants to rip the skin open and claw my own flesh out.

"Ella?" a female voice calls from the other side of the closed door.

I sit up quickly, my legs tangling with the blanket as I swing them over the side of the bed. The door creaks open, and a young woman with deeply tan skin and wavy dark hair enters. She holds a tab-screen in one hand, idly tapping at it, and glances up to look at me in a bored way.

"You okay?" she asks as if she doesn't really care one way or another about the answer.

I nod warily.

"Ella Shepherd, right?"

I don't answer. The woman looks up from her screen.

"We scanned your cuff," she says.

"Yeah," I confirm.

"You collapsed," the woman says, eyes back on the screen. "The meds said you were dehydrated."

I glance at my cuff; everything seems perfectly normal. My health stats are fine.

"The representative offered his office for you to recuperate," the woman continues. She sounds exhausted from the effort of paying me any attention. "Your emergency contact has been reached, but—" She glances up at me, meeting my eyes directly, and for the first time I feel like her attention is entirely on me. "The representative wants to speak to you."

"Representative...?" I ask.

"Representative Administrator Santiago Belles," the aide says. "He's on his way; he should be here in a few minutes."

"Why—?" I start, but she cuts me off.

"He was nearby when you fell, and, after the meds scanned your cuff, vouched for you and requested that you be brought here to await your guardian's arrival."

I blink rapidly. This is obviously a lie—while I was inside Representative Belles's mind, he has no idea who I am. But if they scanned my cuff, they must have seen I'm an intern at Reverie Mental Spa, and Belles obviously recognized that. I can only guess what he wants from me.

She turns and leaves, but doesn't close the door behind her. Now that I have more context, I realize I'm in Triumph Towers—in the representative's personal office. He must sleep here sometimes. I get up and follow to where the aide left. Representative Belle's office is richly appointed and reeking of authority. It's all steel and mahogany, a blend of modern and traditional. A heavy wooden door is on the other side of the room, and I hear the faint click of a lock as the aide traps me inside.

My cuff buzzes and I glance at the screen. Ms. White.

"I'm fine," I say before she can say anything.

"What happened?"

"I'm fine," I repeat. "I just got a little... dizzy. But, look, I'm in Representative Belles's office. I'm going to snoop around, see what I can find."

"Be careful," she says, and I cut the screen off.

The representative's aide said Belles would be here in a few minutes, and I'm not about to waste any of them. I rush behind his desk, scanning the surface for anything of importance, but it's blandly empty. There's a filing cabinet to the left (locked) and a drawer under the desk (also locked). I swipe my hand across the surface of the desk, and it glows as it boots up. The system's not that different from the one we use at Reverie Mental Spa. A screen floats up from the surface, and the top of the desk illuminates a keyboard. A dozen or more holo-icons twirl across the top of the desk, but when I reach for them, they shake. Password protected.

I glance at my cuff—I've already lost a minute. My mind races, and my fingers fly across the keyboard as I try to recall everything I ever learned in any of my interface system classes. I shut my eyes, hoping I can channel some of the representative's thoughts from the reverie we shared.

Beep!

I open my eyes, and see that one of the holo-icons has come unlocked, glowing faintly green. I grab it, and it explodes across the surface of the desk.

Folders. I flip through the tabs, trying to see anything that could possibly be important.

My eyes grow wide.

My father's name. Right there, across the top of one of the folders.

I snatch the holo-folder up, and its contents burst before me. Dozens of papers ranging from news clippings and vid files of Dad to memos from the labs to detailed scientific reports. I try to memorize everything before me, but there's too much. I let my fingers slide over the documents, lingering on one near the top.

Nanorobotics and Cyborg Control in Android Theory: Building a Brain Through Biology and Technology

By: Dr. Philip K. Shepherd

The prevailing theory is that androids simply cannot be equipped with individual thought. While this has proven true through countless tests, it is also true that in order for technology to become what we want it to be, we must alter our quest. Androids are currently ideal laborers and soldiers. They never tire, their work is typically more precise than humans', and they have the advantage of being virtually indestructible through a stronger internal system made of alloy metal rather than bone and flesh.

Human beings have the advantage of individual thought, something that has never been successfully replicated. Androids have the advantage of superior physical strength. It's the classic case of brains versus brawn.

My scientific studies to date have always had the goal of a being with individual thought but also physical strength. I have failed to create an android with a human brain to achieve that end.

THE BODY ELECTRIC

Pain erupts behind my eyes—a blinding sort of migraine. I stagger back, my hand twitching, and the folder closes, the holo-icon dropping back to the desk's surface. At that precise moment, I hear the click of the door's lock. I swipe my hand over the surface of the desk, sending the interface program back into standby mode, and lunge around the desk and into the chair across from it.

The door opens and Representative Belles steps in.

"Hello, Ella," he says, shutting the door behind him.

I stand and extend my hand to the representative's. As we exchange meaningless pleasantries, my heart is racing, my lungs gasping, my mind spinning, but I am confident that the representative sees nothing but my easy smile.

TWENTY-THREE

"HAVE YOU RECOVERED?"

The representative asks, his voice neutral.

I'm not sure if it's entirely true, but I say, "Yes."

"You gave the medics quite a scare. A young girl passing out in front of Triumph Towers."

"I'm sorry; I got, uh, dizzy." I stare into his clear eyes. "Why did you bring me here? I could have waited for someone outside."

Representative Belles splays his hands palm-up on his desk, as if he's offering me peace. "I saw from your cuff scan that you work as an intern at Reverie Mental Spa. Your last name is Shepherd; it wasn't much of a leap to figure out you are Dr. Rose Shepherd's daughter."

I wait, an eyebrow raised. He still hasn't answered my question.

"I recently did a reverie at the mental spa, my first. You can see why I might be… suspicious of someone from Reverie suddenly appearing before me."

"I can see you might be *paranoid*," I say, mimicking his inflection.

The representative snorts in laughter void of humor. "Perhaps I am. But it struck me as unusual, and I wanted to..." His voice trails off.

"To what?" I demand. "Quiz me? Torture me like a spy? Look, I was just in the plaza. I got, uh, dizzy. That's all. And besides," I add, "if you're so worried about spies, why did you leave me here in your office alone?"

The representative smirks. "I have the highest security on my interface system."

I very carefully keep my face emotionless. Highest security my ass; I broke into it with my eyes literally closed.

The representative hands me a glass of water from the bar near his desk. I hesitate; his paranoia is infecting me.

"The medic said you collapsed from dehydration," the representative says, watching me.

I raise the glass to my lips and force myself to drink a few sips before continuing.

"Thank you for not contacting my mother," I say.

The tension in the room crackles around us. "Dr. Rose Shepherd..." The representative sounds contemplative. "The scientist who invented reveries, who is dying of Hebb's Disease."

I flinch at the way he says "dying," as if it's not important at all.

The representative smiles, just the corners of his mouth lifting up before he hides it behind his steepled hands. "I have found it imperative to learn all I can about anyone I associate with," he says finally. "And I have discovered that I cannot afford to trust anyone. Perhaps that has made me paranoid."

I shoot him my best incredulous look, but warning alarms are ringing in my head.

"Your father..." the representative starts, and my head whips around to his. "He was a famous scientist too."

"Yes?" I say tentatively. "I—um—thank you for bringing me up here, but I should get home."

"Oh, please, have some more water first. For your dehydration." He pushes the glass I set down closer to me. I take it, but do not drink this time.

"Dr. Philip Shepherd," the representative muses. "He worked with android sciences."

"And nanobots," I say.

Representative Belles nods. "I've been looking at his research. What I can find of it, I mean."

I place the glass of water back on the representative's desk. I wish I'd had just five more minutes alone with his files.

"He was a genius," the representative says.

"I like to think so."

"Oh, no, he absolutely was." The representative casts me an appraising look. "I'd love to read more about him. Do you have any of his research at the mental spa? Perhaps I could come in one day for a reading."

I hide the smile growing on my lips. This isn't the representative being kind and giving a girl who passed out a glass of water. No... this is an interview. This is a test. This is his feeble attempt to spy on *me*.

"No," I say simply, my confidence rising now that I see what this really is. "He didn't. Much of his research was destroyed in the explosion. You know. The one that killed him."

I'm pleased to see that, despite the blasé way he spoke of my mother's sickness, my reminder of my father's death so bluntly unnerves the representative.

"Probably for the best," I continue. "PA Young warned me personally that terrorists were trying to find Dad's research."

I watch him closely, but his face is utterly blank. "Are they?" he asks, obviously trying to lead me on.

I nod emphatically. "I suppose you can turn any scientific study into some kind of weapon; that's just human nature. Dad wanted his work to help people, cure illnesses. The terrorists think they can corrupt that, I guess. The government, of course, won't allow that to happen."

The representative's eyes slide away from mine. "Of course," he mutters.

I try my best to appear at least a little vapid. "They're after my mother's research too," I say.

Representative Belles's eyes widen slightly, then he leans back in his chair, his face obscured by shadows. "Really?" he asks, his voice feigning disinterest.

My hands curl into fists, but I keep my tone light. Best to make him think I'm nothing but a stupid little girl;

men like him are easier to control that way. I try to look guileless and let the corners of my mouth drift up.

"Do you know why the first lunar colony failed?" he asks finally.

I shake my head, unsure of how the representative has leapt to this topic.

The original lunar colony was located in the "Sea of Tranquility," one of the dark spots on the moon's surface, part of the right eye of the "man in the moon." Covered in domes, the first colony was wiped out after an error, and the new colony—along with new domes—were built over the "Sea of Serenity." The lunar base Akilah serves on is part of Serenitatis.

"The colonists of Tranquilitatis had androids to aid them," Representative Belles says. "The androids were the ones who built the colonial domes—they don't need air to work, they're robots after all—so they built the domes. But there was an error in the construction somewhere. The Tranquilitatis dome was failing, losing oxygen. The colonists had all moved in before they noticed the damage, and if it wasn't fixed, they would all die."

"But they did all die," I say.

"The colonial leader ordered the androids to fix the dome as efficiently and quickly as possible. And they did."

I look at Representative Belles questioningly.

"The androids realized that the seams of the dome around the base were contaminated with moon dust—it's a really fine powder, and it had seeped between the seals.

THE BODY ELECTRIC

To fix the dome, the androids had to lift them up, clean out the seam at the base, and reseal the domes. The colonial leader had told them to fix it as quickly as possible, so the androids gathered around the base of the dome... and lifted it up."

I gape at the Representative. I've never heard any of this. The death of the Tranquilitatis colony was a blow—we had a week of mourning after the news reached Earth that the dome had failed. It happened when I was a kid, but I remember school being cancelled. It was the first time I really understood that bad things happened in the world; the first time I saw adults scared and upset. But while many news sources have questioned how the dome failed, no answer has been made public.

"The androids lifted the dome for exactly eighteen minutes—the time it took for them to clear the moon dust away from the seal and reposition the dome. The average person can't last more than a minute or two exposed to space. All the oxygen left the dome. The domes were also connected to the false gravity in the colony. All the colonists... they died, floating, choking on the vacuum of space."

I can just picture it—the colonists gasping for air, dying in space.

"The decompression in the dome when the androids lifted it caused all the windows in the house to break, and anyone outside was sucked out onto the moon's surface or thrown up to the roof of the dome. It was like a *cyclone*, whirling the bodies around. When the androids reattached the dome and the gravity kicked on, the bodies of those colonists dropped straight back down. The investigators who went to analyze the aftermath said there were dead people everywhere, in the strangest positions. Over roofs. In the hypo-hyrdro trees that had been planted. On the ground, in all kinds of weird positions. It had, literally, rained death."

Androids can only follow directions. They can perform simple tasks. But they can't *think*. Science can do a lot. But it can't make a brain. It can't make something that thinks for itself. I know—I've studied the medical files. Mom's disease lies inside her brain, the drifting synapses and the failing nerves. Any organ in the human body can be cloned—except a brain.

The androids didn't think when they lifted the dome. They don't have a brain. They have a computer. They just followed directions. And that killed the entire colony.

At least, that's what happened if what Representative Belles is telling me is true. Which, honestly, I'm not sure how much I can trust him, or why he's telling me this.

Representative Belles stands up, and for a moment, I think he's going to come around the desk and do something to me. I flinch as he turns on his heel, but then he strides toward the window, not me. I stand up and move closer, gazing down. The Representative has a perfect view of the plaza, the fountain. From here I can see it all, the dark uniforms of security, the hurried walking of businessmen and women, the street androids idly serving customers pastizzi and other snacks.

I'm losing him. Whatever made him talk about science and terrorists before—that's all gone away. He's clamming up. But I try one more question: "What does the lunar colony tragedy have to do with the terrorists the government is trying to stop?" I ask, my voice low.

"Maybe it doesn't have anything at all to do with the terrorists," Representative Belles says as he looks down at the plaza.

I examine his face in the reflection of the glass. He doesn't look like a man who's contemplating treason.

He looks terrified.

TWENTY-FOUR

I STEP OUT INTO THE SUNLIGHT, momentarily blinded.

Well, this day has officially been the strangest day of my life.

Only one thing left to do now. Out of the corner of my eye, I see a street android selling warm, delicious-smelling pastizzi. I may have spent the morning tracking down a lunatic thanks to a holographic image of my dad, hallucinated, and wound up in a potential terrorist's office where I had a super weird conversation, but at least pastizzi are normal.

"Cheese," I say when I reach the front of the line. I tap my cuff against the payment center and wait for the android to hand me the ricotta-filled pastizza.

The android doesn't move.

"One. Cheese," I say again, enunciating clearly. My cuff flashes that my payment was accepted.

"Tranquility through freedom," the android says.

"Excuse me?" I ask. I glance around. There are a few other street androids near the fountain, and all of them seem to have frozen. Their customers look just as confused as me.

"TRANQUILITY THROUGH FREEDOM," the street android bellows. Its voice goes up a notch. *"Tranquility through freedom! Tranquility through freedom!"* it chants.

I back away slowly, dread rising up in my throat.

"The hell is going on?" a man in a business suit asks behind me.

"I have no idea," I mutter. I try to hold the man back, but he shakes me off. "Something's wrong," I say. "We should get help." Out of the corner of my eye, I see that several black uniforms are marching toward us and all the other street androids in the plaza.

The man jerks his arm free and shrugs past me. "No!" I shout. "Stay back!"

He ignores me and grabs the android by the shoulders, as if shaking it will make it work. My feet work of their own volition—I keep backing away, my eyes wide, sure something bad is about to happen. The security is swarming around, but there are more androids than they can handle, and the crowd turns into a mob.

I make it to the gate before I hear the first explosion.

I turn around, my eyes drinking up the horror before me. At least a dozen spots on the plaza are smoking, smoldering chunks of twisted metal. All of the androids exploded. The people nearby... I stare with horror at the spot where I stood with the man in the business suit. All that's left now are red stains on a white shirt, the tattered edges of a dark sleeve, a foot, and, several meters away, another foot. It's like seeing Akilah die earlier, except without the trappings of war. This is every nightmare I've ever had rolled into one: war invading my own home.

"Oh, God," I mutter, staring at the massacre. The black-uniformed security and military people rush forward, trying to stem the flow of chaos. My cuffLINK starts flashing red and a warning message zooms across the screen.

Android malfunction leads to several deaths in Triumph Plaza, Central Gardens, Comino Island, and other areas of New Venice. Citizens should return to their homes. Any androids within the area should be immediately disabled.

My heart sinks, boiling in the acid of my stomach. "Mom," I gasp. *Mom.* And her new nursing android. I left Mom this morning with a walking, talking *bomb*.

I turn on my heel and race through Central Gardens, pushing past the crowds. A definite sense of pure panic rises throughout the city, encompassing it like a tsunami. New Venice has never been attacked before, not like this, not from within.

My fingers skim across my cuff as I run, and I bring up the latest news. The news team must have been ordered to repeat the same message over and over on a loop.

"—no reasoning behind the android malfunction that's led to dozens, perhaps hundreds of injuries and deaths. Sources say Prime Administrator Young did give the command to remotely disconnect all androids operating within New Venice, but the remote kill switch is currently inoperable and countless androids remain online. All citizens are advised to manually disable any android in the area. If the android already appears to be malfunctioning, all citizens are advised to immediately take cover as far away as possible."

Mom can't move fast, not fast enough to out-distance an exploding android.

I blink and turn the news off, pushing myself even further toward Reverie and home and Mom. I try to message Mom, but she's not answering. Ms. White's cuff must be out of reception, somehow, or turned off—none of my messages to her even go through.

When I reach the south gate of Central Gardens, I pass by a group of military elite, guns already out, racing toward the park. Comino Island, a part of the lower city, was also attacked. I think about the children that go to the theme park there. Androids are often teachers' aides. Many use them for nannies or babysitters, even though there are warnings on their labels that children shouldn't be left with androids unsupervised.

How many children were among the deaths? I almost stumble at the thought.

I have to wait to cross the street, ambulances and police cars racing by. The glass front of Reverie is pristine and clear, the neon sheep bouncing across the surface as if nothing at all were wrong. I cringe, waiting for an explosion, half expecting it to happen right here and now in front of me. I close my eyes, trying to stay calm, but all I see behind my eyelids is the glass front shattering, people screaming, running from the building... and Mom. Mom, who named her android, turned to dust and ash, mangled bits of unrecognizable flesh.

As soon as the street is clear, I race across it, sliding through the glass doors of Reverie before they're open all the way. The waiting lobby is empty, sterile, with soft scents and quiet music playing gently. No sign of the chaos outside, no sign of the destruction awaiting upstairs. My breath is jagged and uneven, my footsteps loud. It sounds weird here, where the white tile and serene mood lighting makes everything peaceful. I visualize the serenity torn apart by an exploding bomb, screams cutting through the soft music.

I don't wait for the lift. No time. I take the stairs two at a time, my heart thumping and my lungs screaming for air. I throw myself into the apartment, screaming for Mom as the door slides open. Mom is in the kitchen and struggling to stand, concern etched on her face at my sudden and loud appearance.

"What's wrong?" she asks me, weakly.

I don't answer. I look wildly around. The android Mom named Rosie. Standing in front of the interface screen in the living room, past the kitchen. I lunge around a dining room chair and skid into the living room. Rosie doesn't even acknowledge my presence. The interface screen is open to Reverie's private network, the most secure parts, where Mom's research and the science behind reveries lie. Not even Ms. White has access to these files, just me and Mom. Rosie's not even programmed to go onto the interface, much less hack our system.

Son of a—! "Interface *off*," I command loudly. "Lock screen authorization Ella Shepherd." The screen goes black.

The android slowly straightens. It twists its body, turning its face to me. Its dead, empty eyes stare into mine. Its face is expressionless, as if all the programming to make it appear human has already been deleted.

Rosie's mouth drops open, a movement that is so robotic it breaks any illusion of humanity that could ever be attributed to the machine. Its head cocks a little to the left.

"What's wrong, Ella?" Mom asks again.

"Tranquility through freedom," Rosie mutters, so soft I almost don't catch it.

"Shit," I say.

I spin around to Mom. "Get out!" I scream at her. "We have to go! Rosie's going to explode!"

"What?" Mom asks. She's disorientated. She can't handle this stress, this panic. Her body is always just a shock away from collapsing. Her fingers grip the edge of the table, knuckles white. Her face is pale.

"Tranquility through freedom," Rosie says, louder. "TRANQUILITY THROUGH FREEDOM."

There's no way we can escape in time.

A low buzzing sound emits from the back of Rosie's throat. The same "ZnznznZNznzn" sound that I heard from the other android, seconds before...

I dive for Mom and pick her up, wrapping my arms around her waist and lifting her across my shoulder. "Ella!" she says, breathless and choking on a cough. I don't answer. I run for her bedroom. The building is new, but even though the Secessionary War was a generation ago, nearly every building built since then has at least one special room.

A panic room. And that's the room Mom uses as a bedroom.

As soon as we're through the door, I put Mom down. Her legs give way under her and she collapses on the floor, but I can't stop to help her. I turn around, slamming my cuff painfully against the scanner by the door. The door snaps shut, and I type in the panic code. I can hear the steel bolts shooting through the heavy metal door seconds before the explosion goes off.

TWENTY-FIVE

I SINK TO THE GROUND, MY BACK TO the steel door protecting us. My entire body is trembling, a strange, personal aftershock of the explosion. Even though the panic room is solid and sealed tight, I imagine that I can smell smoke. The idea of it sickens me.

"Mom?" I ask.

Mom doesn't lift her head from where I dropped her on the floor, but her eyes look up to meet mine. "What happened?" she asks weakly.

"I don't know," I say. "Rosie blew up."

I get back up and then help her to stand. Together, we move slowly to her bed. I hook her cuff into the health monitors. Everything's off the charts—her heart, her breathing, her neurons. I quickly schedule an appointment with a Dr. Simpa, Mom's latest physician.

Then I pick up Mom's sleeping pills.

Mom grips my hand. "Ella, don't—" she says. "Let me stay awake. Maybe I can… help…"

But I give her a double dose of sedatives anyway, and I watch as her eyes close in just a few moments. "Get restful and tranquil sleep with our special blend of morphine and melanin!" the label on the bottle of mopheme reads. I rub my thumb over that word: tranquil.

Tranquility through freedom!

I open the panic room door.

The first thing I notice is the smell. Acrid, burning. It's a sharp odor that makes me want to flinch away. But I cover my nose and mouth with my arm and creep forward.

The entire interface window is gone. The glass and the wall framing it—nothing but a jagged, gaping hole. A gentle breeze wafts up, cutting through the burning rubble.

The floor from the kitchen to the where the interface room used to be is blackened and charred, with pock marks made from debris, and a long, stretching series of blast marks.

Rosie the android is nothing but bits of rubberized synthetic flesh, burning circuitry, and barely recognizable pieces.

I have no emotions. I just stand there, in the rubble of my life.

This... this was my home. If it were a person, this would be a gaping chest wound, the kind no one can recover from.

The door slides open and Ms. White bursts inside. She makes a little mewling cry, and rushes for me.

"Your mother?" she asks when she finally releases me from the hug.

"She's sleeping," I say. "I gave her mopheme. The steel walls in her bedroom—that's what saved us."

Ms. White holds me out at arms' length, not willing to let me go. "Oh, you smart, brilliant girl," she says, pulling me in closer and kissing my forehead. Then she pushes me away, examining my face. "Us?" she repeats. "You were here with Rose? I thought you were in Representative Belles's office?"

I shake my head. "I ran here as soon as I saw the androids blow in the plaza."

A tableau of emotion flitters across Ms. White's face, and I cannot read her expression. She swallows, hard. "Oh, Ella," she whispers. "What if you hadn't been here for her?"

My eyes are open and wide, staring at the blast pattern burnt into the floor behind Ms. White. Mom wasn't that far from Rosie, and she was already weak.

A blast like that would have killed her.

Like it killed Akilah.

The shock of the thought surprises me so much that I jerk back, making Ms. White watch me with concern. I don't know what happened to my best friend, whether she died or not, or whether the person I've been talking to for the past year is even the same friend I grew up with.

All I know for sure right now is that Mom almost died.

Ms. White straightens, her gaze never breaking from mine. I can see her jawline go taut, and she nods emphatically, even though neither of us has said anything. "Right," she says. "I'm going to contact some construction workers right away—if they can't fix the hole, they can at least make it safe for you to stay here. Unless you'd rather...?"

"I'm not leaving Mom," I say.

"No, I meant—well, you could stay with me. And your mother... maybe she should go to the hospital... No, not the hospital. It'll be crazy right now, best not to expose your mother to that. I can call Dr. Simpa, arrange a special visit in his private labs..."

"We're not leaving," I say again. "And I've already gotten Mom an appointment with Dr. Simpa."

"I'll arrange for a nurse to come. A real one," she adds when she sees my look. "No more androids."

"Who did this?" I say. For the first time, there's emotion in my voice. "Was it the terrorists?" *Or was it Jack Tyler?* I almost ask, but the words don't form in my mouth.

Ms. White frowns. "It seems likely."

"'Tranquility through freedom.' That's what Rosie said before she blew. Could this have something to do with the Tranquilitatis disaster?" I don't know if I would have made the connection if Representative Belles hadn't brought it up earlier, but it seems far too much of a coincidence to just be chance.

Ms. White's eyes widen slightly. "Have you seen the news already?" she asks.

I shake my head silently, my hand already going to my cuff to bring up the reports.

Ms. White stops me. "PA Young announced that the terrorists might have roots in the lunar colonies, perhaps even traitors from the lunar base. She's had investigators studying the old Tranquilitatis disaster, and she believes that this attack was instigated by the same group of terrorists who caused the deaths of the colonists all those years ago."

I drop my hands and take a step back, surprised at this.

"What?" Ms. White asks, concern etched in her voice.

"I was with Representative Belles just before the attack," I say, even though I know she knows this. "And he mentioned the disaster. Said it was an accident caused by androids."

Ms. White narrows her eyes. "I'll let PA Young know he said that. It's very suspicious he'd be talking about it now, just before the attack..."

I nod, agreeing with her.

"It could be that Belles has already joined the terrorists. Maybe lies like that are what convinced him to join their side."

"Maybe," I say slowly, remembering the way the representative looked so scared.

Ms. White sighs, sinking into a chair at the table. "Who knows, really? This could have just been a stunt to distract the government from a bigger problem, or—"

"It was more than a stunt!" I roar, my voice rising far louder than I intended. Rather than be surprised by my volume, though, Ms. White's face melts with sympathy and emotion.

"You're right," she says simply. "This is war."

TWENTY-SIX

WHILE MS. WHITE HELPS SET UP A NEW— human—nurse with Mom, I retreat to my bedroom, bringing up the news before I collapse onto my bed. Dozens of programs on the android attack pop up in my vision, but they tell me nothing that I haven't already heard or guessed—a terrorist attack from an unknown group. The only thing I didn't know before was the exact number: 104. One hundred and four people dead. Mostly government officials, but one child, aged eight, who had accompanied her mother to Triumph Towers, in order to meet the Prime Administrator as an award for an art contest.

One hundred and four.

I take a shaky breath and silence the news for a moment. "Search: reasons behind android explosion attack," I say, and my vision blurs as the cuff sends the information to my eyes. A moment later, a semi-circle of floating boxes surrounds my head—or at least, it feels that way. I focus on different boxes, reading text and listening to reports, but everything is speculation, and it's all far too weak.

Maybe there aren't any answers. Maybe there never are.

Most of the news reverts back to PA Young's speech about the possibility of the terrorism reaching as far back as the Tranquilitatis Disaster so long ago. When I try to research the failed colony, nearly everything I read has already been altered to include the new information.

I feel so helpless.

I hug my pillow to my chest, silencing the new programs so I'm alone in the darkness, the way I really feel.

"I wish you were here," I say, shutting my eyes and remembering the way Dad looked in my hallucination.

I hear his voice again, so real that I'm worried I'm about to fall into another hallucination. Maybe that's what I really want. If I can only see him in madness, is it worth trying to hold onto sanity?

When I open my eyes, he's not there.

Of course he's not.

Sighing, I reopen the news scans. They all say the same thing, and soon, I notice a pattern. All the government sanctioned channels report first on the total damage, repeating that number—one hundred and four deaths—over and over. And then they zoom in on the little girl victim. They say things like, "dreamt of being a doctor," and "favorite color was pink," and then they all mention that the little girl had gone to see the Prime Administrator—as a prize for a re-envisioned flag symbolically encompassing the colonies—in her bright pink dress, but died in the plaza with her mother before she reached the offices. It's all carefully composed, designed to pull on my heartstrings, and it makes me sick to see the threads of their manipulation so carefully woven around me.

I zoom in on the picture of the little girl, so large that it's like she's standing in my bedroom in front of me.

My heart stills.

I know her.

My interface zooms through information as I look up Representative Belles's history on the interface. It doesn't take long for me to find exactly what I'm looking for: a family photograph. In the reverie during which I spied on Belles, I saw his worst nightmare, his biggest fear. Two children, casualties of war, dead at his feet. And I saw the youngest, the daughter, today, earlier, laughing and playing with the representative before I collapsed.

Before she was killed by an exploding android.

I read what little information is on the interface. Her name was Estella Belles, and she was eight years old. I examine the photograph further—her mother is the same woman in the news reports now, another casualty of the explosions. Belles and his son, Marcos, a scrawny kid who might be fifteen, are all that remains of the family.

In the news, Estella has a bright pink dress on, with a chocolate stain on the front. Her image has been caught mid-spin. "An innocent victim of the terrorist attack," the headline says as I look at the image.

This isn't a picture of a girl walking *into* Triumph Towers. This is the representative's daughter. She hadn't gone to meet the Prime Administrator; she'd gone to see her father. And they were *leaving*, not arriving, when I passed out, which was quite a lot of time for them to get away. And the only image the news shows is of her spinning around when I saw her, long before the attack.

Because... because they don't have any other image of her. I close my eyes, trying to think of the plaza just before the android blew. The little girl was definitely *not* there.

I wave aside the news reports, trying to think with a clear head. If Estella Belles's death wasn't an accident, it was certainly murder. PA Young knew that Representative Belles was considering rebellion, perhaps already working with the terrorists. They had no reason to kill his family... but maybe PA Young did.

I shudder at the thought, wrapping my arms around my body. Am I really contemplating that it was the *government* that killed Belles—not the terrorists? That would mean either the government was using the terrorist android attack to hide their own murder of two innocent people, including a child... or that the android attack itself was coming from the government.

My hand goes instinctively to my cuff, ready to call Akilah and discuss my fears with her, just as I have done with every problem I've ever had in my life. But I pause.

Thanks to Jack, I don't even know if I can trust my best friend.

A whiff of the acrid smell of burnt metal wafts through my room, coming from the remains of the other half of my home. Rosie didn't blow up when the other androids did. She blew up later—because she was busy hacking into our interface system. Exploding androids all across the city would be an effective way to make everyone, including us, forget about how our interface system was hacked.

Was the android explosion a cover-up of the terrorists looking for a way to steal Mom's information, or the government looking for a way threaten Representative Belles?

There's a war going on, that much is clear.

And I'm no longer sure I'm on the right side.

TWENTY-SEVEN

I PULL MY BLUE-AND-BROWN DAMASK covers up around my shoulders, despite the fact that it's not cold. A flicker of movement flashes to my right, and I pick up the framed digi strip I keep beside my bed. In it, Akilah and I are swimming, the summer we turned twelve. Akilah had her mother record it because it was supposed to be a race, and she wanted a record of her inevitable victory over me. But it didn't end up as a race.

We swam and swam, further into the sea than any of us had ever been before. Akilah was far faster than I, but I had more endurance, so by the end, we were pretty neck-and-neck.

"Wait, wait!" Akilah had called, treading water. We were so far out that the waves were just gentle little bumps. Akilah tilted her head back, closing her eyes against the aggressively bright yellow sun.

I swam up and bumped into her, sending her sputtering in surprise. We laughed and splashed, and then Akilah looked back to the shore.

"We came a long way," she says. Water clings to her hair, little droplets like diamonds hidden in the tight curls.

She sees me staring and shakes her head at me, spraying me with water.

I kick up so I can see the shore better. Her mom and my dad are barely visible in the rocky shoreline at the rubble of the area that was once famously called the Azure Window. One of them—Dad, I think—is waving at us.

"Let's not go back," Akilah says. She bobs in the water, stretching out and floating on her back.

"Okay," I say, mimicking her as I let my head fall back and my body float on the surface.

"I mean, ever."

I crane my head in the water to see her. Akilah could switch from fun to solemn and dark without warning. Her father had just left her family, and her mother was talking about having to move to the Foqra District. I'd never been there, but the Foqra District was in the lower city, in the poor section. My parents had already told me that, if she moved, Akilah would have to come visit me. I would not be allowed to visit her.

"Close your eyes," Akilah says. I do, without question. "It's nice, isn't it? Pretending that we can be safe out here. Nothing but saltwater and the two of us, forever."

I peek back at her. In this moment, she looks free. My mother had already been diagnosed with Hebb's Disease by this point, although it wasn't bad yet. Even though I knew what fear was, and loss, I also knew the intense love and safety of my parents. I think it was that moment when I realized that Akilah didn't have the same. Her father had left, and even before that, her parents fought a lot. Akilah was left with a worried, broken parent and a pile of debt that was forcing her to move away from me. After her girlfriend broke up with her, I was one of the few people Akilah had left.

"We keep sending colonies up into space," Akilah says, "and we don't even know what's at the bottom of the sea."

"Yeah, we do," I counter. "Fish and stuff."

Akilah laughs. "We've barely explored the sea. There are places where the water is so deep that it has never seen light." She sighs. "I would like to go to those places. I would like to sink down and down and down and see what's hidden at the bottom."

The sea is a dangerous place because it makes you believe in forever. I stare back at the shoreline, where heavy boulders clutter the shore, a remembrance of the attacks during the Secessionary War. For all the hundreds of thousands of people killed in the war, more are dead and gone beneath the waves of the sea. I tread water, turning slowly, so the island's behind me and all I can see is the blue-green waters. The sea goes on forever and ever. We are tiny, almost invisible specks. It could swallow us up. We are less than the bright stars of the night sky, compared to the vastness of the sea.

And it is this place, as one tiny, barely-visible speck bobbing in the water, where Akilah feels safe.

THE BODY ELECTRIC

Maybe being alone in the sea, with its unexplored depths, its clawing-finger waves, really is safer compared to the land, where there are people and malice and death.

TWENTY-EIGHT

THE NEXT DAY, THE CITY IS SOLEMN. Makeshift black bunting decorates many of the shop windows, and all around us is evidence of the attack, not just in the hole in my apartment or the scorch marks from other explosions, but also from the trash on the ground— no androids sweeping the streets; the lack of street vendors; the chaos in Central Gardens, where all the android vendors have been disabled. People mill around the central plaza, waiting for harried city workers to issue tickets for lift access.

Public access stairs are through a small gift shop at the edge of the plaza. Two men dressed in black military uniforms check cuffLINKs of people going to the stairs— many more people than usual are using them today, since the lifts are such a nightmare. One of the men stops me when he notices my green band, identifying me as a Maltese native.

"Why are you going to the lower city?" he asks gruffly.

I put on my most sympathetic face. "My mom works in Comino Casino," I lie. "She's been told she's going to have a pull an all-nighter tonight since their androids are disabled."

The military man shrugs. "Sorry for it, but there's no reason for you to go down there. We're trying to limit the access in the lower city. People should stay in their homes as much as possible."

"But she needs her medicine!" I say. "She can't work all night without it." My hands grope in my pockets. I always keep a few mopheme pills on me in case Mom has an attack outside of her bedroom. It's rare, but it's happened before.

The military man snatches the small bottle out of my hand and scans the label. His face pales. "Your mother has Hebb's Disease?" he asks gently.

I nod. The tears that spring into my eyes are genuine. I can think of nothing in the world worse than other people's pity.

"I'm sorry," the military man says, handing me back the bottle. "Go on ahead."

I dart through the door, pocketing the pills and racing to the stairs. There are a lot more people here than I expected—the stairwell is dusty and dank from disuse, but people's voices echo and footsteps thunder. After this morning's attack, the tourists just want to get back to their hotels in the lower city.

The upper city rises nearly four hundred and fifty meters over the sea—about the same height as the recreation of the Empire State Building in Nouveau York.

The largest tower in Triumph Towers is taller than that, even—standing in the observation deck at the top of that tower puts you nearly a thousand meters above sea level, so tall that you can see the coastline of Africa to the south if you use the metered telescopes or download amplifications to your eye bots. They say that the glittering tops of Triumph Towers are visible from the shores of Sicily.

Anyway, even though the lower city is so far below, going down the stairs to reach it isn't impossible. But I can't have gone more than halfway before my legs start screaming at me to take a break. All around me, tourists and others with me on this climb down are sitting on the steps, sprawled out and panting. I push through. I need answers.

The stairwell itself is built into one of the pillars that supports the bridge of the upper city, and while there are a few windows every other story or so, they do little more than filter in light from the solar glass ceiling of the lower city. While the top of the stairwell smelled of dust, I'm overwhelmed now by the scent of sweat. My t-shirt clings to my body, and I wish the Mediterranean was clean enough for me to jump right into it when I finally reach the bottom. As I spill out of the door and onto the docking station, I glance behind at the hundreds of stairs I just went down.

I really, *really* hope the lifts are fixed by the time I'm done with Jack, because there's no way in hell I'm going back *up* those stairs to get home.

The stairwell deposits me on the western side of the docking platform, and the giant screen behind the platform flashes a constant stream of news, close-up images of victims before they were hurt or killed, analysts trying to figure out how the government will respond, mournful testimony from witnesses.

And, every few seconds, a picture of Estella Belles. No one's said yet that this is the daughter of a representative—that would be huge news, but it's glossed over. I can't help but wonder if that's part of the plan. Keep the little girl who died in the attack anonymous, keep her hidden. She could be any little girl. She could be yours.

Isn't that what terrorism is? Making people feel terror? It's all manipulation. Like war propaganda.

The lower city is far emptier than it was earlier. I imagine most people are going home—although flights and boats are delayed—but there are some people milling about the docking station, heading into the false façade of the city. Vacations are not to be interrupted. There's still time for shopping.

I pick up my pace, and by the time I reach the main plaza, I'm jogging. It's weird to see no androids. There have always been fewer androids in the lower city—tourists want an authentic experience—but it's strange to see none.

Mechanical pigeons fill the empty spaces once occupied by the androids and the emptying crowds of tourists. The UC has many ways to track the safety of its citizens. There are cameras high above us, in the solar glass ceiling. Recording devices smaller than the eye can see are in every single streetlamp. And, of course, there's a tracker in my own cuff. The government knows where I am at all times. The mechanical pigeons are designed to make the city feel like Old Venice, but their eyes record everything they see, another cog in the UC's attempt at security. They're more focused than typical trackers and scanners. If there looks like trouble—a too-big crowd, a disturbance, a series of thefts—the mechanical pigeons flock to the area. Their presence is just as much a threat as their recording devices. They are a perpetual reminder that the government is watching.

I slow to a walk. A dozen, two dozen—forty mechanical pigeons all twist their metal necks to look at me. I think the pigeons on the roof far above me are real, but none of these are. They're watching. Recording. Me.

I try to tell myself I'm being paranoid. With the recent attack, of course there's more security. But their reflective eyes are zeroed in on me, and I can't shake them.

I curse under my breath. I've not done anything wrong... but I have a feeling Jack has. Not only is he a deserter, but if he's tied with the terrorists that made the androids explode, then he's a serious threat. And I don't want the government to get to him before I can, and I certainly don't want the government to think I'm involved with him if he is the terrorist I think he might be.

I slip into the nearest building. A glassblower is giving a demonstration to a small group of tourists who apparently don't mind that the entire android system in Malta is down right now. It's amazing how quickly people can ignore the threats of the outside world by simply pretending they don't exist.

I can't help but look at them in disgust. How can they just... stand here? It seems so wrong.

One of the tourists, a woman, seems to feel my contemptuous gaze on her, and she turns around to look at me. Our eyes meet. And I see within her a fear that belies her actions. Her hand drops to a young boy's shoulder—her son. She holds him tight—tight enough to make him squirm away.

She knows about the attack. Of course she does; by this point, everyone does. But she has to keep pushing through, she has to keep living her life. She has to pretend, for her son. Maybe if she just pretends hard enough, she can make herself believe this world is still safe for him.

I duck my head and leave the demonstration room. It's connected to a gift shop—of course it is—and I bypass the tourists to go through the shop. There are a few pieces here that are real art—swirling twists of colored sparkling crystal. But there are shelves and shelves of the same thing: a glass rose, a glass horse, a miniature glass version of Triumph Towers. This is what most people buy, and all of this was made in the factories on the southern tip of Malta, far away from the tourists' eyes, cranked out by androids and machines.

"Hey," one of the shopkeepers says as I rush past her, barely missing the shelf of breakable figurines as I head to the exit. I step outside in time to see three mechanical pigeon heads twist toward me, then I slip into the next shop. Several women sit in chairs by the windows, tatting delicate lace. Another show for the tourists—the stuff on the tables in this shop is all factory-made.

"You don't sell jumblers, do you?" I ask the manager, bumping my hip painfully against the corner of one of the display tables as I maneuver around the crowded show room.

The manager raises her eyebrow.

"I just... I'm trying to meet this guy, and I don't want my mom to know," I add, casting my eyes down and hoping that I look romantic. One of the great disadvantages of cuffs is that parents have access to the geo-locator until you're of legal age. My mother would hardly care to look, but it's a good excuse.

The manager's lips quirk up. "I can't sell those; they're illegal," she says, moving behind a counter. She opens a panel behind the display case and slides out a thin tray hidden under a black cloth. "Even if I could sell them, they'd be crazy expensive," she adds, lifting the cloth and showing an array of jumblers. I point to one of the cheaper ones, one that will only scramble the geo-location services of my cuff. The manager types a number into her scanner—250 credits—and then slips the jumbler to me. Without another word, she slides the tray back into its hidden compartment, and I slip out the back exit of the store.

As soon as the door opens, I can hear the click-flap of metallic wings. I duck into a public restroom, slapping the thin rectangle of black onto my wrist. I have to pay fifteen credits for the privilege of washing my hands and waiting for as long as I dare before peeking out the door again.

"Hurry up," a woman waiting for the toilet says. I trade places with her. No pigeons in sight. The jumbler must have confused them. Worse: Now I know they were looking for me. It was no accident that so many pigeons were following me. Someone is watching me.

TWENTY-NINE

I KEEP MY EYES WIDE OPEN AND STICK close to the walls as I creep around the alley to the door with peeling paint. To my left, luzzu boats meander down the waterway. I try to look casual until they pass, then I duck into the alleyway, my heart pounding as I round the corner to the building where I originally found Jack. Directly across from the stoop is a black-and-yellow auto-luzzu, a boat programmed to take tourists from address to address without needing a luzzolier to direct it. It's empty, though, bobbing in the water, thudding softly against the stone and concrete foundations of the city.

This is it. I know it is. That is definitely Jack's door—the same old burgundy paint, although far more scratched and beat up now, the same tarnished door knocker, set askew. I reach for it, kicking through the rubbish littering the stoop.

"I can take you where you need to be!" a cheerful voice says behind me. I jump, startled, and accidentally knock over an empty jar. The glass shatters on the stone step.

When I spin around, though, no one's there. Just the auto-luzzu.

"I can take you where you need to be!" the electronic voice calls again. Just an advertisement. For fifty credits, the boat will automatically take me anywhere in the lower city.

I grab the silver ring of the doorknocker and let it fall against the wooden door. It echoes hollowly. No one answers. I twist the knob. Locked.

"I can take you where you need to *beeeeee!*"

The boat's bobbing seems to mock me. I have no idea what I'm going to actually do—curse out a boat?—but when I reach it, I'm half ready to pay the boat to just go away.

And then I notice the eyes.

All luzzu boats are painted with giant eyes in the prow, a leftover tradition from the old days that the tourists like. But this one...this one has real eyes. Or, at least, mechanical ones. I lean closer, nearly lying on the warm concrete ledge by the water, peering at the electronic eye. Behind the glass, the lens dilates, staring at me.

"Identification: Ella Shepherd. Board now to be taken where you need to *beeeee.*"

I scramble back; I hadn't realized the electronic eye was scanning me while I was looking at it. And it somehow *knew* me.

The luzzu boat repeats its message to me. I look around—there's no one else here. Part of me wants to get in the boat—maybe it will take me to the answers I'm so desperate to find. But I can't trust it. I glance back at the door that once led to Jack Tyler's building. Jack Tyler, with his gold bumblebee pin. The jar of honey that was on the door the other day, the one that's now empty and nothing more than broken glass on the steps. The black-and-yellow stripes of this luzzu boat, the way the electronic, programmed voice says *beeee*. Bee. *Bee.*

This boat is from Jack.

I stand on the edge of the walkway, one foot teetering over the black-and-yellow auto-boat. I have no idea where it will take me, if it'll be safe, and it would be so stupid to just get inside and find out. But if I call PA Young now, she'd send cops. If Jack sees cops coming, he'll never trust me again. This boat might not take me straight to Jack—it could be just the first step of a treasure map where he's the buried gold.

Besides, I'm no longer sure I can really trust PA Young.

I let my weight shift, and step into the boat. As soon as I sit down, the propellers start churning the water. Immediately, I start to program my cuff. I don't want whoever's tracking me to find me, so I keep the jumbler on... but at the same time, I'm not quite sure of what I'm getting myself into. I set my cuff to program my nanobots to record everything, and then make an alarm system message—if I don't turn it off in an hour, everything that's been recorded will go straight to Mom's cuff, and Ms. White's, just in case.

The auto-boat takes me down waterways so tight that I can touch stone walls on either side of me. Garbage floats by, knocking against the wooden sides of the boats. The buildings around us don't have the ornate façades; we're seeing behind the pretty mask of the city.

I gasp, gripping the sides of the boat as it leaves the city's main waterways and picks up speed. We cross the Grand Canal, the stretch of water separating the recreated Venetian city to Comino Island, the only part of the lower city that's not manmade. But rather than veering west, where Comino Casino and the Blue Lagoon are, the boat goes east. We stay close to the coast, as if we're just idly meandering around the island.

The auto-boat slows as we reach the southern tip of Comino Island. The engine jerks, and my heart leaps into my throat as the boat slides behind a natural formation of rock.

"Where are we—?" I start, but my voice fades to silent. There's a cave cut into the limestone wall of the island, an arching, gaping opening. In a moment, we're cloaked in darkness.

"Where are we?" I ask again, quietly, knowing the boat can't answer. My voice sounds weird. So much of the lower city is garish, designed to be awe-inspiring and breath-taking, but it's here, in the silent dark cave, that I feel reverent. This is real. This cave isn't manufactured, it's a part of the island that the beating waves spent centuries making.

I stare into the darkness. There's a small wooden pier built against the wall of the cave, and a worn stone path creeps further into the darkness. The boat bumps up against the pier, and the engine dies.

"No," I say aloud. This is way too creepy, and way too dangerous. There's no way I'm just going to wander around a *deserted cave* in an *uninhabited* part of the island where no one can hear me scream.

The boat, obviously, does not respond.

It also doesn't move. I try finding the controls, but there's no way I could operate the boat even if I could figure out the system. The luzzu rocks as I stand, and I almost fall into the water as I scramble up to the salt-weathered planks of the pier, cursing loudly.

A set of uneven stairs is cut directly into the slick limestone beyond the wooden planks, leading up and up, further into the darkness. The steps aren't even, and most of them are curved in the middle from years of wear. Metal rings are embedded along the side of the wall, and a scratchy, thick rope is strung between them as a makeshift handrail.

"Great," I say, staring into the depths of the cave, where the stairs fade to darkness. "Now what?"

THE BODY ELECTRIC

There's only one answer.
Up.

THIRTY

I USE THE DIM LIGHT FROM MY CUFF TO light my path—making sure that the geo-locator and the recorder is still on. My thighs are screaming at me by the time I reach the top of the stairs. I push open an old, broken wooden door and enter an abandoned, crumbling ruin of a building. There's the barest outline of walls made of stone. Sunlight pours in from a crack in the ceiling so large that a small tree is growing through it. And, sitting under the tree, with his back against the wall and his face half in the shadow, is Jack Tyler.

I cross the room before he opens his eyes and kick his foot. Jack jumps, startled, and it's not until then that I realize he'd been napping.

Napping.

I hear movement behind me and turn, immediately wary. A large man with skin almost as black as his clothing emerges from the shadows. He's well over six feet tall, and his biceps are roughly as big around as my head. A much smaller white girl, tiny in comparison, with laughing eyes and a smirk on her lips, stands next to him, snapping her gum. She wears a yellow sundress and strappy sandals, which show off her array of tattoos perfectly. Bright colors sweep down both her arms, and a single word in calligraphic writing is scrawled across her chest in heavy ink: *Infandous*. I don't know what it means, or even what language it is, but it's oddly ominous on such a petite, pretty girl.

As I stare, the anaconda tattoo curling up the girl's right arm moves, the head whipping around on her shoulder and snapping, exposing two long fangs. A nanobot tattoo.

Jack nods to the two, and they head toward the door on the far side of the room—the one leading outside—silently.

"So you brought a bodyguard with you?" I ask.

"You have been known to hit me," Jack points out. "The kicking is new, though."

"A bodyguard," I say, shaking my head. "You must find me such a danger. He's quite formidable."

"Yes," Jack says. "She is."

I do a double take. The smaller girl turns, still walking toward the door and smirks at me before tripping after the giant. I have no idea where she's keeping her weapons, nor do I know what her hulking companion is there for, and I don't intend to find out. The two of them step outside the door but go no further. While looking back at them, I check my cuff, making sure that it's still recording everything Jack and I are saying.

I turn to Jack. I'm tired. I'm so tired: of the stairs, of chasing him down, of trying to figure everything out.

"Yesterday, androids blew up," I say, cutting directly to the chase.

Jack's expression darkens. For the first time, I notice the dark circles under his eyes, the way he holds his body as if he's even more exhausted than I am.

"Yes," Jack says, confirming my statement.

"One of them was the android my mother uses as a nurse," I say. I force Jack to look me in the eyes; I hardly even blink. The more I speak, the more the rage builds inside me. "My mother—she's sick, did you know? Hebb's Disease."

"I know." There is no smile in his voice now, not even a hint of one.

"She was just in the next room. When the android blew—if I had been just a few minutes later—" I cannot bring myself to say the words. "Even as it is, the stress from the bomb... she's weak. She can't handle things like androids blowing up in her apartment." I cannot read Jack's face. "It could have killed her," I force myself to say. My right shoulder lifts, as if I'm shrugging off what happened as not a big deal. But it is.

"And you." Jack's voice is liquid, but dark. Like slow-pouring honey.

I shrug again. This time I mean it.

"Was it you?" I ask. I have to hear him say it. I need his confession. I need to record it.

Jack's head tilts up and his eyes narrow.

"The bees," I say. "That's a symbol to you, isn't it? The pin you wear, the honey by the door, the black-and-yellow auto-boat. And—" I just realize this, just now, in this moment. "And the sound the androids made. Just before they blew up. *Zzn-zzn-zzzzn.*" My voice quivers with the noise, and I taste bile as I recreate the sound. "Buzzing," I say. "The androids buzzed like bees. And then they exploded. And anyone standing close enough to them exploded, too."

When I look at Jack now, I know he feels the full force of my accusation. My eyes drift to his collar. To the tiny golden bee pin that rests there.

"We are called the Zunzana," Jack says. He runs his fingers through his hair and starts pacing, his boots thudding against the dusty stone floor and echoing around the arching ceiling.

"Zunzana?" My mind races. "Isn't that the old Maltese word for bumblebee?"

Jack nods.

"What a cute name for a terrorist organization."

"We're not terrorists!" Jack stops and spins around to stare at me. "Ella, we're not—"

I cut him off. "Blowing up people is what terrorist *do*, Jack. It's kind of their thing."

"We didn't do that!" he roars.

I cross my arms over my chest. "Prove it."

"Could you really believe I'm a terrorist? Me?"

I snort. Yes. Imagining this is remarkably easy.

Jack pauses. "You really don't remember me, do you?" he asks, searching my eyes. "Are you...?"

I jerk away from him when he reaches for me, putting a couple of meters between us.

"I never imagined that they could have gotten to you too," Jack says softly.

I sneer at him. "No one's 'gotten' to me," I snap. I am not some brainwashed victim like Jack seems to think I am.

Jack shakes his head sadly. "I wish that were true."

"It *is* true!" I shout. I take a deep breath, forcing myself to focus not on my rage, but on the answers I need.

"Someone's made you forget me, Ella," Jack says sadly. "Forget *us*."

THIRTY-ONE

"US?" I ASK INCREDULOUSLY, WAVING my hands at him. "No. I do not have time for your mind games. You are going to answer my questions, and then I'm leaving, and we never have to see each other again."

Jack eyes me warily, as if I am a deadly predator. "But—" he starts.

I cut him off. "Was your little terrorist organization responsible for the androids blowing up?" I ask. I angle my wrist subtly toward Jack. All I need is one confession, and I can go.

"We're not terrorists," Jack says, his voice heavy.

I dismiss this. "Were you?" I ask again.

"*No*," he says emphatically.

I barely restrain from rolling my eyes. If he'd just confess already, we could be done. "Fine, you're not confessing to the android attack. Then who do *you* think did it?"

"The government, obviously."

"Oh, *obviously*," I snap. "Why wouldn't it be the *government*? It's not like we have a perfectly operational *terrorist group* right here to do it."

"The Zunzana isn't a terrorist group!" Jack shouts. His face his red, his breathing heavy. I've touched a nerve.

"What is it then?" I sneer.

Jack runs his fingers through his hair. "We're... we're just.... Look, before—"

"Before what?"

"Before everything. My parents were against the UC since the Secessionary War, and they were trying to change things. *Not* through violence," he adds when he sees my face. "Politically. Then..."

"Then?" I demand.

"Then they started to die. And so did anyone who agreed with them. We're all that's left. Me, Julie, Xavier." He says the last name the French way, *zah-vee-aye*. "Our parents... all our friends... the Prime Administrator had them all killed. Maybe not directly, but it's not that hard to piece together. An accident, a sudden transfer to a Secessionary State, a car accident..." His voice trails off, and I flash back to the obituary of Jack's parents, two aides in the representative administration's office. A car accident. I wonder what happened to Julie's parents, and Xavier's. Jack looks up, his eyes piercing mine. "A lab accident."

I swallow, hard. Dad's death was done by terrorists, *not* the government. He had nothing to do with politics.

But... Estella Belles had nothing to do with politics either.

"Is that what all this is about?" I ask. "Revenge?"

THE BODY ELECTRIC

Jack shakes his head, frustrated. "No, no, of course not," he says, but I'm not sure if I believe it. If I found out the government killed my parents, I'd want a revenge so bloody the sea would turn red.

Jack starts pacing again. "It's not until recently that we started to figure out what happened. I joined the military last year." He eyes me, as if this was a significant thing for him to say, but he continues when I don't respond. "Then I saw what the government was doing. To people—soldiers—people who were from poor homes, who had no one to miss them. People like Akilah."

"She's not dead," I whisper, hearing the doubt in my voice. I say it again, louder. "She's not dead. And she has nothing to do with this."

My mind's reeling. I expected an entire underground movement, a system of spies and rebels—not three teenagers against the entire Unified Countries. I almost scoff at them, but then I remember the gaping, burning hole in my apartment, and I realize just how much damage a handful of people can do.

"Just three of you. Trying to take down the government."

Jack gapes at me. "That's not what we're doing."

"Isn't that what the 'Zunzana' is all about?" I ask, not bothering to hide my contempt.

"We didn't do the android attack!" Jack says, his voice rising. "All we want to do is let people know what's

happening—that something's *wrong*—that people are disappearing!"

"Akilah hasn't disappeared," I say. "But you know who has? The one hundred and four people who died in yesterday's explosions."

Jack paces like an animal in a cage, shooting me frustrated looks. There's desperation in his movements, anger.

"Ella," Jack says abruptly. "Why are you here? How much... how much of me do you remember?"

"Nothing," I say immediately. "Because there's nothing to remember."

His face falls into an emotionless mask. I've noticed that he does that whenever he brings up this supposed past we share. It's his poker face, his way of making sure I can't see the way he's trying to manipulate me.

Well, two can play that game. "Let's make a deal," I say. "I ask you something; you ask me something." He won't learn anything important about me—there *is* nothing important about me—but I might find more information with which to crucify him.

Jack collapses down under the tree again, his body sagging. He pats the stone beside him, but I don't take his offer. I want to be standing. I want to be able to run.

"Is there *anything* about me you remember?" Jack asks.

"I met you a few days ago," I shoot back. "You accosted me in Central Gardens."

"I was *trying* to warn you," he growls. Then his face softens. "You don't remember before?"

"There was no before," I snap. "And it's my turn. Are you the leader of this terrorist organization?"

"We're not terrorists."

I don't bother answering; he can argue semantics all he wants. I half believe him, but I can't risk being wrong based on a gut feeling. Finally Jack sighs and says, "Yes. I suppose that now, after... after everything, I am the closest thing we have to a leader. How much do you know about your father's research?"

The question catches me completely off guard. I was not at all expecting Dad to be brought into this conversation. "His last experiments were focused on making an artificial brain," I answer. Judging from Representative Belles's documents, this isn't a secret or anything Jack doesn't already know. "Which is impossible," I add. Scientists can make something that's exactly the same as a human brain, right down to every wrinkle and crease, but they can't make it *think*. "Androids are nothing but complicated computers dressed up to look human. They can't think for themselves."

Jack nods. "But did you know that he started having problems with the methods the UC wanted him to use? He disagreed with them on some things—I was never really sure what—and anyway, he started having trouble with the high-ups."

I stare at him blankly. "No," I say. I never heard Dad complain about his work. But in my last memories of Dad, I remember him being worried. He lost a lot of weight. For a while, I'd been worried that he was sick, too, like Mom. "What makes you think that?"

Jack looks startled. "Because I was working with your Dad on that research," he says. I remember the photo now, the one of him and Dad in the lab, my father's hand resting gently on Jack's shoulder.

"I was recruited right out of secondary school, for my service year," Jack continues. "I was only supposed to be a lab assistant, but Dr. Philip took me under his wing."

"Dad always liked lost causes," I say.

This earns me a wry grin.

"The month before Dr. Philip died, he fired me. Not for anything I did," Jack hurries to say. "But he didn't want me to get embroiled with the politics, and he worried that he was going to get in trouble for some of his research and didn't want to hurt my name. None of his problems ever came to light though."

Because he died. Because he was *killed*. I can't let myself forget or lose focus on that.

"So after you were fired," I say, "you decided to start up a little terrorist group—"

"A *protest* group," Jack says, his voice rising. "There's a difference."

"Not from where I stand."

"Maybe you're standing on the wrong side."

I roll my eyes.

"There have always been protesters against the UC, since before the Secessionary War. Do you think Malta wanted its capital city named after a city in Italy? Do you think people wanted to be displaced and moved into the Foqra District? The protests started here, in Malta, and as much as she's tried, PA Young can't eliminate everyone." He glances at the door, where Julie and Xavier, the only two remaining members of the group, left.

"We used to be bigger," he continues. "We used to be a network of people throughout not just Malta, but the entire UC. We were organized, and we were strong, and we were going to change the world."

"The Zunzana," I say, tasting the word on my tongue. Could it really be what Jack says it is? Not a terrorist group, but this force of good?

"'Zunzana,'" Jack says in a contemplative voice, "is the old Maltese word for 'bumblebee,' like you said. Bees used to be symbolic of cleverness, and life. And the name of our country, 'Malta'—it means 'honey.' Like bees protect their honey, we protect our country."

"Protect it from what?" I ask.

"From the UC."

"The UC is as good as any government," I say. "And we don't need another war." The Secessionary War was well before my time, but there's a giant, sea-filled crater where the original capital of Malta once stood that never lets us forget about the price of war.

Jack makes a frustrated sound in the back of his throat. "How can I make you see?" he says. "The UC is willing to control us by any means possible. Just look at your cuff—look at the way the government monitors *everything*. You think they do that for your safety? They're lying. This is what the Zunzana are fighting—it's what your dad fought for, before he died. He didn't want us to turn into toy soldiers and puppets."

"Leave my dad out of this," I snap.

"How can I?" Jack roars, leaping up. He rushes at me, stopping just before my face. "You father *died* fighting the government—just like my parents—and you're dismissing his sacrifice like it was nothing. It may have been easy for you to forget the past, but I never could."

"I've not forgotten anything!" I shout back. "I'm just not believing your lies!"

Jack's face grows still. "Really?" he asks, his voice low and dangerous. "Is this a lie?" Before I can do anything more than gasp in shock, Jack jerks me against the solid wall of his body, wraps his arms around me, tilts my head up, and kisses the surprise from my lips.

THIRTY-TWO

MY HANDS ARE CRUSHED FLAT AGAINST his chest, the hard outline of his muscles just beneath my fingertips. For a long moment, all I can think about is his body against mine, his lips against mine.

And then my hands curl into fists and I push him away. I wipe my mouth off and glare at him. "How *dare* you!" I scream.

"Ella, I just thought—" He looks wounded. The son of a bitch looks *offended* that I would push him off me.

I cross the small space between us, raise my hands, and shove him so hard that he falls back against the wall. "Don't touch me again, you creep!"

I turn on my heel and race to the door. I don't think about the way my body feels as if it's on fire, the way I cannot get the taste of him out of my mouth. He had no right.

He catches up to me and grabs my wrist, pulling me toward him. I use the momentum of my body moving in his direction to aim my fist at his face, but he catches my arm mid-throw. "Ella. Ella! I'm sorry, all right? I just thought maybe I could make you remember me."

"Remember you? *Remember* you? If that's the sort of thing you want me to remember, I'm glad I forgot!" I jerk free of his grip, but he lets my wrist slide through his fingers easily. He looks gutted.

"We dated for a year," he says hollowly.

I stare at him.

"You told me you loved me," he said. "We—"

I turn around. "Quit lying. I never met you before this week."

The look he gives me fills me with fear and dread. "I worked with your father. I've eaten dinner at your house with your family—that's how I met you. We were together for an entire year. I was with you when you were assigned to be an intern at Reverie for your service year, when Akilah was assigned military duty. We were... together." The way he says that word, *together*, makes me know he means something special by it.

"No."

Jack shakes his head. His hand moves to his own wrist—where his cuffLINK would be if he had one. But whatever evidence he wanted to show me, it's long gone now. His hand drops away. "How can you have forgotten me? Us?"

"Because I never met you before this week." He sounds so lost, looks so confused. My voice softens. Maybe this isn't some sort of elaborate trick. "I don't know who you think I am, but I'm not the girl you knew a year ago. We've never met before."

"You are Ella Shepherd, and I am Jack Tyler." He says the words loudly, as if he's affirming their truth through his speech. "We were together for a year. You broke up with me, and I joined the military. I know you as well as I know myself. Your father was Philip Shepherd, and he was a neuro-scientist specializing in nanorobotics and android intelligence. Your mother is Rose Shepherd. She has Hebb's Disease, but before that, she developed the technology used in Reverie, the world's leading mental spa. You're in your service year, and in a few weeks, you're supposed to decide whether you're going to go to university or enter employment, but you decided the day your father died you wouldn't go to uni. Your best friend is Akilah Xuereb, and you cried for a week when she was assigned to the military rather than as an intern like you. You wear a fortune-cookie locket your dad gave you when you moved away from Akilah when you were eight years old, and inside it is a digi file of the two of you playing in Central Gardens, catching fireflies after the Summer Festa."

The world spins around me. "How do you know all that?" I whisper.

"You have a mole behind your left knee shaped like a chocolate chip," he continues, louder, as he steps uncomfortably close to me. "You used to have a teddy bear with a green bow-tie, but the dog you had when you lived in Rabat ate it. When you moved, you had to give the dog to your neighbor, and you didn't talk to your father for a week after."

"How—?"

"You used to want to be a cellist even though you don't know how to play, but you never told your parents that, because your mom would talk about how you'd follow in her footsteps as a scientist, and after she got sick, you didn't want to tell her that the last thing you ever want to study is science or medicine."

I don't even have the breath to speak any more. I collapse into a puddle on the floor. Jack squats in front of me and leans toward me. "I know *you*, Ella Shepherd. The question is, why don't you know me?"

THIRTY-THREE

"THIS IS IMPOSSIBLE," I SAY SOFTLY.
I'm gasping at air as if I'm drowning, but it's not enough.

"You really don't remember me at all?"

I shoot him an exasperated look. "I think I'd remember someone as annoying as you."

"But you don't. Despite my devastatingly handsome—and unforgettable—smile." He grins toothily at me.

I push his chest with both hands so that he stumbles back, giving me some space from him. "This isn't some kind of joke," I say angrily. Something is seriously wrong. He knows way too much about me—stuff *no one*, not even Akilah, knew. Maybe my memory really has been wiped... but no. You can't just selectively wipe a memory. I've not *forgotten* my past. My stomach twists. Maybe he can do what I can do. Maybe he's somehow found a way into my mind with reveries, and rooted around in them... but I don't remember having done a reverie with anyone other than myself... but...

"This is similar to what happened to Akilah," Jack says. "The same thing that happened to many of the people I met in the military." He searches my eyes. "That's why I left. Why I joined with Julie and Xavier. The government has some sort of plan—it makes people forget things..."

My mind is chaos. Everything Jack's saying is *impossible*. But... it *feels* right. I clench my teeth. I wish he would quit talking. I need to figure this out—is he lying to me about all this, or has my memory been altered? And if it's been altered... by who?

"What happened to Akilah?" I say. "I saw the digi file you gave me, but I don't understand. She was killed and then... what? Who did I see in the next video?"

Jack runs his fingers through his hair. "I wish I knew. I've been researching it as best I can, but it defies the laws of science." I remember then that Jack worked with my dad—he must be far more intelligent than he seems. "The... the *thing* Akilah became. She can't be a clone— clones grow at a normal rate, and even with growth accelerators, they couldn't have made a clone of her so quickly. And, regardless of that, it seemed as if she retained most memories. You can't just flip a switch and *bam!* A perfect copy of a person.

"The new Akilah, though, while she was still Akilah, was... harder. More focused on fighting—and better at fighting, stronger, faster. But also... cruel." He says that last word softly, as if he wishes it could disappear like dissipating smoke.

Jack looks up at me. "Akilah wasn't the only one. I can't tell you the number of people I saw who... changed. I can't explain it. But the longer you're in the war, the less like yourself you become."

"So you left." I stare at Jack's blank wrist. A deserter. A traitor. ...Or maybe not. Can you betray a government that's already betrayed you?

"I left."

Something inside of me is pulled taut. My heart feels like it's being crushed under an invisible weight. And I realize: I'm starting to believe Jack. The doubts I've been having line up perfectly with what Jack's been telling me.

I grit my teeth. I have to pull myself together. I can't let myself be swayed by this guy. I might not be able to trust the government, but I can't trust him, either.

"So?" I ask, putting my hands on my hips.

"So what?"

"So how do we save Akilah? If that's why you left the military, why you decided to join this 'protest group,' this 'Zunzana,' what have you learned? How do we save her?"

Jack's face pales. "I don't know. Xavier was a medical student; he has some theories, but..."

"You don't know. You tell me Akilah's messed up, but you don't know how and don't know how to fix her. You tell me *I* am messed up, but you don't know how. You tell me that you had nothing to do with the android explosion that almost killed my mother, but *you. Don't.*

Know. Who. And you tell me I should trust you, but you know what? I don't know how."

"I need you, Ella." Jack's voice cracks over my name. It's enough to make me pause.

He steps closer to me, but I instinctually move back. He may not have caused the android attack this morning, but he's still tied up in the whole mess, he's still got some blood on his hands. I'm just not sure whose.

"The Zunzana needs you."

My fingers curl into fists. If all this is just some way to convince me to join his group, then—

"You don't trust me." He says the words hollowly.

"Of course not," I say immediately. "I don't know you."

"What do you want me to do?" Jack throws up his hands. "If I could crack open my skull and let you read my brain like a book, I would!"

My breath catches in my throat. Because I... I could read his brain like a book. And I could find all the secrets of the Zunzana—I could learn everything he's *not* telling me, the truth of the entire situation. That would be the final piece of evidence I would need to hand to Ms. White and Prime Administrator Young and whatever little war Jack thinks he's fighting—whatever web Akilah is caught up in—could be over.

He's just handed me access to the most important information we could have ever gotten. Forget

Representative Belles and the other little government officials dabbling in rebellion. Jack's on the inside.

"I have a way," I say.

Jack looks at me curiously.

"I mean, I can find out if you're telling me the truth or not."

"I'm too scared of needles to let you inject me with truth serum," he says sarcastically. "And my face is too pretty for you to beat the truth out of me."

I force a laugh. "No more of that. It's... it's something at Reverie."

A mask falls over Jack's face. "Not sure I trust anything at the mental spa."

"It's a... simple procedure. You get a reverie, and we have monitors that tell whether you're telling the truth. It's really simple." I shake my head. "I said that already. Anyway. It's true. Simple. And then I'll know if you're..."

"Telling the truth or not?" Jack says when my voice trails off.

"If you're psycho or not."

"Same difference." That stupid smile is plastered on his face again.

"Can you get to Reverie on your own?" I ask. "Tonight?"

Jack nods. He's sensed the urgency in my voice. "I'll meet you at our old place."

I stare blankly at him.

Something dark flashes in Jack's eyes. "Right. You don't know our old place."

I shake my head.

"On the roof."

"Part of it is gone," I say. "It blew up."

Jack's eyes widen slightly—I don't think he quite realized just how close to home the attack had been.

"But the garden's safe," I say. At least, I think it is. The roof is terraced, so it should be fine.

Jack stares into my eyes for several long moments. "I don't trust the mental spa. But I do trust you, Ella."

"Even if I don't trust you?" I can't help but say.

"Even then."

THIRTY-FOUR

JACK SHOWS ME A HIDDEN LIFT INSIDE one of the pillars used to hold up the bridge of the upper city of New Venice. It's clearly designed for workers who have to maintain the electrical and sewage needs of the city, but I don't care; I'm just grateful I don't have to walk back up the stairs to return home.

The lift deposits me near Triumph Towers, and as I walk past the plaza, I'm overwhelmed by the odd mixture of flowers and burning. There are deep black scars in the marble and limestone of the plaza, and yellow tape blocking it all off. Crowds of people gather at the small space between the partitioned area and the gate to Central Gardens, leaving flowers and notes, candles and prayers.

I try to avoid the crowd—I only have to cross Central Gardens to get back home—but then I see a face I recognize.

"She was your daughter, wasn't she?" I ask in a low voice.

The man in the rumpled, dirty suit looks up at me. Representative Belles's eyes are dry, but I can see that's only because he has no more tears to cry. He's been staring at a white teddy bear with pink bows, exactly the color of his daughter's dress.

"How did you know?" he asks, his voice raspy. I wonder how long he's been here, standing vigil for his daughter.

"I recognized her picture from your profile," I lie. "The one we had for your reverie."

The representative grabs my elbow and steers me further away from the crowd. "A reverie," he says, light filling his empty eyes. "Could I see her again in a reverie?"

"Er..." I hesitate. Going into a reverie now would probably be easy for him, and the perfect cover for me to sneak into his mind and see what he's been hiding from PA Young.

But it feels... so wrong. So very wrong, to use this man's grief at the loss of his wife and daughter so I can spy on him.

"Please," he says, and I notice the haggardness of his face, the dark circles under his eyes.

My spine stiffens. Regardless of who the terrorists killed in the android attack—of who the terrorists truly are—the guilt of what he's done lies at his feet, just like that teddy bear with pink bows and the wilting flowers littered with flickering candles. I can't let pity blind me to the fact that he got himself tied up with treasonous plots and terrorists, and that his family paid the price. He's the one who played with fire, who considered joining the terrorists. I can't think in terms of the Zunzana or the terrorists or the government—I just need to find the murderers.

It's my job to stop them.

That is something I can do.

"Come with me," I say. "We can give you a reverie session now."

When we reach the Reverie Mental Spa, I breathe a sigh of relief that Ms. White is there. To her credit, she immediately engulfs the representative in sympathy as she leads him to the reverie chamber—giving me time to slip away and enter the hidden chamber.

My hands shake as I prepare the reverie chair for my entry into Representative Belles's mind. I swallow down the lump rising in my throat. I can't let myself slip into nightmares like before. I can't afford a hallucination, not here, not now.

A faint hum fills my ears as the sonic hood warms up. It reminds me of the sound the androids made, just before they blew up.

I lower the sonic hood over my head, and then I'm gone.

There is a storm inside Representative Belles's mind. As soon as I enter his dream, I can sense it. The air is heavy with the scent of warm, wet earth, and I can hear—though I cannot see—crashing waves and distant cries of fear.

It's all dark. This is a big storm, the kind that floods the streets and drowns the boats. At first, because of the darkness, I fear it's what the old people call *xita tal-ħamrija*—a storm where sands from the deserts to the south are carried in clouds and dumped upon Malta. Slowly, the world brightens. The light is eerie, almost green. The city is abandoned—I don't even see Representative Belles here.

A giant raindrop falls on my shoulder. I wipe my hand on my skin, and it comes away red. Definitely a soil storm, then—sometimes people call it "blood rain" because the earth is reddish and leaves everything—windows, cars, clothes—stained a dusty, deep pink.

More rain falls. It falls in sheets, like an avalanche of water, and it's sticky, viscous—not grainy like *xita tal-ħamrija*. And then I realize: this isn't dirty water falling from the sky.

It is—literally—blood.

I look up, and a droplet of blood splashes directly into my eye. I curse, rubbing my face, trying to get the blood out, but it's everywhere, it's like trying to dry off in the middle of the ocean. Shielding my face as best I can, I stare up into the sky.

I am in the center of a cyclone.

Giant white clouds swirl like a spiraling galaxy above me, the eye a tiny dark speck. The storm rages, throwing out bloody rain like punches, the wind so vicious it tears my clothes and cuts my skin.

Representative Belles's mind is swirling with dark thoughts—bloody thoughts—and they have created the biggest storm I have ever seen.

I shut my eyes as thunder rolls overhead, lightning fizzling and cracking so close to me that the hairs on my arm stand up. Representative Belles is here, somewhere in this storm. I have to find him. I have to stop the cyclone. I have to get him into a peaceful reverie, something that he can hold on to while I root around his brain, looking for answers.

I focus all of my concentration on stopping the bloody rain. The drops come slower and slower. I take a deep breath, imagining the clouds breaking up, spinning into fluffy bits of cotton-candy like clouds. I don't open my eyes until the sounds of beating rain disappear and I can feel the warmth of the Mediterranean sun on my face.

When I look up, though, the swirling cyclone is still there—it's just bright white clouds, no rain. It hangs over us, a reminder that the representative's mind cannot be entirely cleared of his pressing thoughts. But since it's no longer raining down blood, thunder, and lightning, I leave it.

Sunlight beams from the clouds, perfectly illuminating the representative. He's crouched on the ground, covered in blood.

At first I think he's injured—a rare thing to see in any reverie, whether it be happy or not. But then he blinks, the whites of his eyes standing out impossibly bright against his dark-red stained face, and I realize—he's not soaked in his own blood. This storm was the chaos of his mind; the blood was that of his wife and daughter, lying dead on the ground before him.

"I'm sorry!" he screams at their bodies. "I'm sorry!"

The representative wanted a chance to see his wife and daughter again in a reverie, but it wasn't to relive a happy memory. It was to apologize, and apologizing means he remembers what happened, and that means being trapped in a nightmare that's already come true. I have to make him slip into a different reverie, one where he can forget.

I shut my eyes, focusing on my concentration—

"What are you doing, boy?" a gruff voice asks.

The representative looks up at his grandfather. As he stares at him, the city fades away into an orange grove, and Representative Belles's sorrow melts away to a time before he was a father, before he had responsibilities, before he became guilty of not fulfilling them.

But the bodies are still there. He almost trips on them as he approaches his grandfather.

"They're gone," Representative Belles says hollowly.

"Family is never really gone," his grandfather says.

THE BODY ELECTRIC

Before my eyes, the blood slowly fades, and with it, the last of Representative Belles's fears and worries. For just this moment, he's caught up in the reverie. He's reliving his childhood. There are dark clouds on the horizon—he's not quite forgotten everything—but it's enough.

I can get to work.

THIRTY-FIVE

LAST TIME, I WAS SEARCHING BLINDLY, hoping to stumble upon something I can use. But this time, as I mold Representative Belles's dreamscape, I know exactly what I'm looking for.

I turn a corner of Representative Belles's mind into an office filled with filing cabinets. In each cabinet, there's a folder. In each folder, there's a memory. I crack my knuckles and start rifling through his mind.

Music wafts through the air. I... I know this song. "Moon River," Dad's favorite tune.

I turn slowly.

Far away, almost out of sight, the representative is speaking with the memory of his grandfather. But here, close to me, is...

"Dad?" I ask.
But no one's there. Just the music, and a feeling like I'm being watched.

I shrug it off, turning again to the files of Representative Belles's mind. Then I see exactly what I was looking for. A filing cabinet with a label across the top. The label is hand-written in green ink the same color as the reverie drug.

JACK TYLER

Locked. My fingers strain against the metal, tugging at the drawer, but it's impossible. I can't open it.

"Now, why do you suppose that is?" a voice calls.

I spin around, my heart racing.

Far away, almost out of sight, the representative is speaking with the memory of his grandfather. But here, close to me, is...

"Dad?" *I call out to him.*

Dad doesn't stop as he twirls Mom—young Mom, healthy Mom—around in tune to the music. They sway together, swirling and laughing and ignoring me.

The dream stutters. Their movements jerk left-right-left-left. The image of my parents dancing pauses and restarts, a few seconds off-time, like a scratched digi file.

They're not real.

I mean, I know they're not real. Nothing's real here in the dreamscape. But they're not even a real part of the dreamscape.

Of course not.

They're not a part of Representative Belles's dreams.

They're part of mine.

"Go away," I say as firmly as I can.

I hear a low buzzing in the back of my mind.

"Can't!" Dad calls over Mom's shoulder. She leans against him, as if she hasn't noticed me, or even that Dad is speaking. "This is your reverie. You control us."

"This isn't my reverie!" I march closer to Mom and Dad, but every step I take puts them another step further away from me. It's an elegant movement, a part of the dance, but they are always out of reach from me.

"It's your filing cabinet, too," Dad adds, nodding his head to where I was working. I spin on my heel, just in time to see the locked cabinet labeled with Jack's name disappear in a puff of green smoke.

"It wasn't mine," I say. "I'm in Representative Belles's reverie."

"You, Ella, you are the one who dreams in filing cabinets." Dad twirls Mom on her heel, and she giggles. "It's because filing systems are the way computers are organized. A long time ago, when computers were first invented, the developers organized the systems like filing cabinets, because that's what they used to categorize and keep records. We don't use filing cabinets any more, but the computers still do. It's an efficient way to organize."

"Gee, thanks, Dad," I say, moving past him. "Way to make me sound like an android with a computer for a brain."

"That was what my research was focused on. Android brains and nanobots, nanobots and android brains."

"I. Know." I try to back away from Mom and Dad, but, just as before they swirled outside of my reach, now their dance steps bring them closer and closer to me.

"Go away," I say again, but this time the words come out desperate. "P-p-p-please." Stutter-jerk-jerk. My body twitches.

I'm wavering in and out of existence.

Oh, God. I stare up into the bright white, swirling clouds of the cyclone overshadowing this whole reverie. What if I wake up while I'm still in Representative Belles's mind? What would happen to him?

What would happen to me?

"Elllllla!" Dad calls as he twirls Mom around. Her dress swishes around her ankles, black and red and beaded, twirling into poofy white, a wedding gown that evaporates before my eyes, leaving behind nothing but a salt-water soaked sarong that falls off her hips, exposing a slinky silk number.

"Da-ah-ad?" I stu-stu-stutter.

I clutch my head. "What's hap-hap-happening?"

The music stops. My parents are gone.

Silence. What the *hell* was that?

I take a deep breath. I don't have time to go crazy. I have work to do, and the representative will wake up any minute.

I turn to the filing cabinets again. There's no longer a drawer labeled with Jack's name, but I throw open the one labeled "Z."

A misplaced file folder—a misplaced memory—flops out onto the floor as if it were moving of its own volition. I pick it up and read the label.

Nanorobotics and Cyborg Control in Android Theory: The Tie Between Biology and Technology

Something like a raindrop falls on the back of my neck. I rub it, looking up. The cyclone is darker overhead— is Representative Belles falling out of his reverie and into a nightmare? But when I look past my workstation, I see him, still talking to his grandfather, completely ignorant of the darkening sky.

And then I see what's made the sky so dark.

A swarm of bees swoop down in a funnel cloud. The cyclone is not made of clouds, no, it's made of bees. They are a swirling mass of black and yellow and stinging. They buzz so loudly that my entire body thrums with it.

I scream, cover my head, drop to the ground.

THE BODY ELECTRIC

The bees roll over me like boiling water. I scream again, and the bees fill my mouth, the musty-fuzzy bodies pushing against the inside of my cheeks, the stingers clacking against my teeth. They spill down my throat, and I am choking on bees, swallowing them, their stingers scraping my esophagus, their buzzing filling my belly. The bees chew—they chew and sting my cheek-flesh, they are chewing a hole in me, a stinging, chewing hole, and they spill out of the empty recesses of where my face is. Pus and blood drip off me of me so profusely that it feels as if I am melting.

The bees burrow into my flesh, under my skin. They crawl up my sinuses, their little feet tugging at my nose hairs. They ram their fat bodies into my ear canals, filling my brain with buzzing, scraping their stingers along the sensitive skin of my ear.

They spill from my eyes like tears.

The bees, the bees, the bees are everywhere, and they are eating me alive.

I scream, but the sound comes out as bzznnznznnnnzbznnzbzz.

"Ella?" My father's voice. "Ella, get up. What are you doing on the floor?"

I open my eyes.

There are no bees. Beyond us, Representative Belles is completely undisturbed in his own reverie.

My father stands over me, looking disappointed.

"Really, Ella," Dad says, his voice dripping with derision. "You're going to have to *zzz* wake up. *Zzz.* Or *elzzze.*"

Tears and snot stream down my face. "Or else what?" I whisper, my voice cracking, swollen from a hundred bee-stings.

"Or *elzzze,*" he says, sneering at me as a single bee crawls over his face, its pointy feet pricking the skin under his left eye, "you'll *zzz* go *mad.*"

THIRTY-SIX

I WAKE WITH A JERK AND THROW BACK the sonic hood. My chest is heaving, and my heart is racing. My eyes are wide, looking at nothing.

I have to consider the very real possibility that I am literally going insane.

I curl up onto my side, drawing my knees to my chest, painfully pressing them against the mechanics of the reverie chair. It's getting worse. Longer hallucinations, more vivid horrors. More uncontrollable. *Like a storm, a cyclone.* Maybe it wasn't Representative Belles's mind that was so chaotic and violent. Maybe *I* was the one who was tainting *his* mind.

What happens when I lose control? What happens when I can't pull the storms back, when I can't escape the nightmare?

I stare down at the reverie chair in horror. What if I get stuck in a reverie? I cannot imagine a more perfect hell than being trapped inside my own mind.

"I'm so glad your experience this time was peaceful and calming!" Ms. White's voice trills through the secondary chamber room. I freeze. I'd been so anxious to just *get out* that I forgot how important this session was.

Representative Belles's answer is too low for me to make out, but he seems fairly positive about the reverie. I turn on the video feed and see Ms. White is scheduling more appointments for him. I'm seized with anxiety—more appointments means more times for me to go into his reverie, which means more chances for me to get stuck in my nightmares. My skin crawls with the feeling of imaginary bees roiling over my body.

I'm still in the reverie chamber when Ms. White slides open the door. "Ella!" she exclaims. "Oh, you darling girl! What did you discover?"

I dodge the question. "Did Belles have a good reverie?"

Ms. White's smile falters. "Is there a reason why he shouldn't have?"

"I had trouble getting into his mind," I say.

Ms. White sits down heavily beside me. "Nothing unusual on the scans," she says. "I did notice that during the reverie, the representative moved his hands a lot, like he was trying to swat away bugs."

Or bees, I think.

"He was outside with his grandfather in the dreamscape," I say. "There were bugs there."

And a hundred million bees.

"Did you discover anything useful?" Ms. White asks. "I think the grandfather reveries are coming from his thoughts on family—understandable, given the circumstances."

Understandable—but he had a reverie about his grandfather *before* his family was attacked. Were they threatened prior to the android explosion?

"Ms. White?" I ask, searching her eyes. "Are you... are you worried?"

"Worried?"

"That what we're doing... is it right?"

Ms. White sits down slowly. "I... I'm not sure," she confesses. "I want to protect our nation, our family, to make sure the Secessionary War never happens again, but..."

But.

She rubs her arm, her cyborg arm, replaced after she lost it in the war. "It was terrible," she says, her gaze dropping from mine. "The war. I didn't even see any battles, not really, but I was there when Valetta was bombed, I saw the city sink into the sea." Her voice cracks, and I see unshed tears in her eyes. "Yes—yes, this is worth it. If we can ensure that a war like that never happens again..."

I bite my lip. "I'm not sure. Maybe some wars are worth fighting."

Ms. White drops her hand to my knee. "These are the terrorists that killed your father, Ella," she says. "What greater war could there be but to fight them?"

I nod, but I don't meet her eyes again. This feels wrong. Jack didn't seem like a terrorist, and I don't think he was involved in Dad's murder.

"Anyway, the reverie," Ms. White adds, "Remember, reveries can often be symbolic, like dreams. If he had a pressing thought about something, it should show up in the reverie."

I stare at her blankly. I feel so *drained.* "The reverie started with a storm," I say.

"A storm?"

I nod. "A cyclone. But seeing as only blood fell from the skies, I'm pretty sure that was linked to how his wife and daughter were killed yesterday."

"Oh, Ella," Ms. White says, wrapping her arms around me. "How horrible." Her cyborg arm squeezes me even tighter, pressing me close to her.

I push her away. I don't want to be touched. I don't want to think about the cyclone, the bees, my father. Ms. White looks a little hurt when I distance myself from her, and I feel immediately guilty. Ms. White is here only to help my mom and, after she discovered what I could do, to help the government. It's not her fault that I'm now starting to question everything, including the government she works for. That *I* work for, I remind myself.

At least for now.

Tonight, I remind myself. I'll get answers tonight, when I break into Jack's mind. My skin tingles, and I remember the sensation of a thousand bees stinging and eating me from the inside out. And suddenly I'm terrified. Maybe I've lost whatever skill I had in entering other people's dreamscapes. Maybe if I go into Jack's mind, I'll never be able to leave. I'll be swallowed alive by the bees.

I will—as Dad said—go mad.

I bite my lip. *Dad* didn't say anything. It was all a hallucination—including him.

Maybe I'm already crazy.

THIRTY-SEVEN

I'M USUALLY A BIT OF A NIGHT OWL, but I start drinking coffee at ten. I don't want to slip up in front of Jack because I'm sleepy. By the time midnight rolls around, I'm a jittery bundle of nerves.

I shouldn't do this. I shouldn't let a member of the Zunzana into my home, where Mom is, where Reverie is. I should punch in the panic code of my cuff the second I see his face.

I should.

Instead, I climb the short ladder at the end of the hall that leads to the rooftop garden. Mom used to love it here, and filled the terrace with peppers and tomatoes, beans and peas, with climbing yellow roses and sprigs of forget-me-nots tucked into the corners. The garden now isn't as flourishing as before Mom got sick, but there's still a few signs of life.

The bench by the water basin is usually cluttered with a dirty trowel, a few buckets, and a basket I use to collect the vegetables in. Right now, it's full of Jack. Even though I was expecting him, it feels strange to see him here, this person I associate with terrorism, sitting in the garden on my roof.

A fat bug flies by my ear and I swat it away violently, jumping from the sound. It was nothing more than a beetle, but my heart's racing.

Bees. Bees, everywhere. Crawling under my skin, chewing through my flesh.

I repress a shudder. "Let's get this over with," I say.

Jack stands up. "So... all it's going to take is me having a reverie, and you'll believe me again?"

Something like that. "Yeah," I say.

Jack claps his hands as if he's just finished building something and is proud of his accomplishment. "Fine! The sooner you start trusting me again, the easier this will be. Although, honestly, I have no idea how you can *not* trust me. I mean, look at me." He juts his chin out, grinning. "I've got a very trust-worthy face, don't I?"

"Remember that time I punched you in front of my father's grave?" I ask in a sentimental voice.

"Ye-es," Jack says warily.

"You looked good with a split lip."

"Shame it healed. Made me look a bit dangerous, yeah?"

"I can give you another one if you like."

Jack throws his hands up. "Oh, no, I couldn't bear to inconvenience you so."

"It would be my pleasure."

Jack barks in laughter as we reach the ladder. "Be quiet," I order.

He raises his eyebrow. "Don't want anyone to see you sneaking around with such a handsome devil?"

"I don't want to wake my mom."

To his credit, Jack sobers immediately. He is silent as he follows me down the ladder. We creep past Mom's room, through the apartment. The only time Jack shows any reaction at all is when he sees the gaping hole where our interface room once was—the burned-out remains now covered with a tarp.

Jack opens his mouth, but no sound comes out. He just stares at the destruction, until I pull his arm and tug him to the door and then the lift that leads down to the reverie floor of the mental spa.

"So, this reverie...," he says, a nervous catch to his voice as the lift doors slide open.

"Reveries are easy," I respond. "As easy as falling asleep."

"Oh, I know," Jack says. "I had one before."

I stare at him incredulously.

"The military has something similar, I mean," he elaborates.

"No way, this stuff was invented by Mom; she hasn't sold her formula."

Jack shrugs. "They had relaxation chambers, for after intense training or skirmishes."

"This is much different," I say as we reach the basement floor of the building. "Okay, so, reveries are basically dreaming about memories. I'll need you to focus your thoughts on memories of me. We have monitors that can indicate whether you're dreaming about something that really happened or whether you're making it up."

"I could always *tell* you I'm dreaming about when I met you, but really dream about something else. Then you won't know if my dream is real or not."

I grin at him evilly, opening the door to the reverie chamber. "Oh, I'll know."

Jack jumps into the sensory chair as if it were a lounger and holds out his arm for the electrodes. He doesn't have a proper cuff, so it complicates the reverie process, but it's not impossible.

I lower the sonic hood over Jack's head and give him a puff of the bright green reverie drug. As he drifts off, I slip silently out of the sensory chamber and into the control room. I bring up his brain scans, and set up the monitor that shows brain activity to record. I want to know if the memories I'm about to spy on come from truth or imagination.

When I get to the secondary chamber, I work quickly, hooking myself up to the machinery and dosing myself with more reverie drug. It doesn't matter that I had four cups of coffee—as soon as the green drug hits my system, I'm out.

I'm overwhelmed by the sights-smells-sounds of everything in New Venice. The lights are brighter, the air drips with the smells of pastizzi and honey rings, the blasting horns and sirens are so jarring that I clap my hands over my ears. I cannot think in this cacophony.

In the center of the pandemonium is Reverie—but not quite the Reverie I know. The leaping neon sheep is bigger and shinier, the flashing slogan blinks erratically.

This is Jack's memory, and to him, New Venice was a swirling mass of chaotic sights and sounds. I wonder how long he's been in the city at the time of this memory. I wonder if he still thinks New Venice is like this. To me, the city is as comfortable as my apartment.

Jack starts to enter the Reverie Mental Spa, but he hesitates. He seems scared. He pauses by the window, nervously running his fingers through his hair, trying to smooth it down. He's wearing a wrinkled suit and recently polished shoes. He tries to adjust his tie in the shiny surface of Reverie's window.

And then—

I walk toward him.

Me.

It's not me—it's a memory of me. The memory-me is more perfect than the real me. She's more of what I wished I looked like than what I really do look like. The memory-me is wearing a black tank top and jeans, sneakers, and my fortune-cookie locket. My hair is in a messy ponytail. I think I've been doing yoga in Central Gardens—I used to do that, before Mom got worse. Memory-me is pre-occupied with her cuff, flicking through messages.

I watch, unable to take my eyes off the me of Jack's memory.

And then Jack looks up from the window, where he'd been fixing his tie, and he sees me.

The entire city disappears.

The dreamscape is gray and empty—not barren, just vacuous. At one moment, the city was there, overbearingly present, and the next second, it's gone.

It happens so suddenly that I'm left gasping.

It was true then. Jack really did meet me before. And when he saw me for the first time, everything else in his world faded away.

THIRTY-EIGHT

I CAN'T REALLY COMPREHEND WHAT I'm seeing.

I... I had no idea that I'd ever even met Jack. But the first time he saw me, he saw nothing *but* me. And the me through his eyes—it was the me I wanted to be. He saw me better than I even saw myself.

I watch, barely breathing, as the memory-me chats idly with Jack. The world springs up around Jack and his memory of me slowly, but the edge is gone. The lights are dim now, barely visible. The sounds are muted. The scent of lemons and lavender—like my shampoo—is stronger than the smells of the food sold by street vendors, the ever-present saltiness in the air.

I changed the way Jack experienced the world.

His memories speed up—as he follows the memory-me into Reverie, he meets Ms. White. They talk—an interview. My eyes dance over a tableau of Jack's memories in the first days of his job working at Reverie as an assistant to Ms. White. She never let him do anything serious, but he maintained the charts and data, helped her with clients—spa clients, not reveries.

And, in the background, he watched me.

It's weird, now, with me watching him watch me in a memory. Voyeuristic. But I can't help but see the way Jack thinks of me in his memories. Wherever memory-me is, the world is brighter, sweeter. It's dim and shadowy outside my glow.

Jack's memories slow down soon—probably a month or so after he started working at Reverie. He catches me crying. I remember that night. Not Jack—but I remember crying, on the bench at the roof of our apartment. That was the night Mom's doctors started talking about end-of-life care, and their treatments were all about making Mom comfortable, not trying to find a cure.

That was the night the doctors gave up on her.

I shut my eyes, recalling my own memory of that night. I climbed the ladder to Mom's garden—woefully neglected at that point, nearly everything was dead and there was algae in the hydroponics system. I sat on the bench. And I wept. I didn't hold anything back. Even though I was outside in one of the biggest cities in the world, it felt like the most private place I could be—out of earshot from everyone else, in a place Mom couldn't get to any more.

When I think of that time, I remember how very, very alone I felt.

But in Jack's memory, he's there. He'd heard me from the street, and he climbed the fire escape ladder. And found me.

In Jack's memory, he's there. In mine, I'm alone.

Every detail is right. I wore those clothes that day. There was a mustard stain on my pants, right there. That was the summer of my unfortunate bangs, and there they are, flopping in memory-me's face.

But Jack isn't in my memory of that night.

In this memory, his memory, the one I'm watching, Jack puts his arms around me, and he holds me until I'm done sobbing, and then memory-me looks up into his eyes, and then we kiss.

I remember crying myself sick that night, then going to bed alone.

But my lips feel bruised. I touch them now, as I watch Jack and memory-me kiss. I shut my eyes.

I think I can remember the feel of his lips against mine. The pressure, the taste of him.

No.

I open my eyes. This isn't real. We're going to wake up from Jack's reverie, and the screens will tell me this is all in his imagination.

But a part of me wishes it was real. The part of me that remembers crying, alone. I wish there had been someone there that night, someone to kiss away the pain.

Jack's memories progress. In his mind, we became close—closer than I've ever been with anyone else in my life, even Akilah. Months pass. I tell him my darkest fears and he whispers his to me. We kiss. We do more than kiss. My cheeks grow warm and my eyes grow wide as I see Jack and memory-me stripping our clothes off, our hands and eyes and lips hungry for more, more, more. I cannot tear my eyes away; I watch it all. I watch him. I watch the way he looks at me, the love in his eyes. The gentle touches. The hungry touches. The way he holds me, the way he lets me soar.

I swallow hard. I have never... I've never done that. Not with him. Not with anyone.

Lies. This is all lies.

This is Jack's sick imagination. His obsession. None of this happened.

I would *know*.

I turn away. I try to build a wall between Jack's memories and me. No, not his memories, his hallucinations—but either way, I can't tear myself away.

The weather gets colder. I can feel it in my bones, even though I'm not really here, it's not really winter, all of this is happening in Jack's mind.

I see Akilah, and I gasp aloud. I'd forgotten the way her tightly-curled hair bounces when she walks, her penchant for too-slick bright red lip gloss. Jack hangs in the background as Akilah tells me she's leaving for the military.

I remember this, too. The moment when I realized my friend, my last friend, my very best friend, was going away. I had been so upset that I didn't eat for days.

But in this memory, Jack's there. He cheers memory-me up with stories and jokes, distractions to pull me out of my funk.

Winter Festa. I remember going out, alone, and coming quickly back home. A festa is no fun without people to share it with.

Jack remembers it differently. He remembers going with me, sharing a honey ring and warm, sweet-roasted walnuts and fizzy spiced cider. We watched the parade together; he gave me the luminescent plastic snowflake he caught from one of the floats. We watch the fireworks, and we gasp in awe as the memory tree is lit in the center of Central Gardens.

I choke back a sob. I can't take much more of this. This... this is a life I wish I could have had. This is a life without the loneliness, the aching longing for someone, anyone to understand me.

This is a life I've never had, that I've always wanted, and it's painted so vividly here that I could almost believe in it. That's what hurts. Seeing it, and knowing it isn't true.

Something changes.

A different sort of cold.

Darkness. The blackness of void.

Raised voices.

My voice.

I can't hear the words. Just the tones, the sounds.

And they are *furious*.

And then, in the foreground, I see two long, rectangular shapes emerge. Everything is darkness now, but the black of those rectangular boxes is like a black hole, sucking away light and turning everything into nothingness.

With a sickened twist in my stomach, I realize what those black, rectangular boxes are.

Coffins.

There are no lids. I creep forward in Jack's memory, and peer down at the faces of his parents. I remember the obituary I found before, the one that lists his parents, both workers in the UC, killed in a car crash in Gozo. They are bloody and mangled here, barely recognizable, with a sheet covering everything below their chests. This is the last image he had of his parents, when he identified their bodies in the morgue, mingled with the day of the funeral, when their coffins must surely have been closed.

I look up and see memory-me and Jack, both dressed for the funeral. He wears a black suit and black shirt; I wear a dress I do not recognize, one made of black and silver.

"We are *done*," memory-me says. "I never want to see you again." Any doubt that remains that this could be real is gone now. I would *never* have done anything so callous as to break up with someone at his own parents' funeral.

"What—why? Ella, why?" Jack's voice is a plea, and it quivers. With fear, I think. Or sorrow.

The next words mumble and fade. Jack doesn't remember the exact things we said, just the fight.

Then one sentence rises from the chaos of sound.

"They deserved to die, and so do you!"

And then.
Silence.

It's over.

THIRTY-NINE

I WAKE UP.

My eyelids feel heavy, and when I touch my cheeks, my fingers come away damp from tears.

I stand, my body still shaking.

What *was* that?

That last memory, when everything went black.

If all of Jack's memories of me are false, why would he create something so horrible?

I rip the electrodes off my skin. I feel wobbly on my feet, but I cross the chamber quickly. I have to see it for myself, confirm the truth I know. The door slides open and I push past it, dropping into the chair in front of the control panel. I swipe my hands along the monitor recording Jack's brain scans.

My world bottoms out.

Jack's memories came from the place of truth.

None of it was his imagination.

The memories are real.

"Impossible," I whisper. None of that happened, none of it. And especially not the end. I would never do something like that. I know what it's like to lose a parent. I wouldn't... I couldn't...

But his memories were real.

But *my* memories are real.

I close my eyes, my fists curled up under my chin, pressing into my chest. I feel hollow inside, as if there's a black hole where my heart was, as if I am caving in around myself.

"What's impossible?" Jack stands in the doorway of the sensory chamber, watching me. His face is somber; he just woke up from that last, horrid memory too.

I look at him, and I find I'm unable to hold anything back. "You... you have memories of me. *Real* memories. But... I never met you before this week. How is that possible?"

Jack spins the other control room chair around and plops down into it. "Told you so," he says, but his voice is sad.

"It's not like my memory can just be wiped. Memories don't work that way. You can't just erase a person from your past."

Jack looks at the monitors and brain scans. "Maybe you can."

I roll my eyes. "The mind can lose memories— amnesia is a scientific possibility. But it's not selective. I mean, it can be, but not like this. I *have* memories of the past few years. They're just... different from yours. The brain doesn't function that neatly. Real science is messy. This isn't a sci fi novel."

Jack raises an eyebrow. "We're doing brain scans in a mental spa, love."

"So? And don't call me 'love.'"

Jack runs his fingers through his hair. "I don't know," he says. "Xavier's brilliant, and I'm no idiot, and we've not been able to figure out how this is happening. We just know what it's not—it's not cloning, it's not being replaced by an android. The people who come back—"

"Like Akilah," I interrupt. *Like me?* I want to ask.

"Like Akilah. Those people are still *people*. They're just... missing parts. In their brain—like memories, but also other emotions."

"I have emotions," I whisper. I am nothing but a black hole of emotions.

Jack shakes his head. "I don't understand it," is all he says.

"The reverie drug is designed to enhance memories you have, but there's not a drug that can just erase them, rewrite them."

"But I knew you," he says gently.

And—as impossible as it is—I cannot deny it.

FORTY

THE NEXT MORNING, I WAKE TO THE smell of bacon.

I stretch and throw my comforter back. I stare at the blue-and-brown damask pattern. Jack knew this comforter. Jack knew this bed.

I shudder, heat rising in my cheeks.

Jack *knew* me.

After the reverie, Jack left, telling me that, should I need to find him, I could go to the lower city and hire the black-and-yellow auto-boat again. I had thought that I would uncover the secrets of the Zunzana, and that I could hand them straight to Ms. White and the UC... but I no longer know what's right or wrong, what's true or not.

And I no longer know who—*what*—I am. I'm still me, of course. But those missing memories bother me, nagging at the edge of my mind like a buzzing bee in my ear. Has something happened to me to make me...*other*? Is that where my memories went?

The bacon is burning. I taste bile on the back of my tongue as I remember the last time I smelled burning, the explosion of the androids in Triumph Plaza, that one stump of a foot of the man I'd spoken to moments before. The explosion in my own home, the gaping hole, now covered with tarp, where our interface room used to be. I can't let myself get distracted by whatever Jack is, or what I am, or what we used to be. I have to focus on finding whoever is attacking my nation—and my family.

Bacon... burning. I shoot out of bed and race to the door. Mom shouldn't be up, shouldn't be making bacon. She's too sick, too weak. I slide on the slick tile floor as I race down the hallway to the kitchen, where I can hear the sounds of grease popping. We've not had bacon in the apartment for... for ages. More than a year. Mom's had trouble with greasy food, and it was just safer to serve her protein in pill form and give her soups and vegetables.

But when I step into the light, blinking, I see Mom standing over the stove, a cast iron frying pan sizzling with slices of bacon. She's wearing blue jeans, the ones with the holes in the knees. The ones she's not worn for years, forgotten in her closet as she opted for stretchy pants that were easier to get on and off. There's no sign at all of the nurse Ms. White hired for Mom.

"Mom?" I ask in shock.

She turns, a huge grin plastered on her face. She's paler than usual, and still too-skinny, her cheeks sunken in that hollow sort of way that shadows people with a long-term illness. But she's standing on her own, cooking.

"Mom?" I whisper, creeping forward, cautious joy rising in my throat.

"I didn't want to get your hopes up," she says. "After my relapse, Dr. Simpa tried me on a new therapy and medication."

"You're... better?" I can't seem to grasp simple things, like words.

Mom's smile falters. "Not entirely. I'll always have Hebb's. But... I'm a little better. Better enough to do this." She flicks a piece of crispy bacon from the pan onto a paper-towel covered plate, then plucks it up and pops it in her mouth. "Mmm," she says, grinning. "Life's not worth living without bacon."

Mom hands me a plate of already cooked pancakes and deposits a healthy portion of bacon on the side. I drown everything with syrup and stuff it in my mouth. Mom only eats one more piece of bacon and one pancake, but it's more solid food than she's had in weeks.

"This is... sudden." I think back to only a few days ago, when the only thing that would help her sleep at night was a reverie and a pile of pills. She could barely stand then, and now she's cooking breakfast?

"I didn't want you to expect this," Mom says. "My Hebb's seemed to be going back into remission, but we weren't sure about it... and I was definitely getting worse before I got better."

"Remission? Is this something permanent, or...?" I don't know if I can handle seeing Mom sick again, not after this glimpse of her almost well.

Mom smiles. "It's still too early to tell, but the scans have been good. I hope, one day, one day soon, this will be normal."

There are tears of happiness in her eyes—and mine, too. I let my fork drop on the table. "This is just... it's so quick!"

"I'd slowly been feeling better for a while now," Mom says. "But like I said, I didn't want you to get your hopes up, not if it wasn't going to work."

I don't even know what to say. Hot tears slide down my cheeks, and I realize quite distantly that these are tears of joy. For the past year, as Mom has fallen further and further into the clutches of her disease, I'd nearly given up. I'd been waiting for the day when the doctors told me to quit bothering with the medicine, that it would be better for Mom to just silently slip away. I'd been prepared for the goodbyes—as prepared as anyone could be, I guess— but I wasn't at all prepared for a hello.

I throw my chair back and wrap my arms around Mom. Already she feels more substantial. Before, when I helped her into the reverie chair, just a few days ago, she'd felt almost wraith-like, already half-ghost. But she's solid now, real. She's more my mom in this instance than in all the year previously.

"I just can't believe it," I say snottily into her apron.

She strokes my hair. "Believe it. It's about time we've had some good news, no?"

I nod, holding her tighter. This is all I've ever wanted to do: Hold my mother against me with the promise that she wouldn't go away.

When I let her go, I feel a hundred pounds lighter. I had not realized how heavy the weight of her disease was on my shoulders.

Mom smooths down my hair, an indulgent smile smeared across her face. "Let's go out," she says, her voice giddy and young. "A picnic. In the lower city. We'll hire a luzzu and sail around the waterways and then eat sandwiches and watch the tourists get sunburned. What do you say?"

I'm dressed and ready to go in ten seconds flat.

We meander through Central Gardens toward the lifts. Mom's chatting happily, and I'm barely even listening to the words, just the sound of her voice, rich and whole and not cracked with tiredness.

Someone big bumps into me, so violently that I nearly fall to the ground. A mitt of a hand grabs me as I stumble, jerking me upright.

"Sorry about that," the man's voice says in a deep rumble with a French accent.

I start in surprise. This is the giant Jack has working with him—what did he call him?—Xavier. My eyes widen in shock, but Xavier dips his head close to me and whispers, "Shh."

From the opposite direction, a small girl in a bright orange sundress bounds forward, seemingly distracted by her eye bots. As she passes Mom, the large anaconda tattoo coils up her arm, circling the girl's neck and hissing near her ear. I see a flash of something metallic in Julie's hand—a scanner, flashing red.

"Are you okay?" Mom asks, knocking Xavier's hands away from me. All of this has taken place in just seconds, and even as I stand there, Xavier and Julie disappear into the crowd.

"Yeah," I say slowly, staring at the crowd.

It's still too early for many tourists, but at least the lifts are operational again. We get one fairly quickly, mostly to ourselves. I watch as the upper city fades away and the sprawling water world of the lower city blossoms on the other side of the glass lift.

"It's pretty, isn't it?" Mom says softly, leaning against the glass. "Especially from up here, where you can't see the people properly."

I press against the glass, peering down at the glittering waters of the Mediterranean, and for just this moment, I allow myself a moment of joy.

My cuff vibrates on my wrist.

I look down and read the screen.

That woman with you is not your mother. Be careful.—Jack

FORTY-ONE

WHEN THE DOOR DINGS OPEN, MOM'S the first one out, already heading to the row of luzzu boats lined up. The luzzoliers cat-call at Mom, which makes her smile. She relishes the attention—the first attention she's had in a long time that's not pity or concern.

"Oh, this is delicious!" Mom says, grinning hugely. I stare at her. She's never used "delicious" as an adjective for anything other than food.

"Something wrong?" she asks, motioning for me to catch up.

I swipe the screen of my cuff blank, and look into my mother's eyes. Her wide, bright eyes, set in full cheeks that do not look like they belong to a woman who, days ago, was counting down the days to her death. "The eyes are the window to the soul," my dad always said. But I don't see her now.

"What's wrong, Ella?" the woman who looks like my mother says.

I shake my head.

I *want* to believe it.

Even if...

Even if her cure was a bit too miraculous. Even if a small part of me has doubted this from the start. I think about the flashing red screen on Julie's scanner.

No. *No.* She's Mom.

She has to be. She has to be.

Mom leans forward, concern etched on her face. "Ella?" she asks again.

I force a smile. "Sorry, Mom," I say. "I was just thinking about the last time we did this." I wave my hand at the luzzu boats and the touristy crowd.

"When was the last time we did this?" Mom asks curiously.

I laugh, my voice too high. Inside, I'm screaming, screaming. "Oh, Mom! You always called it 'your last good day,' the day you and me and Dad came out here to the lower city, just before you were diagnosed with Hebb's Disease."

"My last good day?" Mom asks, a slow smile playing on her face.

I nod. "Don't you remember? You and me and Dad came out here for a picnic on the beach. It was before you got ill."

This is a lie. All of it. We've never been on a picnic in the lower city, and even if we had, this is not Mom's last good day. Not by a long shot. Her last good day is the one she repeats in every reverie she does, over and over. The house in Rabat, dancing with Dad when I was a little kid.

BETH REVIS

I try not to look obvious as I wait for Mom's answer. I feel as if I am on the edge of a knife, my feet being sliced by the blade, teetering toward one side or the other.

"Oh, of course!" Mom exclaims, her voice trilling with laughter. "How could I have forgotten?"

And now I know. Really know. This woman is not my mother. I don't know who she is, but I know absolutely who she is not.

"Come on, let's go! I have a surprise for you."

She starts to pull me toward a luzzu, but I hang back. "A surprise?"

"I want to take you somewhere."

My stomach twists in dread. Go somewhere? With this... thing? This thing that looks like Mom? The terrorists are clever—clever enough to make a copy of Mom, to find a way to get me alone. What do they want with me? To hold me for ransom so my mother will hand over her research?

"Ella?" Mom asks when I don't move, and she sounds and looks and smells so exactly like my mother that I take a step toward her.

"Let me take you where you need to be!" a cheerful electronic voice calls.

A black-and-yellow luzzu bumps up against the dock. The human luzzoliers try to shove it aside—they don't want to lose their fare to an automated boat, but I lunge for it.

"Where are you going?" Mom calls after me as I leap off the dock and land into the boat.

-240-

I slam my cuff against the meter, and the boat's electronic voice says, "Identification: Ella Shepherd. Emergency evacuation initiated."

Before the thing that looks like Mom can say anything, the luzzu roars to life, knocking other boats out of the way and sending a tourist couple splashing into the water. I glance back behind me, a spray of seawater obscuring my vision. Auto-boats are only supposed to travel at a sedate pace, but this one's practically flying across the water. From the dock, I can still hear Mom screaming my name.

My wrist buzzes again, and I accept a com from Jack. His face fills my vision as my eye bots project a holographic image of him across from me.

"You made it to the boat," he says.

"What the hell is going on?!" I scream.

"I'm sorry—we don't have time. Look under your seat—there should be a burner cuff there for you. Cut off your own cuff and drop it into the water."

The boat is taking me straight out, away from Malta, away from Mom. I'm blinded by sunlight—real sunlight, not the false light from the solar glass that lines the roof covering the lower city. Ahead of us is nothing but waves.

A siren cuts through the noise, and I twist in my seat. A pair of police boats are making their way toward me.

"Jack—what—"

"Ella! Cut off your cuff! It has geo-locators in it! You're going to have to run!"

I drop to the boat's floor and peer under the bench seat. A knife and a cuffLINK is taped to the wood. As the sirens grow closer, I slip the knife edge between the thin tech foil and my skin, slicing through the cuff. It takes some sawing, but a moment later, I've sliced through the mechanics. I gasp in pain as I yank the cuff off—the tiny needles connecting the cuff to the nanobots inside my body aren't noticeable until they're torn out of my flesh. My arm feels naked and weak without it, the skin where the cuff had always been too pale next to the rest of my body.

I drop my cuff into the Mediterranean.

The burner cuff is one of those temporary things that you wear if you somehow break your cuff. I slip it on—it feels alien against my skin, too rough, not like my cuff. When I swipe my finger across the screen, I see that the cuff identifies me as Carly Pucket, native of Gozo, orphan, factory worker. It's a good hack—it looks legit, down to the photo on the ID screen.

As soon as it's on, a program downloads to my nanobots. The boat veers sharply right, heading back to the island, and the police boats change course.

My hands clench into fists, my fingernails digging into the skin of my palms. I have two options. I can make sure the police catch up to me. Go home. Forget about this all. I could jump out of the boat; I could tip the boat over.

Or.

Or, I could run.

FORTY-TWO

PANIC RISES UP IN ME AS THE BOAT
automatically speeds up, aiming not for the touristy area of
New Venice, but the Foqra District, the poor area behind
the shiny surface of the city. I've never been there before,
but Akilah lived here before she went to the military.

Akilah—cutting my cuff cut my communication with
her, too. But... she was like Mom. The same, but different.

Something made that thing that looked like Mom. If
Jack's story is true—and I'm inclined now to believe it is—
the government is really responsible for the android attack.
And the android attack was, in part, focused on my own
home and the Reverie Mental Spa internal interface
system. And Mom—she'd been seeing a new doctor, one
who worked at the UC labs. Her "cure" must have come
from there.

A flood of questions rises up inside me. Do they have
my real mom as a prisoner somewhere? Jack said that the
soldiers, the ones like Akilah... they died in battle before
they were turned into the doppelgangers. My eyes burn.
Does that mean Mom was killed? No—not if they want her
research. Surely they wouldn't kill her.

After all, a very small voice in my head says, *they did something to my memory, and I didn't die for it to happen.*

Over the sound of the crashing waves and the rising sirens behind us, I can hear the buzz-*zzz*-buzzing of a bee in my ear. I swat at my face, but there's nothing there.

I take a deep breath, quelling the panic that's choking me. I can't break down. Not here. Not yet.

The boat swerves behind the docking station, the long platform that extends the entire width of the lower city. In the center are the rows of lifts that connect the lower and upper city, and while luzzi crowd the open area at the front of the docking station, the entire back of it is made of giant electronic displays advertising hotels and restaurants, spas and tourist attractions.

I've never been *behind* it.

As the boat approaches, the program automatically downloaded from the burner cuff lights up. It's similar to the one I used when I followed Dad's ghostly image to Jack. But as I see just what the Foqra District is, I find it difficult to focus on the program.

Because the Foqra District is a city. A city made of boats.

Hundreds—no, *thousands*—of luzzu boats crowd behind the docking station all the way to the natural coastline of the island.

I never imagined Akilah made her home in a place like this, huddled under the shadow of the bridge of the city where I made my home. Even though I knew that the

Foqra District was where the poorer people lived, I never really realized just where it was. Or what it was.

A floating city, made of boats.

Massive pillars of steel and concrete, wrapped in rubberized wires and pipes, extending from the dark ceiling down to the water. The sewer system, I realize. And electricity, and freshwater. The light is dimmer here, hiding the squalor of the Foqra District in shadows. On the other side of the docking station, the touristy section is clean and sunny, thanks to the solar glass embedded in the roof. No solar glass here. If the lower city is perpetually sunny, the Foqra District is perpetually in dim twilight, the only light coming from fires in the boats or random beams of sunlight that have crept through the darkness.

I squint at the dark ceiling, bumpy with exposed pipes and wire. The map program labels what's on the other side of the bridge. *Central Gardens*, it says near the point where the advertisement wall at the back of the docking station is. My eyes skim forward, to one of the support pillars nearest us. *Reverie Mental Spa*. The word flashes across my eyes. On the other side of that ceiling is my home.

I never knew this was below my feet.

My boat knocks into another one, and my attention is brought slamming back to the water level, where the thousands of boats are clustered around the pipes and pillars. There are actually thin clear spaces in the water, designed to let boats go through. The auto-boat veers into one of these narrow waterways so quickly that it sends the nearby boats thumping and clattering against each other, the people inside the boats shouting at me.

My eyes fall to the pillar that leads directly up to the upper city, probably close to where Reverie is. One of the nearby luzzu boats flashes green. Not really—the map program synced with my eye bots make it appear as if a green light silhouettes one specific boat.

"MISSING PERSON!" a voice booms, both loud and oddly muffled. My head swivels to the source of the sound—the wall hiding the Foqra District from the touristy part of the lower city, the wall behind the docking station full of advertisements. "ELLA SHEPHERD, DAUGHTER OF RENOWNED SCIENTISTS PHILIP SHEPHERD AND FOUNDER OF REVERIE, ROSE SHEPHERD, KIDNAPPED TODAY LESS THAN THIRTY MINUTES AGO."

Kidnapped? Hardly. But the fact that this government-issued alert is announcing this lie makes me question even more how much of the terrorism I've supposedly been fighting comes directly from them.

"LIFTS CLOSED UNTIL FURTHER NOTICE."

They know I'm here, in the lower city. Closing the lifts keeps me on the water. Makes me easier to find.

Red and blue lights start flashing near where I entered the pathway into the Foqra District. The police boats have caught up to me.

My heart is banging inside my chest as I stand. I glance back behind me, once. My mother—no, the thing that looks like my mother—is standing in the prow of the boat, pointing right at me.

I turn my back on her, toward the boat illuminated in green with the map program in my eyes. I can hear the thing that looks like my mother shout as I leap from my boat with a thud on the wooden floor of the other luzzu, worn and beaten, with peeling paint and spots of cracked wood. An older woman with a crook in her spine throws a dirty shawl over my head and shoulders.

"You're with Jack, yeah?" the woman says in a raspy voice. She looks over my shoulder to the police boats winding their way through the pathways.

Before I can answer, the closest police boat is on us. A loud boom echoes across the water, and for a moment, I see nothing but small, glittering, crystal-like substances flying from the wide-mouthed gun at the prow of the police boat.

The old woman collapses. Her body convulses, bucking against the wooden floor of the boat in loud, sickening thuds. Her side is littered with the crystals—taze stuns. Electricity is pouring into her, incapacitating her.

"Get her!" one of the policemen on the other boat shouts.

"Run!" the old lady gasps through the pain.

I don't pause—I just leap onto the next boat, racing across the wooden planks to the next and the next.

The map program in my eyes points me to the left, deeper into the Foqra District. Behind me, I hear the sirens drawing closer, and I dare one more look over my shoulder—a look that makes me almost trip and fall out of the boat. A young man grabs my arm and steadies me, but at the same time pushes me toward the next boat. "Don't hesitate," he says urgently. "Never hesitate."

"Why are you helping me?" I ask, my feet pounding across the floorboards of the boat.

The man doesn't answer me as he helps me over a pile of rope and fairly pushes me to the next boat; he just makes a low sound in the back of his throat. It's not until I land in the next boat that I realize what the sound was: *Zzn, zzn.* Buzzing. The Zunzana is small, but the people still support it.

I leap into the next boat, skidding on the wet floor and crashing down. My knee burns against the rough, painted wood, and a row of scrapes blossom in blood on my palm. I turn my head as I struggle to stand and see the people who live in this boat. A girl sits on one side, holding two small kids in her arms. I'm not sure if she's the mother or the older sister, but she looks terrified. "I'm sorry," I feel compelled to say as I race past. She doesn't acknowledge my words, she's just staring at the police.

I can hear them now. Their heavy boots stomping on the wooden floorboard. The sirens slicing through the air. Shouts and calls, focusing their attention after me.

"Ella Shepherd!" a loud, deep voice shouts through an amplifier. "Stop running. You are wanted by the Unified Countries government."

At my feet, the girl holding the children gasps, a little sound of vocalized terror. I leap from her boat to the next, the effort already making my legs strain and ache. This isn't just a small local kidnapping—these cops aren't trying to save me. They are trying to *capture* me.

I look around wildly, trying to figure out where to go to next. The next boat I need to get to is too far away to reach in one jump. I make a snap decision, crashing into the nearest boat.

A man, his mustache peppered with bits of dried food, lunges at me, grabbing my elbow and yanking me back. "Bet there'll be a reward for ya," he snarls, dragging me to the other side of the boat, away from the one I need to get to.

One of the little kids the girl in the other boat was holding breaks away. "Let her go!" the little boy says indignantly. His mother or sister grabs him, pulls him down, but I can still hear the kid calling to the old man who's gripping my arm, "Let her go! She's Jack's friend!"

He doesn't know me—or, at least, I think he doesn't. But the little boy knows Jack, and that's enough for him.

The cops are getting closer. I can see them individually now. They have more taze stun guns, but also real guns. At least the thing that looks like my mother isn't with them. I don't know if I could face her.

I smash my foot against the old man's instep and break free, throwing myself across the boat and racing to the other side, leaping blindly to the next boat. I land so hard that my bones rattle inside me.

What are they going to do to me? This is the government, the side of the government I've never seen before, the side that makes doppelgangers and uses an entire squadron to bring in a teenager.

I look up, and it's not until I'm scanning the boats in front of me that I realize the map program isn't working. I stare down at the burner cuff—the screen is blank. I don't know if I've somehow broken it or it's been remotely disconnected, but it doesn't matter. The end result is the same: I don't have a safe route to follow any more.

I'm on my own.

FORTY-THREE

I SPIN AROUND WILDLY, LOOKING FOR someone to help me, but this boat is old and empty. I can hear the cops louder now—they're shouting about a reward. Whoever captures me and turns me in will get ten thousand credits.

That old man was willing to turn me in for free.

Where do I go? *Where do I go?*

One of the boats not too far away is yellow and black, just like the auto-boat was. I clench my teeth and hurtle toward it. Inside, a woman nods at me, urging me to the other side. She points to another boat—it's painted in traditional red and blue and green—but there's a small bee painted on the prow.

"Stop, Ella Shepherd!" the police shout behind me.

I keep low, running as quickly as I can. Jack's program is completely dead, but between the Zunzana symbols and a few people willing to point to the next friendly stop, I can keep going. The boats are fewer and further between now, and some of the people in the boats I have to cross over grab at me—perhaps eager for the reward, or just wanting to get on the good side of the cops.

Then—there—I see it—a boat close to the end of the water, near the gray sands of a beach shadowed by the bridge city. I leap closer to it, stumbling and nearly falling. A woman—young, about my mom's age—stands in the boat. Next to her is a boy about a decade younger than me, but tall and slender. He urges me closer to their boat, shooting frantic, worried looks at the cops behind me. I take a breath and hurtle myself over the water toward their boat. I crash into a pile of rags, then glance behind me. At least a dozen black uniformed officers, all chasing me. They're closing the ground rapidly, like vultures swooping toward an injured rabbit.

"Quickly!" the woman in the boat tells me. I jerk around to face her just as she yanks me down. What is she thinking? There's no way I can hide here; the cops are too close. They know where I am.

"Charlie!" the woman snaps. The boy drops to the deck beside her. She frames his face with her hands and kisses him quickly on the forehead. "Run, baby," she says, snatching the dirty dark shawl off my head and wrapping it around him. She keeps one hand on my shoulders, pushing me down, and Charlie—dressed in my shawl—takes off at a run, leaping to a nearby boat. The cops shout at each other, and I hear a whistle blowing, cursing, yelling.

"Deep breath," the woman tells me.

"What?" I gasp.

THE BODY ELECTRIC

Her hands are under my shoulders, lifting me up, and she throws me in the water with a splash drowned out by the cacophony of the chase.

I bob up, gasping for air, and the woman, leaning over the edge of the boat, pushes me back down. "Shh," she whispers, eyes wide. I nod and sink low into the water, clutching the side of the boat. I move as silently as I can around the boat, hoping I'm out of view of the cops.

The woman starts screaming. "That way! She went that way!" I hear her footsteps clacking on the wooden planks as she races to the opposite side of the boat, pointing to her own son, already several boats away.

I can see land nearby, a narrow strip of beach crowded with people and huts, lit up by small campfires. I could swim that. It wouldn't be hard. But there are less boats here. I'd be too easy to spot.

The waters of the Mediterranean are gray, almost black, speckled with litter and refuse. I hang near the prow of the woman's boat, clinging to the wood just beneath the luzzu's painted eyes. The wood is cracked and the paint is peeling, large chunks of dingy yellow flaking off in the water.

The boat rocks so violently that I nearly lose my grip. Dirty salt water fills my mouth, and I spit it out, scrambling to hold onto the wooden planks again.

"She was here," a deep male voice barks. Shit. It's one of the cops.

"She jumped in, yes, she made a mess of my bed." Those pile of rags I crash-landed into—that was her bed?

A loud smack resounds, followed by a heavy thud. The cop's hit her so hard that the woman fell down against the boat.

"Know what I think? I think maybe you're helping her run. Is she hiding here?" the cop growls.

I cower in the water. I sink so low beneath the surface that only my nose peeks out. I should be brave. I should help defend this woman, who sent her son running in my place to distract the cops. I should... I don't know what I should do. But it feels wrong, hiding here, while she's being beaten.

I close my eyes and pray I'm not discovered.

I hate myself.

I'm such a coward.

Rags and cloths spill over the side of the boat, and the woman screams. He's dumping her belongings out. The cloth was just worthless scraps, but it was also her bed, one of the few things she owned, and he's dumping them into the water. A water-drenched photograph of a baby—Charlie?—drifts by. My hand snakes out and I grab it. I can't do much, but I can save that at least. The woman starts to scream, pleading with the cop to stop.

Another crack of fist meeting flesh. She stops speaking, but I can hear her silent sobs. They're the loudest thing I've ever heard.

Heavy footsteps grow closer to me. He's going to look into the water.

I take one deep, silent breath, and plunge under the surface. I hope the junk in the water is enough cover to hide my kicking legs as I force myself below the boat.

I count the seconds. One... two... three...

Ten...

Twenty...

When will it be safe for me to surface? Will I rise from the water only to be captured?

Forty...

Sixty seconds—a full minute.

My heart's thudding, and I clutch the picture of baby Charlie in one hand, the other hand touching the bottom of the woman's luzzu boat.

Eighty...

One hundred...

One hundred twenty—two minutes.

I would have thought my lungs would burn from holding my breath so long, but I'm okay. I can do this. I can hide.

One hundred and fifty seconds.

How long should I be able to hold my breath?

Three minutes.

Shouldn't I need air by now? Why am I able to hold my breath this long? My heart's still racing; I feel panicked—shouldn't I *need* to breathe?

Four minutes.

The boat feels stable and quiet, but even though inside I'm panicking at the thought of being underwater so long, I stay. The longer I'm here, the further the police will be when I surface.

Five minutes.

I don't even feel pain. I remember learning to swim as a little kid, the way I'd try to stay under longer than Akilah, the way my lungs would ache, my face would burn. But here, now—nothing.

Six minutes.

I should be dead, shouldn't I? Six minutes under water... surely that would kill me.

Seven minutes.

Out of habit, I glance at my cuff, looking for the official time. Maybe I'm just counting down the seconds *really* fast, maybe it hasn't *actually* been seven minutes. When I look at my cuff, though, I see what made it malfunction. A tiny taze crystal is embedded in the thin tech foil. I hold my arm out, marveling at what I see. A dozen or more taze stuns prick my flesh, studding it with crystals.

I pluck one from my arm and squeeze it between two fingers. The thing shatters underwater, emitting a brief flash of sparks.

It was working. It was working, and it was in my skin, and I didn't feel a thing.

I look up at the bottom of the boat I'm hiding under. It has to have been at least ten minutes. Ten minutes under water, and I don't feel a thing. I'm fine. I was hit by a dozen or more taze crystals and I didn't even notice.

That's... that's not human.

FORTY-FOUR

I LET A FULL HALF HOUR SLIDE BY, THEN I let go of the boat, bobbing up next to it. I shiver in the cool, shadowed water. On a boat closer to the bay, an old man stands up next to the edge and pees directly into the sea. His watery eyes drift to me, but he doesn't seem to care about a girl clinging to the side of an old luzzu.

I kick up in the water enough that my hand can slap the water-logged photograph of the baby I salvaged onto the wooden railing.

A tiny squeak of surprise comes from the boat, and a small hand clasps around my wrist. "Thank you," the woman who owns the boat whispers to me. "I don't know how you saved this, but thank you."

"Thank you for protecting me," I say. Her face is bruised, her lip is cut. A sodden pile of rags leaves a dark stain on the floor of her boat—the belongings she was able to salvage from the water.

"Is Charlie—?" I cannot bring myself to voice the question.

"He'll be fine," the woman says, but I'm not so sure of that, and I don't think she is, either.

THE BODY ELECTRIC

My skin is wrinkled and my hair is stiff with salt—and whatever else is floating in this dirty water—by the time I finally swim to the narrow, crowded beach. As I approach, a few people look up, but they don't seem to particularly care about me or my presence. They're caught up in their own microcosm, and even the reward offered by the police is not enough to entice them to get involved with my affairs. In the distance, at the edge of the boats, I see flashing lights, police boats, and men and women dressed in military-grade black. But they hang on the edges of the Foqra District. Even they know that this is a no-man's land.

Houses made of trash—scrap tin and broken boards that clearly came from luzzu boats and cardboard and plastic tarps—are built right up to the water's edge, every spare bit of space used. Despite the fact that it's summer, there are glimmers of small campfires throughout this makeshift city.

I cough. The stench of smoke—both from old engines and from cooking—is overwhelming. It clings to me, slimy on my skin as I start to dry. I glance down at my clothes. They're ruined, soaked through with the polluted sea water. Bits of trash stick to my body and are caught up in my hair.

But I don't care about that. I only think about how I don't need to breathe air, how taze stuns didn't even make me twinge with pain.

I'm not human.

The words resound in my head with every step I take up the shore.

I'm not human.

A human couldn't do those things. And more—I think of how, when the androids first issued their warning, I threw Rosie down to rip off her bypass panel. I shouldn't have been strong enough for that. I threw Jack off me when he attacked as if he were nothing, injuring him despite the fact I've never fought anyone in my life.

I'm not human.

I stare down at my own hands. What is under my skin—wires and circuitry or flesh and bone?

I'm not human. I can't be human. But then...

What am I?

I choke back a sob. All I want is to strip down and take a scalding shower, then wrap myself up in my fluffy bathrobe and curl up in Mom's bed with her. But that reminds me of the woman who wore Mom's face, and my stomach churns. I don't even know what's *real* any more.

"Ella?" A man stands up, moving around a lean-to toward me.

Jack.

There's nothing about the way he looks that implies he should belong in the Foqra District, but despite this, he walks as if he's inherently at home here.

"Jack," I say, relieved, rushing toward him. The mad dash through the boats left me breathless, but my lungs reject this thick, polluted air, and I would hold my breath if holding my breath didn't remind me that I was other. He holds his arms out as if to embrace me, but I stop short, suddenly conscious and self-aware.

"They almost got me," I say, pointing back to the now-silent boats in the bay.

Jack nods grimly. "I know."

"And Mom? What happened to my mom?" The words spill out of me. "What was that... that thing? What happened?" My voice cracks, and for a moment, I'm afraid I'll cry. I shut my eyes, willing the burning inside them to not spill out.

Jack touches my arm, and when I open my eyes, I see his sad look. "She might still be okay," he says. "This— thing—it's not your mother. But you have to believe that she's still out there, that she's going to be okay."

I can do that. I can pretend. I've spent the past few years of my life pretending that nothing was wrong with my mother.

That there's nothing wrong with me.

I swipe my hands over my eyes, swearing silently to myself that I will discover what has happened to Mom. I will save her.

"How?" I ask softly, and even though Jack hasn't been privy to my own silent ruminations, he understands my question.

"I don't know how we can save her," he says. "But we will. *That* is what the Zunzana does, Ella. We're not terrorists. But we don't accept what the government tells us to be true. When we see something wrong, we try to fix it."

Like my mother. *Like me.*

I still don't know if I trust Jack and his Zunzana. But I know I don't trust the government, not after they chased me down like a criminal, not after seeing the thing with my mother's face, something that only the government labs could have made.

I will trust myself, whatever I may be now. And I will save my mother. My *real* mother.

I square my shoulders, then look around. "Where are we?" I finally say.

Jack barks in a bitter laugh. "It's called Paradise Bay." He sees my look and adds, "No, really. It was named before New Venice was built. It used to be a really beautiful beach."

Those days are long gone, that's for sure. In the water, the boats are so close together that it was easy to leap from one to the other. That had felt crowded, each wooden side bumping against another, but it was nothing to the claustrophobia here. People are *everywhere.* We have to squeeze past roughly hobbled-together walls of the makeshift housing. In some cases, Jack lifts a part of a shack out of our way and then replaces it behind us. Screaming children dart impossibly through the debris, but the one baby I see—a thin little girl nursing with her mother—seems to have already acquired an apathetic acceptance of her lot in life. Her eyes are listless, her body already huddled and defeated.

There are—I don't know, at least a thousand or more people destitute on this beach.

I look back at the boats crowded around the pillars in the water behind us. The boats further out are nicer. I can see their brightly colored finishes even from here. But the boats closer to shore are dingier, faded, damaged, broken. Like the people.

It's even harder for the people not on the boats, the ones crowded on the shore and up against the cliffs that encircle it. There's little space here, and little warmth, and no joy at all. I glance down at one of the pots over the fire. Food—scraps, really, carrot peelings and something I'm fairly sure is grass along with meat that I assume (I hope) was once a rabbit—simmer in an earthenware pot over a small stone kenur hearth. A girl about my age pokes the food around with a stick, fanning the steam with her hand.

She looks up and sees me staring at her. Her eyes grow narrow and mean, and she snatches the pot away from the flames and hides it behind her. She spins her stick-spoon around in her hand and jabs it toward me.

I put up both my hands and step back. She watches me suspiciously, then returns her pot to the fire.

I move closer to Jack. His face is grim, his jaw clenched as he leads me toward the towering cliffs at the end of the beach.

"How are there so many people here?" I ask. I wrap my arms around my chest and hurry to keep close to Jack.

"Some were born here," Jack says. "Some families have hidden here since the Secessionary War." Jack pauses, looking around. "Most, though, are just poor, and they're not willing to do what the government wants them to do so they can stop being poor. Money doesn't mean anything if you have to give up what you believe in to get it."

The cliffs are spotty and even darker than the rest of the Foqra District, hollow caverns cut into the outer edges. Jack leads me past most of these, then stops in front of a narrow opening on the western side, so close to the edge of the water that I can see shafts of sunlight peering down.

It's not until we are nearly at the cavernous opening at the cliff that I notice some of the people gathered at the entrance. Most of them are men, but there are a few women, too. All of them have sharp eyes, and those eyes are trained on us. Lumps with hard edges—weapons— move under the cloths in their laps.

Jack raises a hand, flashing a burner cuff on his wrist. "She's with me," he adds. The suddenly tense air around the cave relaxes. I remember what Jack said about the Zunzana—although the core group is reduced to just the three of them, the network created by it was vast, with friends throughout the Unified Countries and beyond. People may not be willing to stand up and fight the government, but they are willing to help those who are.

Jack steps aside, letting me enter the cave first. I step into the darkness.

FORTY-FIVE

A METAL DOOR JUST INSIDE THE CAVE slides open, and we step inside a room so bright that I have to blink rapidly until my eyes adjust.

Rough-hewn limestone walls curve around us, extending far beyond what I can see. This isn't a cave—it's a tunnel. I stumble as I step forward, and it's only then that I notice the long magna-track embedded into the floor. On top of the track is a worn-out carriage—little more than a giant metal tub set into the track—and in the center of the carriage, where the power supply is supposed to be, is a glowing glass brick.

"Solar glass," I gasp, peering closer. Solar glass comes from one of the interstellar colonies—the perfect fuel source. Set it out in the sun for just a little while, and it stores enough energy to pull a train across the world. The glittering tops of Triumph Towers supply all the energy for the upper city of New Venice, and the solar glass bricks embedded to the bottom of the bridge spanning the short stretch of sea between Malta and Gozo—the roof of the lower city—provides an alternate for sunlight and power for the entirety of the lower city.

But on its own, as single bricks used by people and not giant powerhouses, solar glass is rare and super expensive.

Jack's friends, Xavier and Julie, step forward, casting long shadows that dance down the tunnel.

"What... what is this place?" I ask.

"Originally, Paradise Bay was going to be a bit of a tourist attraction," Jack says. "This was going to be a train stop. But then the plans fell through, and the homeless moved in, and ultimately, the tunnel was abandoned. It goes all the way to the Silent City."

"It has been convenient," Xavier says in his rough voice. "The resistance movements have been using the tunnels since before the Secessionary War. The government has been kind enough to forget it existed."

"Since before—?" I ask.

"Ever since the Financial Resource Exchange started in the middle of the 21st century, people have seen what was coming and worked to prevent it." Jack starts to lead me to the metal carriage on the magna-track.

"What was coming?" I struggle to keep up; Jack's long legs make his strides twice as long as mine.

"A unified government. Which, yeah, doesn't sound bad. But the thing is, if a government gets too big... well, it forgets about the people."

The Foqra District is proof enough of that, I guess. There aren't supposed to be poor people in New Venice—not poor like that. Akilah's family was never well off, but they always had a home and enough food to live on. Or, at least, I thought they did. She never told me... I never knew... No wonder she wanted to escape to the military.

"Sacrificing the few for the good of the many is fine, until you remember that we're talking about people," Jack adds, a bitter note in his voice.

"Sacrificing the few for the good of the many." I parrot his words right back at him, stopping in my tracks.

"The android explosion wasn't the Zunzana's fault," Jack says immediately.

"Oh, I believe you on that," I say, stopping him from speaking again. "But...." I think about Akilah, about Mom. About Dad. About Estella Belles and the one hundred and three other people who died in the android explosion. And then I think about the hundreds of thousands of people who died in the Secessionary War. Of the pockmarks caused by bombs that dot the island, of the cities wiped out. "I don't want my friends to die. My family. *I* don't want to die," I say. "But I don't want another war, either."

"Ella, we *can't* let the government take away our humanity," Jack starts.

"They started it!" Julie says, her clear voice ringing. "If it takes a war to stop those—ugh! *C'est vraiment des conneries! Pute!*" She rambles in more French that I don't quite pick up, and Xavier draws her aside, calming her down.

Jack turns to me, an argument on his lips.

I throw my hands up. "Look, I'm not trying to get into another argument here. I was just calling you on your bullshit. Whatever—don't try to be noble when you have blood on your hands. You're rebelling against the government, and even though you haven't resorted to their methods yet, where do you think this is heading? If you want to overthrow the government, you're going to end up in the exact same place as them." I look away; I can't bear to look at his face like that. "There are no winners here. There is no good or bad. By the time this is over, we'll all have blood on our hands."

Jack tilts my face until I meet his eyes again. "Ella," he says, his voice dark and grave. "I realize that you don't remember me. But if you did, you'd know that I would *never* become the kind of person you seem to think I already am. But I will *not* let myself be turned into… whatever those things are. If I have to kill, I'll kill—I'll do what it takes to protect myself, and humanity. But if it does resort to violence, you can rest assured I will not just explode half the city and kill innocent people. If I'm going to kill someone, then I'm going to look that person in the eye when I do it, and they are going to know why I am doing it."

He pauses, and his hot, angry gaze sweeps up and down the full length of my body. "Besides," he says, "every hero I know is soaked in blood."

I swallow down the lump in my throat, because, judging from the way he talked about him earlier, Jack counts my father as one of his heroes.

"We should go," Xavier says in his low, gravelly voice. He opens the carriage door for us, and Julie scrambles in, giving me a foul look as I follow her. She is spitfire and rage, and the fact that I don't want the world to burn like she does is enough to make her question my worth.

Jack sits beside me, and Xavier moves to the helm, starting the carriage up and whisking us into the dark tunnel. The solar glass brick not only powers the carriage, but also casts a radiant glow of light around us, illuminating the tunnel minutes before the magna-track rushes us through the shadows.

"I don't want a war," I whisper.

"What?" Jack asks. I turn away—I hadn't realized I'd spoken loud enough for anyone to hear.

Jack reaches for me. "I didn't ask for this," I confess. "I just..." I don't know why, but I'm shaking my hands, as if they're wet and I'm trying to dry them. The motion becomes more violent, and I'm thrashing my arms against my body. I can't control it. Across from me, Julie stares, eyes wide. I am overwhelmed with this knowledge that nothing—*nothing*—is the way I thought it was, that even I am not who I thought I was—that I'm not human, I'm not even a person, I'm some thing, a thing that doesn't need air to breathe, that can turn off pain, that may as well be an android, a monster, a soulless shell, like the thing my mother has become that maybe Akilah has become and I'm alone, I'm a soulless monster and I'm alone alone alone.

Jack wraps his arms around me and holds me until I still.

He doesn't say anything. He just holds me.

"I didn't breathe," I say after I calm my heart, voicing my confession.

"What?" Jack pulls back, confused.

"I hid under the water. And I didn't breathe."

"Good," Jack says, slowly, still confused. "I'm glad you weren't caught."

"I didn't breathe for half an hour."

Jack's eyes widen.

I rip away from him and huddle against the carriage wall. The limestone zips past us, leaving the scent of petrichor in its wake. "That thing that wasn't my mom... Akilah, who's no longer Akilah... I'm afraid I'm something like that. I'm... I'm afraid." I turn and look into his eyes. "You say I'm missing memories. Maybe... maybe I'm just breaking down."

The sound of a hundred million bees descending on me from a cyclone fills my ears.

But then Jack's voice rises above the sound. "I don't know what you are, Ella Shepherd, but I'm sure that you're still Ella Shepherd. Those things that the government's been creating, the ones that look like people we know but aren't—they didn't have emotion. They didn't have fear. They were empty inside. And you are not."

"But—"

Jack silences me. "We'll figure this out. Together."

I snort. "Just like we'll win a war against the world's largest, most powerful global government?" I say incredulously.

"I never said we could win." Jack bites the words off one-by-one. "I just said I wouldn't quit fighting."

And for the first time, I really appreciate how dangerous Jack Tyler is. He may have only a handful of people on his side and the ghosts of his parents to back him up, but he will never stand down.

He will never give up. Not on the war.

Not on me.

FORTY-SIX

XAVIER STOPS THE CARRIAGE SO suddenly that I nearly lurch out of my seat. I think for a moment we've arrived wherever it is that we were heading—we must have travelled at least ten kilometers. But rather than open the carriage door, Xavier curses and shutters the solar glass brick with a metal cap, sending us all into pitch black darkness.

"What's wrong?" I ask. From the glow on their cuffs, I see that Xavier, Jack, and Julie all have silver eyes—they're seeing something with their eye bots, a program that they share and I do not.

"We've been followed," Jack answers me.

"Five kilometers away... four and a half... *merde*, they're going fast," Julie whispers.

"No other carriages on the tracks—they're running," Xavier says. He pauses. "Two people, definitely two people. But—"

"No human can run that fast," Julie says.

"Shit," Jack curses. "We have to hide. *Now*." He throws open the carriage door, pulling me out behind him. Julie and Xavier rush to follow.

"We should stay in the carriage, yeah?" I ask, but even as I say it, Xavier starts the carriage up again, and it speeds away into the darkness, without us. I guess they think whoever is chasing us will chase after it without realizing that we're missing.

"The Templar tunnel's around here," Jack mutters.

"Three kilometers away," Julie says, a panicked edge to her voice.

The only light we have now is from the glow of our cuffs. I look around at the oppressively small tunnel and swallow down the hysterical laugh rising in my throat. "Where can we go?" I say quietly.

Jack grabs my wrist and pulls me into the wall—or, not the wall, exactly, but a crack in the tunnel, a slim passageway that we barely squeeze through. Xavier follows us, and Julie brings up the rear. The crack in the tunnel reveals a niche perfect for hiding in. It's clearly manmade—narrow, but uniform, and just the right height for a small person and extending further back than I can see. Xavier has to hunch, and the footing's uneven.

"One kilometer," Julie whispers.

Whoever is chasing us is speeding insanely fast.

"Cuffs out," Jack orders in a low voice. Julie and Xavier immediately turn their cuffs off, but I hesitate. The light from the cuff is so dim, but it's better than nothing. Julie reaches over and force closes my cuff.

The stone in the crevice is wet and dank, and when I touch it, slime leaks from the stone and onto my skin.

BETH REVIS

A slant of light leaks through the tiny cave Jack pulled us into. Whoever's been chasing us has caught up.

Voices.

The sounds are muffled, but it's two women.

Jack grabs my forearm, his fingers digging into my flesh. I can feel the fear emanating from him.

And then I can make out one word from our pursuers.

"Here."

They've found us.

Jack slips his hand over my face, clamping my lips shut. And it's not until then that I realize what voice I heard before, the person who said, "Here."

Akilah.

I creep closer, shaking off Jack's hand and moving toward the light. From the narrow crevice in the wall, hidden from view, I get a glimpse of Akilah's face. This is my friend, my very best friend, my sister. My eyes are thrown wide open, drinking up Akilah's image in the pale light of the lantern clipped to her side. She's aged, just a little, some of the baby fat around her cheeks gone, replaced with sharper lines. Her eyes are deep brown, but hooded and shadowed. Her hair—she always used to wear it in twisty braids that snaked down her back, or in a poofy cloud around her head, but it's shaved off now, nothing but curly black tufts close to her skull.

She looks different, but also exactly the same.

"She's nearby," Akilah says in a harsh, emotionless voice.

"A tracker," Jack whispers.

My heart sinks. I quietly pat down the clothes I'm wearing—a simple tank top and jeans, no different from what I usually wear. And I can't find a tracker on them. Just like Jack had a tracker on him that enabled me to find him, I must have something on me—something that led the enemy straight to me. Enemy... she's the enemy now. My stomach sickens to know that I think of Akilah as a person to fear and avoid.

"But I can't see her." Akilah continues. She must be speaking to someone—whoever is issuing her orders. There's a pause as she waits for commands, then I hear her say, "Yes, ma'am."

I shut my eyes. Prime Administrator Young. She's controlling Akilah; she's sent her on a manhunt.

"Ella!" Akilah shouts. "Ella, where are you?"

And she sounds so much like my friend that I ache to call back. Jack's grip around my mouth tightens so forcefully that my entire body is drawn back against his.

"Ella!" Akilah calls. "I escaped the military! I... I need your help!"

Her words sound sincere, but her face is utterly blank.

"I'm hurt!" Akilah says. If I shut my eyes, it sounds just like the Akilah I knew. But if I watch her, I can see—

there is absolutely nothing left inside of her of the person I used to know.

She isn't my friend. She isn't Akilah. Not anymore.

"Ella, please!" Akilah's voice breaks over my name, and it sounds as if she is in true pain.

I peel Jack's hand from my mouth. He resists, but he has nothing to worry about.

I'm not going back to her. I've seen exactly what Akilah has become, and it's not anything I recognize.

Akilah pauses—receiving new orders from PA Young after I don't fall for her tactic. Akilah mutters her consent to something, then turns.

It's only then that I remember that it was two people in the tunnel, two pursuers chasing us in the darkness. The second woman steps forward, and I see her through the sliver of rock we're hiding behind.

Mom.

FORTY-SEVEN

AKILAH'S VOICE CUTS THROUGH THE dim tunnel. "Ella, we know you're nearby. We don't want to hurt you. We just want to take you home."

I don't move. My fingers curl into fists and my teeth clench, but I don't move.

"You give us no choice," Akilah says. "If you don't come out or reveal your location in thirty seconds, I will kill your mother."

I am stone. I am stone. That woman is not my mother and I will not move I will not go to this thing that wears my friend's face I am stone I am silent I am immoveable.

Through the narrow slit in the tunnel wall, I see Akilah raise her gun and press the barrel to my mother's head. Not my mother, not my mother, that thing isn't my mother.

"Ten seconds," Akilah says in a voice devoid of all emotion.

I am stone.

Akilah pulls the trigger.

My mother's head bucks back—but doesn't break. The flesh of her face splatters and shatters, revealing a glint of metal beneath.

Not bone.

Metal.

"Ella!" the thing with no face calls using my mother's voice.

My heart thuds in my chest. I taste bile.

Akilah aims the gun again, pointing for my mother's left eye. She pulls the trigger again, and I hear the bullet ricocheting around the solid metal of my mother's skull. Her body convulses chaotically, the bullet pulling her head left and right. And then her body collapses, as empty as a rag doll. She falls to the stone ground of the tunnel, broken and gone and dead.

It's not my mother, it's not my mother, I know it's not my mother—but I cannot choke back the sob of grief rising in me.

Akilah's head whips around, her eyes falling on the hidden passage in the wall. She holsters her gun, then pulls another weapon from her hip.

It's a small gun, and the bullets inside it glow like solar glass, glittering in shimmering gold.

"Shit!" Jack shouts. "Move! Move! Move!"

Behind us, Xavier and Julie scramble deeper into the cave, but it's too late for Jack and me, so much closer to the wall. Jack throws me down and covers my body with his just as Akilah pulls the trigger, and the stone wall of the tunnel explodes in rubble. Dust clogs the air and debris rains down. A heavy rock slams into Jack's back, so violent that I feel the force of it through him.

Akilah steps through the smoking rock.

"Hello, Ella," she says. She lifts Jack bodily off me, and tosses him against the wall.

I cower at her feet. I do not understand what happened to her, all I know is fear.

Something—someone—Julie—slams into Akilah's side, throwing her off-balance and forcing her to stumble back. Quick as lightning, Julie kicks Akilah in the side, then slams her fist into Akilah's solar plexus. It doesn't incapacitate her, but Akilah moves back, raising her arms warily in defense.

I scramble over the broken rock to Jack. "Are you okay?" I gasp, running my hands over his body. Between the rocks crashing on him and Akilah throwing him, I expected at least a broken bone, but while he's dirty and grimy and his clothes are shredded, he is, thankfully, miraculously, fine.

I pull Jack deeper into the tunnel, out of the way. Akilah and Julie circle each other like starving wolves, each about to strike. Akilah tries to move toward me, but Julie blocks her, using her distraction to slam her elbow into Akilah's collarbone. It is Julie, though, who screams in pain at the move—Akilah's bones must be made of that same impenetrable metal as Mom's.

I see the determination in Akilah's eyes; I see the exact moment when she decides that she will end Julie quickly and get it over with.

I cry out a warning, but it's too late—Akilah leaps at Julie with speed I didn't think was humanly possible—*it's not humanly possible, she's not human*, I remind myself—and Julie crumples to the ground. But—not quite. Her leg sweeps out at the last moment, knocking Akilah off balance.

As soon as her body hits the ground, Xavier erupts from the shadows. He slams himself on top of Akilah, and in the dim light, I see a glint of something silver.

A needle.

He plunges it into Akilah's skin. Akilah has just a moment to curse—and then she's out.

I stand, half expecting her to jump up and attack again.

"Is she—?" I ask.

"Asleep," Xavier grunts.

"It's okay," Jack says. "Xavier's a med."

Xavier shrugs. "Or I would be if I'd finished school."

My eyes drift past the broken wall, to the tunnel with the magna-track and my mother's body.

Jack reaches for me, but out of the corner of my eye, I see Julie hold him back. I stumble over the wall, and kneel beside my mother's body.

Not my mother. I have to remind myself of that. Beneath her neck, where the bullets didn't strike, she has every appearance of Mom. The tiny mole in the hollow space where her collarbone connects. The soft hands, the long fingers.

But her face was blown off by Akilah's gun blast, and beneath it is metal.

There is blood—so much blood—or, at least, something red and sticky like blood. And there is flesh here, and skin, the skin feels real. But her skull is metal. Her eyes—her eye, there's only one left now—looks like a human eye. It dangles from veins, like a human's eye would. But there is an odd sheen to it, and I think I can see the edge of a lens embedded behind her pupil.

Sparks of electricity flicker, and through her skull, I can still see the small whirr of gears. She is not yet dead, even now.

"We have to go." Jack's voice cuts through all the dark, horrific thoughts cluttering my brain. "There will be more coming, now that these two are down."

"Trackers," Xavier says in his gruff voice.

"Where?" I ask. "I looked, I don't have any on me."

"Come here." Xavier lifts the flap of one of the pockets on his cargo pants, and pulls out a flashlight and a small med-kit. He sets the flashlight on its end, illuminating a sphere around us. Snapping the med-aid kit open, he pulls out a small scanner and runs it over me.

"*Damn*," he mutters, reading the scanner.

"What?" I ask. I try to look over his shoulder, but can't see anything.

Xavier silently hands over the scanner to Jack.

"*What?*" I ask again, growing nervous.

"You have a significant proportion of bots," he says. "I haven't seen this high of a presence of nanobots since my time on the lunar warfront. I'm surprised you don't have bot-brain, to have this many nanobots in your system."

I bite my lip thinking about the way I injected myself with the extra dose of nanobots earlier. Maybe the nanobots I injected in myself were the result of the weird abilities I've been having, as well as the hallucinations. I had been so careless, just thinking of giving my mother some happy memories and time away from her disease. I glance down at the broken body of the thing that looked like Mom. How long has Mom been... this? Did I give myself a chance of bot-brain to make this robot have a reverie? No—that's impossible. Robots don't have memories; they can't have reveries.

I rub my bare arm self-consciously, the movement becoming more anxious. My fingernails dig into the skin on my arms. I want to peel it away, rip the nanobots from my flesh and crush them under my heel. But of course, it doesn't work that way. Nanobots can't be seen, much less pulled out.

"And there are tracker bots in her system," Xavier adds.

My eyes shoot to him. He nods. "You don't have trackers on you," he says, rummaging in the med-kit. "They're *in* you."

"How?" I gasp, holding back a gag of disgust. How could someone have *injected* nanobots into my system without my knowing? And who? Who would want to track me that way? I'm not important.

Xavier holds up a syringe he found in the med-kit. "I can't get them out," he says. "But I can kill them. This will only destroy any nanobots that are designed for tracking purposes—it kills any geo-locating signals, nothing more. The rest of the bots in your system... I'll have to analyze them before we do anything else."

I hate the idea of dead nanobots floating in my system, but I hold my arm out. Xavier slips the needle into my skin, and I gasp with pain—needles are almost never used now, and I've only seen them when Mom had an IV or something from the hospital. Xavier swipes the puncture mark with antiseptic and sprays it with Band-All before packing away the med-aid kit again.

"We should go," Julie says. She pushes off from the wall she'd been leaning against. Her lip is split, and angry red marks already indicate the developing bruises all over her body. Even Xavier, caught in the debris, has not escaped unharmed. "They might not be able to track the princess over there now, but they know where these things were for sure, and now that we've taken them both offline, they'll be sending in replacements."

Jack nods. "Right," he says. "Let's split up. Xavier, can you carry Akilah?"

Xavier nods and picks my friend—the thing that looks like her—I don't even know any more. But he picks her up easily.

"You and Julie go to war. I'll take Ella, and we can go to sleep, then stay awake."

"Sleep?" I ask.

"Code, stupid," Julie says, already pushing Xavier further down the tunnel. "That thing is still alive, it might be recording." She jerks her head to my mother. While the lens in her eye is shuttered and she is completely motionless, there is still electricity sparking in her gaping skull. It may not be beyond repair.

"Come on," Jack says, pulling me back into the hidden cave that we'd been crouching in before Akilah and Mom arrived.

The darkness envelops us.

FORTY-EIGHT

"THROUGH HERE," JACK SAYS, PUSHING me into a narrow space. It's not until I stumble over them that I realize there are steps. We're not just in a small crevice in the tunnel system; we're in a separate cavern, a whole new tunnel, far older than the ones the Zunzana used. As I inch my way up the uneven steps, Jack follows, near enough that I can feel his body heat in contrast to the cold, damp stone.

"They won't be able to find us here," Jack says, trudging up the steps behind me. "I think."

"You think?"

Jack's long strides make me pick up my pace as I follow him up. "I mean, I hope. But..."

"But...?"

"But we should keep going, that's what I'm saying. Come on."

The only sound in the cramped, narrow space is my and Jack's footsteps on the slick stone. We slide on it every once in awhile, and my hands and knees are bruised and scratched by the time I climb the last stairs. This tunnel is ancient—so old it feels almost as if it were made by nature, not man, but the stairs we just climbed were clearly manufactured, albeit several centuries or more ago.

Jack grabs my arm and pulls me closer to him as he flicks on a small penlight I didn't know he had.

"We're finally here," he says, his voice ragged from the exertion of climbing the steps.

"And where is here?"

"The cata—the exit," he says quickly, but I already caught the word he was trying not to say. I take the flashlight from his hand and cast it around the tunnel.

It is filled with dead bodies.

Well, not bodies.

Skeletons.

Hundreds and hundreds of them.

"What is this place?" I whisper.

"Saint Paul's catacombs," Jack answers. He crosses the cavern and sets up his flashlight in the center of the room on a raised, circular dais. It casts light and shadow around the room. The entire area is carved directly from the rock. The smooth, slick floor, the low ceiling, the indentations in the walls filled with bones.

Through a stone window, I can see a long row of rectangular indentations carved into the rock, almost like narrow beds, each one filled with a skeleton. Many of the skeletons are too big for the indentations, and whoever laid the bodies there bent the arms and legs so they would fit.

"It was made in the Roman times," Jack says. His voice is soft, but it bounces around the stone walls so that it sounds like each of the skeletons whispers to me. "The ancient bodies are long gone, but when the Secessionary War broke out, they started using the catacombs again, putting bodies in the loculi after they died."

"They?" I ask.

"The poor. The ones who can't afford cremation. When the bombs hit Valetta and the other towns, whole families were killed. But their friends and relatives didn't have the proper materials or knowledge for preparing the bodies, and people who came here to entomb the dead started to get sick. The Zunzana closed off the catacombs again, fairly early on, and people had funerals at sea instead. That's what the poor still do, the ones in the Foqra District."

I'm reminded of what Jack said about the Zunzana, that it had existed for years before him, an organization that worked silently, correcting the mistakes of the government. It had once been vast and influential enough to help people bury their dead in wartime—and now it was just three teenagers, struggling to show the world an unspeakable evil.

The skeletons here are all blank, devoid of any personal features, most of them wrapped in a thin linen cloth. Some are only bones, but there are still several that have a slimy, waxy sheen to them. It is dank and dark here, but also cool, and the bodies do not rot as quickly as they would above ground.

I'm starting to envision faces on the cadavers. They didn't die that long ago. These are not bodies from the ancient days; these people could have been my relatives. My grandparents, the uncle I never met, the cousins I never had.

And then I see a small hole carved into the wall, no longer than my arm, and a tiny skeleton inside it, and my heart cries out in horror. My hand shakes as I raise it, resting on the damp stone wall just below the baby's tiny, bone fingers.

Beneath it is a slightly smaller crevice, and inside, the skeleton of someone a bit younger than me. A glint of gold shines in the light—a tiny metal bumblebee like the pin Jack wears, resting where the kid's heart should be. These bones belong to someone like Jack. Someone like Charlie, the kid who ran off and distracted the police so I could escape. I gasp, overwhelmed by the emotions I've been trying to hold back for so long. I swallow down the lump in my throat. I cannot cry. I cannot cry.

I cannot stop crying.

Jack rushes around the table and touches my shoulder, hesitantly. I jerk away from him. I don't want his comfort. I don't *know* him, even if he thinks he knows me. But my eyes are blurry and burning, and I can't choke down the sob rising in my throat.

THE BODY ELECTRIC

I don't know what it is. Seeing the dead bodies of children who died before I was born, victims of a war they never had a chance of winning? Or knowing that, when my body is dead and I start to rot, maybe it won't be a human skeleton that will rest in my grave. I might not rot at all. I might be nothing more than an android, and death is as simple as a kill switch behind a bypass panel. What else can I be, to have a nanobot count like I do, to be able to do the things I have done?

Androids don't feel, I remind myself, and there is nothing I would like to do more now than to *not feel*.

I sink to the floor, the wet stones soaking the seat of my jeans, and draw my knees up to my chest, hugging them against my body as my head sinks down, my short hair barely covering my face. I just want to be alone, but I feel the death of the tracker nanobots in my blood, and I cannot be alone, even from them. I am surrounded by death, inside and out, and all it does is remind me of how futile everything is, everything ever was.

I feel rather than see Jack sit down beside me. He doesn't touch me. He just sits there, beside me, the only warmth in this cold, dead cave.

I look up when I feel a cool breeze on my skin, making goose bumps race along my arms.

"There are ventilation shafts," Jack says, pointing up. I follow his finger, but see only darkness. I feel like I've lived in this darkness for so long that I will be blinded by sunlight.

"She's really gone, isn't she?" I say softly, staring at a glint of a copper ring around the finger of one of the skeletons resting in the wall across from me. It reminds me of the rose-gold ring my mother wears. I try to remember if the doppelganger of Mom had her ring, if that's one more piece of her lost.

It takes Jack a moment to realize what I mean. "Your mother?" he asks.

I nod my head. "And Akilah."

"I think so." We both know that Akilah's body was gone—we both saw it destroyed. But I had hoped that there was *something* left, something that was my friend. Something left of my mother beyond the metal skull and sparking electrical wires.

"How?" I ask simply.

Jack stares blankly ahead. "I'm not sure. At the Lunar Base, when a soldier died—and it happened far more than the news lets on, there are a lot of 'accidents' during training missions, and skirmishes from Secessionary States. Anyway, if a soldier died, he'd be replaced fairly quickly with a doppelganger. It didn't take long for me to figure out something was wrong. All the soldiers in the Lunar Base were young—some of them younger even than the military should allow, mostly from the Foqra District, or other poor areas. There weren't a lot of soldiers, but as soon as one was killed or seriously wounded, the replacement... it looked just like the person, knew the person's memories, but..."

"They weren't the same." I'm not speaking about the soldiers.

"No. None of them were ever the same."

We're silent for a long time after this.

"Is that what happened to my mother?" I ask in a very soft voice. "Did she die? Was she replaced with... that?"

"I'm not sure," Jack says again.

And then, because I can't help myself, I say, "Is that what happened to me? Is that why I can't remember you?"

Jack doesn't answer.

The corpses around us wait for us to speak again.

"Here's what I know," Jack says finally, his low voice a rumble among the bones. "All the ones who died and came back—they were fundamentally different. Some memories were there, most weren't. They were *extremely* patriotic. They were blindly obedient to superiors. They had no emotional attachments—to anyone. They weren't themselves."

Jack turns, looking me in the eyes. "But you're still you, Ella," he tells me, sincerity ringing in his voice. "You're just missing one piece."

"You."

"But everything else is there. Your memories of me didn't define who you were. Who you are. You're still you, whole and complete, and everything that made you *you* is still there."

And I wonder if he means, *everything that made me love you is still there*. But those are words that cannot be spoken, not here, not now, not by this version of me that doesn't know that version of him.

"Am I human?" I ask, my eyes drifting to Jack's bag, and the nanobot analyzer that told him how much of me is microscopic robots. This is not a fear I have quite been able to voice yet, but it is the deepest terror within me. I grew up in a world where things can look human but aren't, but I have never once questioned my own humanity. It was just so clear that androids weren't anything more than dressed-up robots. But seeing Akilah and the doppelganger for Mom, seeing my own super-human abilities... I'm questioning everything, starting with myself.

"You're *you*," Jack says, but I notice that this doesn't really answer my question.

FORTY-NINE

JACK STANDS, THEN OFFERS ME A HAND to pull me up. "Ready to go?"

I stare around at the skeletons littering the catacombs. "Is this what you meant?" I ask. "When you told Julie we were going to sleep? You always meant to come this way?"

Jack stares at me, his face flickering in shadow from the flashlight. "Yes," he says. "And now it's time for us to stay awake."

"Where's that?"

Jack tries to smile. "You'll see."

"And you told Julie and Xavier to take Akilah and go to war..."

Jack heads toward the far side of the catacombs, and another set of stairs. "There's an old World War II bunker on Gozo—the tunnel cuts back around, and they can get there and then to a safe house."

I follow him up a set of stairs—old, but more modern than the ones in the secret tunnel. A wooden handrail used to exist, but it's nothing more than rotting splinters now.

"Why did you separate us?" I ask.

"What?" Jack calls back down.

I speak up. "Why did we have to split up?"

Jack pauses for a moment, but doesn't turn around. "I wasn't sure it was safe."

"I don't care if it was dangerous—I could have gone with Akilah. Even if she's… different… I'd rather be with her than not."

Jack still doesn't turn to face me when he says, "I thought it wouldn't be safe for them."

I stumble on the steps. My nanobot count, the tracker bots that were inside of me, my inhuman abilities… I don't know if I can't be trusted because of what I am or because he doubts what side I'm on, but at the end of the day—I'm a liability.

Jack opens a door at the top of the stairs, kicking against it when it sticks. We step out into the cool night air. I drink in the fresh air, filling my lungs until they ache and sighing the air out in one long whoosh.

Stars twinkle overhead, barely visible. I can see the lights of the city of Mdina nearby, so bright that they wash out the sky. We're in Rabat, and while we've just emerged into a fairly large town, no one notices us. People keep to themselves here. I lived in Rabat with Mom and Dad before Mom developed the technology for the Reverie Mental Spa, and we had a small house with ivy and dusty limestone walls. This part of Rabat, however, is desolate. A few children race by, one on a bicycle, lugging a heavy cart behind him. Although they're young, these children are working, not playing, and the curve of their backs and the cracks in their hands imply that they're already far older than their ages allow.

In the distance, I can see the outline of St. Paul's Cathedral, the namesake of the catacombs. Its roof is caved in, the sign is broken, the big door in the front is missing, exposing a shadowy, bare inside.

The UC never banned religion, not like some of the Secessionary States did. It just engendered apathy. Rather than actively discouraging people to drop their religion, the government simply ignored it. Holidays were changed from religious memorials to festas and parties. Tax exemptions were eliminated; no special allowances were given to any religion. When a religious statue was damaged or broken, it wasn't repaired—it was replaced with something different, something neutral.

It wasn't that the government made the people give up church; it's that the people simply forgot to care. When Mom was first diagnosed with Hebb's Disease, I caught her praying. I guess it's only natural to pray at a time like that. But we both were embarrassed, as if I'd seen her naked, and I've never known her to pray since.

There are still a few cathedrals and churches scattered across Malta—St. John's always has a big charity drive for the Foqra District every year—but for the most part, people don't bother. I've never really cared about religion one way or another—neither of my parents were deeply religious, although Akilah's family was—but seeing the hollow remains of St. Paul's Cathedral, especially after stepping out of the catacombs filled with its own remains, makes me a little sad.

It feels as if everything in my life is nothing but rotting bones.

Jack takes me a few blocks away from the catacombs, and he accesses a street-level garage with a retina scan. The locks to the metal door slide open, and a few minutes later he emerges with an antique black electric-model all-terrain Vespa with gold trim. It's beat-up and old, but when he starts the engine, the thing is silent, and the tires look new. It looks inconspicuous, old, and worthless, but the bike is probably powerful enough to scale a mountain on.

Jack swings a leg over the seat and scoots forward, making room for me. "I don't get my own?" I say.

"There's only one, love."

"Then let me drive," I say. "And don't call me love."

Jack moves back in the seat, but just before I clamber on, he adds, "Of course, you *do* know where we're going, right?"

I growl and climb onto the Vespa behind him. I don't put my arms around his waist, instead opting to hold onto the fender behind me. Jack glances back at me, shrugs, and the scooter purrs to life, lurching forward and bouncing over the pot-hole-ridden street in front of the garage as the doors close automatically behind me.

I'm so turned around that I'm not sure where we're going, other than away from civilization. Jack avoids all the bigger towns and cities on the way. Mdina fades into the background, although the bright lights of New Venice— including the sparkling tips of Triumph Towers—are still visible to the northwest.

When Jack veers off the road and into the rocky terrain of a warehouse packing district, I grab his waist to avoid falling off the back, clinging to him as we bounce painfully over the streets that were probably never properly paved. Jack drops one hand on top of mine, holding me against him, and I start to pull away, but decide against it. It's warm, next to him, and it makes me feel safe.

After a while, I realize where we're going. The land is more and more deserted, not even factories venturing this far north and east. Hollow remains of buildings stare blankly at us as Jack risks the bumpy streets again. The roads were once well-travelled and popular, but hardly anything of that time remains.

We're heading into the former war zone.

The Secessionary War was hard on every country involved. There is a mark in every land. In Malta, our biggest scar is the former capital, Valetta.

Jack stops before we reach the ruined remains of the city. He pulls up to a twisted iron gate that blocks a series of broken stone steps. A blue-and-white tiled sign speckled with age announced that we're at **SENGLEA**.

Underneath the city is a phrase written in Latin: *Città Invicta.*

Jack sees my gaze. "It means, 'the unconquerable city.'"

What a joke. Every city falls.

I jump off the Vespa, rubbing my sore butt as Jack uses an old-fashioned key on a metal lock at the top of the stairs, and the gate swings open. The dim night sky is full of more stars than I have ever seen. I push past Jack, my eyes to the heavens, and step forward onto a plaza made of smooth, pale bricks, many of which are cracked or missing. A low wall made of similar bricks lines the side of the plaza, and I rush to it, breathing in the heady scents of saltwater as I gaze up.

Above us, the moon is a sliver, nothing more than a tiny scratch of white in the sky. The constellations stretch out far over the sea, and the waters glitter beneath them.

"It's beautiful," I breathe. I never see the stars in New Venice.

I turn to look at Jack. But he's not looking at the sky. He's looking at the water. He's looking at the hole in the world, an entire city leveled and filled in with the sea.

"That's where Valetta used to be," I say, even though we both know. The once great city, the former capital of our entire nation. Nothing but a sunken circle of black water. All that remains of the city—all the remains of the hundreds of thousands of people who used to live in the city—is under the sea.

I look around me with fresh eyes, eyes that are aware of where we are. There are bricked-in olive trees arching over us, a sort of memorial made of stone balls in the center—but past the garden I can see the relics of old buildings, the crumbling foundations of a church, a clock tower that was knocked sideways in the force of the blast that destroyed Valetta.

"When the capital was bombed during the Secessionary War," Jack says somberly, "Everyone there died immediately. It completely wiped out the whole city. But some of the cities nearby, like this one... some of the buildings survived. Most of the people didn't, not if they didn't make it to a shelter."

I feel dangerous just standing here, overlooking the remains of a city long-dead. The bomb was a solar-flare; the radiation poison might make a person sick, but it rarely killed, not like nuclear bombs of the past. Still, I feel as if we shouldn't be here, a wrongness that reminds me of my reaction to the catacombs.

And then I recall what PA Young told me, about how she was in Valetta just before the bomb, with my parents and Ms. White. I imagine what it must have been like as they huddled in a bomb shelter for protection. The terror, the horror. Ms. White, nearly bleeding to death after her arm was lost in the blast. My parents, not even married yet, unsure of if they would survive. And Hwa Young, the woman who would one day rule the entire UC, crouched in a shelter, listening to the sounds of a hundred thousand people dying.

Maybe if I'd been there, I would understand why she is willing to turn people into soulless shells in order to avoid such violence again.

Jack and I lean over the wall at the top of the garden in Senglea, looking across the Grand Harbour at where Valetta once stood. Jack makes a sort of growling angry noise, and turns his back on the emptiness that was once the capital, staring instead at the scattered remains of the city we're in, destroyed not by the bomb, but by the blowback and tsunami that followed it. "It's worse, I think," he says in a low, almost inaudible voice, "to leave something more than a gaping hole."

FIFTY

JACK WALKS UNDER THE WIND-SWEPT olive trees toward a tower built into the wall at the very edge of the city. We're high up overlooking the harbor, and I'm momentarily filled with vertigo as I watch Jack jump over the pavement broken by tree roots and age, nothing more than a twisted, rusted iron railing protecting him from the deadly drop over the side of the walled city.

A small tower is built into the wall, no more than the size of my closet. Neat, rectangular windows are cut directly into the stone bricks that make the hexagonal room, capped with a pointed dome roof that ends on a geometric sort of a design that I can't quite fully see in the dark. Over top each of the windows of the tower is an additional carving, alternating between a giant ear and an enormous eye. A bird, its long neck craning down, is carved into the stone.

Jack notices me staring. "This used to be a watch tower, like a thousand years ago. The eyes and ears represented how the guards of the city were always watching and listening."

We were asleep—among the closed-eyes of the dead

in the catacombs—now we're awake. Jack's code finally makes sense.

As Jack approaches the tower, the stone bird over the door comes to life. Jack stands still, his eyes wide, as the bird's head moves up and down. The bird snaps back into place, every appearance of stone. The eyes and ears carved into the tower flash once, bright red, and then they, too, fade back into stone.

"I don't think that's from a thousand years ago," I say, staring at the stone bird, the electronics inside it now invisible.

Jack snorts with unamused laughter. "The Zunzana may have done a few updates. It's a bug-out tower now, for if one of us has to go on the run."

I step inside the small room under the stone roof. The windows are open, as is the door. It's small, but there's plenty of room for both of us standing.

Jack works quickly, first typing a code into his cuff, then touching a hidden panel under the lip of the stone wall. Silvery material drops like curtains around the building.

"Anti-tech cloth?" I ask, touching the slick material.

"It's the closest thing we have to an invisibility cloak," he says. He nods toward the door. "Go look."

I step outside the tower room and look back at it. The anti-tech cloth lines the inside, keeping any geo-locators or nanobots out. Meanwhile, the outer shell of the curtains is made of a thin, malleable screen that projects the image of an empty tower. When I'm right next to the curtains, I can tell that they're hiding the tower, but even from a few steps back, it looks as if the tower is empty, all signs of Jack gone.

When I step back inside, there's barely room for me to stand. Jack has opened a hidden compartment in the floor and withdrawn two instabeds. He pops open the packages, and two foam mattresses spring to life.

I lean so far against the window that I'm practically hanging out it, my shoulders against the anti-tech cloth. The instabeds are narrow and thin, much like this tower room. When Jack lays them down, they're side-by-side. It's more like one large bed than two small ones. I can't take my eyes off the nonexistent space between the mattresses.

Jack looks up and notices my nervous face. "I don't bite, love."

I whip around. "I told you to quit calling me that." Jack opens his mouth to speak, but I don't let him. "I don't care what kind of person I am in your memory. Because I'm not that person *now*."

Jack looks as if I've smacked him across the face. He turns silently back to the beds, pushing them as far apart as possible. My heart is racing; I feel like I've run a marathon.

I snatch the second thin pillow and metallic blanket from his hands, spreading them out over my foam mattress, and then lay down as far away from Jack as possible, my body scrunched against the angled stone wall.

Part of me feels stupid. But part of me feels scared. I don't know who I am anymore, and I don't like the way Jack seems to know me in a way I don't know myself. I don't pretend to understand the situation. Jack has memories of me—*a blue-and-brown damask bed cover, a night together, kisses that stop the whole world.*

But... *I* don't have those memories.

"I'm sorry."

I peek over my shoulder; Jack has his back to me and spoke the words to the wall.

"I forget," he says, still without turning. "You—I forget you're not my Ella anymore."

"I'm not," I say softly. I don't know what I used to be, I only know what I am now.

"I know."

The night is silent. Although I am not touching Jack at all, I'm deeply aware of his presence, just a few inches from me.

"You don't know what it's like," he says finally, his voice so low I can barely hear it. "To have loved you the way I loved you, and for you to not even remember who I am."

I roll over, facing the center of the tower, and, after a moment, Jack shifts too. He watches me intently, his face cast in darkness, his eyes unreadable.

"I'm sorry," I whisper. The words feel feeble and useless, but they're all either of us has.

We both turn away from each other, and we let the night encase us.

FIFTY-ONE

I WAKE UP IN HIS ARMS.

For one brief moment, I panic. This isn't my bed, my home. I freeze, and my brain whirls into motion.

It's barely dawn. I can't see the sun, just that everything's a little brighter, a little less midnight blue and more orange-gold. I'm tangled up in two blankets, mine and his, and Jack's barely covered at all. His arms are around me, one under my head, the other thrown over my body. His face is centimeters from mine.

This is a comfortable position. It is one, I realize, that we must have practiced. My body knows how to meld against his.

I stare at his face as the world grows lighter. His eyelids twitch, clinging to a dream. His mouth murmurs, and even though I cannot hear the sound, the shape his lips form is my name.

How does he know me? I want to reach into his mind and know not simply what he knows of me, but how. I want to see myself through his eyes; I want to know the Ella he cannot forget.

I close my eyes and try to think of that year Jack and I supposedly spent together. I remember that year… trips to the doctor's with Mom, trying to hold everything together. Giving up on dreams of going to university, losing Akilah. I don't remember much of that year; it was not a year I wanted to remember.

And Jack wasn't in it.

Except… he was. His memories of that year are different from mine, but they both seem real.

It doesn't make sense. Either someone added me to his past, or took him from mine.

When I open my eyes, Jack's are open too. I watch as his pupils focus on me, the corners of his lips tilting up. "Good morning," he says warmly.

And I try to remember if this happened before, because this is a memory I would want to keep.

But there is no echo of it in my mind.

FIFTY-TWO

I SIT UP SUDDENLY, EMBARRASSED BY how close I was to Jack. He seems to realize the awkwardness of the situation, because he doesn't say anything as he packs away the beds. He uses his burner cuff to contact Julie and Xavier, who spent the night hiding in the old bunker from World War II, then moved to a hidden house where there are apparently medical facilities to examine Akilah.

"The tunnels are entirely compromised," Jack says after he turns off his cuff. "UC officials were seen near the catacombs, too. I have a boat coming to pick us up here, but we're going to have to be careful. The UC knows too much." He looks around at the small tower that was our home last night. "There are other safe houses we can hide in."

"Hide?" I say.

"What do you want to do?" Jack says. "Launch a full-scale attack on the UC? Because I'm all for that, except I'll have to find some more weapons somewhere. A missile launcher would be nice."

I honestly can't tell if he's being sincere or not. "No," I say, just in case.

Jack shrugs and returns to his work, making sure we leave no trace behind at the tower. But... I don't want to hide. I want to go home.

Home... an empty apartment with the remnants of a mother I didn't know.

"Ms. White!" I gasp.

Jack jerks his head around to me.

"She doesn't know Mom was a whatever! She'll just go into work today—and there won't be anyone there, and she won't know what happened, and—"

"Not just that," Jack adds darkly, "If the UC wants you that badly, they might threaten her."

They already did something to my mother—maybe even killed her when they made that thing that looked and sounded so much like her. They could do that to Ms. White, too...

I have to save her—I have to save her, and Mom, and Akilah. And I have to stop whatever PA Young's doing. I'm not sure why she wants me so much. It has to do with the fact that I could go into other people's reveries. Maybe she wants to turn me into her perfect spy. Maybe there's something else that reveries can do, something I've not yet discovered, but PA Young wants me to exploit. Whatever it is, it's clear that PA Young will stop at nothing to get to me, and will hurt everyone I love in the wake of her cruel disaster.

Jack sits on the floor of the tower and motions for me to join him. Using the projector built into his cuff, Jack logs onto the security feed outside of Reverie Mental Spa.

"How are you doing that?" I ask wonderingly. This vid feed is from the light pole across from the spa, one of countless feeds controlled by the government.

Jack shrugs as if hacking into UC-controlled security feeds are nothing and zooms in on the front door of Reverie Mental Spa. The building is still dark. Through the big glass windows, behind the front desk, I can see that Ms. White's office door is still closed and locked.

"She should be there by now," I mutter, worry rising in my throat.

"Do you know where she lives?" Jack asks.

I give him the address quickly, and Jack gets to work. His fingers slide over the projected keyboard from his cuff, and he mumbles to himself as he works on this new hack. Within moments, though, he shows a house in the suburbs of New Venice, nearer to Mellieha than to the main city. It's a crowded street filled with row houses that all look nearly identical: dusty limestone, traditional terraces, cut-out windows.

One door on the street hangs open, the bright blue wood swinging over the stone steps of the stoop.

"That's the one," I say, pointing at the screen.

As we watch, a man in military-grade black leans over the steps and slams the door shut.

I recoil as if I'd been hit. My body vibrates, a long, skin-crawling *buzz* that rattles my bones and electrifies my flesh.

Someone from the military just shut Ms. White's open door.

Jack meets my eyes.

Don't say it, don't say it, don't say it, I think over and over again in my head.

"They have her now, too," he says.

Somehow, Jack secures the tower, making it look like nothing more than a dusty relic once more. We walk for a long time, making our way to the coast, then meet up with someone in a boat. No one talks as this stranger, this friend to the Zunzana, blends in with the fishing boats and circles around the island to a small, hidden dock leading to an isolated house in Gozo.

"This is a safe place," Jack says after he pays the man who took us here. "But maybe you should stay inside and hidden until we know more."

Julie and Xavier see us as we approach and throw open the door, embracing Jack happily. It feels weird to me to be so removed from this happy reunion of friends. I notice the cuts and bruises on their faces and bodies—not only from the fight and destruction yesterday, but also from transporting Akilah.

Jack leads Julie and Xavier to another room so they can discuss plans, but he leaves me in the kitchen first. They have a kitchen android that offers to make me a meal, but even though my stomach growls, I refuse. There's a bitter taste in my mouth that I can't escape.

I wander the house. It's surprisingly large—bedrooms on the top floor; a large kitchen, dining area, and office on the ground floor. Behind one door, I can hear the low rumble of voices as Jack discusses options with Julie and Xavier.

Ha. Options. What options do we have? We have nowhere to go. There's nothing we can do—just four teenagers against a global government with the power to replace people with doppelgangers?

Nothing.

There's one more door, made of rough-hewn wood. A cold breeze flows under the door, and I'm not surprised to find steps when I push it open. I descend into the basement, my fingers on the stone wall. This area, like the tunnels we were in yesterday, is cut directly from the stone foundation of the island.

The bottom of the stairs is a cluttered, cobwebbed mess, but there's a clear path in the grimy floor—footprints and scuffmarks. I follow it a few steps to another door. This one is covered with wood, but I suspect it's made of steel. A keypad is lodged in place by it—this is the panic room nearly every house in Malta has since the Secessionary War.

THE BODY ELECTRIC

It's not locked, though. I push it open with both hands pressed against the heavy door.

Light spills out of the room, momentarily blinding me. This room, unlike the dirty, cluttered basement, is sterile and bright, lined with steel and fluorescent lights. It reminds me a bit of my mother's room at our apartment— it, too, is made from a panic room, and it, too, is cluttered with the accoutrements of a hospital. I'm reminded of how Xavier was a med student—that desk cluttered with documents and diagrams must belong to him. The cabinets over it are well-stocked with first aid and emergency supplies, but I'm not focused on them.

In the center of the room is metal gurney, a long, chrome slab on wheels.

And strapped to the top of it is Akilah.

FIFTY-THREE

I TOUCH AKILAH'S HAND, COVERED BY tech foil restraints. Her body is warm; she looks peaceful, asleep. At my touch, her body twitches.

"Wake up," I whisper. And then, louder, "Wake up."

The back of my tongue aches, and my eyes burn with unshed tears. The irony is not lost on me; the echoes of those same words reverberate in my mind from the dreams of my father.

My cheek touches Akilah's as I draw closer, whispering directly into her ear. "Wake up."

I feel movement.

My body snaps back, instantly wary.

Akilah's eyes are open, staring at me. For a moment, I see nothing but rage and murder. And then she blinks. Her face grows softer.

"Ella?" she whispers.

"Akilah!" I throw myself on her restrained body, hugging her. "Is it really you?" I ask.

"What's happening?" Akilah tries to move her arms and legs, but can't.

My mind goes blank. How much do I tell her? If she's just waking up from this weird nightmare, what words do I use to tell her that the true nightmare is just beginning?

"How much do you remember?" I ask gently.

"I—I was at the lunar base." Akilah looks around, her eyes rolling as she strains to see more. "Am I in the infirmary?"

"No," I say softly.

Akilah's quiet for a moment. "No, I didn't think so." Her eyes seek mine. "But I remember... there was a skirmish. Some Secessionary Rebels attacked. There was— they said, when I was assigned military for my service year, they said there was no violence, that there had been no fighting since the war. But they lied. There was fighting all the time—just on the edges, where most of society didn't see it."

I squeeze her fingertips.

"Why am I bound?" Akilah asks.

"What else do you remember?"

She shuts her eyes. "I think I was hurt," she says. "I remember pain."

Her eyes open. "Is that why I can't move? Am I hurt? Did they send me back to Earth? Or are we still on the moon? How did you get here?"

I open my mouth still unsure of the answers.

And then Akilah says, "I want my mom." The words are almost whispered, but there is such emotion in them, such desperate longing.

"Oh, Aks," I say.

She meets my eyes, piercing me with my gaze. "Am I hurt? Is that why I can't move?" she asks.

I shake my head.

"Then why?"

"It's..." My voice trails off. "I mean, you were hurt. In a way. It's hard to explain."

"Please, Ella, please. *Please*. Help me. I want to get up."

My grip on her fingers slide away. "I can't, I'm sorry, I can't."

"*Please*."

I take a step back, still shaking my head. Tears spring into my eyes.

"Ella." My name is aching longing.

I lean in closer. I stare straight into her eyes. *Eyes are the windows to the soul*, that's what Dad always said.

And her eyes are lens. I see the false pupils dilate and focus, I see the too-gleaming glassiness across the tops. There is a light inside these eyes, but it is not her soul, it is manufactured from a bulb.

I feel the exact moment when I accept that this thing before me is not my friend, and I see the exact moment when she realizes it.

Her body bucks wildly, thrashing against the metal gurney, straining on the tech foil restraints. A stream of vicious curses follow me as I scramble away from her.

"I *will* get free, and I *will* rip your head from your body!" she screams, slamming her head back against the gurney so hard that she dents the metal. Her jerking motions are enough to make the gurney move, scratching against the tile floor.

There is nothing of my friend in this thing. All that before—the softly spoken words, the confusion—it was all a ploy to try to trick me into releasing her.

Xavier bursts into the room, snatching up a bottle from the table and sending a cloud of pale green mist at Akilah's face. It seems to calm her—or at least slow her—long enough to him to jab an IV needle in her arm. Soon, her body is motionless.

"I keep having to increase the sedatives," he says in his low, gravelly voice. "The nanobots in her system are smart and adaptive. Soon, we won't be able to keep her unconscious."

I look at him with hope in my eyes, but he shakes his head. "She won't wake up, Ella, not really, not ever."

We both know what he means: even if her eyes open, even if she's conscious, she won't be in control of herself.

"If she wakes up and we can't contain her," he says wearily, "we'll have to…"

"Don't say it," I snap.

Xavier nods, acquiescing. But he adds, "We will, though."

We'll have to kill her. Before she kills us.

"We should do it now," Julie says. I hadn't noticed her—she's leaning against the doorframe. Jack's behind her, scowling. "It's dangerous," she adds when we don't respond. "She'll bring the government here."

"Her geo-locators are dampened," Xavier says.

Julie rolls her eyes. "The government has the best hackers. They could override our systems at any time, and be here before we have time to piss ourselves."

My eyes dart fearfully from Julie to Xavier. I don't know if I could stop them if they tried to kill Akilah.

I don't know if I should.

"We're not going to kill her." Jack's voice is low and gravelly. He scowls at us. I remember then that she was his friend, too.

FIFTY-FOUR

AN ANDROID SERVES US LUNCH. I STARE at it as it places sandwiches in front of us, wondering what the android does when no one is here. This is a safe house, used only in emergencies, a throw-back to the days when the Zunzana had power. When Jack, Julie, and Xavier are somewhere else, does the android just shut itself up in the charging closet and wait? Or does it piddle around the house, keeping everything tidy, just in case?

I stare at the sandwich—sliced meat and lettuce between two slices of hard bread—as Julie argues that we should keep moving.

"If you won't kill that thing downstairs"—Akilah, she means Akilah—"Then we should at least leave it and hide somewhere else."

My eyes shoot to Jack, and I know he's thinking the same thing I am.

Xavier puts down his sandwich, watching us all silently as the tension builds in the room.

"We've been hiding since we came back from the lunar base," Jack says. "I'm ready to fight."

"Fight what?!" Julie slams her back against her chair. "The 'government?' That's too nebulous; we can't fight something without a face."

I shut my eyes, trying to think as Julie and Jack argue. I don't know what I am. I'm not an android like the one who served us this morning. But I'm not human—at least, not entirely. Something happened to me, something changed me. My body is different—and my mind. The hallucinations, the fear. It's all turning me into something I'm not. And, somehow, Jack's wrapped up in this, and Dad, and Mom. Something made me forget Jack. Someone.

What does the government want? PA Young has tried everything—manipulation, hacking, violence—to discover some aspect of my parents' research. Some part of Dad's nanobot and android technology, some element of Mom's reverie chairs. Something—something—in all of that is the key for whatever it is PA Young wants to do.

"I need to go back to the Reverie Mental Spa," I say. My soft words cut through the angry yelling from Julie and Jack, and they both turn to me, eyes wide.

"No. No way. That's the *last* place you need to go." Jack glares at me.

"I know," I say. "But I need to go into a reverie. If I could think about this while I was in a reverie, I could make sense out of it." I've spent far too long exploring other people's minds in reveries. It's time I explored my own.

"You can't go back to Reverie." Jack says this as if it's a command. My back stiffens. Sensing my disagreement, Jack quickly adds, "But I know where there's another reverie chamber you can use." I quirk up an eyebrow, waiting for him to continue. "At your father's old lab."

"The one that blew up?"

Jack shakes his head. "Only one room was damaged. The laboratory facilities are huge, built underneath Triumph Towers."

I roll my eyes. "Oh, because it's going to be a lot simpler to break into the *world's most secure building* than to sneak into my own home."

"They expect you to go back home," Julie says.

"But they'll never expect us to break into the labs at Triumph Towers," Jack counters.

"Because that's *insane*." Julie leans over the table toward me, a glint in her eye that I'm not sure is disbelief or approval.

"We need someone on the inside..." Jack mutters. "We need someone in the UC, or at least in the labs, that can get us in. That would be the simplest way."

Xavier shakes his head. "Julie reached out to some contacts, but we're having trouble finding anyone who'll help us."

Jack frowns. "But what about—"

"The android attack was effective."

Xavier explains. While the exploding androids seemed random and many innocent civilians were killed, most of the androids that exploded were not random at all. It wasn't just Representative Belles who was affected. There were others. Contacts that had remained loyal to the Zunzana were either killed or directly affected by the android attack. Friendlies who are scared aren't friendly any more. Everywhere Julie and Xavier went, all they got were warnings and closed doors.

When he quits talking, silence envelops us. It's hard for me to understand the power that PA Young has, and how effective it is. This is all another form of manipulation. Separate us, make us believe we're alone, and what else can we do but give up?

A sunbeam trails between the curtains of the window, all orange and green from the trees outside.

"I think I might have the connection we need," I say.

Julie delivers the message for me while Jack and I make our way as inconspicuously as possible back into the heart of New Venice. When we reach Central Gardens, we go straight to the groveyard, to Dad's grave.

And then we wait.

It's not long before Representative Belles shows up.

"It worked," Jack mutters. "I can't believe that actually worked."

"Jack?" Representative Belles says, anger in his voice. "I told you never to contact me again; your organization is too risky." I leap up, noticing that the representative's hand is already on his cuff, poised to call for aid. Then his eyes fall on me. "Ella Shepherd," he says, his voice low. "They say you were kidnapped. There's a reward for you."

"I think we both know I wasn't kidnapped," I say flatly. "Just like we both know the death of your wife and daughter was no accident."

"I didn't even do anything," Representative Belles says in a low, emotionless voice. "All I did was *think* about opposing the PA, and she had them killed. *Make an example of me*, that's what she said." His eyes meet mine, and they are empty, like the hole in the world where Valetta once stood. "I still have Marcos, though," the representative says, referring to his son. "And I can't risk him, too. Don't contact me again."

He turns on his heels, practically running in an effort to distance himself from us.

"She killed half your family!" Jack calls out, and the representative pauses. "Don't you want revenge?"

Representative Belles turns, his eyes blazing. "*No,*" he says vehemently. "I just want to save the only family I have left." A wild look passes over his face as his eyes dart left and right. I'm glad I picked the groveyard as the meeting spot; there's no one here to disturb us and raise his suspicions further. "Have you seen what they do in the labs?" He continues in a lower voice. "How they can control anything... anyone...?" His eyes lose focus, then his head whips around to me. "I still have my son. I'm not taking any risks. Leave me alone. Don't contact me."

Jack lunges forward, trying to grab the representative, but he whirls out of his grip. Without thinking, I shout, "Do you know how my dad died?" The words twist out of me, bursting violently from my lips.

Both the men freeze and turn to me.

"Your dad?" Representative Belles says. For the first time, I recognize his Spanish accent, so heavy in his reveries but nearly gone in real life.

I point to the holly tree. "My father, Philip Shepherd."

The representative and Jack both stare at me, waiting for me to continue.

"They killed him," I say, and as I speak the words, I realize for the first time that my beliefs have shifted. Faceless terrorists didn't kill my father. Prime Administrator Hwa Young did, just as she killed Jack's parents, and the representative's family. Just as she has killed every single person who has ever stood in her way.

"He objected to what the government was doing with his research—research so top secret that we don't even know *what*, exactly, was happening. Just that... it hurt people."

I take a few steps closer to the representative. He no longer looks as if he will run away. He is frozen in his fear.

"I saw him die," I say, my eyes never leaving the representative's. "I saw the bomb tear him apart. But I'm still going to fight the PA. Because he can't, not any more." I struggle to recall what the representative's grandfather told him in his last reverie, but the words I speak ring with my own truth. "I fight for him. I fight for my family. Because family is never really gone."

Something inside the representative breaks. He doesn't move, but there's something in his eyes, something that gives me hope.

"I can't join the Zunzana," he says, his voice pleading. "It's too dangerous. The PA knows everyone who joins, and they... they disappear."

"I know," Jack growls.

"We don't need you to join us," I say. "But can you get us into the labs? The labs where my father worked?" As soon as I say the words, I know they were the right ones. My eyes dip down to Dad's memorial plaque. Truth doesn't lie in the heart of fortune... it's under Triumph Towers, where the labs are.

FIFTY-FIVE

AN ANDROID DELIVERS A MESSAGE TO the safe house that night.

"He was scared," Jack growls, looking down at the envelope in his hands. "He might try to rabbit."

I shake my head as I open the envelope. Two identification badges spill out—one for me, one for Jack. Two cuffLINKS drop out next, followed by two fingerprint pads. I press my finger against the skin-colored slip of silicone and it sticks to me, giving me a new, fake fingerprint.

I examine the cuffLINKs. These are fancy, more advanced than any of the ones I'd had before. Representative Belles said that all the labs are marked with tap-touch locks, something Jack confirmed from his time in the labs. To get in, we have to tap approved cuffs against the locks, then touch the fingerprint scanner by the lock. At any point, the plan may fail. Someone could notice the fingerprint pads, or the cuffs may malfunction. And we'll already look suspicious enough, two teenagers entering the labs at dark.

Still—I'm hopeful it'll work. Representative Belles could have reported us—or even just me. But he didn't. He thinks this will work.

"We go in tonight," Jack says. "The sooner we get to the labs, the better."

Part of me wants to wait, plan everything, slow down. But he's right. We need to go in now, while we still can.

Jack looks at me. "Do you really *need* a reverie?" he asks. "This seems like... it's a ridiculous amount of risk, just to plug you into a reverie machine. It'd be quicker to go in, find what we can at the labs, and leave."

I bite my lip. It's more than that. For the first time in a long time, I feel like what I'm doing is *right*. I guess it's a gut feeling; but I've never had one so strong. It reminds me of how I felt when I followed Dad in the map program that led me to Jack. And, well... he led me to where I needed to be.

And besides— "In all my past reveries, I've seen Dad," I say. In the hallucinations, too. Jack's full attention is on me. I think about the last reverie with Representative Belles, the one that threatened to engulf me. "He's trying to tell me something."

"Ella... he's dead." I hate the blunt way he says the truth.

"I forgot you, didn't I?" I snap at him. "Isn't it possible that I've also forgotten something Dad told me?"

Jack frowns.

Ella, wake up. I thought he meant that I had to wake

up from the reveries I was in, but what if Dad needed me to wake up from the idyllic life I'd been living? What if he needed me to break through the lost memories?

"I'm sure—I *know*—if I can just get one more reverie, now that I've learned so much, I can figure out what he needs me to know. Dreamscapes are confusing; there's a lot to sort through in a person's mind. But I have something to focus on now." When Jack hesitates, I snatch up one of the burner cuffLINKs Representative Belles sent over and snap it on my wrist. "I'll go by myself if I have to."

"I'm definitely coming too," Jack says immediately, grabbing the other cuff.

"It's honestly more dangerous for you," I say. "If I get caught, I'm valuable. They want to use me... for something. But if you get caught..."

The Prime Administrator has a way of making people she dislikes disappear.

"You're right," Jack says. "I think there's more to the labs. Your father's work was obviously important to the UC. You get your reverie; I'm going to try to access his data files. If we can figure out just what the government *wants*, then we have a chance of preventing them from getting it."

"Tonight," I say.

Jack nods. "Tonight."

Jack gets us janitorial uniforms. He also has a pair of lab coats folded up into small squares and stuffed in the waistband of our pants, hidden by the too-large, button-up work shirts. The first goal is to get in without raising suspicion; the second is to blend into the labs so it looks like we belong.

The entrance to the lab is through the main tower—the one were the Prime Administrator works. We fall in line with a group of custodial workers, and a security guard by the door scrutinizes our ID badges. We have to tap our cuffs against a scanner before we can board the lift. Jack goes first. He keeps his sleeve pulled down over his arm as much as possible. My breath catches when the scanner processes his information, but then it beeps and flashes green. He gets on the lift.

A few more people go by, then I approach the scanner. I tap my cuff against it, and look up just as Jack's lift doors close. He opens his mouth—but he can't say anything. He can't call attention to himself. The lift descends, taking Jack away from me.

"Go on," one of the workers behind me after the scanner light flashes green. I file through the doors and rush into the waiting lift. Twelve more people scan in and get on the lift before the doors close. It's an excruciatingly long time. Jack can't just wait for me at the bottom. He's probably already in the lab now.

Unless he's already been caught.

The lift jerks to a start and begins to descend. There are no buttons—this lift is specific to the laboratories, and works automatically. The lift jerks to a start and begins to descend. My ears pop, and I start to count the seconds it takes for us to fall. Ten seconds... fifteen... twenty... thirty... a full minute passes, and we're still falling. Just how far beneath the Earth are the labs?

Far enough for an explosion to happen, one big enough to kill my father and four other people, and not disrupt the daily operations of Triumph Towers.

But the lift couldn't possibly descend so far—New Venice is built on a bridge. There's nowhere for the lift to go. And then I realize where the labs *really* are. This lift must go through one of the pillars that supports the bridge. We're not just below Triumph Towers—we're below New Venice. We're below the *sea.* This lab was built so far underground that it's beneath the waters of the Mediterranean.

The doors slide open with a soft whoosh, and the workers in front of me file off the lift. A guard stands by the doors, examining every badge. I look down, making sure my badge shows, and try not to make eye contact or call attention to myself.

Giant steel doors stand opposite the lifts. Everyone must go in one at a time, after scanning the cuffLINK and fingerprint scanner. I shove my hand in my pocket, working the fingerprint pads on my fingers as I try to will myself invisible in the crowd of workers, hoping and praying the guard doesn't notice me.

One-by-one, the workers tap the scanner and press their finger against the touchpad. The doors beep, the person enters, the next moves forward and taps and touches.

The guard shifts behind me, cocking his head, listening to the earclip in his left ear. His eyes scan the remaining workers in front of me. I shuffle forward. The guard's eyes rest on me. The person in front of me steps through the giant steel doors. The guard's gaze intensifies, and he steps toward.

Tap-touch. I move quickly. The doors whisk open and I step through.

FIFTY-SIX

I BLINK IN THE BLINDINGLY WHITE LAB.
Bright solar glass lights illuminate the wide hallway, with
frosted glass doors on either side.

Jack is nowhere to be seen.

I'd been relying on him and his knowledge of the
lab—and we'd both been hoping that the lab hadn't
changed too much since he left it. Of course I memorized a
map, but it feels strange here, without Jack. I take a few
tentative steps forward, and one of the other workers
stares at me. I can't hesitate. If I look like I don't belong,
they'll realize that I really shouldn't be here. I have to move
forward. I have to pretend like I know where I'm going.

I stride forward purposefully. My eyes flick back and
forth—there are small black-and-gold placards by each
door. Some have names on them—Dr. Adams, Dr. Martin,
Dr. Ashby. Most are labeled with the type of research that
happens behind the door. Biological weaponry. Virus
manufacturing. Solar energy. Solar weaponry.

A door behind me bursts open, and I turn, surprised,
just as an arm grabs me and yanks me into a lab. I open my

mouth, a gasp already rising in my throat, and a hand clamps over my face.

"It's me," Jack growls. He spins me around, and I gape at him. He's discarded his custodial uniform and wears the lab coat he snuck inside. "Damn, I was worried," he continues. "When we got separated..."

I swallow down my racing heart. "Where are we?"

I'd expected another research room, but this door has opened into a hallway. "Android sciences," Jack says. "So far, it looks like nothing much has changed since I worked here."

"Good," I say. I shimmy out of the uniform shirt—my black tank top underneath is disgustingly dirty—and slip on my own lab coat. Jack examines my appearance, and it seems to satisfy his critical eye.

"This way," he says.

Even though we're here at night, there are still plenty of people around. We walk down the hallway as if we own the place. Jack nods at people we pass, although we're careful not to make real eye contact and invite conversation. When we reach a door labeled "Nanorobotics & Artificial Intelligence," Jack puts his hand on the door.

It doesn't open.

"Shit," he mumbles. I knock his hand aside, pointing to the tap-touch lock. An extra layer of security for this lab. For Dad's lab.

We both scan in, and the door opens. The lights automatically cut on in front of us—at least no one is already inside. I feel Jack start to relax. I think he expected trouble.

This lab has several more frosted glass doors in the far wall, each one neatly labeled. We're clearly at the hub of the android and nanorobotic research. One door—also with a tap-touch lock—is labeled **CYBORG-CLONE DEVELOPMENT**.

Another is **ANDROID ENGINEERING**, then **AI RESEARCH** and **NANOROBOTICS**. The door to the far left is **REVERIE TRANSFER**. Beside it is a door—the only one without a window—labeled **KTENOLOGY**.

Jack stares, open-mouthed. "This is so different," he says in a low voice. "I mean, not these—" he indicates the android, AI, and nanobot doors, "—but these other ones. They're all brand new. What even is ktenology?"

I don't answer him. I'm distracted by the first door, the way the words barely fit on the label. I approach it slowly. Jack reaches for me, but I'm just a step away.

"We should go here," he starts, heading toward the door marked REVERIE TRANSFER.

I raise my hand, examining the CYBORG-CLONE DEVELOPMENT door. I cover up the "borg" part of the label.

CY███-CLONE

"Cyclone," I whisper.

"What?" Jack asks.

THE BODY ELECTRIC

I put my hand on the lock.

"Wait!" Jack hisses at me, but it's too late. I've opened the door.

In the center of the room is a giant tube, tall, but narrow. If I were to try to swim in it—for it's filled with a blue liquid that glitters—then I could touch the sides of the glass tube with my arms, even though the liquid would go over my head. I lean in close, peering into the sparkling blue inside the tube, but there's nothing in there but the liquid.

When I turn around, I jump in surprise. A perfect skeleton lies on an examination table near the tube. It's definitely human, and, judging from the size, not yet an adult. But it's also not real. The bones are made of some sort of metal that is so shiny it's nearly white, held together with medical-grade flex-alloy strips for tendons.

"Ella," Jack whispers.

I ignore him, fascinated by the skeleton. One arm dangles off the table, and I pick it up, slipping my fingers through the cold, metal bony fingers of the hand of this strange creation.

"Ella," Jack says.

I turn.

He stands in front of a low vat covered in a clear glass top. The vat is filled with a clear liquid that might be water, but it's what's inside that stops me in my tracks.

At first I think they're jellyfish. Even though the bodies are too bulbous and defined to be jellyfish, there are long tentacles come off each spherical, floating object, drifting down to the bottom of the tank. But then I see the single heavy, long tentacle coming out from the center of each of the things, and I realize what they are.

Brains.

They're beige and pink, with tiny lines of blue veins. I always imagined brains as gray and mushy, but these are firm, bobbing along in their vats. The spinal cords—which I'd mistaken for tentacles—reach straight down to the bottom, where they're plugged into metal tubes and clamped in place. All along the spinal cords are tiny tufts, almost like sea anemones. As I watch, I see little white sparks of electricity flickering between the nerves, traveling up the spinal cord and flashing in the brains like lighting. When I lean down closer, I notice small microchips embedded into the wrinkles of the brains. I wonder, if I put the brains under a microscope, if there would be nanobots connecting the synapses. It's an eerie, creepily beautiful image of the biological blending with the mechanical.

"This is impossible," Jack says. "Your dad—Dr. Philip tried for years to clone or manufacture a human brain, but he said it was impossible."

I turn around slowly, drinking in everything. The metal skeleton, the vat of brains. Beyond them, a wall with tiny refrigerator doors, each one labeled with a different organ. A smaller vat in the corner filled with long strips of beige material and labeled simply, "syn-skin." A cabinet with a sign on it that says, "flesh stimulator." Pipes run along the ceiling, leading to the giant tube in the center of the room. They're labeled with different versions of nanobots: NB-126, NB-252, NB-378.

"All of this… It's all the pieces of a human," I say in a hollow voice. Bones of metal, fake skin, cloned organs. Piece them together, and you have a Frankensteinian monster.

I touch the glass of the tube, wondering at the android that's stuck inside it. No—not an android. A cyborg-clone, according to the label on the door. A cy-clone. Representative Belles learned about cy-clones, and his mind was troubled by what he learned. Maybe that was the real reason why he came in for a reverie, to forget about whatever cy-clones really are, and how they're made.

A terrible thought floods my own thoughts: did *Dad* have something to do with this?

"Hey, Ella," Jack says from across the room. I walk over to him—he's scanning the information in the interface system, documents and images flashing on the monitor screen as he selects information to copy and send to the Zunzana computers.

"They're working on a rush order," he says. "Yesterday, there was an order for a 'new one.'"

"A new what?" I ask.

Jack shrugs. "'A new one,' that's all it says. And this model needs a remote kill switch, and some other features, like an increased amount of some sort of chemical compound called PHY-DU5."

I voice the thing we're both afraid of saying. "Is this what Akilah is?" I ask. "Some sort of man-made monster? And my mom?"

Jack whirls around. He looks me right in the eyes. "No way," he says. "You said it yourself—you can't make a brain think. Look at those." He points to the vats of brains. "Do you think you could just pick one of those up and stick it in that skeleton and make it think for itself? Science has come far, Ella, but you can't just manufacture *this*."

I stare down at the vat. Despite the flickers of electricity, there's no evidence that these brains can think, even with the microchips.

As we leave the room, I'm filled with an unexplainable sense of dread. I glance back behind me. Even though the skeleton is made of nothing but metal, it feels as if it's watching me, mocking me.

Jack slides the door shut, and the last image I have of this strange room is the flickering sparks of electricity pulsing through brains that cannot—*cannot*—think for themselves.

Jack latches on to my arm and drags me to the lab marked "Reverie Transfer." I think he's afraid I'm going to wander into the other labs, but he shouldn't worry about that. I can't shake this feeling, a sort of ominous déjà vu, from my shoulders. I'm definitely going to be glad when we can escape this lab, but I'm getting my answers first.

On the far wall of this lab are a series of small, square doors, each neatly labeled with a few words I cannot read from here. The little doors are made of heavy steel, with a locking metal handle. They stack one on top of the other, like morgue doors. This room is cooler, and I think, judging by the condensation near the wall, the little rooms behind the little doors must be refrigerated.

In the center of the room is a reverie chair—a pair of them, connected by wires, much like the two reverie chairs in Reverie are connected, although our second chair is hidden in a different room. These reverie chairs look old and uncomfortable, none of the plush lining or little comforts we have for our clients.

One chair is empty and shiny, newly polished. The only flaw in it is a small, misshapen hole in the center of the chair back that looks a bit like a bullet hole.

The other chair is not empty. A body is slung across it, arms and legs dangling lifelessly. The head is tilted back, almost falling off the back of the chair. But there's not a full head, not on this body. There's a gaping hole, and through the flesh and metal, I can still see the whisper of a spark in my mother's mechanical brain.

FIFTY-SEVEN

I HEAR A BUZZING IN THE BACK OF MY head.

Jack looks around for something to cover my mother's doppelganger body with, but there's nothing there, and it doesn't matter. I've seen it. And it's not my mother. But I've still seen it.

I can smell it now. A sort of sweet scent, with a rancid edge.

Rotting meat.

"We should go," Jack says immediately. He's speaking so fast. I can barely keep up with his words.

"Why are there two chairs together like that?" I ask. Connected reveries are rare; Mom only theorized about them. I thought the mental spa was the only place to have some. Everything feels slow, like I'm sloshing through water. There is something... something important. I just... I can't seem to *think*.

I feel like I'm missing something.

"Your father was working on a theory of your mother's—at least, he was before he fired me. Using reveries on androids, trying to find a way to make them really think. Judging from this and the vat of brains, it looks like the UC has continued his research."

I start, then look guiltily at Jack. I only understood half of what he said. "Do you hear that?" I ask, craning my head, listening.

Jack stares at me. The lab is eerily silent.

"Never mind," I say. "It was nothing."

"Anyway," Jack says slowly, still staring at me oddly, "your father thought *zzz* that it might be pozzible to tranzfer thought through something like reveriez. He'd zometimes experiment, putting an android *zzz* in one chair and a perzon in the other. Put them both in reveriezzz, and zee if any intelligence could be tranzferred. Ella?" Jack snaps his fingers in front of my face. "Are you *zzz* listening?"

"The buzzing," I say softly.

"What?" Jack asks. But I can barely hear him.

The buzzing is so loud.

I clamp my hands over my ears.

It's still. *Zzz*. So. *Zzz*. Loud.

"Ella?" Jack asks. Or, at least, I think that's what he asks. I can't hear him. I can only see his mouth open and close around the syllables of my name.

"Where are the bees?" I ask loudly. Jack clamps a hand over my mouth—I don't know why he thinks *I* am too loud. I could barely hear my own voice, the buzzing is so deafening.

Jack mouths something else, but I can't hear it. Juzzzt buzzzzzzing.

I whirl around. How can there be this much buzzing, and no sign of bees? They must be everywhere... but I can't see them at all.

Jack grabs my shoulders and spins me about. He opens his mouth.

Bees pour from it. They swarm in front of his face. They knock against his teeth. They crawl up his nose, over his eyeballs.

I scream and fall back. The bees follow me. I swat at them, waving my arms about and taking the lab coat off, trying to beat them away. They ignore me entirely. I can feel their heavy bodies against the bare skin of my arms. Their pointy, sticky feet prick my clothes, snagging in the threads. Their slightly fuzzy bodies leave goose bumps on my shoulders.

They crawl over me, their wings beating against my skin. They crawl through my hair. I bend over, scratching my head with both hands, trying to get the damn things out, but there are more bees than I have hair, bees, bees, everywhere *beezzzzz*.

Jack grabs my wrist, crushing the bodies of bees between our skin, and jerks me forward. It does no good— the bees follow. I squirm, twisting around, swatting at the bees everywhere.

Jack throws me into the reverie chair—the empty one, not the one with a body in it.

THE BODY ELECTRIC

He lowers his face in front of mine. He speaks—I cannot hear his words, not through the sound of the bees, but I can see his lips form my name.

A bee lands on his lower lip. I watch, eerily fascinated, as the stinger punctures the pink skin. The bee jerks, leaving the stinger in Jack's lip. The bee falls against Jack's teeth, drops from his lips to the ground, where its body is swallowed up by the thousands of bees swarming on the cold tile floor. The floor used to be white, but now it is black-and-yellow, swirling, whirling, massive bodies of bees writhing along the ground, crushed under Jack's feet, smeared into the tile as more bees swarm over the dead ones.

Hands grip my chin, turn my face.

Jack's mouth is open so wide that I think he's shouting, but there's no point. Can't hear anything, not over the buzzing, buzzing, *buzzbuzzbuzzbuzzing.*

I'm screaming. When did I start screaming? Opening my mouth left space for the bees to get in. They dive-bomb down my throat, scratching the sensitive flesh of my mouth with their stingers, their thin little legs getting stuck between my teeth. I claw at my mouth, trying to get them out, and then firm hands pull my arms away from my face, and they're strapped down, held against the metal arms of a reverie chair—*how did I get in a reverie chair?*—and I turn my head, and there's the other reverie chair, the one with the dead body of the thing that looks like my mother, and I can't get away because I'm strapped down, and the bees are too heavy anyway, their bodies piling over mine, pressing me down, and I can't breathe.

And then one of them stings me.

A giant one, with poisonous green venom.

No.

Not a bee.

A needle.

Not venom. Reverie drug.

The bees melt like candle wax into the shape of a man. Jack stands before me, holding a needle. I look down at my arm.

He drugged me.

I slip into a reverie.

FIFTY-EIGHT

THE BUZZING BEES ARE SOFTER NOW, IN the background, like music.

"Ella."

I am still strapped down in the reverie chair, but there's nothing in the dreamscape except the darkness and my father.

"Where am I?" I ask.

Dad bends over the chair and starts to loosen the straps. I rub my wrists. My mouth is sore. I touch it gently and can feel the raised skin of my own clawing.

"You are in a reverie chair," Dad says.

"No, I mean... where am I now?" I look around me. I'm in a reverie; this is a dreamscape. This isn't the lab. Jack's not here. Just me and the chair and Dad.

"Where do you go when you enter someone's reverie?" Dad asks idly, as if the question were rhetorical.

"I enter their mind."

Dad looks off into the blackness of the dreamscape. "You enter someone else's mind. Someone else's memories, someone else's dreams." *His eyes turn to focus on mine.* "I suppose you're in someone else's mind right now." *He giggles.* "Which means you're not in your right mind."

I stand up—not only is the reverie chair hard and uncomfortable, but I want to get some distance between myself and this dream of Dad.

And then what he's said hits me. I'm not in my mind at the moment—I'm in a reverie, dreaming someone else's dream. But the person—the thing—the thing that looks like my mother—in the other chair isn't alive. All that was left was a few electrical sparks in a rotting body.

"Is this what death looks like?" *I mutter to myself.*

"Depends on what you think death is." *Dad sounds cheerful now, like the man I remember before we moved to the city, before he started working with the government.*

"I don't understand you."

"You—your thoughts, your being, your self—are right here, correct?" *Dad waves his hands in front of me. Of course I am not really here—I'm in a chair in a lab with Jack. But I am also here, in a dreamscape with Dad.* "Which part of you is you—that body you left behind, or the girl in front of me now?" *Dad asks.*

I think about it a moment, then say, "I guess me. Here. Now. A body isn't a person. A person is..." *I struggle to answer him. It's hard to put it in a definition. But I think about the digi file Jack showed me, of Akilah's death. Even on a screen, I could tell the difference between Akilah alive and Akilah dead. Dead, she was empty. She was nothing.*

She was like she was in the tunnel. A shadow of herself. She wasn't her body.

Dad grips my shoulders, his fingers pressing into my skin. "Remember that, Ella. That part is important."

"What part...?" I ask, but Dad releases me so suddenly that I'm left breathless.

He spins away from me, and I hear his voice, heavy and sad. "Ella, you have to wake up."

I march over to him. "You keep saying that!" I scream at him. "But what do you mean? What am I supposed to wake up from? What do you *really* mean?"

Dad takes my former place in the reverie chair. He looks up at me.

He looks so tired. Wan.

His cheeks are sunken. His eyes are red-rimmed. His lips are cracked.

He looks dead. Almost.

"You were my key. I hid the truth in you." As he talks, the flesh falls away from his face, until there are gaping holes where his cheeks should be, his clacking teeth visible.

I start to cry. The tears are hot and burn my cheeks as they fall. They remind me of the bee-stings.

"When you wake up, your face will be dry. But that doesn't mean you didn't cry."

The buzzing grows louder. It's not background music any more. It's the sound of me losing my mind.

"I'm going crazy, aren't I?" I whisper. The fear of it dawns on me like a horrific revelation. Before, in the lab. There were no bees. I realize that now. There were no bees. Just me. Crazy me.

Or... maybe I'm not going crazy. Maybe I'm some sort of android-cyborg-clone-thing, and I'm just breaking down.

I'm not sure which way is worse.

Dad laughs. As he does, the rest of his skin and flesh cracks and falls away from his head, exposing his grinning skull. His eyes roll in their sockets, then fall, dangling from a string of red vein. The veins snap and his eyes splatter on the ground.

"You're not in your right mind, dear," he says. "No, no, no, you're not."

And he still laughs. He laughs until there's nothing but the noise of his teeth clacking together and the never-ending sound of a million bees buzzing in my ears.

And then—
—Silence.

Dad fades away. The reverie chair disappears.

There's just blackness. I remember then that I am in the reverie of something dead. Whatever that thing was, it was dead.

And, just as I'm starting to wonder if, perhaps, I have died, too, I see a light, far away in the corner of the dreamscape. The light isn't soft; it's not glowing. It crackles like silent lightning, burning with electricity, sparks flying out and fizzling in the dark.

I don't know why—it makes no sense, the way dreams often don't—but I want to touch the light.

So I do.

The light arcs from the corner of the dreamscape, connecting with my fingertips. It burns me up inside, lightning bouncing around my organs, pinging through my blood.

I hear a voice. A voice I know, a voice I love.

"Mom," I whisper.

And there's something within me, some indefinable knowledge that I cannot explain, but when the light answers me, saying my name, I know that it's my mother's voice. My mom. My real mom—not the thing that looked like Mom, the thing that wore her face and sounded and smelled and seemed like her.

This is my mother's voice.

"Ella," she says again, the word resounding through my soul.

And then I realize: something's wrong.

"Mom?" I ask. My voice crackles with fear and electricity.

"I held on as long as I could," my mother says. "But you have to let me go now. Let all of me go. Because there's nothing left. Not here. Not anymore."

My eyes snap open. Jack stands over me, concern etched on his face. "Ella?" he says, and I know he's saying my name to see if I can respond, to see if I'll answer him with screaming or a buzzing sound.

"I'm fine," I say, even though I'm really not.

FIFTY-NINE

MOM USED TO SAY THAT THE THOUGHTS in our heads were nothing more than electrical impulses. I remember Dad and her talking about this over dinner. It frustrated Dad that the human brain can fire electrical sparks and *think*, but that the electricity he'd pump into an android brain would never give it independent thought. The body isn't that different from a machine. Humans and androids both run on electricity.

That lightning spark of energy I saw in the reverie.

That was my mother's last thought, an echo of electricity, something that sparked when I entered her dreamscape.

That spark is gone now. Her life is gone now. Everything that made her, her, is gone now. Faded into nothing. "Ella, we have to go," Jack says. He speaks as if he's afraid his words will break me, but I cannot process his gentle tone. He looks down on the burner cuff on his arm. "We have to go," he repeats. "I stationed someone to watch the security system. People are heading toward this lab. We have to go."

When I don't move, Jack bends over, whips the black tarp on the floor up, and re-covers my mother's body. "Ella. *Ella.* We have to go."

But then we hear the sounds of footsteps. It's already too late.

"Shit!" Jack says softly. His eyes dance around the room—there's nowhere to hide, no exit except through the door we entered, the one that leads to the entry lab.

"Here," I say. I feel as if I'm finally waking up from a long, long sleep, one where I dreamed about crazy things and my mother died and my father rotted before me.

I cross the room, careful to avoid any contact with the black tarp, and approach the labeled doors, the little ones that look like they belong in a morgue. They each have a neat label on them. One is slightly open. The label reads: **Shepherd, Rose, Vers. 12.**

My mother's name. I swing the door open, and a blast of cold air hits me. Inside, the little room shows a narrow, flat tray that easily extends out. Jack scrambles onto the table, then scoots to one side. There's a sliver of room left.

"Come on," he says.

"I'll open another one—"

"What are the chances they're all empty? Come *on.*"

I jump up on the table. It's impossible to lie on the tray and not touch Jack. Jack reaches both arms over our heads, straining to scoot the tray, now bearing the weight of both our bodies, back into the refrigerated section. I catch the door with my foot and swing it closed behind us—but not fully shut. I dare not click the door closed—what if it locks? We'd die in here.

Die. Like my mother.

I choke down a sob, and Jack wraps his arms around me, pulling me even closer. "Shh," he murmurs in my hair. His breath comes out in a puff of steam. Goose bumps prickle my arms, and I start to shiver. Jack holds me even tighter, so tight I can barely breathe, but warmth rises between us. I close my eyes, breathe in the scent of him.

"The lights are on." A gruff voice I don't recognize fills the room. I clutch Jack's arms, hanging on to him as if he can save me just with his presence. He has one arm around my head, pressing me to his chest, one arm around my waist and back. I feel his arms go rock hard, his breath catch in his throat. I glance up at him, and see, for the first time, fear in his eyes.

"This lab is spooky," a second voice says. "The stuff they do down here... ain't natural."

"You think anything that requires thought 'ain't natural,'" the first voice mocks. "Nothing about this lab is scary, man."

"Yeah. Because that dead body right there is perfectly 'natural.'"

My mother's body.

"They say this lab's haunted. By those women."

My mother? And another woman? Maybe Akilah?

"Don't be stupid."

Footsteps as the two men walk around the lab. "Looks messy. Like someone trashed the place."

"It's always like this, after a transfer."

The footsteps come closer. Jack's eyes are wide and staring, his grip on me viselike, his muscles tense. I don't even feel the cold any more, just the fear.

"This door's open a crack," one of the guards says. He's close. He's right outside the morgue chamber we're hiding in. He could pull the door open, drag our cold bodies off the slab, kill us like my mother's dead.

I hear the metallic sound of the latch.

Or he could slam the door shut, and we'd freeze to death.

"Don't mess with it, man," the first guard says. "They hate it if anything is disturbed. Just leave everything like you find it."

"What are you doing here?" a female voice I almost recognize says. I scramble up, sliding closer to the door, craning to see.

"There was an alert—"

"These labs are off-limits, even to security." I peer out of the crack at the door and strain my eyes to see who's talking.

I gasp, and Jack's arms tense around me. His eyes widen, and he shakes his head slightly. But I ignore him. Because I've finally recognized the woman. She's the plump nurse, the one Ms. White hired to take over care of my mom after Rosie the android exploded. Except she's not a nurse. She's a scientist, one of the ones here. Not a nurse at all.

After a few more moments, the footsteps walk away from us as the scientist escorts the security away.

Jack breathes a sigh of relief, forming a cloud around our heads. He doesn't release me, but his muscles go slack.

I shift when I hear the door zip closed behind the guards, but Jack shakes his head. Of course—stupid me—they're examining the other labs, too.

"One... two... three..." Jack whispers, counting, his voice barely making a sound. I focus on his mouth, watching numbers spill from his lips, disappearing as the condensation from his breath evaporates.

When he reaches two hundred and fifty, I feel as if my eyelashes are made of ice, my lungs are filled with snow. Jack slides down, kicking the little door fully open, and pushes the tray and our two frozen bodies back into the warm lab. I stand there, shivering, but it's not because of the refrigerated air that's followed us into the lab. It's because of how bereft I am without him holding me against his body.

SIXTY

"WE SHOULD GO," I SAY. NOW THAT we've come so close to being caught, all I want to do is escape. There's so much we've not examined yet—only this one tiny section of the lab—and I may never have another chance to see the place where my father worked and died (and my mother, her body is there, it's right there), but I cannot get over the feeling of wrongness this place gives me.

"We have time," Jack says, checking his cuff. "The guards marked these labs as clear."

"We should still go," I say, looking at my mother's body.

"Transfer," Jack says. He waits until I meet his eyes. "This lab is labeled 'Reverie Transfer.' That must mean something. And the guards—they mentioned transfers."

"It's not that big a deal," I say, moving toward the door.

Jack reaches for me, but I sidle away. "Do you know what a reverie transfer is?" he asks, searching my eyes. "Do you know why the two reverie chairs are connected? I've never seen that before."

I heave a sigh. "Yes, you have. You just didn't know it. The chairs at Reverie are connected."

Jack's eyebrows furrow in concentration. "Chairs?" he asks. "There's more than one?"

I nod. "There's a second chamber behind the control room. And a chair there that's connected to the first."

"What's it used for?" When I don't answer, he asks it again, his voice urgent.

"My mother had a theory," I say finally. "That some people can enter others' reveries."

Jack snorts. "That's impossible. You can't just go into someone else's mind. Right? Ella?" He stares at me. "You... you can, can't you?" He speaks the words slowly, not believing them even as he says them. "Can you enter other people's minds? Is that a transfer?"

I look down. There's no reason to be ashamed of this, but I am. "It's how I knew what to say to Representative Belles."

"You'd been in his mind?" Jack sounds disgusted, horrified.

I nod. "I call it the dreamscape. It's not like I break into other people's heads; if they're in a reverie, I can plug myself up to a connected chair and enter their reverie."

"Do they know you're there?" Jack asks, and then, before I can answer, I see the horror filling his eyes. He looks at me, disgusted. "You've been in my reverie, haven't you? When you plugged me up before. You said you could tell if I was telling the truth about knowing you, and you could—because you entered my mind and rooted around in my memories!" There's accusation in his voice, as if I've done something vile.

Because I have.

"What did you see?" he asks, his voice suddenly hollow. "When you were *spying* on my brain, what did you see?"

"Memories," I say simply. "Memories I don't have. Because someone's done it to me, too—someone's entered my mind and erased my memories."

"Who?" Jack demands.

"I don't know. It's the only answer, though." That, or I'm just a machine with missing bits, erased data.

Jack runs his fingers through his hair, his blue eyes glittering. He starts to pace. "I don't understand this, any of this. This... this stuff should be impossible."

"It's not."

"Can anyone else do it?"

"I didn't even know the UC labs had a reverie chair— maybe they've figured out how." Maybe that's what happened to my memories of Jack.

Jack starts pacing again. "But this room—it's labeled 'Reverie Transfer.' Not 'Reverie Spying.'"

I flinch.

"Transfer implies moving something from one vessel to another, not just a temporary observance," Jack continues. I'm reminded that he's a scientist, like Dad, brilliant enough to be considered as a replacement.

He freezes, and I can tell that he's realized something. His eyes dart to the wall of morgue doors.

"What?" I ask.

Jack strides over to the doors. "Those brains in the vat—in the other lab. Your dad. You can't make brains think for themselves." His words rush together, confused. When he sees I'm not following his train of thought, he swings open the little door we hid behind and stares into the cold abyss.

"Your father tried everything he could to make an android brain that could think for itself. But it never worked." Jack slams the door shut and runs his fingers over the little label, the one with my mother's name. "He worked for years on developing a true android brain—a brain in a robot that thought for itself. But he *couldn't*— because it *can't* be done."

I examine the other nearby doors, and for the first time, I read the other labels on each door. The door we hid behind was **Shepherd, Rose, Vers. 12.** Above it is **Shepherd, Rose, Vers. 11.** And then **Shepherd, Rose, Vers. 10.** The column beside that was labeled **Shepherd, Rose, Vers. 1** all the way to **Shepherd, Rose, Vers. 9.**

"'Vers.' means 'version.'" I say slowly. I'm not processing the words I'm saying.

Jack opens the 11th door.

On the metal slab is a perfect copy of my mother. It lays motionless, as if sleeping, but there's no life in her. She looks like a mannequin.

I reach my hand out to the door labeled **Shepherd, Rose, Vers. 1.**

The body inside is my mom's. It's been frozen, like the others, the flesh solid and unforgiving. I touch the hair. It's brittle and crumbles in my hand. Her flesh is hard, like ice, and her hands are folded over her stomach. I glance behind me at the dead copy of mom on the reverie chair. There was something inside that corpse that was my mother, but maybe that was the only thing. Just another version. Whatever science this is, it rips a soul from a person and puts it in a hybrid of human and machine. A cyborg-clone with a human soul.

I look down at my hands, where the pieces of my mother's hair clings to my fingertips. "And this one, Version 1. Do you think this is my real mother? The original?"

Jack doesn't answer.

I look down at the frozen body.

"How long...?" I start to say, but the words die in my mouth. How long has my real mother been dead? How long have these replacements been in my home instead? My heart bangs against my chest, and my breath comes out in shallow gasps. I think I'm having a panic attack.

Jack picks up a chart clipped near the door. "It says that with each transfer, your mother lost stability. They weren't able to clone out the Hebb's Disease, so she stayed sick." He flips through the pages. "They were planning to phase out the 'Rose model' soon, anyway, because they couldn't keep up with production." He stops abruptly, slamming the charts down on the ground.

Cool air swirls around us as Jack closes the morgue doors in the wall, sliding my mothers back into their refrigerated graves.

And then I see it.

If before I was having a panic attack, all my organs banging around chaotically, now it feels as if my insides have shriveled up and withered away. Everything is silent and empty.

Something changes in Jack's demeanor. His eyes get hard and cold, his body shifts. He's looking past me, at the thing I'm looking at.

"Ella—"

But it's too late. We have both already seen it. Three doors, three neat labels, in the column beside my mother's.

Shepherd, Ella, Vers. 1
Shepherd, Ella, Vers. 2
Shepherd, Ella, Vers. 3

SIXTY-ONE

I DON'T REMEMBER LEAVING THE LAB, or running through the upper city, or winding up at the Zunzana safe house.

I only remember the three doors, the three labels.

The three versions of me.

Jack tries to talk to me. He tells me I'm human. Not some pieced-together monster. That whatever type of "transfer" the reverie transfers in the lab detailed doesn't involve me. That we didn't look behind those doors labeled with my name, that I'm assuming the worst.

He doesn't understand that I can't even comprehend the worst. There are copies of me.

And… maybe I'm a copy of me.

If we had opened those doors, would "Version 1" be empty—meaning that I am the original? Or would there be a body with brittle hair and frostbitten lips in the door marked Version 1—and would it be Version 2 or 3 that was empty?

Jack, Julie, and Xavier retreat to a part of the house to discuss "plans." I'm not stupid. They're discussing me. What I am. If I can be trusted. If I should be put down, like Julie wants to do with Akilah. Maybe it'll be simple, like unplugging a toaster.

Maybe I won't feel a thing.

I sit at the kitchen table, feeling everything and nothing at the same time, like someone who's been hurt so much they're just numb to the pain now. The android is in the kitchen, working. I watch it. When I blink, it blinks. A programmed reflex.

I try to see where the human façade ends and the android begins. Androids have always reminded me of death, never more so than now, as I stare at this one, and realize that the most unnatural thing about its appearance is simply that its chest doesn't move up and down as it breathes. If it had that one single additional feature, then it would appear alive.

My mother's chest moved. I know. I watched her like a hawk when she was sick, waiting for that moment when the inevitable end happened. She had a particularly bad attack just after my father died. I wonder now if that was the first time she was transferred to a cyclone body. She started seeing Dr. Simpa at the government labs around then. But anyway, Mom was sick, or the Mom I thought was Mom was sick or malfunctioning, or something—and I watched her. All night long. I counted her breaths, thankful for each one.

And then I saw Mom's body. Bodies. Lots of them. All unbreathing, unmoving.

I take a deep breath, my hand on my chest, relishing the feeling of my lungs expanding, my ribs moving beneath my skin. I try to tell myself this is real, but I don't know what to believe any more.

I try to figure out the facts of what has happened, and who I am. It's been a habit of mine, breaking the world down into fact and fiction. But this is not a matter of black and white, right and wrong, android and human. Nothing is so easy, and besides—only androids think in nothing but facts.

"Who are you?" I ask the android softly. The lens in the android's eyes shift as it zooms on my face, searching it for the clues it needs to properly respond.

"I am a Helpmate Model K, International Model. I have been given the user-friendly name Kim." The android picks up a knife and starts chopping carrots, but while its head tilts down in a mimicry of humanity, its eyes still watch me. This model is androgynous, and could be made to easily look like either a boy or a girl, with short, black hair, high cheekbones, and a small frame. When I drop my eyes to the android's hands, Kim follows suit, looking down as its knife speeds across the cutting board.

When I asked who it was, the android gave me a name. I am more than a name. I feel, I think, therefore I am.

Right?

"Kim, what happens if you slip?" I ask.

"Pardon?" the android says, sliding another carrot under the blade of the kitchen knife.

"What happens if you cut yourself?"

"I am programmed to handle all cooking tasks, including chopping."

"But you could make a mistake."

"Any errors in my program resulting in damage to my body would be covered under the Helpmate International Warranty. Would you like me to tell you about the warranty program?"

"No," I say. The carrots are done. Kim scoops them into a bowl and turns to the stove, where a large pot of boiling broth awaits. It drops the carrots into the hot liquid, its hands closer to the steam than a human's would be.

"Does it hurt?" I ask softly.

"Please repeat your command," Kim says, turning back to me.

"Can you feel pain?" I ask. Because I can.

"I am equipped with a standard application of electro-stimuli programmed throughout my body that will alert me if I am near to damaging myself," Kim states. It picks up a large wooden spoon, stirring the carrots, and adds rosemary and thyme to the mix, crushing the herbs between its mechanical fingers before dropping them into the boiling soup.

"What would happen," I ask, "if you put your hand inside that pot?"

"The pot is full of boiling liquid," Kim replies automatically. "I am programmed to avoid hazards."

"Would it hurt?" I sit up, leaning over the table that divides us.

"My electro-stimuli would register that my hand should move away from temperatures that may jeopardize my warranty." Despite my questions, there is no fear in Kim's voice, nothing but factual responses to my questions.

"Would it really damage you?" I ask.

"My synthesized silicone-based skin is designed specifically to be able to handle extreme temperatures in the event of an emergency. An emergency situation would not void the warranty if any damage were to happen."

So, no. I'm talking to an oversized potholder.

"Stick your hand in the soup," I say.

"There is no emergency situation that would warrant such an action," Kim replies, utterly emotionless.

"Command: stick your hand in the soup."

Kim holds the spoon with its right hand, but its left hand hovers over the edge of the pot.

It hesitates.

"Why aren't you doing what I ordered?" I say, throwing back my chair and staring at it.

Kim's eye-lens shift, staring from me to its own hand. "I... am not in an emergency situation," it says. "Such an action may void any warranty—"

"I gave you a direct command, regardless of the warranty," I say. My voice has grown eerily calm. I don't know why this means so much to me. The android can't feel pain. The heat won't damage it. This will prove nothing—but I have to see it happen, regardless.

The android still hesitates. I can see steam condensing on its false skin, and its fingers shake, but its hand doesn't lower.

"Are you... *scared?*" I ask, my eyes growing wide.

"I am programmed to avoid damage," the android states in its utterly void voice. "My electro-stimuli system is warning me that this action is unnecessary and potentially dangerous. My senses have been increased, causing my system to lock up. I have registered your command, but my programming is overriding my obedience."

"That's what fear is," I say. I feel tears welling in my eyes. "Kim, I release you from all my previous commands. Continue with your processes."

The android takes a step back, dropping its left hand to the side and stirring the soup again. There is no tension in the way it stands before the stove, no anger or rebellion. Just acceptance.

SIXTY-TWO

THERE IS ONLY ONE PERSON WHO knows what I may be, and she wants to kill me.

Still, I make my way downstairs, to the panic room and the shell of my former best friend. As I reach the solid steel doors, though, I hear voices. I don't intend to eavesdrop, but as I reach the bottom step, I hear Jack say my name. I lean against the wall by the door, focusing on the low voices in the room.

"So... she's an android?" Julie asks.

"The labs called them 'cy-clones,'" Jack answers. "A sort of combination of machine and person."

"Machines can be hacked." Xavier's voice is so low I almost can't distinguish his words.

"We're not even sure she *is* a so-called cy-clone," Jack answers, his voice raised in anger.

"I can do some testing." My heart stops at Xavier's words—testing? Like I'm some sort of lab rat?

"You might have been a med student, but that doesn't make you a doctor," Jack snaps. "And besides, we don't have the resources."

"You said she had a higher nanobot count than normal, right?" Julie says. "How high?"

Jack doesn't answer—or at least not loud enough for me to hear. When I was born, I was a collection of blood and bones and flesh. Would the addition of tiny, microscopic little robots change me all that much?

"That could be how they're created," Xavier says after a moment. "You said in the lab you saw evidence of cloned organs and synthetic, cyborg parts. Add in nanobots as the glue to hold the human pieces together with the machined parts, and you get a person."

"Half human and half machine," Julie says in a low voice.

"Oh, I don't know if it's fair to call anything like that human at all." Xavier's words cut me to the bone—even if I don't know if my bone is real or metal.

"She's not some monster!" Jack says, his voice rising again. "She's still Ella—still *human*."

The others don't answer.

I look down at my hands. Metal for bones, hidden behind real flesh. The ultimate android. A *thinking* robot. Is *that* all I am? A clone, a copy of my original self, strategically enhanced through a mix of cyborg technology—alloy bones, additional processors in the brain, things like that. And, of course, nearly every neuron in the body with a nanobot attached to it, keeping me together.

"Look at this," Xavier says, and the room goes dark. I press my face against the crack in the door, peering inside. Akilah lies on the gurney, still knocked out from the sedatives. A holographic projection hovers above her—her body, shimmering in the light. Xavier reaches his hands into the hologram, and then throws his arms apart. On one side is the muscular structure of Akilah's body, on the other, the skeletal.

"Her bones are all made of titanium alloy," Xavier says. "But her body is mostly cloned—human. However, look at this. Computer: display nanobot percentages." He touches the hologram of Akilah's flesh, and it sparkles and shines as if someone coated it with glitter. "Nanobots," Xavier says. "Billions—trillions of nanobots. Enhancing every muscle, every organ. Even the brain."

I can hear it, the buzzing in my head. The whirr of tiny little robots, churning in my brain.

I swallow down the hysterical laughter rising up within me.

When Dad first combined nanobots to his studies on androids, people thought he was crazy—a tiny machine enhancing a far larger one. When he turned around and applied that area of study to Mom's disease, they called him a genius. The nanobots he used are self-replicating, each one designed to make the synapses in my mother's failing body work as they should. It's that same nanobot technology that enhanced android technology, cyborg development... Dad's work changed everyone's world.

And ruined mine.

I realize—he made this tech for Mom. He wanted to save her. *He* turned her into... that. He kept her alive, as much as he could. And he did it before he died. He knew what she had become, and he loved her anyway.

But then the government stole his tech. And killed him.

So... when was *I* made?

"There were three doors in the lab marked with her name—she could still be the original, with two copies in the lab," Jack says, and my heart soars at the thought. Maybe I'm still me.

"Unlikely." This from Julie. "You said they kept making copies of her mother, right? Because they kept breaking down, were unstable from the disease, whatever. And it looks like they can only really make one copy at a time. So it seems like what they have is the original and any used-up copies in storage, kept on file, so to speak, and then one spare copy."

My mouth is dry as I strain to hear Jack's answer. "So, what you're saying is, Ella is dead. Version one, the real person. Is dead."

"And Version 3 is the spare copy in case anything happens to Version 2—which is what Ella is now."

Dead.

I'm dead.

Before, when I was running from Akilah, I kept thinking about how I wasn't human. And now I'm not even alive.

I shut my eyes, pressing the thin skin of my forehead against the cool metal door.

Akilah died. She died in battle, like a hero, and she rose again, like a phoenix.

Is this what immortality is? A sort of hollowness inside me, where I think my humanity must once have been, filled now with nothing but electronics.

What happened to me? How did I die? Why... why was I brought back? Akilah's a soldier, and, according to Jack, is an even stronger solider now that she's a cy-clone instead of a human. But why was I brought back?

My heart stutters—not *why?* or *how?*—those are not the important questions. The really important question is: *by whom?*

Could it have been my own father? Did Dad do this to me—to Mom? Is this the research the government stole from him—killed him for?

To make a cy-clone, the scientists need two bodies. One human, one synthetic. And the human body has to die for the synthetic one to live. If I'm not *me*, then that means I died... I was *killed*.

By... Dad?

Was he so obsessed with science that he would let me die to prove his theories? Maybe I became a cy-clone a long time ago, as a test subject to see if it would work on

Mom. I wasn't infected with Hebb's Disease, my synthetic body would last longer.

I clutch the fortune cookie locket Dad gave me. Dad loved me. He wouldn't...

Would he?

SIXTY-THREE

"I CAN EXAMINE HER." THE VOICE IS loud and deep—Xavier's. The sound cuts across my thoughts. "I'll examine her, determine if she's a threat to us."

"Ella is not a threat!" Jack roars. "And no one's *examining* her. She's Ella, and she's on our side, and that's final!"

Silence follows.

I straighten my spine, and I don't care if it's made of bone or metal. I want the truth. I shove my shoulder against the heavy door, and it swings open. The others in the room jump in surprise, but I stride across the tiled floor, pushing the gurney with Akilah's sleeping body to the side as I lie down under the scanner and holographic projector rigged in the ceiling.

My insides float above me in a hologram. I marvel at it for a second.

I take a deep breath.

"Computer," I say. "Display nanobot percentages."

THE BODY ELECTRIC

The image of me lights up like the sea at sunset, sparkling and glowing, alight with the fire of countless nanobots, crawling under my skin.

Xavier reaches out, separating the bits of me that are human and the bits of me that are mechanical.

Everything I feared is true. I am not human.

I am a monster.

Xavier turns to his computer system. After a moment, he says, "This scanner is linked to the genome database at Triumph Towers. You're a match for Ella Shepherd." He turns the screen around, showing my ID profile.

"So, she's Ella," Jack growls.

"Her DNA is," Xavier says. "She's a cy-clone, though. A clone of the real Ella, enhanced with a cybernetic body."

Tears burn the back of my eyes. *The real Ella.* Not the original. The real one.

I stare at my hands, wondering at how I am trapped within this manufactured prison that looks like my own body.

I stand up slowly. Julie watches me with wide eyes, and I don't know if it's because she's afraid of me or if I should be afraid of her. Xavier silently turns off the program, and the damning hologram disappears.

"Leave," Jack says in a low voice, and Julie and Xavier scamper away. I stand still, trapped in Jack's gaze.

I don't want to be a thing. I want to be a person.

"You're Ella," Jack says, striding toward me. I blink at him. "You're Ella," he repeats. "You're you. You're human."

"Prove it," I say.

Jack sighs. "You can think. Androids can't think."

But the copy of my mother that I met in my kitchen could think. She decided to make breakfast. She decided to go to the lower city.

Or... maybe? Perhaps she was just given very specific details, a program that told her things like, "if your daughter questions you, play along."

I sigh, and the sound seems to wrap around me, like a rope made of my own self-doubt, strangling all my hopes with it.

Jack's expression is fierce. He moves closer, but I back away, my heart thudding, until I'm pressed against the wall and he towers over me. His arms drop down, caging me in.

I only have time to squeak in surprise as Jack swoops down, his face millimeters from my own. My eyes are wide, staring into his.

My gaze drops.

His lips are right there, right in front of mine. They part slightly, and I smell the apple he just ate on his warm breath. I imagine tasting that apple, too.

"You have no idea how difficult it is," Jack said that night in the tower. *"Loving you the way I loved you, and you not even remembering who I am."*

Jack lifts his hand and presses it against my chest so hard that I can feel the full outline of his hand, burning through my shirt and into my flesh.

"Feel that?" he asks, but I have no answer for him, because everything I've ever felt is racing through my entire body, fear and desire and panic and lust and doubt, all of it, all at once, bubbling up around his hand like a pot of boiling water.

"Science can make a heart beat," Jack says softly, each word falling on me like a caress. "But it can't make it race."

He steps back. Bereft of his touch, there's a cold spot on my chest where his hand once was.

But at least I know now. A robot can live, it can even maybe think, but it can't *feel*.

Not like this.

Right?

SIXTY-FOUR

JACK WAITS FOR ME TO RESPOND.

But I don't know what to say.

How to feel.

How to be.

With my back against the wall, I slide down, down, down, to the cold tiled floor.

I stare at my knees.

"El—" he starts.

"Please," I whisper.

He waits.

"Please, just leave."

He opens his mouth, but no sound comes out. After a moment, he walks to the door. He pauses once. I don't see it—I just feel his eyes on me, burning into my false skin.

But then he's gone.

I shut my eyes, and I force myself to feel myself. You never really think of what it's like to be in your body, but even with my eyes shut, I can feel the boundaries of my skin, real or not. Everything that's me is contained inside this body, and I feel it all. The heartbeat I cannot control. The mind that may not be mine. I am here, in this moment, in this body. All that I am—maybe not all that I ever was, but all that I currently am—is right here.

I stand and walk over to where Akilah is, heavily sedated. I push her gurney back into the center of the room, under the scanner and holographic projector, straighten so it was just like it was before I entered.

"I miss you," I tell her face.

My fingers trail on the thin tube delivering the sedatives into her system.

And then I crimp the tube, stopping the flow of the medication.

I stare at her. Waiting.

Her eyes flutter open.

I lean in close.

"Ella?" she asks, but this time I can hear the falseness in her voice.

Eyes are the window to the soul. That's what Dad always said. And right now, more than anything else in the whole entire world, I have to know one thing.

Is there anything left of my friend inside her body?

As she wakens more, Akilah starts to squirm. Strains against her restraints. Thrashes on the gurney, her body bucking, thudding hollowly against the metal.

I lean in even closer.

"Let me go!" Akilah screams, and I almost release my grip on the IV, worried that she will break the techfoil and escape.

But I do not break eye contact with Akilah.

My eyes burn, a deep hotness that licks at my sight like fire. Akilah stills. She stares back into me, as if we are both seeking a humanity that neither of us has.

She blinks.

And for a moment, just one small flash—I see my friend.

I'm so surprised that I drop the IV as I step away, but I am certain of it. I had her back. As the sedatives rush back into her bloodstream, Akilah starts to protest, demanding her release, but the sound is nothing but buzzing in my ears.

She was there. She was Akilah again. In this world where everything I thought was certain is now nothing more than false promises, I know that moment was real.

That spark inside her, the thing that makes Akilah my friend—it's *not* gone. Buried under programming, drowned out by computer commands, bleached from her mind—but still, irrevocably, *there*.

Hope isn't lost.

There is still an Akilah to save, and I can save her.

I just have to figure out how.

SIXTY-FIVE

IT IS JULIE WHO COMES TO MY RESCUE.

"Let her try," she tells the boys after I explain my plan.

"It's too dangerous," Jack says immediately.

Xavier watches silently.

I don't know if they believe me or not—they did not see the light of life come back to Akilah's eyes; they have no reason to trust me anyway—but at least Julie says that I should try.

"It's too late, anyway," I say, speaking for the first time since I explained my plan. "I've already contacted Representative Belles."

"What?" Jack says, glaring at me.

I put my hands up. "I only asked him to read up as much as he can. He has access to documents that we don't, all the stored research, possibly the plans from the government."

"But even if he reads it all, how can he get that information to us?" Xavier asks, his voice low and calm.

"If it's in his head, I can get it out."

There's a hard set to Jack's jaw. "It's dangerous. We can't go back to the labs and that reverie chair."

"We can go back home," I say.

The Reverie Mental Spa is the only other place in the world with two reverie chairs connected. If Representative Belles is in one, I can link to him in the other and see everything the government is planning. Even if he hasn't consciously memorized the bulk of what he read, his subconscious has absorbed more than he can tell.

It's too late to save Mom. But maybe I can still save Akilah.

Maybe I can save myself.

"But how can we get in?" Julie says.

"My biometric scan is programmed into the security," I say. "It's my home—I can get in."

"There will be guards," Jack growls.

"I can take care of those." Julie grins, as if she's looking forward to the fight.

"I will stay with Akilah," Xavier says. "She should not be alone."

"I'm staying with you." Jack glares at me. "I don't trust that representative."

"He's on our side," I try to protest.

"He's not fighting for us," Jack says. His voice is low, even, and he doesn't break eye contact with me. "He's fighting for his family. What's left of it. He may agree with us, he may hate the government, but in the end, all he will ever want to do is protect his family."

"The freedom of our people is more important!" Julie says fiercely. "We will never stop fighting, never stop working for what is right!"

Jack just smiles at her. "That's a nice lie to believe," he says.

My cuff buzzes. I read the message, then meet the others' eyes. "Tonight," I say. "He's ready tonight."

It feels so strange to be heading home. It's only been a few days since I left, but it feels like a lifetime. I clutch my fortune cookie necklace, the only thing I really have left of the person I used to be. It feels weird that I could just walk away from my home. I briefly consider going back to my room, but what would I take? There's so much I don't want any more. The photos of my family are tainted with doubt and questions. The small gifts my mother made, the mementos of my father. None of it feels real.

Jack, Julie, and I stop short when we reach the gate to Central Gardens, directly across the Reverie storefront. The neon sheep bounces cheerily over the slogan, illuminating the dimming twilight with garish colors and a glossy glass surface. But when I look past all that, through the glass to the waiting lobby, the building is dark and empty.

"Wait for my word," Julie says, slipping into the shadows. Jack and I wait, nervously, and in a few moments, Jack's cuff buzzes.

"All clear," he says.

Representative Belles waits for us at the street corner.

"Ready?" I ask him.

He nods. His body is tense, and his mouth is drawn tight.

"Here's hoping this works," I mutter as we reach the door. I press my finger against the touchpad, and the doors slide open.

SIXTY-SIX

REPRESENTATIVE BELLES LOOKS NERVOUS as Jack plugs him into the reverie chair. I guess if you know someone's going to break into your mind, you're not quite so eager to go under.

"Just think about the research you did," I say. "I can access your memories. You won't feel a thing."

The representative nods tightly and shuts his eyes as Jack administers the reverie drug to him. We both leave the representative, but Jack touches my arm to hold me back before I can go to the next chair.

"Be careful," he says. There's real concern etched on his face, and perhaps fear.

I slip into Representative Belles's mind as if it were a comfortable T-shirt.

There are no oranges, and it feels odd to be here without the scent of the grove filling the air.

In the background, I can hear the soft sound of a boy's voice, barely audible, singing to the tune of a guitar.

Representative Belles stands before me, looking sheepish. "My son," he says. The music fades to nothing.

His dreamscape is of his office. Through the window, the sky is blue and cloudless, overlooking the upper city of New Venice. In the center is a giant desk, the glass surface already filled with digi files and documents, and two raised screens displaying data.

I sit down in the representative's chair and start reading.

Nanorobotics and Cyborg Control in Android Theory: Building a Brain Through Biology and Technology

By: Dr. Philip K. Shepherd

My scientific studies to date have always had the goal of a being with individual thought but also physical strength. I have failed to create an android with a human brain to achieve that end.

However, my current research indicates that I can approach the solution differently by reversing the starting point. Namely, a human being with an android body, rather than an android with a human brain.

Obviously, a human cannot be fully robotic. Cyborg technology in the past three decades has advanced by leaps and bounds, providing paraplegics with fully functioning limbs, but that is not the same as a full android body.

Full replication of android biomechanics is not feasible. But the advantages of an android's body can be replicated by other means through the use of nanorobotics.

Dad's research is dense. He used to speak that way, too, circling the issue, and providing the information, waiting for me to discover the meaning behind his words.

Across from me, Representative Belles stares out the window of his office.

This isn't really the representative—he's dreaming of himself here with me now.

I hear soft singing and a guitar playing again.

He turns around me, his smile apologizing for their distracting noise. "My son," he says again.

I turn back to the desk.

Internal Report: Update on Dr. Philip Shepherd
Please note: The doctor's wife, inventor and scientist Rose Shepherd, has been diagnosed with Hebb's Disease. Dr. Shepherd has not asked for leave from his scientific research, but instead requests further funding for nanorobotic research in conjunction with his current theory and development.

Representative Belles touches the window, and I see that, despite the fact we're nearly at the top of the tallest Triumph Tower, there's a bumblebee beating against the glass, trying to get in. "I really do support what you're doing," the representative says. "As soon as I read your father's research and realized what the UC was doing to people, I knew I couldn't do nothing."

Another file slides across the representative's desk.

Memo
To: Jack Tyler, Research Assistant
From: Dr. Philip Shepherd

Effective immediately, you are dismissed from my employment. Should you need further information or answers pertaining to our past research together, you may consult my daughter, Ella Shepherd.

Ha! I don't have any answers at all.

I look up, and realize that Representative Belles has moved away from the window. His eyes are zeroed in on me, and he stands uncomfortably close.

"Yes?" I ask.

"My son," Representative Belles's says for the third time. "He's all I have left."

I turn my full focus on him.

Everything goes blindingly white, then solid black.

Sparks flash in the darkness.

"My son," Representative Belles says. "My son. My son. He's all I have left. My son."

"What did you do?" I whisper.

The sparks flash and die, flash and die.

"My son. My son. My son. My son. My son."

"What did you do?" I shout.

The sparks. Just like the last one I saw in my mother's replicated body.

It's thought.

And the darkness means his thought is dying. Representative Belles is dying.

I look up at him, his face illuminated by the flashes. Blood leaks from a hole in his skull, dripping down his nose, spilling on either side between his eyes, falling like tears over his face.

"I think I've been shot," he says. His eyes focus on me. "If I die, do you die, too? I'm sorry. My son. He's all I have left."

Oh, God. If he dies, do I die, too? Can he trap me in his dying body; will mine rot away, empty?

"Maybe I can live if I go back the way you came. Maybe I get to have your body, and you can stay in mine until it's dead and gone."

Representative Belles struggles toward me, lurching like a zombie. The bright, shimmering sparks fire rapidly, like a strobe, and he gets closer with every flash. I turn on my heel. I have to escape. I have to leave his mind, find mine.

You're not in your right mind, Ella.

Dad's voice cuts across my thought. Shit! I can't have a breakdown now, no hallucinations, no bees buzzing through my brain.

Representative Belles grabs my wrist, leaving a hot, red smear of blood on my skin. I slip away, running. I can hear his footsteps coming closer, his breath on the back of my neck. The sparks of his thoughts sizzle now, burning out like a snuffed candle rather than a flash of lightning. I hear sounds behind me: children's laughter, sobbing, inscrutable words, muffled moans, joyous shouts.

And then I hear nothing.

That's the first to go, then, sound.

I slow to a stop. Representative Belles is still chasing me, but it's like he's running on a treadmill and I'm standing still. No matter how much he runs, he can't reach me.

I smell oranges.

Representative Belles stops.

"I don't want to die," he says.

"Neither do I," I whisper.

Darkness washes over us.

SIXTY-SEVEN

I DON'T KNOW WHERE I AM.

"Ella!" a voice shouts. I don't recognize the voice, but it fills me with warmth and comfort. I shiver in its absence.

"Hello?" I call. "Where am I?"

"Ella!" the voice yells, but I cannot tell where it is coming from. The sound wraps around me, spreading like spilt water and then evaporating into silence.

"Where am I?" I whisper again.

The darkness stretches out for eternity.

I take a few steps forward, but the feeling is surreal— I cannot tell if I've actually moved or not, because everything is nothing. I feel something wet and warm slide down my cheek, and I touch the tear with my fingertips, swiping it away.

Representative Belles is dead. I'm certain of that now. He's gone. I'm… I'm in the place where he was, and now he's gone, and now I'm stuck. I'm stuck in the nothingness of a dead body, and I don't know how to get out.

My heart thuds against my chest, and I gasp for air. What if I can never get out? What if eternity is nothing more than me, alone, in the darkness? Trapped in someone else's death.

I collapse, but it's not like I fall on the floor. There is no floor. There was the illusion of one, but as my body gives way, I realize that I'm floating. I stretch out, my fingers and toes aching to feel, but there's nothing, nothing at all, and I draw myself into myself, hugging my legs, my knees tucked under my chin.

I'm alone.

Maybe when Representative Belles died, I died too.

Maybe this is it.

"ELLA!" the voice roars again, and finally, I recognize it.

"Jack?" I say, lifting my head and looking futilely into the darkness.

"Ella, wake up, please, please, wake up." His voice is softer now, almost gone.

And then one last whisper wraps around me.

"I need you."

I open my eyes.

I expected the first thing I'd see to be Jack, but he's not beside me. He's broken a piece off the reverie chair— one of the arms, the one not connected to my cuff, and he's ramming it into the control panel by the door. I rip the electrodes off my skin and leap up from the chair.

"What's happening?" I gasp. I clutch my head, momentarily overwhelmed with dizziness.

"I heard a gunshot," Jack says. "I went across the hall and I saw—" He turns then, and sees me. "Are you okay?"

I wave him aside and stand. "I'm fine. I—that's never happened before." When I saw the last spark of life in my mother fade, that was different from this tsunami of pain and regret, this sudden flash of darkness and death.

The sliding door that leads into the reverie chamber creaks as the mechanics try to open it. Jack curses, driving the bit of the chair deep into the electronic tap-lock. I hear the heavy thud of bolts shooting down into the floor, sealing the door closed.

Jack whirls around. "It was a trap. All of this—it was a trap."

I stumble again, and sit back down on the reverie chair.

"The Prime Administrator was here. She killed Representative Belles," Jack says. His eyes are wild, panicked. "I saw—I saw the gun in her hand. The bullet hole…"

"He had a son," is all I can think to say.

"Ella!" I can hear her now, PA Young, calling to us from the other side of the door Jack's sealed closed. "Open the door, please, dear."

I hear the echo of Representative Belles's voice, pleading for me to understand. He was scared. He didn't want to betray us... but he did. He had to. PA Young forced him to bring us right here, right to the exact place where she had control, and then she killed him. Because he had a son, the last of the family she'd already nearly destroyed.

"I couldn't wake you," Jack says. "I couldn't get you out." He sounds defeated, as if he's doomed us all.

I look around the room wildly. The things that were all designed to provide us comfort—the chair, now broken, the walls of sensory screens and soothing lights—it's all just the trappings of a prison.

He couldn't wake me, so he locked us in here.

"There's no other door," I say, turning to Jack. "That's the only way in or out."

Jack's jaw hardens.

The door echoes with a thud.

I raise my wrist, my fingers sliding across the screen of my cuff, hoping to call for help. But nothing happens.

"I tried that already," Jack says, nodding at my cuff. "But we got that from Representative Belles."

"And he got it from Young," I say.

Jack nods once, strained. "It was all a setup."

The door shudders. It's made of solid steel and reinforced with lockdown rods.

Then silence.

Then soft clicks of metal-on-metal. PA Young is attaching something to the steel doors.

Jack whirls around and grabs me by the shoulders, yanking both of us to the corner, as far away from the door as possible. "Ella," he says, more emotion in that one word than I've ever heard before. "Ella, the door won't hold. She's going to get in. She's going to get us."

His fingers dig into my shoulder, and while it's painful, I relish the sensation. As long as he's holding on to me, he's here, and that's enough.

"They might kill me."

"No!" I say. The word rips out of me with a force I didn't know I have. The idea of Jack, dead, Jack, gone—it fills me up with the same sort of darkness as I felt when I was lost in Representative Belles's empty shell of a body.

"I'm not important," Jack says. "They don't need me. They'll probably—"

"*No!*" I scream the word, shutting my eyes and shaking my head.

"Listen," Jack hisses, pulling me closer, his fingers tightening even more on my shoulders. "Listen, Ella. No matter what happens to me, *you have to escape.* You hear me? You have to escape."

Now I hear soft beeps.

A countdown clock to whatever explosives have been strapped to the door.

"Your father knew," Jack says. My focus whips back to him. "He knew something was wrong, and they killed him for it. You have to figure it out, Ella. You have to stop them. You are the key."

"I'm not, I'm nothing, I'm not," I say, tears burning my eyes.

The world rips open.

The flash of light is so bright that I'm momentarily blinded. All I can do is clutch Jack as we both scream over the sound of the metal wall disintegrating—the solid steel door with bolts in the floor that is supposed to be impenetrable. The metal at the edges glows orange-red.

As the smoke clears, PA Young's image appears. And behind her—

Androids. Of course, androids. At least these are true robots, without the face of anyone I know or love. But still, she controls them. She controls everything.

"Ella, you are the key," Jack says urgently, forcing my attention back on him. "Your father knew he was being targeted. He told me before he died; he told me he would hide the information *inside* of you. I didn't understand that before, but now I do. That's why I came back to warn you; you're the key, you're the key to it all."

I nod, tears dripping down my nose.

"He hid information for you, I'm sure of it, something only you can find. *Find it.* Whatever happens to me, don't give up. Ella, I believe in you. I know you can finish what your father started. I—"

The androids move closer, their footsteps heavy on the tiled floor.

Jack wraps his arms around me, pulling me close and whirling me away, protecting me with his body.

For one brief moment, it is only him and me as the world falls apart around us.

His head dips close. "Don't forget, Ella," he says in a low voice, only for my ears. And then his mouth comes crashing down against mine, his kiss panic driven and desperate, his arms clutching me against his rock-hard body, supporting me as my own legs turn to jelly. He holds me as if he wants to crush our bodies together, but his grip isn't strong enough, and silicone-covered metal fingers worm their way between us, and Jack is yanked back, thrown against the floor so violently that his body bounces.

"Really, we don't have time for this," PA Young says dispassionately as two androids hold Jack against the ground. I stumble away, my body confused by his sudden absence. Jack bucks against the floor, trying to throw the androids off, but PA Young swoops down.

And then I see what's in her hand.

A small spray bottle, filled with bright green liquid.

I try to twist away, but she's too quick. The reverie drug puffs into my eyes. The last thing I see before being enveloped in darkness is Jack's still body being dragged away.

SIXTY-EIGHT

MY EYES FLY OPEN, AND I'M AWAKE.

And alone.

In the reverie chamber. Why did they leave me here? How long have I been out?

My first thought is of Jack. I scramble up from the wreckage of the reverie chamber and look frantically around. But he's gone. And so is PA Young and the androids.

They left me.

But then, why did they drug me? Maybe I've only been passed out a few seconds—maybe my inhuman body found a way to bypass the drug.

My mind races. Julie can't be far away; if I could find her, we could perhaps save Jack. Save him from a megalomaniac who rules the entire civilized world and an army of androids.

Shit.

I creep deliberately over the debris, careful to make no sound. I slink to the doorway, peering outside, but there's no one there.

THE BODY ELECTRIC

The door to the other reverie chamber, the one where Representative Belles was, is open. A light is on.

I see a shadow.

I move forward. All the monitors along the control room show nothing but blackness and static. There is no sound, outside of my thudding heart.

I peer into the other reverie chamber.

The first thing I see is the chair, and the blood. It leaks through a hole in the center of the headrest, a thick, viscous liquid that moves slowly, like syrup, but I know what it is.

A fat bumblebee meanders across my vision. I snatch it from the air, crushing its fuzzy, crunching body between my fingers. I do not have time to hallucinate right now.

"Ella!" a voice gasps, and on the other side of the room, I see Ms. White. We rush to each other, both babbling in frantic relief.

"We have to get out of here," I say as she glances around wildly, telling me how she escaped PA Young.

"There are guards everywhere. Why are you here?" Ms. White gasps.

I think of what Jack said. "It was a trap."

Ms. White clutches me harder. "I was trying to get out—they locked me in your mother's room, hoping you'd return and they could use me against you. Some androids brought a boy about your age into your apartment to lock him up, and I used their distraction to get out. But there's a whole army of androids blocking the exits. And then I came down here, and I saw... and I thought..." Her voice is choked with unshed sobs as her eyes skim from me to the bloodstained reverie chair.

"We have to get out," I repeat, only half-listening to her. My mind is racing, trying to figure out an escape plan.

"And Hwa," Ms. White continues, her eyes distant as she talks about PA Young. "I thought she was my friend. Oh, God, Ella—I used to think... some people contacted me, a few weeks ago, with information about Hwa's method of ruling... and Ella... she's a tyrant, she's nothing like what I thought, and I tried to get out, to get both of us out, but she must have guessed, she must have realized..."

"This isn't your fault," I say, grabbing Ms. White's arm. "It's mine. I found the Zunzana, the group that's been fighting PA Young here in Malta. Everything we thought about PA Young and my father's research... it was all wrong."

Ms. White grows very still. Then she tilts her head, staring into my eyes. "Your father's research," she says. "Do you know... what does that have to do with anything?"

"I'm still trying to figure that out," I say. "But PA Young somehow combined Dad's research in cybernetics and Mom's research with reveries to make... these things. They're called cy-clones. Cyborg-clones. Part machine, part person. As strong as an android, but with human intelligence."

And I'm one, I think, but do not say.

Ms. White starts pacing.

"I can see how that would work..." she says. "Your father had long been experimenting with bio-engineering and cybernetics. But—" She turns to face me. "You said 'clone.' To make a clone, you need a person to be cloned. And to make a thinking robot, you need..." She gasps. "They use your mother's reveries, don't they? They make a body, then use the reveries to transfer a person's soul from their human body into the engineered one."

I nod silently.

"But that means..." Ms. White pales. "The person who is transferred dies, doesn't she?"

I try to speak, but I can't—my mouth is full of honey. I smack my lips, trying to eviscerate the sweet taste. I focus on Ms. White, still marching around the room. I *cannot* go crazy, not now, not with so much on the line.

"Akilah...," I manage to say, barely able to spit out the words. "Mom..." *Me.*

Ms. White's face is pale, her eyes unfocused as she thinks. She hasn't noticed my struggle to speak. "I suspect that the government's been able to figure out at least a rudimentary method of creating cy-clones. It makes sense—they've figured out an alternative formula for your mother's reverie drug, and patched together at least some of your father's lost research. That's what I could piece together from what I overheard while being held prisoner, at least."

"They have?" I gasp, shocked.

Ms. White nods absent-mindedly. "So now the government's figured out a way to copy some of what your father developed. But copies and imitations are never as good as the original version."

Version.

I blink, and for just that moment—the space between shutting my eyes and opening them again—I'm back in the labs where my father was killed, where my mother died, where I saw three little icy morgue doors, each labeled.

Ella Shepherd, Vers. 1

Ella Shepherd, Vers. 2

Ella Shepherd, Vers. 3

And then my heart slams into my chest with the force of a defibrillator bringing it back to life, and I'm back in the reverie chamber with Ms. White.

"Are you okay?" she asks. She's stopped pacing. She's right in front of me, even though less than a second ago she was on the other side of the room.

"Fine," I say, over the sound of buzzing.

Her mouth moves, but I cannot hear whatever she's saying.

I can only hear the bees.

"STOP!" I scream

Silence.

Ms. White stares at me, worry etched into each line of her face.

"Are you okay?" she asks again.

"No," I whisper.

I'm going mad, I'm going mad,
I'm
going
mad.

Ms. White frames my face with her long, slender fingers. "Ella," she says. "We have to save you."

"No," I say, "We have to save Akilah and Jack."

But then I realize that the words never left my mouth. My lips are sewn shut, not with thread, but with bee stingers, piercing the soft, pink skin that, just hours ago, Jack kissed.

Ms. White brushes my sweaty hair off my forehead. "Ella, your father was a genius. He developed the nanobots that saved your mother, and the technology that recreated her when she could not be saved any more. He made the first cy-clone. He gave your mother a piece of immortality."

She peers deeply into my eyes.

"But he was only thinking of saving your dear mother, my best friend. And I loved him for it. But the government... it wants the formula. If they can make cy-clones out of healthy, young people, not people who were already sick like your mother, they can create the perfect soldiers."

"Ella, dear," Ms. White continues, oblivious to the one-sidedness of our conversation. "Your father knew what the government wanted. Knew how much the government would pay for his research. And he destroyed it all."

"And then the government destroyed him." The words fall out of me, each one escaping my mouth like a tiny bumblebee soaring past my lips.

Ms. White nods. "They killed him before they realized the research they had was falsified and useless."

I open my mouth, my jaw cracking like plaster. "But they made cy-clones. Akilah."

"Oh, yes. Your friend Akilah. And dozens of others. But none of them are good. They are poor copies of your father's original work. The government hasn't been able to recreate the methods perfectly. Eventually, all these models break. They last maybe one or two years."

I struggle to move, but can't.

"I think—I'm just guessing here, but I think that PA Young and the government believes there's some key hidden inside you."

That's what Jack said too, almost exactly.

"If we could figure out the information your father left you—"

I cannot speak, I cannot move of my own free will, but my body shakes violently, my head whipping back and forth, *no, no, no.*

Ms. White frames my face with her hands, stilling me. "Perhaps he told you something, some memory you can no longer access."

I can no longer access Jack.

Ms. White's eyes shift back to the reverie chair. "Ella, I think... if we can find that secret inside of you, we... we might just have the weapon we need to fight PA Young and the corrupt government she's building."

"Run..." I manage to say. *We have to run.*

"Run where?" Ms. White asks, her voice even.

I blink—*the safe house, the android Kim, the lab where Jack kissed me, Akilah strapped to a gurney*—and then I'm back in the reverie chair, Ms. White leaning over me.

"Go..." the word is a struggle to say, almost impossible to hear.

"Go where?" Ms. White repeats. "Go to sleep?"

What? No. That doesn't make any sense.

Ms. White leads me to the reverie chair. She pushes my shoulders gently, trying to get me to sit down. A bee lands on her face, walking over her eye, trailing its stinger along her lashes.

"I don't know if this is real," I whisper, but the sound is lost in the buzzing of bees.

SIXTY-NINE

A HOT TEAR SLIPS DOWN MY CHEEK, and with it, the hallucinations fade.

"Ella?" Ms. White asks. She is the model of concern.

I look down. Without realizing it, I'm already strapped into the reverie chair. I can feel the drying blood from Representative Belles's gunshot wound on the back of the headrest. I blink and the restraints are gone. Blink again, and they're back, but they are black and yellow and fuzzy and sting my skin.

"I think I'm going crazy," I say.

Ms. White blanches. "It's all the nanobots inside you. You're getting bot-brain."

But it's not the nanobots. The nanobots are a side-effect of being a cy-clone, not the cause of my madness.

"What's happening to me?" My words come out slow, dripping from my tongue like honey.

Ms. White leans back. Her dress is green—why didn't I notice that before?—the same poison green as the reverie drug.

"Ella, dear, you know I love you. And your mother."

I nod. I try to pull away from the restraints on the chair. I can't see them, not always, but I can feel them.

"But you're not you any more, are you?"

My eyes widen with shock. I feel as if there are bees crawling under my skin, trying to vibrate their way out.

"You're a computer. One with a very valuable file locked up inside your mind." Ms. White steps closer, her eyes wide with sympathy. "I know," she says gently. Kindly. "I've known for a while. It doesn't matter to me. But I'm afraid of what will happen if we don't get that file out of you. Ella, I need for you to go into a reverie. I need for you to find the information your father hid inside of you. That's how we escape this nightmare, Ella. That's the only way."

I try to shake my head—*No, this cannot be it, this feels like giving up*—but then I see a figure moving behind Ms. White.

Dad.

You need to wake up, Ella, he says, but Ms. White doesn't notice him.

It's all in my mind.

I'm in my right mind now, and my right mind is crazy.

You need to wake up, Ella.

The words are a command I cannot obey.

"Have you ever wondered why you always access reveries through filing cabinets?" Dad asked.

When I access memories, I look through them as if they are a filing cabinet. A system that humans no longer really use—but computers do. Computers like me. Dad...

Dad *programmed* me. That's why I could hack Representative Belles's computer so easily—because my brain is a processor. It talks to computers as easily as it talks to other people.

Dad *made* me. And he made my brain programmed to discover the truth. The hallucinations, his constant message—*You need to wake up, Ella.* He's been trying to get me to find the truth for as long as I've been made.

My eyes open wide. I know what I have to do. I have to wake up.

And then Ms. White puffs the reverie drug into my eyes, and I fall instantly asleep.

I am standing in a room—the laboratory under Triumph Towers. I stand on the other side of the frosted glass door that leads to the lab marked **Reverie Transfer.** *Through the glass, I can hear people shouting.*

One of them is my father.

"NO!" he bellows. "It's unethical, and I will not do it!"

Something nudges me in the back. I turn and see Ms. White. But not the Ms. White who I just found in the reverie chamber. This is Ms. White from last year, with last year's haircut. She's calmly holding a gun, the barrel of it resting against the small of my back.

"Go on in, dear," she says kindly.

THE BODY ELECTRIC

My legs tremble as the door slides open. My eyes go to my father. I see the fear in his face, anger. Defeat.

Ms. White pushes me forward, and I stumble into the lab.

"Ella, baby, I'm sorry. I'm so sorry," Dad says. "I didn't know..."

I look frantically around the room. Perhaps if I could make a weapon... One wall is covered in unlabeled morgue doors, many of which are open and empty. The desk to the side of the wall is bare, except for a microscope and several glass vials marked "Phydus Prototypes." Perhaps I could smash one over Ms. White's head...

Ms. White pushes me into the reverie chair standing in the center of the room. It's connected to another reverie chair, but that chair is empty.

"Philip," Ms. White says genially. "We've tried negotiating with you. We've tried bribing you. I want you to know that, really, this is your fault."

She raises the gun to my head. I can feel the hard metal rim of the barrel pressed against the thin skin over my skull. She pushes the gun against my head so hard that I'm forced back against the chair, my skull trapped between the metal chair back and the metal gun barrel.

"Jadis, please!" Dad says. He's begging.

"Will you give us the formula and procedure notes you used to transfer your wife into a new body?"

"My wife—your friend!"

Ms. White nods. "My friend. The one who never shared her reverie formula with me. The one who won't go public with the mental spa. The one who only gives me a salary, not a true partnership."

"You love her! You're Ella's godmother, for God's sake!"

Ms. White shows no emotion on her face. "Loved, Philip," she says. "I loved her. But she's a shell of who she was now. I gave her everything, even my right arm. But I've learned. If I want anything, I have to take it for myself." Ms. White presses the gun against me harder, and I cannot bite back a whimper of pain.

"Would it help," Ms. White continues casually, "if I told you that we know most of the formula already? We know that the transfer only works in a clone of the same person—we can't swap bodies. We know that the percentage of nanobots in the clone must be high for the transfer to work. We know that clones have the ability to be enhanced with cyborg parts and are stronger, faster, and smarter than their original counterparts, and have the potential to live longer. As long as they're not already afflicted with Hebb's Disease, of course."

She snaps the fingers on her free hand, and someone I can't see walks to the back wall. I can hear a door zipping open, the metal slab sliding out, a thud of a body, a grunt of someone picking it up. Ms. White slides the gun down the side of my face, forcing my head to turn to the left and watch as a perfect copy of myself is dumped gracelessly into the reverie chair beside me. The replica-me has glassy eyes and her head lolls listlessly as a scientist I don't recognize straps her body into the reverie machine.

"Thank you, Dr. Simpa," Ms. White says absently.

I stare at the body on the chair. She's empty. A shell of a person. Made up of cloned material, but also cyborg parts, metal and wires and computers beneath skin and flesh. Ms. White wants to force Dad to move me, the real me, into this manufactured replacement body.

"If I give you the formula, I'm handing you the most effective weapon the world has ever known," Dad says hollowly. "You'll make perfect soldiers. This would be more devastating than Einstein's formula for the atomic bomb."

Ms. White stares at him blandly. "I won't do any of that. I'm just selling the formula. I don't care what they do with it."

Dad shifts so that he can meet my eyes. "Ella," he says. "I'm sorry."

And I know he won't do it. He won't trade me for the whole world.

Ms. White slides the gun down the side of my face, into the hollow between my collarbones, pressing the metal barrel painfully into my chest, resting over my heart.

"Last chance," she says idly.

"I can't," Dad whispers. "Ella, I'm sor—"

Ms. White pulls the trigger.

Everything goes dark, and then I open my eyes.

Dad leans over my body. "Ella?" he asks. "Are you in there?"

I nod my head, then look to the right.

I am dead in the chair beside me. There's a hole in my chest, and blood, so much blood, and too-white bone, and murky grey-ish pink bits of me dripping from the chair.

My hands go unconsciously to my mouth as I gasp in shock, tasting bile. But then my fingers wonderingly explore my face—my face. I'm dead. Right there is my body. But I'm here. Not dead.

Dad wraps his hands around either side of my face and forces me to look at him. "Ella," he says. "I couldn't not do it. I had to save you. I had to. But baby, I'm going to make sure you have the truth. And control." He takes a deep breath. "I am going to make sure you can do what I couldn't."

SEVENTY

HE DIDN'T DIE IN AN ATTACK FROM terrorists. He wasn't killed by a rogue android sneaking into the labs—that was all manufactured. I try to remember the video PA Young showed me—just Dad talking with his colleagues, a brief image of the android, a flash of light. That could be faked. And I fell for it.

Dad didn't kill me. He saved me.

I open my eyes blearily. Ms. White hovers over me, anxious. "What did you discover?" she asks.

My mouth opens. I try to shift my arms, and realize they are still strapped down to the chair, immobilizing me.

"I discovered that you *killed* me, you bitch," I snarl, struggling against the chair.

Ms. White rolls her eyes. "Oh, not this again."

"Again?" I strain against the restraints, trying to break free.

"I loved your mother. And I love you, Ella. But we've had this argument before, whether you remember it or not."

It's not until that moment that I recall how my memories have been tampered with, that someone erased Jack from me. And, apparently, more than just him.

"I offered you money. I offered you a home, with me."

I spit in her face.

"You did that last time, too." She sounds bored. "It really would be easier if you'd just tell me your father's method. How did he make you? Did you discover anything new in that reverie? The secrets are locked inside of you, I'm certain of that."

"I will never tell you anything," I snarl.

Ms. White calmly rears her cyborg arm up, crashing it against the side of my face so violently that my head snaps back. I taste blood in my mouth. I may be a cy-clone, but her arm is cyborobotic, and it hit me with the force of a wrecking ball.

"You will tell me everything, one way or another," she says with certainty. "You're just a glorified computer, and computers can be reprogrammed. They can be hacked."

Something about the cold, emotionless way she says this breaks me. Hot tears slide down my cheeks, veering down my face at an odd angle since I'm still strapped down to the reclining chair. "Why?" I ask, all my hopes and fears bundled into that one word.

"When your father cured your mother, all he saw was her. But I saw something more. A chance at peace, at immortality."

I stare at her, horrified.

"Think of how nice the world would be if everyone is a cy-clone. Humans who allow themselves to be gently guided into doing the right thing. Terrorism will be a thing of the past. Anger, hatred—it will all fade away. True equality, true peace, true prosperity."

"You don't want citizens," I say flatly. "You want slaves."

"Androids are slaves. That's what the word 'robot' means, you know, slave. But—"

I interrupt. "That's what you want to turn people into."

"No—no," Ms. White says, frowning. "Not at all. Cy-clones are not androids. There's a difference."

"Not when you control them."

Ms. White makes a frustrated noise. "Either way, there will be peace. No more threat of war. No more terrorism."

"No more freedom."

This is why the government—controlled by Ms. White—was willing to stage the android explosion and wrap it up in the pretense of a terrorist strike. People do desperate things in war. They sell out the causes they believe in, like Representative Belles did, or they take stupid risks, like Jack and the Zunzana. But one of the first things to go in a time of war is simply freedom.

This—this long, long nightmare—has all been about the manipulation. And didn't PA Young tell me that from the start? I just didn't listen.

"Your mother and father were so... limited... in what they were willing to do with their technology," Ms. White says. "I can sell cy-clone upgrades to the rich as immortality. Cy-clones are nearly impossible to kill, and they live much longer natural lives. And of course, the peace and prosperity—not just for me, but for all."

And then I realize: This is not just about war. This is about the fame, the prestige. My mother never allowed Ms. White to have full access to the reverie system and the formula for the reverie drug. My father blocked Ms. White utterly from his cy-clone research. They may not have known how corrupt she was, or maybe they did and it was too late, but either way, Ms. White has been blocked by my parents. Mom only ever intended reveries to be used to help people relive their happiest memories. Dad only ever wanted to use cy-clones to save Mom. It was Ms. White who saw the advantage of combining the two procedures to develop something that will turn a profit and give her the ultimate control of the entire Unified Countries.

"Ella, you have no idea, no idea at all, how rich war can make someone. I know. I saw what happened to the leaders of the Secessionary War, the ones who made weapons, the ones who fed off the fear of others."

I stare at Ms. White's arm. She was in the science labs at the Lunar Colonies when she was my age, just like Dad and Mom were. I usually think of my parents at the colonies in a sort of idyllic way—it's where they met, where they fell in love. But they were there because they were geniuses in science, and so was Ms. White. My father was a master of robotics, and Mom invented reveries. But Ms. White... Ms. White is where the cyborg part came from.

There will be terrorism. Ms. White and the android explosion has seen to that. And that terrorism will make people scared, and that will make them get reveries, and that will make them accept the procedure to become cyclones. And Ms. White will pull all the strings. She will manipulate the entire country... the entire world... right into the palm of her hand.

"And in the end," Ms. White says, "wouldn't I deserve it? This war really *will* end all wars, and we'll have world-wide peace."

"A brainwashed peace," I say.

Ms. White waves her hand as if this doesn't matter. "It's so simple. Make a war, make some money. End the war, make more money. Give people the chance to live in utter bliss. Peace and prosperity."

I don't know which she wants more: world peace, or a throne of gold. But either way, she'll get them both. "Don't try to dress this up as nobility," I snarl.

"What did you think?" Ms. White says. "That this was some elaborate action-thriller? You against the world, you versus the big, bad government? I have news for you, dear. It's never the government that's evil. It's not like the world is divided up between good and bad like that, and no one cares if you're willing to fight the good fight, because there is no good fight in the first place. It really is as simple as this: we do what we have to in order to get what we want."

"And you want money."

"Gobs of it. Don't you?"

"Not at this price."

Ms. White shrugs. "And now we are at a crossroads—and a decision."

"A decision?"

"Actually, it's more of a final chance. You see now, don't you, Ella?" Ms. White asks softly. "Give me your father's formula. If we know how he made you, we can recreate the process, make better cy-clones. Ones that will last longer, ones that will work perfectly. None of the ones we've made so far have been as successful as you. None are stable."

I think, then, of the flash of reality I saw in Akilah's eyes. Ms. White believes that all the cy-clones she has made so far are breaking down, but maybe they're just breaking free.

"Let me go," I growl, jerking my arms and legs against the restraints futilely. Because the only thing I know for certain now is that I cannot let Ms. White have the information she wants.

"If you tell me your father's method of making cyclones," she says idly.

"I thought you said you could hack a computer," I say bitterly. Because isn't that all I am to her? A computer?

"What do you think I'm doing?" Ms. White says, dosing me with more reverie drug.

SEVENTY-ONE

WHEN I OPEN MY EYES, I AM STANDING in the reverie chamber. My body is on a chair—not struggling against restraints, but asleep. I know, even though I cannot see, Ms. White is plugged into the other chair.

None of this is real. We are in a reverie. We've been in a reverie the whole time, ever since I "woke up."

When PA Young broke into the reverie chamber, she took Jack, and she dosed me with the drug. And then someone strapped me into the chair. And Ms. White plugged herself into the other chair, the one Representative Belles had been using. And from the moment I "woke up" to right now, I've been inside Ms. White's reverie. She's been manipulating me, tricking me, trying to find a way to discover whatever the hell it was my father hid inside me.

But now that I *know* I'm in a reverie, I can see through the fabric of lies she's woven around me.

I understand now, in a way I did not before. This is all in my head.

Including Dad, who is standing beside me.

"I tried to save you," he says.

"I know." And I do. All that he did for me, all of it, was just to save the people he loved. Mom. Me.

He made sure I had access to the memories I would need. The hallucinations I had in the reveries before—it was me, trying to access the hidden parts of my mind. It was Dad, protecting me. When I needed the information, he tried to help me get it. The images of him in the reveries were files of himself he saved in my mind.

He hid the truth inside me.

"Truth lies in the heart of fortune," he says.

But that is not one of his sayings. Dad was always full of pithy saying—*Eyes are the window to the soul; Get knocked down twice, stand up three times*—but "truth lies in the heart of fortune," wasn't one of his sayings.

It was just the thing we printed on his tombstone.

We. Mom and me.

But. Mom was sick. When Dad died. She couldn't do anything.

I arranged the funeral.

I picked the tree—a holly—to commemorate Dad. I picked the casket he was cremated in. I picked the songs played at his funeral.

I picked the memorial engraved on his plaque.

Dad's been giving me clues this whole time. The bees, the hallucinations. I didn't know what I was before, and, just as Kim had automatic defenses to prevent it from sticking its hand in a pot of boiling soup, I had unconscious automatic defenses to keep me from learning the horrible truth about myself. Only in moments of panic and fear did my true nature shine—the way I attacked Jack when I first saw him without really knowing anything about self-defense, the way I never let my mind really question how I could do reveries and no one else could, the way I had the strength to save Mom and myself when Rosie blew up, the way I could hold my breath forever. My true nature flickered if I needed it, just on the edge of my consciousness.

And when I started to question it, when I came a little too close to the truth… my mind and body fought me, too. The seizures, the hallucinations. All designed inside my head, like a choreographed dance, showing me just enough to find the right path to the truth.

But that clue—*Truth lies in the heart of fortune*—that was left for me, by me. Dad was dead. He couldn't tell me that secret.

I grip the little fortune cookie charm I wear around my neck—the one Dad gave me, the one I always wear. I remember putting a digi file of Akilah and me playing when we were younger into the locket.

Truth lies in the heart of fortune.

But… I've never actually looked at the fortune cookie locket for… a long time. I don't recall *ever* opening the locket. Every time I came close, I would have a piercing pain in my head or a seizure or a hallucination, and I would forget.

I don't have pain now.

I know what I have to do. To find the last secrets in my mind, all I have to do is open my locket. Open the secret I hid for myself. I slip my fingernail in the crack around the edge of the metal fortune cookie. It pops open, and a single, scrolled piece of paper flops into my hand.

I tremble as I slide apart the tiny scroll. A bot code is written across the front in black ink, one designed to automatically launch a program when it's linked to my eye bots.

"The eyes are the window to the soul," I whisper, staring down at the code. A tiny spot in my head between my eyebrows starts to ache with a sharp pain that quickly fades to throbbing.

And then everything shifts.

My brain is a computer, and nothing on a computer is ever really erased. In the darkness, I see a filing cabinet.

A plain filing cabinet with a hand-written label in green ink. **JACK TYLER.**

Standing on one side of the filing cabinet is my father. In his hand is a silver key.

"You locked away my memories of Jack?" I ask.

Dad hands me the key. "I couldn't have," he says.

And then I realize: that is true.

I met Jack—I dated him, I fell in love with him—*after Dad's death.*

No.

I stare down at the silver key.

No.

No.

I couldn't have.

Only one person can alter memories.

I slide the key into the lock, and the drawer slips open easily. The memories spill out like photographs, moving in quick scenes. An awkward meeting. First kiss. Last fight. Then I see the one that's all black, sucking away the light of the others like a black hole.

I touch it and slip into a memory so visceral that it feels as if I'm living it.

In my hand is the open fortune cookie locket. I look up, having just experienced the memory it hid.

I had done this before—I had sought the truth, and I had found it. That was one more thing, like Jack, that I forgot about.

Ms. White stands in front of me. Not the Ms. White from today, or the one from the other reverie, but a Ms. White I recognize from the more recent past.

Angry tears spring to my eyes. "You killed me!" I accuse. "You killed my father."

Ms. White waves her hand, dismissing me.

"I won't let you control me," I say.

Ms. White pinches the bridge of her nose. "I don't want to control you," she says. "I just want to get paid. I've invested a lot of time and energy into you, you know."

"Dad would never want—"

"Your father didn't want to die, either. We'll figure it out, one way or another. Once I have your father's formula, I'll give you some of the payout. You can go. You can do whatever you want."

And the worst part is, I'm tempted.

"If I tell, you'll go to prison!"

"No, dear, I won't." Ms. White looks bored.

"I'll take Mom and run!"

Ms. White's bemused smile mocks me. "You can't run away with your mother. She's so sick, you see." More manipulation, although I had not realized it then.

I swallow, hard.

"I'll still go," I say softly.

Ms. White's eyes widen a little, and then she gets a manipulative, knowing look. "It's that boy isn't it? Jack."

"I love him!" I shout. The feeling wells up inside me, threatening to break through me like a flood.

Ms. White laughs. She laughs. "Well," she says, "we can't be having that. If he's going to encourage you to leave me, I'll just have to kill him. Like I killed his parents."

Horror washes over me. She could. She would.

"No!" I protest.

"Really, dear, you've given me no other choice."

"I'll stay!"

She shakes her head in mock-sorrow. "I just can't trust he wouldn't entice you to leave again."

"He doesn't entice me!" I shout.

Ms. White looks truly apologetic. "Just by existing, he does," she says. "He reminds you of freedom, and I can't be having you thinking that you can just leave me."

"I won't," I whisper. "I swear."

"Your promises mean nothing."

I stop, thinking. I am realizing all the power I have, and how it's all in her hands, as long as she holds Jack's life over me.

"I know a way," I say.

The screaming fight at his parents' funeral. I burn with shame and revulsion at my own actions—but I know the only way to truly keep Jack away from me is to hurt him so bad that he'll hate me.

"I never want to see you again!" I scream the lie, and I put all my love behind it.

Jack's plaintive plea. His question.

"Why?"

I sit down in the reverie chair, trembling. Ms. White looks down at me doubtfully. "Are you sure you can do this, dear?" she asks.

I know what she's thinking. If I mess up, she can just start again, this time with a fresh version of me.

"I can do this," I say. "I'll erase Jack entirely."

"You could just give me your father's research instead," Ms. White says.

My eyes burn with fear and frustration. "I don't know my father's research!" I plead. "I don't understand it at all. But if I make myself... acquiescent... I'm like a computer, that's what you said. You can hack into me. You can find what you need to know. Just... don't hurt Jack. Let me stay with Mom, and don't hurt Jack."

Ms. White contemplates my offer. Dad's information is hidden far, far into my subconscious, and the only chance she has of hoping to find it is by breaking into my mind. And that will take time.

"I have you, for as long as it takes," Ms. White says. "That's the deal. I have you until I have the information inside of you."

I nod, agreeing. "You'll make it so I don't know you're examining me?"

Ms. White's emotions bleed through her stony face for just a moment. "Yes," she says. "I can do that. I can run tests at night, when you're asleep, or when you're in reveries."

I look down at my hands. "Thank you."

"But if you try to leave me," Ms. White adds in a terrible cold voice, "I will assume you simply cannot be hacked, and I will perform a vivisection. You know what that means?"

I swallow hard. "I won't run," I say.

"If you don't do this, I know I won't be able to trust you, that that boy, Jack, is a distraction I must eliminate." She stares into my eyes. "It will be easy. I want you to know that. He signed up for the military after you broke his heart. Did you know that? I want you to understand how simple it would be to arrange his death. A little friendly fire, a little accident..."

"I can do this," I repeat.

I open my eyes.

"Hello dear," Ms. White says, smiling down at me.

"Hi!" I grin and start to take off the electrodes.

"Did you have a nice reverie?"

A small frown mars my blank face. "I don't... I don't remember."

"Are you going to see Jack later?" Ms. White asks.

"Who?" I say.

I did it.

Only one person can alter memories.

Me.

Only one person could have planted the tracker on Jack, left the tracker program in my private files for me to find him. Only one person could have laid down the groundwork for me to rediscover my own past, the past I erased.

Me.

I destroyed my own memories of Jack.

I did it to save him, to save me. But I'm the one who wiped him from my mind.

And it didn't save him, or me.

SEVENTY-TWO

I WAKE UP IN THE REVERIE CHAIR WITH Ms. White of today hanging over me, the restraints on my arms. Behind Ms. White, I see my father, smiling, reminding me that this isn't real, this is all a hallucination, all one more way to try to manipulate my father's secrets out of me and into her hands.

"This isn't real, either," I say, and the restraints melt away. I stand.

"Ella," Ms. White says, "Don't you see how much better we can make the world? Give me your father's formula. If we know how he made you, we can recreate the process, make better cy-clones."

And I do see—or rather, I hear. I hear the tiniest quiver in her voice.

She's scared of me.

Despite the bravado, despite her plans, there is one flaw.

Me.

She cannot have her perfect cy-clones without me. No one will sign up to become one if all they see is soulless, empty Akilah as an example of what they would become.

Behind Ms. White, I see my father, smiling, reminding me that this isn't real, this is all a hallucination, all one more way to try to manipulate my father's secrets out of me and into her hands.

We are in a reverie, and I am in control of the dreamscape.

"My father knew what you were, and he hid his research in the only place he knew you couldn't get to. Inside of *me*."

"Give it to me!" Ms. White screams, rushing at me.

But I just shut my eyes.

Ms. White tricked me into believing a reverie was real. And it was smart of her to make me think that. Because if there's one thing I can control, it's reveries.

I open my eyes. Ms. White stands before me, her face pale. I reach out and touch her forehead. "Time for you to open up to me," I whisper.

Her mind fights, but it is no match for me. Her memories spill out around us. Ms. White's mind swirls with thoughts—some of them no more than nebulous feelings, like guilt or love—some more distinct. Memories of me— as a baby, growing up—flicker in and out, like lightning behind a storm cloud.

"Did you ever really love me?" I wonder. Images rain down. All those times Ms. White urged me to go to college—part of it was manipulation. But part of it was a wish for me to escape. And when she saw me with Jack, there was, hidden beneath waves of grief and sorrow, a very small part of her that wished she could let me go, that didn't want to use me in her plot.

But there is a hollowness inside of her, and when she saw the chance to bridge it with money and power and control, she took it.

Jack. I can't save Ms. White—I can't save Mom or Dad. But I can still save Jack.

"Time to wake up," I say, and I slam the heel of my palm against her forehead.

This is real. I am in the reverie chair from before, and it feels like the dream, but this real. I try to stand, but there are straps here, too, holding me down. I feel my jaw clench. As if mere straps could restrain me.

I'm not human.

I'm better.

I lift my arms, and the straps snap away. Androids, followed by PA Young, pour into the room. They move as one, arms outstretched to hold me down, but my body is programmed with knowledge I'm not aware of. I let it take control. I strike and kick, punch and hurl, and the androids lie around me like more debris.

PA Young shifts her position, ready to strike me. "What are you doing?" I scream at her. "How can you be on Ms. White's side with this? You ended the Secessionary War—surely you can't—"

She doesn't speak; she just attacks. I race across the room, yanking out a piece of metal from the debris made when PA Young first broke into the room, and I slam it against her back, making her fall to one knee. I use the momentum to swing up, aiming for her head, but she dodges away, and I just clip her shoulder.

The sharp metal rips her silk blouse to shreds, slicing through the exposed skin underneath—the skin, and the glint of wire and bone mingled with blood and flesh. Sparks of electricity shoot through the pool of red blood dripping down her arm.

PA Young curses low under her breath.

I move instinctively, twisting the metal around her arm, winding it back, and bending it as if it were twine. Before she can move, I rip off a piece of the reverie chair and wrap the steel around her ankles. I may not be able to defeat a cy-clone, but I can at least capture it.

As I stand panting over the struggling form of the Prime Administrator of the entire Unified Countries global government, Ms. White calmly walks into the room.

"Even her?" I gasp, pointing.

"Don't you remember our talk with her, when you first met her at Triumph Towers? She said everyone has to pay a price for war. That was her price: becoming a cyclone."

I wonder how it happened. Did PA Young volunteer herself for this? Did she allow herself to die, for the chance to be immortal, in its own limited way? Did she know Ms. White would be able to control her like a puppet? Or did Ms. White force her to change?

"You're getting better," Ms. White says, surveying the damage I've done. "I did not expect you to wake from that reverie, or do all this. Your father would be proud."

I narrow my eyes. She is *not* allowed to speak of my father, never again.

She knows I'm a cyborg-clone. She knows that my bones are made of metal, my flesh enhanced with nanobots. She knows I could snap her like a twig.

But she strolls into the room as if I was as harmless as I once thought myself to be.

My hands clench around a part of the reverie chair I just awoke from, and the metal gives way, crumpling like tinfoil.

I will *crush* her.

I will watch the life flicker out of her like it faded from the shadow of my mother.

"It was so much easier when your mother was here," Ms. White says. "You really did have a blind spot for her. You were willing to stay without question, and you slept so soundly while I did my tests on you every night. We'll just have to find another way. Eventually, I will discover your secrets. Perhaps a vivisection, as I promised. Perhaps first with that boy you like, just for fun."

My fists clench. "You can go fu—"

Ms. White cuts me off. "Ella, dear, you know the great thing a computer can do, besides being hacked? It can be controlled."

She raises her arm and slides her fingers over her cuffLINK.

My muscles goes rigid, but my body thrums with some sort of energy I've never felt before.

"I control you, Ella," Ms. White says. "It will be easier for both of us if you accept this now."

I try to shake my head *no!* But I can't. I try to run away. But nothing inside me moves without her permission.

Ms. White sighs, sorrow in her eyes. "I don't want to do this, darling. You're like a daughter to me—or, at least, you were, before you became something not quite human. It—it hurts me when you have to be reprogrammed, when we have to modify you into something more compliant."

Ms. White stands up. Despite the fact that I am entirely immobile, she draws closer, so that our faces are mere centimeters apart. She stares into my eyes, as if she can see an answer within them. And then she leans back, resignation smeared across her face. When she speaks again, she has the slow drawl of someone who's hiding her pain behind mockery.

"It will be tedious if, from now on, I am forced to control you in this way. It hurts you, I know, and it's extra work for me. And I *do* care about you, darling, of course I do. Your cooperation will make our future much better. Cyborg-clones that acquiesce have a much better life. Just the same as people that do."

I struggle to just open my mouth and shout at her, but I cannot even twitch. My automatic functions—my heartbeat, blinking, breathing—that all happens. But even though I feel as if my heart should be racing, I can feel that it's not. I wonder if that's a part of her control too. If she could force it to stop, just with a command from her cuff.

SEVENTY-THREE

"NOW, ELLA, HERE'S WHAT'S GOING TO happen," Ms. White says. "You give me your father's secrets. And we'll make sure that the formula works. Representative Belles still has a son—let's try it on him. And when the formula works and you've given me what I need, I will let you go. And your little boyfriend. And I'll even give you enough money to leave this godforsaken island and do whatever it is you want with your life."

Before I can say anything, she adds, "*Or*, I can kill your little boyfriend in front of you, and you can do all this for me anyway."

No, I won't tell you anything, I won't, and you can't make me.

But, of course, she can.

"Remember, dear," Ms. White says. "I control you."

Something clicks in my mind. If she can control me, she wouldn't have needed all the subterfuge and lies. She wouldn't have already tried to trick this information out of me. She wouldn't be afraid right now.

All Ms. White is, is lies and manipulation.

She is trying to control me with fear, because she cannot control me any other way.

My eyes open wide. They *burn* as if they are on fire— no, as if they are made of fire. *Eyes are the window to the soul.* Something of the flames inside me must show, because Ms. White scrambles up and takes several steps away from me.

I turn my head to face her.

Ms. White's fingers tap frantically on her cuffLINK, but to no avail.

She no longer has *control.*

"I know they're going to try to use you," Dad whispers. "I've done what I can to make sure that I can save you. All the technology they forced me to make... I gave it a fail-safe." He looks into my eyes. "You."

I blink at him. I'm so confused. There's me, dead, and there's me here, and there's him telling me things I don't understand.

"Computers are faster than humans," Dad continues. "Steel is stronger than bone. And I made sure your brain cannot be controlled. You bypass their tech. They don't know it, but you do." He laughs softly. "There's so much they don't know. They didn't know I knew they were making a cloned version of you, that they wanted to use you as leverage to get my formula. Well, so they have it now. But I have something better."

He leans down, his mouth inches from my ear. I feel warmth encircle me—he's hugging me.

"I have you. For this moment, at least, I have you."

When he pulls away, there are tears his eyes. "You're the key to it all. You are stronger than them. You cannot be used by them. You can break the system. If they ever try to make you do something, I'll make sure you find a way to access your advanced tech, so you can—"

"Dr. Shepherd?" Ms. White's voice calls from the far side of the room. Footsteps echo throughout the room as she comes closer.

"You are the queen bee," Dad whispers just before Ms. White pushes him gently away from me, and her smiling face fills my vision.

"Oh, good, you're awake and not dead, Ella. I suppose that means the formula and procedures Dr. Shepherd showed us were legitimate?" She glances at Dad. "I must say, I'm glad you didn't let her die. It was such an inconvenience to make her cyborg-clone without you finding out."

"Now you know how I did it," Dad says, straightening his shoulders and staring Ms. White down. "Let my daughter go. She and my wife have nothing to do with this. You have me."

Ms. White runs her finger along the barrel of the gun. "Yes, but now I don't need you," she says. She glares back at her colleague. "Gather up any of his little seditious friends and bring them here. We'll want to make this look like an accident." She turns her attention and the gun back to Dad's face.

"This is because you took Rose from me," she says, no emotion in her voice.

The gun blast is too loud and too long and I'm screaming, the sound piercing through my eardrums—

The silence in the vacuum of the absent scream reverberates in my mind as I stare at Ms. White. She looks panicked and flustered, her fingers skimming across the surface of her cuff.

That was the last gift of my father. Because of him, my life was taken away. Because of him, control over myself is solely mine. Ms. White cannot control me.

I take a step forward.

"Stay back!" Ms. White shouts, her voice trembling with fear.

It's so unusual for me to see her afraid.

And empowering to know I caused that terror.

"You killed me," I say. "You killed my father."

"Ella, dear…"

Dad was right. His technology is far more destructive than any bomb. Not because of who it can kill, but because of what it can destroy without killing.

"Stay back!" Ms. White screams again as I take two more steps closer. She's still trying to use the controls on her cuff; she cannot believe the truth that I'm unaffected by them. But as I grow closer, her eyes narrow. Ms. White turns on me, her right arm raised, and she seizes my throat.

And then I remember. Ms. White isn't a cy-clone, but she does have one cyborg part: an arm. An arm she lost in the Secessionary War, saving my mother.

My eyes bulge, and my mouth opens in a pitiful mewling sound. I gasp for breath. I don't need breath—I proved that when I hid under the boats in the Foqra District—but it's uncomfortable now, and it hurts, and I wonder if Ms. White's cyborg arm is enough to crush my cy-clone throat.

I feel the light flickering in my eyes.

I cannot let her win.

I channel all my strength into my arm, all my hope, all my power. And I slam my hand against Ms. White's arm, using all the force I have within me.

It snaps like a twig, breaking off in one swift motion.

Wires sparking electricity dangle from her elbow as bio-gel leaks from the place where her arm was. Ms. White backs away, screaming in agony. I use my hands to untangle her fingers from my throat and throw the piece of arm on the ground.

Ms. White has disengaged her cyborg arm from the shoulder, which also disengages it from her nervous system. But she is pale and shaken, still feeling the phantom pains of the severed arm. She leans against the door frame, panting, her hair sweaty against her skin, her eyes glassy.

I use her pain to my advantage, shoving past her and racing toward the steps. I have to find Jack, I have to escape—somehow.

SEVENTY-FOUR

"NO!" MS. WHITE SCREAMS, AS I LUNGE away. I have little doubt as to what she'll do with me. Transfer me into another version of myself, wipe my memory again, so I'll be complacent. I'll spend the rest of my life just like I spent the last year without Jack. Blindly doing what Ms. White says while she secretly pumps me full of tracker bots and does tests on me while I'm in reveries or asleep, trying to break into my mind as if it were nothing but a locked box.

My desperation to avoid this fate makes me stronger. I rip around the steps, taking them four at a time. Ms. White grabs at me, but I leverage my body weight against my attacker, throwing her off me and down a flight of stairs.

I am deeply aware of the thuds of her footsteps on the stairs behind me, just out of reach.

I wrench open the door and race down the lobby. I can make it. I can escape.

But androids fill the lobby. Their dead and empty faces turn to me as one, and they start to march toward the stairs, toward me, their footsteps heavy, making the walls vibrate with their even rhythm. I turn on my heel, but Ms. White's right there, so close that her fingernails leave long, jagged scratches on my arm. I lunge for the stairs again, going to the only place I have left—my home. I race up the stairs, slamming my hand against the lock—it doesn't work; I have a different cuff now, a different ID— but I kick the door down, something I wouldn't have been able to do with simple human strength.

I don't know what I was thinking. I was blindly running. But as I turn and see Ms. White and an army of androids standing in the doorway, I realize: I've trapped myself.

Ms. White shoves the androids aside. She seems uneven without one arm, and there is rage in her face unlike anything I've ever seen before.

And then I hear footsteps down the hall, coming from, of all places, my own bedroom.

Boots thud hollowly on the floor, and Jack emerges from the shadows.

My heart leaps into my chest—with hope, with something else, something stronger—

More than a year ago, I was killed, my memories forcibly jammed into a cloned body enhanced with cybernetics, pieces of me disappearing bit by bit. Including my memories of Jack.

So why does my whole soul react when I see him?

Because...

Because he still loves me, even after I forgot him.

I don't have any memories of Jack. I have no reason to save him because of a shared past. Those are memories I will never, ever get back. All I have of Jack are the past few weeks. The way we slept side-by-side while on the run. The way he pressed his hand against my heart, certain that it proved my humanity despite my cy-clone body. The way his kiss seared into me, desperate and passionate, as if he were trying to put everything he ever felt into the pressure on my lips.

I don't care about how he used to make me feel; I want to save him because of the way he makes me feel *now*.

Now. Now in this very moment, when I realize that he needs saving.

Because his eyes are glassy. His skin sallow.

And I recall the way Julie and Xavier were beat up after the fight with Akilah, but Jack and I weren't. I recall the way Jack was in the military, the same unit as Akilah. I remember all the little things, the moments when he wasn't tired or wasn't hurt or wasn't... human.

"How long?" I ask, backing away slowly.

It is Ms. White who answers. "We turned him before we turned Akilah."

So, from the moment I met him, Jack was a cy-clone, too.

The perfect spy into the Zunzana. Into me.

Always able to stay one step ahead. Always, unknowingly, giving Ms. White our exact location, the exact information she wanted. Jack's arrival pushed me to discover Dad's secrets in my subconscious more than anything else. Whatever tests Ms. White did on me didn't work—she needed me to find the information and hand it over to her. She knew I wouldn't give it to her blindly, so she used Jack.

"Did he know?" I ask. He steps closer. Closer.

Ms. White barks in laughter. "He was as ignorant as you." She sounds amused. This is entertainment for her.

Something cold and bitter and hard snaps in place inside my soul.

And that is the moment he attacks.

SEVENTY-FIVE

"I DON'T WANT TO HURT YOU," I SAY, panicked.

"Get her!" Ms. White screams from the doorway, her breathing jagged.

Jack charges forward, but I dodge him, throwing the kitchen chairs at him. He smashes them aside, advancing, advancing. He moves as quick as lightning, leaping over the end of the table, using the momentum to slam his feet into my stomach. I double over, gasping for air, and he rams the flat of his palm into my chin. I reel back, the pain of the blow reverberating through my whole body.

I feint toward the hallway, then lunge out of Jack's grip, slipping on the tiled floor. My mind spins at the possibilities before me. I can't hurt him. Even knowing that Jack's not really Jack, I can't hurt him.

I try to run.

Ms. White is in the doorway now, with her army of androids. I spin on my heel, heading for the tarp-covered gaping hole in the wall, the scar in the side of the building caused by the android explosion. Jack sweeps at my legs, knocking me down. My head cracks painfully against the tiled floor, and I taste blood in my mouth. I concentrate and realize that I can turn the pain sensors in my brain off. Handy.

He leaps on top of me, his knees pressing painfully into my chest. I try to throw him off, but his hips shift down and his biceps harden as he forces my arms down. My back bucks, and I slam my head into the floor, cracking the tile, trying to gain some traction.

It's useless.

"Jack," I gasp. "Please."

Please. I think I love you. I know you love me. Please. Don't hurt me.

Don't be this hollow shell.

But nothing happens.

He is controlled—absolutely, utterly controlled by Ms. White. And this is what she wants to do to people. Let them have their own lives, until she wants them. Give them the strength of giants, but not the power to control it.

The pressure on my chest intensifies.

Ms. White walks casually forward. "So," she says, as if dictating an agenda to a secretary android, "it has become painfully clear that I cannot rely on you to give me your father's formula either consciously or subconsciously, so I will just have to take it from your body. A shame really, but it can't be helped. And as you so graciously took my arm, perhaps I should have this boy do it."

THE BODY ELECTRIC

His fingers dig into my skin between my breasts, and it feels as if he would like to rip the beating heart from my chest and crush it in his hands.

I close my eyes for one second—no more.

My father gave me what I needed to survive.

When I open my eyes, I know what I have to do. My body—my body that is just a copy of myself, filled with nanobots and steel bones and parts manufactured in a factory—my body will not fail me. Because even if it was pieced together, it was made by my father, and my father will not fail me.

I shift my weight, springing upward, throwing Jack from me. I leap up from the floor, sliding down on one knee as I jab stiffened fingers into Ms. White's solar plexus, sending her flying across the room, gasping for air. I twirl around Jack, grabbing the back of his head with one hand and slamming my other hand against the side of her neck. Jack is faster and stronger than I had thought, able to slip from my grasp despite the blow I've given him, but he's not fast enough. I drop to both knees, sliding under his open-legged stance and kicking up from the floor, pushing him away in the same moment. He drops heavily, and I throw myself on top of his body, much like he'd pinned me to the ground before.

We're close to where Rosie the android exploded, the gaping maw of a hole in the apartment opening up mere meters away. It still smells of destruction and burning. Scorch marks smear the ground, and the giant tarp covering the hole flaps in the wind.

But rather than try to hurt him, I stare into his eyes. They are empty and dead inside, pools of bright blue color that do not have a single spark of emotion.

Eyes are the windows to the soul.

I frame his face with both my hands, staring into him. I pour in every emotion I have: love and trust and hope, but also fear and pain and sorrow. My eyes burn the way they did before, when I first realized the power my father left for me. When I stared into Akilah. My entire body stills—and so does his.

He blinks. And when he opens his eyes again, I see him, the real him, the Jack I have fallen in love with all over again.

"No!" Ms. White screams, and she does something—some sort of remote command or something—and the life snaps out of Jack like a rubber band breaking.

He tries to shove me off, tries to pull my hands away, tries to break my arms.

But I don't let go.

I can do this.

I hacked into Representative Belles's computer. I hacked into my own mind. I can hack into his.

Jack's arms snake up, his hand wrapping around my throat.

Squeezing. Squeezing.

THE BODY ELECTRIC

How ironic it would be, to die at his hands while trying to save him, when he first came to me because he was trying to save me.

Black spots float in front of my eyes. I can't breathe. This is more than when I was hiding underwater, able to hold my breath. Jack is choking not just air from me, but my very life.

The black dots merge, striped with yellow.

You're the queen bee, Dad said. Funny that.

Bees have been following me everywhere.

I taste honey in my mouth.

No, that's not honey.

It's blood.

A buzzing fills my ears.

You're the queen bee.

But Dad wasn't a part of the Zunzana, he didn't know about Jack's secret code.

Queen bee.

Queen... of the hive.

All the computers in the world are on a network. They're linked by our cuffs. But I'm a computer. Jack's a computer—Akilah—PA Young—all the cy-clones. We're all computers.

You know the great thing about computers?

They can be hacked.

SEVENTY-SIX

LINKED COMPUTERS ARE LIKE BEES IN A hive, connected to each other, despite being separate.

And I'm the queen bee.

My eyes flash open, and I feel the burning inside of them, like fire, like rage. I stare at Jack, and his eyes fly open, too. I connect to him wirelessly, remotely, our eyes portals into our operating systems. I see—no, I feel—the string of commands that makes Jack controlled by Ms. White.

Fire and electricity and passion boil inside of me, inside of Jack, and I sever the connection.

His hands drop from my throat.

But I'm not done. My power extends far, far beyond just us. I sense PA Young, tied up with metal bars and steel downstairs, where I left her. *Snap.* I free her mind from Ms. White's control. My reach goes further. Dozens in the capital building, sleeper cells in Triumph Towers, people who don't even *know* that they're cy-clones, just doing their jobs and going home at night to their families without even realizing that one day Ms. White would call on them and force them to become this inhuman monster to do her biding.

Snap. They don't even know they were trapped, but I've broken the bonds around them.

Further. The safe house. There's Akilah. I fill her mind with fire, I burn away the ties twisting her brain into something it's not.

Snap.

Further, further. To the lunar base, the soldiers Ms. White used for experiments. *Snap. Snap. Snap.* The spies she placed in the Secessionary States, awaiting a time when she might need to use more terrorism and war to convince people through fear and manipulation to willingly come into her grasp. *Snap. Snap. Snap.*

Free. They're all free.

It is only then that I stand, only then that I turn to Ms. White, with the fire of my power burning in my eyes.

"We are free," I say, my voice buzzing with the sound of the hundreds of people she'd turned into cy-clones. We were a part of the network, a part of the hive, but it was not Ms. White who had control.

It was me.

And I have freed them all.

"We cannot be controlled," I say. My voice is loud and low, and through my mouth, all the others speak as well. We are all united in this moment, all united against this horrible woman who thought to control us all.

Ms. White cowers in terror.

BETH REVIS

"We cannot ever be controlled!" I roar, my voice rising among the horde.

But this much power, it burns through me like a fire. I was not meant to hold the strings of every single person to me. I tremble, the power inside me scorching my veins.

"Please," Ms. White begs. She's scared now. She's really, truly scared. I don't think she ever saw me as anything other than her little robot or the container that hid Dad's research. She forgot that I was a person, and that my father gave me a very specific set of skills, skills designed to stop her.

"Ella," Ms. White says. "Think now. Think about what you're doing. You're not one of them. You have seen the possibility of war. You know what the consequences can be. Don't—" Her voice cracks. "Don't throw away all we've worked for. We are on the brink of a peace the world has never seen."

"Control is not peace," I say.

"You think you can stop this?" Ms. White says. Her knees quake, but she stands anyway. "There is no stopping technology. The Secessionary States already have similar tech. Someone else will make cyborg-clones, someone else will be in control. All I want is peace. Yes—I wanted a peace where I profited, but still, peace. If you stop me now, the next person to rise up won't want peace. They'll want war."

I feel the ripple of fear that passes from me into the hive of all the other cy-clones. The fear of being used. The soldiers' fear of battle.

But I pull it all back into my heart, and I lock it up inside of me.

"I will never allow you—or anyone—to take away our humanity," I say. "We are not robots. We have a human soul, if nothing else, and I will never, ever allow this power to be used in any way."

Ms. White smiles sadly. "You already are," she whispers. "You think I can't see it in the way that boy stands behind you? You're connected to all the cy-clones. You didn't sever my control of them; you just shifted it to yourself."

My stomach drops. She's right. I can feel all the other cy-clones she made, I have access to them, their thoughts, their actions, their voices. I could, with merely a thought, make Jack stride over to Ms. White and snap her neck. Or jump off the side of the building. Or kiss me. I could do it to them all. I control the Prime Administrator. I could release her from her steel bonds and put her in her office and control the whole entire world.

I could.

And the power is intoxicating. It courses through me. It burns, yes, but it burns so beautifully.

And that is the very reason why I gather all the strings of the power tightly inside of me.

And that is the very reason why I have to let it go.

I release them all. I cut the bonds I have made between all of us, and I let it all go.

And just when I stumble and think I'm about to fall, I feel Jack's strong arms wrap around my own, holding me up, keeping me steady. Not because I forced him to. Because he loves me. Because that is what love does.

And I know.

I will never fall again.

EPILOGUE

PRIME ADMINISTRATOR YOUNG LOOKS as if she has been shaken to her very core. I don't know if she would have believed me if I'd just gone up to her and told her she was no longer human, but a cy-clone capable of immense strength... and capable of being controlled. But she felt it, felt *me*—all of the cy-clones did.

She knows.

"I had no idea," she says. "I think I can see it now, in some of the decisions I've made this last year, some of the laws I've put through, but at the time... it felt like *I* was the one deciding. I didn't realize the level of control Jadis exerted over me."

I nod. She seems different now, free of Ms. White's influence. Perhaps a little more aged, but also a little more scared. This suits a person who faced war the way PA Young did. Not all confidence and bravado, but a little fear for her own consequences, for the people she would affect.

Her clear eyes meet mine. "I'll have to step down, obviously."

"But—" Jack starts.

PA Young is already shaking her head. "I cannot run the risk that someone else figures out a way to hack, er, *me*. It's too dangerous. For the good of us all, I must step down from my position as Prime Administrator."

And now I see why she was elected, and why she has been the strongest leader the Unified Countries has ever known. The Vice Administrator—a slightly older man originally from Mexico—seems to be a good man, but he will always be in PA Young's shadow.

The androids, previously under Ms. White's control, are all turned off. They're piled into one corner, their bodies stiff and oddly-angled, their eyes still open wide and staring at nothing.

"I'll have to take Ms. White into custody," PA Young says. "Obviously. The trial will be a fiasco. I don't know how we'll keep cy-clones from the media... and that worries me, because the more people know about the possibility of... of *us*, the more likely they'll try to emulate what Ms. White has already done." She pauses, fear evident on her face, but she also looks resigned. "Where is she?"

Jack and I exchange glances. "I didn't know what to do with her," I confess. "And I wasn't sure who to trust, at least not at first, so..."

PA Young narrows her eyes. "What did you do?" she asks.

THE BODY ELECTRIC

Jack and I lead her down into the basement of the Reverie Mental Spa, into the reverie chamber, where Ms. White is plugged into the machine.

"I've rigged it to give her a continual dose of the drug," I say.

"That's not much of a punishment." PA Young scowls at Ms. White's sleeping form.

"She's not reliving happy memories," Jack says.

PA Young's eyes dart back and forth between us.

"I've made her relive, over and over, the last few days," I say softly, watching Ms. White's body. "I've had to fill in the blanks with my own feelings and experiences. She's spiraling around those last moments, those times when she went against me, and she's feeling it from my side, the pain, the betrayal."

She thinks she's awake. I'm doing to her just what she did to me. I'm making her feel what it was like to slowly go crazy, to question everything. To watch my mother die. To fight for my life against my best friend. To feel the man who loved me try to kill me.

To know that the woman I trusted as much as my own mother betrayed me.

That's what I'm making her feel.

I've turned her into me, and made her live the life she forced me to live.

Over and over and over again.

As PA Young leaves—escorted by a frantic security detail that had no idea where she'd gone the night before—Jack and I stay behind. He leads me to the roof of the apartment, the place that was, in another life, ours. It's hard to see the stars in the perpetual twilight made by the lights of the city, but we squint up at the sky anyway.

I lean into his hard chest. Akilah is awake and herself again, and she and Julie and Xavier are coming here. They are the only family I have left, and joy bubbles up inside me at the knowledge that, despite everything, I am not alone.

I lean back in the warmth of Jack's arms, and the infinite sky stretches out before me, and for the first time in my life, I finally feel free.

A fat, fuzzy bumblebee meanders by, buzzing softly as it dips among the flowers in the rooftop garden.

Answer.

That you are here—that life exists and identity,
That the powerful play goes on, and you may
contribute a verse.

　　　—*Conclusion of Walt Whitman's "O Me! O Life!"*

A SINCERE THANKS TO ALL MY READERS

This book, quite simply, would not exist without you. Thank you for reading and supporting my writing. I deeply appreciate you, and hope you enjoyed *The Body Electric!*

Never miss a new book! You can subscribe to Beth's monthly newsletter and never miss news on her latest books. Newsletters are packed with fun info about writing, exciting links to new science fiction news, YA book recommendations, and much more. To subscribe, simply visit Beth's website at www.bethrevis.com or subscribe directly at http://bit.ly/bethnews

There's more to read! If this is the first book by Beth you've read, make sure you check out her first science fiction trilogy. *Across the Universe* is the story of two teens trapped aboard a generation space ship bound for a new planet, and the sequels, *A Million Suns* and *Shades of Earth,* show their struggle to escape the ship and find a new home.

Get a signed copy! You can purchase a signed copy of any of Beth's books (including this one!) from her local independent bookstore in Asheville, NC. Visit Malaprops in person or online at http://malaprops.com to order your copy today.

Please review! Readers find books through reviews. Please consider sharing your honest thoughts—positive or negative—in a review.

PRAISE FOR BETH'S WORKS

The Across the Universe Series
--Three weeks on the NY Times Bestseller's List
--Two Kirkus Starred Reviews
--Romantic Times Seal of Excellence
--Two-time recipient of Romantic Times YA Futuristic Book of the Year
--YALSA Teen's Top Ten Award of 2012

Across the Universe

"Cunningly executed thriller...a compulsively readable crowd-pleaser."
—-Booklist

"...a believable romance and a series of tantalizing mysteries that will hold readers' attention."
—Publisher's Weekly

"Who Should Read This: Well, sci-fi and mystery fans will love it, but so will any girl or boy who's ever sat in a room full of quiet conformists and wanted to scream at them all, 'Wake up!'"
—MTV.com

A Million Suns

"Revis has penned a fast-paced, action-packed follow-up with her dystopian, sci-fi thriller...that explores not only the nature of authority and loyalty but fear of the unknown and fulfilling one's personal destiny."
—LA Times, 8 January 2011

"There literally isn't one dull moment in the entire story!"
–Seventeen.com

"Setting and plot are the heart and soul of this ripping space thriller, and they're unforgettable."
–Kirkus, starred review

Shades of Earth

"A tense and delicious ride — one that satisfyingly brings the series full circle." –The Examiner

"[Revis has a gift] as a propulsive storyteller with a knack for jarring surprises and raising the stakes." –Booklist, Dec. 1, 2012

"[Shades of Earth] brings it home on a planet far from home." –Kirkus, Dec. 1, 2012

ACKNOWLEDGEMENTS

This book came from two things I love most in the world: reading and traveling. The first time I left the continent was in college, with a trip through my education program organized by Dawn Shepherd. She led us fearlessly to a little island none of us had heard of before. Malta left an indelible print upon my soul, and I have been forever, irrevocably entranced with this beautiful, unique country. Subsequent trips—notably to the Italian version of Venice—helped me to see the world in a new perspective and invent a new one of my own.

But of course, *The Body Electric* is more than a world—it is also a story. And while Ella and Jack and the rest are fully mine, I was inspired, like many other modern science fiction authors, by the work of the brilliant Philip K. Dick. Ella Shepherd is an homage to Dick's *Do Androids Dream of Electric Sheep?* and the Reverie Mental Spa owes a debt to the novella *Total Recall*.

I have so much gratitude to the people who helped me produce this book. Merrilee Heifetz and Sarah Nagel at Writers House are my very own knights in shining armor, and among the few people who inspire me to never give up. I will never forget how awesome you are. Thanks go also to Gillian Levinson for reading and providing editorial feedback. Hafsah Faizal developed a beautiful cover and interior design for the book, and I'm so honored to have the chance to work with her.

Carrie Ryan and Lauren DeStefano are my heroes; thank you for the countless emails, the tea and sympathy, and the encouragement as I wrote this story. Elana Johnson and Natalie Whipple are both fantastic writers and incredible people; thank you for giving me information, advice, and cheers as I started to turn this story into a book. Extra love to Alan Gratz and the Bat Cave group for helping me to revise the story, especially Megan Miranda and Megan Shepherd for reading the whole thing; Heather Zundel for being so enthusiastic for this tale; Christy Farley for willing to drop everything to read for me; the Breathless Girls, who have become my sisters: Andrea Cremer, Marie Lu, and Jessica Spotswood. I know I'm forgetting people—I'm sorry! I have the best friends in the world, and my life is better for it.

Huge thanks to my local independent bookstore, Malaprops, for always wanting my next book!

There are three people who are more important to me than all the words on all the pages: my parents, Ted and JoAnne Graham, and my husband, Corwin Revis. I will never forget your love.

Thank you, thank you, thank you.

ABOUT THE AUTHOR

Beth Revis is the *NY Times* bestselling author
of the Across the Universe trilogy, hailed by the *LA Times* as
"fast-paced [and] action-packed." The complete trilogy is now
available in more than twenty languages throughout the world. A
native of North Carolina, Beth loves to travel, and first visited
Malta when she was in college. She currently lives near the
Appalachian mountains with her husband and dogs, and is
working on several new books.

Find her online at www.bethrevis.com
or on Twitter @BethRevis.

Printed in Great Britain
by Amazon.co.uk, Ltd.,
Marston Gate.